PENGUIN

THE LOST WORLD AND OTHER THRI...

SIR ARTHUR CONAN DOYLE was born in Edinburgh in 1859 and died in 1930. Into these years he crowded a variety of activity and creative work that earned him an international reputation and inspired the French to give him the epithet of 'the good giant'. He was educated at Stonyhurst and later studied medicine at Edinburgh University, where he became the surgeon's clerk to Professor Joseph Bell whose diagnostic methods provided the model for the science of deduction perfected by Sherlock Holmes.

He set up as a doctor at Southsea and it was while waiting for patients that he began to write. His growing success as an author enabled him to give up his practice and to turn his attention to other subjects. He was a passionate advocate of many causes, ranging from divorce law reform and a Channel Tunnel to the issuing of steel helmets to soldiers and inflatable life jackets to sailors. He also campaigned to prove the innocence of individuals, and was instrumental in the introduction of the Court of Criminal Appeal. He was a volunteer physician in the Boer War and later in life became a convert to spiritualism.

As well as his Sherlock Holmes stories, Conan Doyle wrote a number of other works, including historical romances, such as *The Exploits of Brigadier Gerard* (1896) and *Rodney Stone* (1896). In the science fiction tale *The Lost World* (1912), he created another famous character, Professor Challenger, who appears in several later stories.

Sherlock Holmes first appeared in *A Study in Scarlet* in 1887. The Holmes stories soon attracted such a following that Conan Doyle felt the character overshadowed his other work. In 'The Final Problem' (1893) Conan Doyle killed him off, but was obliged by public demand to restore the detective to life. Despite his ambivalence towards Holmes, he remains the character for which Conan Doyle is best known.

PHILIP GOODEN read English at Magdalen College, Oxford, and now teaches in the English Department of Kingswood School, Bath. He is the author of *The Guinness Guide to Better English*, editor of *A Warning to the Curious and Other Stories* by M. R. James and *The Open Door and Other Ghost Stories*, as well as being a contributor to various short story anthologies. His novel, *Sleep of Death*, the first of a projected sequence set in Elizabethan–Jacobean London, was published in 2000.

ARTHUR CONAN DOYLE

The Lost World
and Other Thrilling Tales

Edited with an Introduction and Notes by
PHILIP GOODEN

PENGUIN BOOKS

PENGUIN BOOKS

Published by the Penguin Group
Penguin Books Ltd, 80 Strand, London WC2R 0RL, England
Penguin Putnam Inc., 375 Hudson Street, New York, New York 10014, USA
Penguin Books Australia Ltd, 250 Camberwell Road, Camberwell, Victoria 3124, Australia
Penguin Books Canada Ltd, 10 Alcorn Avenue, Toronto, Ontario, Canada M4V 3B2
Penguin Books India (P) Ltd, 11 Community Centre, Panchsheel Park, New Delhi – 110 017, India
Penguin Books (NZ) Ltd, Cnr Rosedale and Airborne Roads, Albany, Auckland, New Zealand
Penguin Books (South Africa) (Pty) Ltd, 24 Sturdee Avenue, Rosebank 2196, South Africa

Penguin Books Ltd, Registered Offices: 80 Strand, London WC2R 0RL, England

www.penguin.com

The Lost World first published 1912; *The Poison Belt* first published 1913;
'The Terror of Blue John Gap' first published 1912; 'The Horror of the Heights' first published 1918.
This collection published in Penguin Classics 2001
2

Editorial material copyright © Philip Gooden 2001
All rights reserved

The moral right of the editor has been asserted

Set in 10/12.5 pt Monotype Baskerville
Typeset by Rowland Phototypesetting Ltd, Bury St Edmunds, Suffolk
Printed in Great Britain by Clays Ltd, St Ives plc

CONTENTS

ACKNOWLEDGEMENTS

I am very grateful to Dr Peter McDonald of St Hugh's College, Oxford, for discussion of this edition at an early stage and for his helpful suggestions and reference-points for the Introduction; to Richard Lancelyn Green for clarification of the circumstances of the first US publication of *The Lost World*, and for information on the illustrator and the photographer for the first British edition; and to John Edwards, Trustee of the Bath Postal Museum, Richard Simpson of the Royal Air Force Museum (Hendon), Dr Neil Young of the Imperial War Museum, and to Alexandra Gooden, for their help over various queries, particularly those relating to the final story in this collection, 'The Horror of the Heights'.

INTRODUCTION

The Lost World *and Time-Travel*

Speaking at a Royal Society's Club lunch held in 1910 to honour the
American explorer Robert Peary's return from the Arctic, Arthur
Conan Doyle referred half-humorously to the pressures put on writers
like him by successful expeditions like Peary's: 'The question is where
the romance writer is to turn when he wants to draw any vague and not
too clearly defined region.'[1] The world was shrinking, and so was the
adventurer's room for manoeuvre. ' "The big blank spaces in the map
are all being filled in, and there's no room for romance anywhere" ' says
Ned Malone's news editor (*The Lost World*, Ch. II), taking up his creator's
words. It is a response that is echoed in other Victorian–Edwardian
accounts, and it suggests a fundamental, if intermittent, ambivalence
about development.[2] The nineteenth-century belief in progress demanded
that civilization's lighted torch be directed into every corner, even while
pastoral sensibilities might have preferred some of those corners to
remain obscure and unspoiled. The increasing difficulties of creating a
piece of romantic real-estate which had some vague geographical basis
were the professional concern of writers like Conan Doyle, but they also
provide an oblique confirmation of the late Victorian rush to explore
(and exploit) virgin lands. If geographical space was filling up, however,
a rather different kind of arena was becoming available to at least some
literary explorers towards the end of the nineteenth century.

Educated opinion before the beginning of the Victorian era held that
the earth was no more than a few thousand years old. In 1654 Bishop
Ussher of Armagh had fixed the moment of creation at nine o'clock

on the morning of 26 October 4004 BC. For well over a century this whimsically precise date (arrived at by totting up genealogical lists in the Bible) was 'accepted without question by most English-speaking Protestants'.[3] As the world was, so it had always been. That species might appear and disappear or that continents might coalesce and separate with infinitesimal slowness were ideas almost beyond thought. Then, impelled by palaeontological and geological discoveries by individuals like Baron Cuvier and George Lyell, the short vista down a few thousand years was extended to an inconceivably far-off starting-point. The bottom – or the beginning – dropped out of the world. A *chronological* framework, with its emphasis on change, development and mutation, and the less welcome corollaries of instability, decline and extinction, became the dominant mode of understanding the world, superseding older, more static and hierarchical modes of thought.

It is at this point, therefore, even while geographical horizons are shrinking, that temporal boundaries are undergoing a perhaps not altogether welcome expansion. Travelling backwards in time becomes, in literary and imaginative terms at least, a feasible and worthwhile enterprise when there is somewhere – or nowhere – to go. The journey is not likely to be pleasant. To travel back is to explore shadowy and frightening Darwinian origins rather than to hit the comforting, God-made buffers of 4004 BC. Even though the most famous time-travelling story of all, Wells's *The Time Machine* (1895), goes *forward*, indeed as far as to the end of the world, what the unnamed inventor finds when he reaches it is a vision of entropic collapse whose terms suggest that the imagined end is a replay of the beginning:

Then like a red-hot bow in the sky appeared the edge of the sun. I got off the machine to recover myself. [. . .] As I stood sick and confused I saw again the moving thing upon the shoal – there was no mistake now that it was a moving thing – against the red water of the sea. It was a round thing, the size of a football perhaps, or, it may be, bigger, and tentacles trailed down from it; it seemed black against the weltering blood-red water, and it was hopping fitfully about. (*The Time Machine*, Ch. 11)

Superficially, *The Lost World* is not a time-travelling novel. But in recapturing a past that was almost unimaginably remote – if one more or less confirmed by Victorian palaeontological discovery – Arthur Conan Doyle's characters are, in effect, making a journey down the geological ages that in its scale dwarfs the few thousands of geographical miles they have to travel round the globe. On the South American plateau, where according to Professor Challenger 'the ordinary laws of nature are suspended', imagination may juxtapose forms of life which, in sober geological reality, never met. In the study of his Sussex home Arthur Conan Doyle kept two iguanodon fossil feet. The prints of this herbivorous dinosaur from the Jurassic period lay beneath a table on which was displayed a flint arrowhead from the Stone Age. An aeon or two separated the relics of man and dinosaur, but it was Doyle's achievement in *The Lost World* to bridge the gap between the disparate worlds of reptile and human with the same imaginative nimbleness that his travellers show in felling a beech tree to cross from a rock-pinnacle onto that mysterious plateau.

Doyle's sweep in *The Lost World* does not extend as far back as the unthrilling amoeba or Wells's tentacled 'round thing' but he does cover a remarkable spread of periods – from the Mesozoic (the 'Age of Reptiles') to the Cenozoic (the 'Age of Mammals') – as well as whisking us through the human gallery from the pre-Neanderthal to the primitive community of the plateau Indians to modern man. There is even a miniaturized primordial ocean in *The Lost World*, in the shape of Lake Gladys. This telescoping of the historic and prehistoric could be interpreted as a strategy for dealing with the challenge to vestigial religious faith – or to simple human discomfort – posed by the realization that the earth is almost unimaginably older than we thought. Tens of thousands of millennia are concertinaed here, so that human beings and dinosaurs share the same living-space; the wastes of time are domesticated.

Indians, Dinosaurs and Anthropoids

The explorers encounter three distinct, living groups in the Lost World, and feel affinity with only one of them. These groups are the Indians, who Challenger decides must be comparatively recent immigrants to the plateau; the ape-men, apparent descendants of the anthropoid ape; and the dinosaurs. As far as the Indians are concerned, there is a rapid establishment of familiar Victorian–Edwardian colonial relations. Commended for their fighting spirit, the 'little red warriors' have the aesthetic edge over the ape-men, being 'wiry, active, and well-built' while their faces are 'hairless, well formed, and good-humoured'. More noble than savage, they are properly grateful for the intervention of the explorers in their perpetual war with the ape-men. It is the arrival of Challenger and the others, with their 'tubes of strange weapons', which tips the balance, at last giving the Indians control of the plateau. There is a certain irony in that the adventurers provide the technological means by which the more recent 'native' immigrants are enabled to exterminate the indigenous inhabitants, a task normally reserved for the whites. Significantly, it's in another time-travelling novel that we find a similar scene – at once vainglorious and shifty – of extermination aided by superior, imported firepower. Mark Twain's *A Connecticut Yankee at the Court of King Arthur* (1889) climaxes in the annihilation of the ten-thousand-strong chivalry of England by thirteen gatling guns. Twain's satire, however, is anti-chivalry and probably anti-colonial too, precisely the things that the author of *The Lost World* could never be. Even though Conan Doyle plays the massacre straight, the victorious Indians of *The Lost World* are unlikely to enjoy for long their hegemony over the plateau. One can only wonder what will be their fate when, as foreseen by Malone towards the close, the 'dreamland of glamour and romance' gets opened up and becomes 'vulgarized, the prey of hunter and prospector'.

Curiously, the dinosaurs are not perceived by the Indians as being as much of a threat to their existence as the ape-men. This despite the testimony of Malone and the others to the fearsome qualities of the carnivorous reptiles. Some of the most successful episodes in *The Lost World* are in these human–dinosaur encounters: the first sight of the grazing iguanodons or the rookery of pterodactyls (Ch. X), the night-time glimpse of a 'bloated, warty, blood-slavering muzzle' provided by the flaring torch of Lord John Roxton (Ch. XII), the pursuit of Malone by the same toad-like monster across moonlit countryside (Ch. XII), and, a supreme moment, the unveiling of the young pterodactyl back in London (Ch. XVI). Such passages demonstrate the transformative capacity of Conan Doyle's imagination, fleshing out fossils. Yet it is hard to avoid the conclusion that these episodes are a form of what is, essentially, the primeval picturesque. The monsters, however closely based on real science (and many are taken from one of Doyle's principal sources, Sir Edwin Ray Lankester's *Extinct Animals* (1905)), have a fantastic, chimerical quality. They are the stuff of Bosch and bad dreams: 'a strange creature, half-seal, half-fish'; 'a great running bird, far taller than an ostrich, with a vulture-like neck and cruel head which made it a walking death'; 'the toxodon, the giant ten-foot guinea pig, with projecting chisel teeth' (Ch. XV) – this last, incidentally, sounding like a distant relation to Holmes's giant rat of Sumatra (see 'The Sussex Vampire' in *The Case-Book*).

Most imaginative recreation of the dinosaur era lapses into wonder. Dinosaur-land may be arrived at in various ways: through travel, as in Jules Verne's *Journey to the Centre of the Earth* (1864) or Conan Doyle's *The Lost World*, or through the magic of cloning, as in Michael Crichton's novel *Jurassic Park* (1991),[4] or through the unapologetically antihistorical sequence of Hammer films beginning with *One Million Years BC* (1966), in which primitive humans (with a rather advanced grasp of underwear) are casually lumped together on the earth with the big lizards. But, however the 'Age of Reptiles' may be recreated, the reaction of the human beings who find themselves in it is generally – and sensibly, one might think – to stop and stare, while hoping they won't be noticed. A staple of any decent dinosaur saga is a fight to the finish between two monsters. *Journey to the Centre of the Earth* provides an early example of this in the underworld sea-battle between an ichthyosaurus and a plesiosaurus (Ch. 33). The first film version of *King Kong* (1933), heavily indebted to *The Lost World*, features a similarly titanic struggle. Unlike the conflict between the Indians and the ape-men on Doyle's plateau, the struggles of the dinosaurs, enthralling though they may be, are nothing to do with us. They are pure spectacle, nature red in tooth and claw, diverting but alien. In a similar way, the quantity of time given in Steven Spielberg's film versions of Crichton's *Jurassic Park* (1993) and *The Lost World* (1997)[5] to simply looking at these creatures – and, in the publicity, to dwelling on the elaborateness of the special effects required to create them – shows how much we are satisfied with them as sheer spectacle. We don't require dinosaurs to do much, they just have to be.

With the ape-men things are different. The real anxieties of the text are to be discovered here, and they reflect late Victorian apprehensions about the 'Missing Link', the discovery of which (or whom) would establish man's descent from the apes once and for all. From their arrival on the plateau Lord John Roxton and Ned Malone, the more intuitive and practical members of the expedition, share 'the same feeling of mystery and danger'. Tellingly, it is located not where we might expect, on the ground level occupied by dinosaurs, but up in the gloom of the trees. The first actual sighting is by Malone and it validates his constant 'feeling that something malevolent was watching us'. He climbs a tree to obtain a vista of Maple White Land, but before reaching the summit which would give him a commanding overview of where they are, and hence more control over their situation, he has an alarming encounter:

A face was gazing into mine [. . .] It was a human face – or at least it was far more human than any monkey's that I have ever seen. It was long, whitish, and blotched with pimples, the nose flattened, and the lower jaw projecting, with a bristle of coarse whiskers round the chin. The eyes, which were under thick and heavy brows, were bestial and ferocious, and as it opened its mouth to snarl what sounded like a curse at me I observed that it had curved, sharp canine teeth.   (Ch. XI)

In Challenger and Summerlee's argument over classification these ape-men are pigeon-holed as 'dryopithecus' or 'pithecanthropus', while for the pithier Lord John they are 'red-headed devils' or 'Missin' Links, and I wish they had stayed missin''. But the real argument, of course, is not over what these disturbing beings should be called; it is over the degree of kinship which they may claim with the twentieth-century travellers. There is a parallel encounter in Swift's *Gulliver's Travels* (1726), also a narrative of tours to wonderful places. In the country of the Houyhnhnms, the rational, talking horses whom Gulliver so much admires, the traveller sees some unpleasant-looking animals sitting in a field:

Their Shape was very singular, and deformed [. . .] Their Heads and Breasts were covered with a thick Hair, some frizzled and others lank; they had Beards like Goats, and a Long Ridge of Hair down their Backs, and the fore Parts of their Legs and Feet; but the rest of their Bodies were bare, so that I might see their Skins, which were of a brown Buff Colour.   (*Gulliver's Travels*, Part IV, Ch. I)

The animals are, notes Gulliver, tail-less but equipped with claws which they use for climbing trees. The itemization is echoed in *The Lost World* when Challenger quizzes Malone about what he has seen up the tree ('Had it a tail?', 'Was the foot prehensile?'). For both Gulliver and Malone, the repulsive exterior is all too clear a sign of the 'bestial' or 'abominable' animal within. Gulliver is forced to acknowledge kinship with the Yahoos, as the Houyhnhnms term them, when he is brought not so much face to face as side by side with one:

. . . our Countenances [were] diligently compared, both by Master and Servant, who thereupon repeated several Times the Word *Yahoo*. My Horror and Astonishment are not to be described, when I observed, in this abominable Animal, a perfect human Figure . . .   (Part IV, Ch. II)

In *Gulliver's Travels* the shock of recognition intensifies, if anything, Gulliver's detestation of 'that cursed Race of *Yahoos*'. Conan Doyle's tactics in *The Lost World* are more evasive. Some fun is had with the likeness between Professor Challenger and the leader of the ape-men. Roxton notes that their chief had 'every one of our friend's [i.e. Challenger's] beauty points, only just a trifle more so' and when Malone is in a position to make the comparison for himself, he catalogues the 'same short, broad figure, the same heavy shoulders' and so on. The only difference – but a key one, plainly – is in the cranial developments of the Professor and the king of the ape-men. That the scene is being played, essentially, for laughs is confirmed by Challenger's huffing approach to Malone after the rescue: the great academic is concerned about his image, and he dismisses any talk of resemblance as fanciful, although adding that the ape-king 'was really a creature of great distinction'. Challenger can come close to being a figure of fun in a way that Conan Doyle would never permit for Holmes (and, one might almost say, in a way that Holmes would never permit for himself). Malone's encounters with the anthropoids, by contrast, are treated without levity. As if to convince the reader that the ape-men aren't really a laughing matter, their influence on the narrator is straightforwardly visceral: when firing into the thick of them, the tyro war-correspondent is transported by 'the blood lust'; climbing up the look-out tree he experiences revulsion at his first sight of one; caught in an ambush, drawn up inexorably into thick green foliage by a pair of muscular arms (an image of assimilation rather than capture), Malone finds something hypnotic in the terrible blue eyes of his overhead assailant.

Conan Doyle can find only one solution to the problem of the ape-men. It is Kurtz's scrawled message in Conrad's anti-romance, *Heart of Darkness* (1902): 'Exterminate all the brutes!' The time between the discovery of the 'missing link' and its extinction – about three days – must be something of a record in European colonial annals. Except that the extinction isn't quite complete. The Indians destroy the male ape-men, a process justified in terms of retaliation and also in the larger progressive context provided by Challenger ('Now upon this plateau the future must ever be for man'), but the surviving females and young are led off to a life of servitude and, in a comparison that perhaps suggests some residual unease on Conan Doyle's part about the situation which his white characters' guns have helped to engineer, they are likened to 'the Jews of Babylon or the Israelites in Egypt'.

Characters and Sources

As explorers, Conan Doyle's foursome divides into thinkers and doers, at least on a superficial level. The vantage-point is very much that of the practical Malone and so a good deal of humour is extracted from the tendency of Professors Summerlee and Challenger to drop into abstraction or argument at perilously inappropriate moments. Conan Doyle's attitude is ambivalent: the two professors possess 'that highest type of bravery, the bravery of the scientific mind' (Ch. VIII) but they are childish in their constant bickering and one-upmanship as well as child-like in their enthusiasm and capacity for wonder. At first sight of the iguanodons (Ch. X), Summerlee and Challenger 'unconsciously seized each other by the hand, and stood like two little children in the presence of a marvel'. Roxton has the wit to be awed but he also thinks how envious the 'Somaliland–Uganda crowd' would be if he returned with a dinosaur head to hang on his Albany walls. If Challenger is sometimes the parody odd-socks professor, he can also, at the necessary moment, show himself to be as practical and energetic as Roxton or Malone, while Summerlee continually surprises the narrator with his stamina and 'surly courage'.

Malone's unqualified hero-worship is reserved for Lord John Roxton, and in Doyle's portrait there are no nuances or ambiguities. A man's man, Roxton is a soldier-adventurer, a harrier of slave-drivers, a bluff romantic, an English gentleman – and, to judge by the pictures and furniture in his rooms, a species of aesthete (perhaps of the no-nonsense variety). The loyalty and love which Malone has given to his fiancée Gladys, devotion to whom propelled him into the Lost World in the first place, is displaced at the end onto Lord John. Failing to win Gladys's hand – most likely a 'cold and hard' one, by association with her nature – he gains instead Roxton's 'brown hand [which] stretched out to me across the table' in token of another joint expedition but, more importantly, as sign that Malone has been admitted to the fraternity.

Conan Doyle's decision to make his narrator a journalist has several sources. One was that such a figure could plausibly find himself recruited for Challenger's expedition, despite being neither a scientist nor an experienced explorer. Another was the glamour that had by this time attached itself to the most dangerous branch of the profession. Peter Keating makes the point in *The Haunted Study* (1989) that improved communications in the later nineteenth century combined with a new phase of imperial expansion, and with such conflicts as the Crimean and Boer Wars, to place a dramatic emphasis on the messenger: 'The international demand for news made public heroes of the special war correspondents: they were dashing, adventurous, competitive, desperate to be first to reach their paper with a news story, and they were personally named.'[6] That this role was regarded as a supreme test of – as well as an accolade to – journalistic skill is indicated by Malone's comment, before reporting the final battle between the plateau Indians and the ape-men, that 'Often in my dreams have I thought that I might live to be a war correspondent.' Malone's credentials as a brave but modest young man are sketched in at the very beginning when he off-handedly reveals to Gladys that he helped at a mining accident, while his Scots news editor's compliment on his 'true descreeptive touch' points to his narrative capability. The narrator's tone throughout is one of gratitude for being allowed to participate in a great adventure, and, while laughing from time to time at the foibles of his travelling companions, he is also generously active in finding occasions to praise their courage, quick wits, or sportsmanship.

Conan Doyle also had a specific individual in mind in creating E. D. Malone, whose likeable and enthusiastic character is a tribute to the original. From 1909 the world-famous writer had been involved with a young Franco-British journalist, Edmund Dene Morel, in the latter's campaign to expose the brutality of King Leopold II of Belgium's regime in the Congo. This vast area of central Africa had been, in effect, the personal fiefdom of King Leopold (although he never once set foot in the territory that he had appropriated largely by fraud). In 1908 control of the territory was formally ceded to the Belgium government, because of growing international unease over the way the hidden kingdom was being run by Leopold and his agents; in return for his 'generosity', Leopold was paid millions of francs.[7] However, the change was largely cosmetic. The ruthless treatment of the indigenous inhabitants of the Congo basin in pursuit of the region's resources of ivory and rubber – horrific even among colonial records – continued after the hand-over. That it became a *cause célèbre* was thanks largely to Morel's crusading journalism and campaigning.

Another figure involved in the Congo campaign was, at least in part, the basis for Lord John Roxton. In 1903 Roger Casement had reported to the British government on the atrocities perpetrated against the Congo tribes. More relevantly for *The Lost World*, Casement, who became Consul-General at Rio de Janeiro in 1909, was directed by the British Foreign Office to investigate charges of ill-treatment of the natives by the Peruvian Amazon Rubber Company. After a visit to the Putumayo River in northern Peru, where the Company held a concession, he accused its agents of 'crimes of the most atrocious kind, including murder, violation and constant flogging' and demanded pun-

ishment for named individuals.[8] The anger and indignation of Casement provided a model for Roxton's response (with the difference that
the fictional peer exacted punishment himself by killing the 'king' of the
slave-drivers after a one-man war). Casement's report was not published
until 1912 but Doyle, who did the bulk of the writing for *The Lost World*
between October and December 1911, would have known of Casement's findings because of the campaigning association between the
two men. Indeed, both Casement and E. D. Morel were Conan Doyle's
guests at a 1910 performance of the stage version of the Holmes short
story 'The Speckled Band'.[9]

The original for Challenger was, according to Doyle himself, Professor William Rutherford, a physiologist who taught at Edinburgh University. Rutherford was like Challenger in having resigned from a
London chair (in fact twice over), and there was also some physical
resemblance. However, Owen Dudley Edwards and other biographers
have found a variety of sources, including George Bernard Shaw and
possibly the charlatan doctor, George Budd, with whom Conan Doyle
very briefly set up in partnership in Plymouth at the beginning of his
medical career.[10] Challenger's name was suggested not only by his habit
of defying orthodoxy but by Conan Doyle's familiarity as a student with
the exploits of Charles Wyville Thomson, zoologist and leader of a
scientific expedition which had covered nearly 69,000 nautical miles in
its exploration of the depths of the sea, on board a ship named HMS
Challenger.

The Lost World *and the Quest-Romance*

The Lost World takes its place among the very greatest of Victorian–
Edwardian romances, and can be seen as the final flowering of a genre
whose practitioners include Stevenson, Haggard, Kipling and Buchan.
Conan Doyle's awareness of the genre, and of his own place in it, can
be seen in the nice little flourish of cod-authentication which has
Malone, in the midst of danger, doubting the survival of 'this bundle
of manuscript' at the same time as asserting 'that what I am writing is
destined to immortality as a classic of true adventure' (Ch. X). The

emergence of the romance at the *end* of the imperial programme is not an accident. As Patrick Brantlinger observes in *Rule of Darkness*: 'Because late Victorian imperialism had little utilitarian or evangelical optimism about converting the heathen, its fanfare often seems compensatory, an attempt to reclaim a waning heroism or an adolescent romanticism before the frontiers shut down.'[11] For Elaine Showalter, the whole enterprise is more narrowly partisan, an attempt to make the novel less of a woman's domain (both in terms of its readership and its practitioners): 'the revival of romance in the 1880's was a men's literary revolution intended to reclaim the kingdom of the English novel for male writers, male readers, and men's stories.'[12] Certainly, Conan Doyle's epigraph to the novel is sexually exclusive in its appeal to 'the boy who's half a man,/Or the man who's half a boy'. The female presence in *The Lost World* is minimal. Gladys Hungerton is there in Chapter I to give a chivalric kick-start to Malone's participation in the expedition, with her demand for a famous man to marry as well as her expectations of ostentatiously heroic behaviour. She reappears at the end transformed into Gladys Potts, with a (presumably unheroic) solicitor's clerk for husband, leaving Malone to meditate on 'the twin shadows of selfishness and of fickleness' which he thinks he may always have detected in her soul. Mrs Challenger is also a marginal presence; she treats her husband as a dangerous animal which she alone knows how to handle: 'Don't wait to argue with him. Several people have been injured through doing that', she tells Malone. In one of the oddest scenes in the novel he puts her – literally – on a pedestal or, as he terms it, 'Stool of penance', because she upbraids him for his brawling (Ch. IV). In both cases, Conan Doyle seems to be parodying the female role in adventure stories, whether as the motivator for the knight-errantry or as the idealized stay-at-home Penelope, the fixed point for the wanderer.

The Lost World conforms to type in its deployment of the props of the quest-romance, such as tantalizing charts, cryptic messages and inscriptions, mysterious forerunners, and the promise of treasure. These accessories of the genre are frequently given pictorial shape or otherwise reproduced in the body of the text (the original illustrations to both *The Lost World* and *The Poison Belt* are included in this edition).

In Rider Haggard's *King Solomon's Mines* (1886), for example, Allan Quatermain comes into possession of a dying man's statement in Portuguese, as well as a map drawn in his blood, both of them reproduced in the text, describing the path across desert and mountain to the wealth of Solomon. In Verne's *Journey to the Centre of the Earth*, one of Doyle's models for *The Lost World*, Professor Lidenbrock is alerted to the hidden route by the discovery of a parchment containing a runic cipher; as his party descend into the earth they are intermittently guided by the marks of an earlier explorer. John Buchan's *Prester John* (1910), a late and much more explicitly imperial work than the others mentioned, is shaped around an even more mysterious forerunner, the legendary, eponymous king, reincarnated in the ambivalently presented figure of Laputa. As with the adventurers in *King Solomon's Mines* and *The Lost World*, the reward for Buchan's narrator is not only renown but treasure. The gold or the diamonds are, however, the icing on the cake, applied last of all in a narrative coda. No Victorian–Edwardian adventurer can expect to be paid in advance.

Another highly significant feature of the romance is the focus on the journey to the promising land. For Buchan's David Crawfurd in *Prester John*, 'The *Pilgrim's Progress* had been the Sabbath reading of my boyhood', and there is a sense in which all quest-romance becomes a secular pilgrimage across a landscape which is full of exotic threats. One might include in this the very extended London-based prelude of *The Lost World*, for almost the first third of the narrative is occupied by Malone's encounters with Gladys, with his news editor, with Challenger and then with Lord John Roxton. The latter two certainly qualify as exotic, in the challenge and appeal they hold for the Irish-born newsman. After that, the actual journey by canoe and then on foot to the plateau (taking about a fifth of the narrative) is the essential preliminary to the core of the narrative, since it both confirms the heroic difficulty of the enterprise and teasingly delays the moment of arrival. As Brian V. Street says in *The Savage in Literature* (1975), talking of Haggard but describing a pattern which applies equally to Conan Doyle: 'The approach to his inland "paradises" is always along devious, hidden routes, which ensure that the hero is one of the few white men ever to reach that land.'[13]

Apocalypse Averted

The quartet was brought back in the year following the publication of *The Lost World* for the novella *The Poison Belt*. Like *The Lost World* this was an immediate success, running to four editions between publication in October 1913 and the end of the year. This time, Challenger and his party do not have to go on a quest; danger comes to them, and indeed to the whole world, in the shape of a belt of poisonous gas or 'ether' through which the solar system must pass. Challenger, Summerlee, Roxton and Malone gather in the Professor's house overlooking the Sussex downs (the room in which much of the action takes place is modelled on Conan Doyle's study in Windlesham) and from there, like spectators in 'four front seats of the stalls', they sit out the end of the world. Challenger's foresight has provided them with the sealed room and the oxygen cylinders which will enable them to outlive, at least by a few hours, the entire human race.

The four characters react along the lines laid down for them in *The Lost World*. Challenger, glimpsing living amoeba down his microscope, takes the (very) long scientific view that the ultimate restoration of 'animal and human life [. . .] will spring from this tiny root'. Summerlee is querulous and combative. Roxton demonstrates a sporting fatalism, while Malone falls back on his vocation as a recorder of events, producing a narrative from 'mechanical professional habit' even though, as in *The Lost World*, he suspects that no one will ever read it. Mrs Challenger's role is amplified after her brief appearance in the earlier narrative. Now she is there to show the great Professor in his role as domestic protector: in the illustration on the dust-cover of the first edition she is cradled in her bearish husband's arms while a band of mist spirals round them. Mrs Challenger also exhibits – parenthetically – the human response repressed by Edwardian male *sang-froid*: 'We could have wept – Mrs Challenger did weep – when we passed a great Council school and saw the long trail of tiny figures scattered down the road which led from it.'

There is a consciously Wellsian quality to *The Poison Belt*. The Home Counties apocalypse, the vision of London arrested in its tracks, the implicit questioning of humanity's place in the scale of things, all are reminiscent of another and more famous narrative of an incursion from outer space, *The War of the Worlds*. But in comparison with Wells's novel of 1897, Conan Doyle pulls his punches. Damage in *The Poison Belt* is sporadic and limited in scale. The most spectacular disaster glimpsed by the watchers from Challenger's window is a train crash, while the foreground is occupied by the fallen bodies of golfers and nursemaids. When Challenger and his party discover that, because the earth has moved beyond the poison belt, the air is once more safe to breathe they travel to London. There they find its inhabitants frozen in their final postures, some panic-stricken but some in 'so natural an attitude' that it is hard to believe they won't resume their daily routine at any moment. Conan Doyle wishes a nightmare quality on the 'dreadful, silent City' but the scenes do not possess the poetic sense of fracture and ruin that we find in *The War of the Worlds*. Doyle's fundamental, if sometimes willed, optimism can find a silver lining even in apocalypse. The experience which the world has endured in passing through the poison belt is terrible but it is also salutary. The summing-up at the end of the narrative of the lessons which have been learned, presented slightly perfunctorily in the form of an imagined *Times* editorial, suggests that humanity has been jolted into a proper seriousness and humility by 'this revelation of the possibilities of the universe'. In any case, death in *The Poison Belt* has already lost its sting: it is a gentle slipping into sleep or – in line with the author's spiritualist beliefs – a transition to a higher plane.

Conan Doyle and the Sceptics

The other two stories in this collection show Arthur Conan Doyle working in territory that overlaps with the Challenger narratives. In 'The Terror of Blue John Gap' (1910) a tubercular patient convalescing in the Derbyshire hills is at first sceptical of local tales of a monster that dwells in the limestone caves. When eventually encountered, the creature is revealed as a throw-back, like the monsters of *The Lost World*; like them too, its survival can be accounted for scientifically but its impact is visceral. In 'The Horror of the Heights' (1913) an early aviator, Joyce-Armstrong, sets himself to reach a new altitude; his aim, however, is nothing so banal as a place in the record books. He is convinced that the upper air is populated, like the depths of the ocean, by giant creatures that are both beautiful and predatory. He is right on each count. His body is never discovered but among his relics are pieces of a shattered monoplane and a blood-stained manuscript found in a field and known as 'the Joyce-Armstrong Fragment', describing his passage through the upper air. 'The Horror of the Heights' is less a story, more the interrupted record of a revelation. Nothing develops out of Joyce-Armstrong's discovery, except his own disappearance. But the revelation – 'I have seen the beauty and I have seen the horror of the heights' – is enough, and underscores the simple, visionary streak in Conan Doyle.

A feature linking *The Lost World* with *The Poison Belt* and the two non-Challenger short stories is that the central characters in each narrative have to struggle to convince a doubting world of the truth of the 'stories' they are telling. A substantial part of *The Lost World* is taken up with Challenger's confrontations with a sceptical Malone and then with fellow academics and members of the public at the Zoological Institute (Chs III, IV, V), to say nothing of the constant sniping from Summerlee. *The Poison Belt* provides something of a reprise of all this, with Challenger, in Cassandra mode, defying the scepticism of his colleagues and the world. In 'The Terror of Blue John Gap' the narrator is himself a disbeliever in the beginning; when, after his first encounter with the monster, he attempts to tell the story he is referred to the 'best mad doctor in Derbyshire' for his pains. In 'The Horror of the Heights' the doomed aviator aggressively asserts his belief in the existence of 'jungles of the upper air'. There is humour in some of this. As Owen Dudley Edwards shows, the *Lost World* scenes in the Zoological Institute are a reminiscence of Doyle's own days as a medical student in Edinburgh.[14]

But there is something more than knockabout argument in the attempts of the narrators, variously arrogant or defensive, to place their fantastic visions before the world. It is tempting to see in the pattern of confrontation and vindication an echo of Conan Doyle's own public career as a combative campaigner and proselytizer for a variety of causes, including his association with Casement and Morel over the Congo; and, of course, there may be an element of wish-fulfilment here too since, in his fiction at least, Conan Doyle always justifies the campaigner/dreamer against the prosaic or blinkered sceptic. The really significant cause into which Doyle threw his energy and influence in later years was the battle to establish some credentials for spiritualism and it is perhaps significant that, for *The Land of Mist* (1926), the only extended fictional treatment which he attempted of this central area of his life, he should select the most pugnacious (and ostensibly scientific) of his heroes, Professor George Edward Challenger.

The struggle against scepticism or sneering disbelief is not only autobiographical in impulse but also good narrative strategy. The reader's necessary inclination to disbelief is grounded or short-circuited by the protests and objections of other – sometimes objectionable – characters within the story. Doubt or outright rejection provides the friction which enables the narrative wheels to turn. Malone joins the South American expedition because Gladys implicitly questions his manliness; McArdle, Malone's news editor, wants Challenger exposed as a charlatan; Summerlee signs up because he is possessed with the desire to prove his old rival wrong. When the vindication comes in *The Lost World* it arrives in the form of generous concession from the sceptics, as when Summerlee apologizes after a passing pterodactyl has seized the explorers' supper ('Sir, I am very much in the wrong, and I beg that you will forget what is past'), or in dramatic showmanship (the splendid scene of the London pterodactyl in the final chapter).

Yet beyond mere narrative strategy in preparing us for the extraordinary there is Conan Doyle's own desire to show us wonders, as if this were the real business of fiction. Three out of the sixteen chapter titles in *The Lost World* clearly signal this: 'The Most Wonderful Things have Happened', 'A Sight which I shall Never Forget', 'Our Eyes have Seen Great Wonders'. For Joseph Conrad's Marlow in *Heart of Darkness*, the voyage into uncharted territory is a trip into some primal self – 'a region of the first ages', a description which could apply to Doyle's Amazonian plateau but which is employed by Conrad in a more profound and double sense than Conan Doyle would have wanted to conceive. In the upper reaches of the Congo, deprived of the 'solid pavement' underfoot and the social and legal nets of 'scandal and gallows and lunatic asylums', Kurtz has already lost (or found) himself, and Marlow comes close to doing so. But for Arthur Conan Doyle's characters the dangers of withdrawal from society are external only. Doubted by others, they never doubt themselves, except in the conventional way of wondering whether they'll be up to the job. What matters is the journey and the extraordinary destinations and sights: the grand, if monstrous, life-forms in the cave or on the plateau or up in the sky. To enter Conan Doyle's world is to enter what is, essentially, a fairyland, with its requisites of innocence and open-mindedness. The approach is secret and the gateway is, of course, well hidden. So Challenger says to the others as they are about to embark on the final stages of their pilgrimage to the lost world:

The secret opening is half a mile onwards upon the other side of the river. There is no break in the trees. That is the wonder and the mystery of it. There where you see light-green rushes instead of dark-green undergrowth, there between the great cotton woods, that is my private gate into the unknown. Push through, and you will understand.   (Ch. VIII)

NOTES

1. Conan Doyle's speech to the Royal Society's Club is cited in the introductory material on *The Lost World* in Richard Lancelyn Green and John Michael Gibson, *A Bibliography of A. Conan Doyle* (Hudson House, 2000).
2. See e.g. three works which bracket the publication of *The Lost World*. The narrator Marlow muses over the map of Africa in Joseph Conrad's *Heart of Darkness* (1902): 'It had ceased to be a blank space of delightful mystery – a white patch for a boy to dream gloriously over' (Ch. 1); while, in his own person, Conrad talks about looking at his 'beloved old atlas' in his boyhood to see that the 'heart of its Africa was white and big' (from 'Geography and Some Explorers', *Last Essays*, 1926). W. H. Hudson's autobiography *Far Away and Long Ago* (1918), describing his childhood in Argentina, is suffused with a sense of pastoral loss for the way in which the large and empty places are now given over to cultivation.

3. See Damian Thompson's survey of millennial fears and hopes, *The End of Time* (1996), for an explanation of the various ways in which the age of the earth was calculated, pre-Darwin.

4. Stephen Jay Gould, in his fascinating essay 'Dinomania' (in *Dinosaur in a Haystack*, Jonathan Cape, 1996), points out that, by remaking literary dinosaurs out of DNA taken from dinosaur blood inside mosquitoes, etc. preserved within amber, Crichton 'used the best possible scenario for making [them]'. At the same time, Gould shows how this process could never work in real life. He also comments on changing fashions in perception of these extinct beasts and how, once ridiculed as too stupid and slow to prevent their own extinction, dinosaurs are now regarded as 'lithe, agile, potentially warm-blooded, adequately smart, and behaviourally complex creatures'.

5. Crichton's appropriation of Conan Doyle's *Lost World* title for his sequel to *Jurassic Park* is homage or lèse-majesté, depending on your point of view. There are a number of similarities between these prolific and globally popular story-tellers, not least the medical training which each received. The later *Lost World* (1995) contains a sly reference to one John Roxton, a palaeontologist described as an 'enthusiastic fund-raiser' but incompetent when it comes to actual discovery.

6. Peter Keating, *The Haunted Study* (Secker & Warburg, 1989), 299.

7. See *King Leopold's Ghost* by Adam Hochschild (Macmillan, 1999), 257–9, an investigation into the Congo slave-state and the part played by E. D. Morel, Roger Casement and others in exposing it to the world.

8. Cited in H. Montgomery Hyde's *Roger Casement* (Famous Trials 9, Penguin Books, 1964), 44–5.

9. *King Leopold's Ghost*, 270–1.

10. See Chs. 7 and 8 of Owen Dudley Edwards, *The Quest for Sherlock Holmes* (Penguin Books, 1984) for an extensive discussion of possible models for Challenger. Edwards also shows how significant were Conan Doyle's years at Edinburgh University in providing him with raw material for much of the academic flavour of *The Lost World*.

11. Patrick Brantlinger, *Rule of Darkness* (Cornell UP, 1988), 38.

12. Elaine Showalter's observations (from *Sexual Anarchy: Gender and Culture at the fin de siècle*, Bloomsbury, 1991) are quoted in Robert Fraser's *Victorian Quest Romance* (Writers and their Work series; Northcote House, 1998), 2–3.

13. Brian V. Street, *The Savage in Literature* (Routledge & Kegan Paul, 1975), 122.

14. Edwards, *Quest for Sherlock Holmes*, 186–9.

FURTHER READING

The Annotated Sherlock Holmes, ed. William S. Baring-Gould, 2 vols. (1968), is indispensable. Richard Lancelyn Green and John Michael Gibson, *A Bibliography of A. Conan Doyle* (2000) is invaluable.

BIOGRAPHIES

There is no sign of the extraordinary interest in Conan Doyle abating, as a cluster of recent biographies indicate, while his principal creation, Sherlock Holmes, seems to grow in mythic authority year by year. Among recent lives of the author are: Charles Higham, *The Adventures of Conan Doyle* (1976); Julian Symons's illustrated summary, *Portrait of an Artist: Conan Doyle* (1979); Michael Coren's concise *Conan Doyle* (1995), which takes a sympathetic and interesting look at Doyle's spiritualist beliefs; Martin Booth's detailed *The Doctor, the Detective and Arthur Conan Doyle* (1997); Daniel Stashomer's *Teller of Tales* (2000); and, indispensably, Owen Dudley Edwards's *The Quest for Sherlock Holmes* (1984), a biography which illuminates all of Conan Doyle's writing by an examination of his early life and which uncovers much new material, as well as showing everywhere its author's profound commitment to Doyle.

For background on the cultural and publishing conditions which obtained in the late Victorian and Edwardian period, see Peter Keating's panoramic *The Haunted Study: A Social History of the English Novel 1875–1914* (1989), and Peter McDonald's *British Literary Culture and*

Publishing Practice 1840–1914 (1997); the latter contains a substantial section on Conan Doyle and the debut of Sherlock Holmes.

By the time *The Lost World* appeared the Darwinian shock-waves were diminishing, but the novel can still be interpreted as a delayed response to Victorian discoveries about earthly (and human) origins. Gillian Beer's *Darwin's Plots* (1983) shows not only how Darwin himself adopted narrative strategies in relaying his insights, but also the way in which these insights informed the work of writers such as George Eliot and Thomas Hardy. *The Lost World* is widely and correctly seen as an example of romantic/imperial literature, and discussion of the novel under this heading is found in Brian V. Street's *The Savage in Literature* (1975); Patrick Brantlinger's *Rule of Darkness: British Literature and Imperialism, 1830–1914* (1988); and Robert Fraser's *Victorian Quest Romance* (in the Writers and their Work series; 1998). There is a section on Conan Doyle's 'Gothic' writing, including some commentary on the two short stories featured in this volume, 'The Terror of Blue John Gap' and 'The Horror of the Heights', in David Punter's *The Literature of Terror: A History of Gothic Fictions from 1765 to the Present Day*, 2nd edn, Vol. 2 (1996).

CHRONOLOGY

A chronology of Arthur Conan Doyle's life and work is likely to be skeletal. As a highly professional writer, a medical specialist, a public campaigner against injustice, a would-be politician, as well as a sportsman, spiritualist, and well-meaning amateur in fields ranging from skiing to weaponry, he threw himself with generous energy into a variety of lives, any one of which would have satisfied most people. A brief account of his activities can, at best, only suggest the range of an extraordinary life.

1859	Arthur Conan Doyle born at 11 Picardy Place, Edinburgh, on 22 May, second of ten children of Charles Doyle, a civil servant, and Mary Doyle, née Foley. (This year also saw the publication of Darwin's *The Origin of Species*.)
1868–70	Spends two years at Hodder Preparatory School, Lancashire.
1870–75	Spends five years in secondary education at Stonyhurst, the leading Jesuit school, in Lancashire.
1875–6	Attends Jesuit college at Feldkirch, Austria.
1876	Enters Edinburgh University to study medicine. Taught by Joseph Bell, a surgeon at the Edinburgh Infirmary, on whom he later bases some of Sherlock Holmes's powers of detection.
1878	Begins first job, assisting a Dr Richardson in Sheffield. Stays with relatives in Maida Vale, London, his first visit to the capital. Writes novel, *The Narrative of John Smith*, which is lost in the post and never recovered. Works as

assistant in doctor's practice in Ruyton-of-the-eleven-towns, Shropshire, and then in Birmingham.

1879   Publication of first story, 'The Mystery of Sasassa Valley', in the Edinburgh weekly *Chambers's Journal* (September).

1880   Serves as ship's doctor on Greenland whaler the *Hope*.

1881   Serves as ship's doctor on West African cargo steamer the *Mayumba*. Graduates from Edinburgh as Bachelor of Medicine.

1882–90   Establishes solo general medical practice in Southsea, a suburb of Portsmouth, after a brief and unsuccessful partnership with Dr George Turnavine Budd in Plymouth (1882).

1884   Publication in the *Cornhill* magazine of 'J. Habakuk Jephson's Statement', widely taken as a true explanation of the mystery of the *Marie Celeste*.

1885   Marries Louise Hawkins. Obtains a doctorate from Edinburgh for dissertation on syphilis.

1886   Writes *A Study in Scarlet*, the first Sherlock Holmes story, which is rejected by the *Cornhill* magazine and the publishers Arrowsmith but is accepted by Ward Lock who hold it over for a year before publishing.

1887   *A Study in Scarlet* is published in *Beeton's Christmas Annual*.

1889   Birth of first child, Mary Louise. *Micah Clarke*, Conan Doyle's first historical novel, is published. At a meeting arranged by the magazine publishers Lippincott, Conan Doyle is commissioned to write what becomes *The Sign of Four*, the second Sherlock Holmes story.

1890   Publication of *The Firm of Girdlestone*. *The Sign of Four* published in *Lippincott's* magazine. Leaves for Austria to study ophthalmology in Vienna.

1891   Opens short-lived oculist practice in Marylebone, London, half a mile east of Baker Street. First six Holmes short stories published in the *Strand* magazine. Abandons medical career and moves to Norwood, south-east London, to take up writing full time. Publication of *The White Company*.

1892   Birth of Kingsley Conan Doyle. *The Adventures of Sherlock Holmes* collection of short stories published.

1893   Louise diagnosed with tuberculosis. More Sherlock Holmes short stories published in the *Strand* and later collected as *The Memoirs of Sherlock Holmes*. In one of these, 'The Final Problem', Conan Doyle apparently kills off Holmes at the Reichenbach Falls. His father, Charles Doyle, dies in the same year. *The Refugees* published.

1894   Makes a very successful US lecture tour with his brother Innes. Publication of *Round the Red Lamp*, a collection of medical stories.

1896   Publication of *The Exploits of Brigadier Gerard* and *Rodney Stone*. *The Field Bazaar*, a Conan Doyle Holmes pastiche and the first new Holmes work since the detective's 'death', is published in an Edinburgh University student magazine. Moves to Hindhead, Surrey.

1897   Publication of *Uncle Bernac*. Meets and falls in love with Jean Leckie.

1898   Publication of *The Tragedy of the Korosko* and *Songs of Action*.

1900   Serves as a volunteer doctor in South Africa during the Boer War and produces an account of the struggle in *The Great Boer War*. Stands (unsuccessfully) as Liberal Unionist candidate for Edinburgh constituency.

1901   *The Hound of the Baskervilles*, set before Holmes's 'official' death in 'The Final Problem', begins publication in the *Strand*.

1902   Receives knighthood. *The Hound of the Baskervilles* published in book form.

1903   Publication of *The Adventures of Gerard*. Holmes properly resurrected in 'The Empty House', published in the *Strand*.

1905   *The Return of Sherlock Holmes*, the latest collection of Holmes short stories that began with 'The Empty House', published in book form.

1906   Stands (unsuccessfully) as Unionist candidate for Hawick on the Scottish Borders. Publication of *Sir Nigel*. Death of Louise Conan Doyle.

1907   Marries Jean Leckie. Publication of *Through the Magic Door*.

1908   Publication of *Round the Fire Stories*. Moves to Crow-
borough, Sussex. A new Holmes short story, 'The Singular
Experience of Mr John Scott Eccles', later renamed 'The
Adventure of Wisteria Lodge', published in the *Strand*.

1909   Joins with journalist E. D. Morel (model for Ned Malone
in *The Lost World*) to campaign against brutality of the
Belgian Congo regime, and writes *The Crime of the Congo*.
Birth of son Denis.

1910   Birth of Adrian. Holmes play, *The Speckled Band*, opens at
the Adelphi, London. Holmes short story 'The Devil's
Foot' published in the *Strand*.

1911   Holmes short stories 'The Red Circle' and 'The Dis-
appearance of Lady Frances Carfax' published in the
Strand. Conan Doyle is converted to Irish Home Rule by
Sir Roger Casement.

1912   *The Lost World*, now the most famous of Doyle's non-
Holmes stories, begins serialization in the *Strand* and is
published in book form in October. Birth of Jean.

1913   Publication of *The Poison Belt*. Holmes short story 'The
Dying Detective' published in the *Strand*.

1914   Conan Doyle forms volunteer force on outbreak of the
First World War. Holmes story *The Valley of Fear* begins
serialization in the *Strand*.

1915   Publication of *The Valley of Fear* in book form.

1916   Conan Doyle makes first of several visits to the front line
areas and produces an account of the British campaign in
France. Joins unsuccessful movement to reprieve Irish
patriot Sir Roger Casement from execution for treason
following the Easter Rising in Dublin (Lord John Roxton
in *The Lost World* is partly based on Casement).

1917   'His Last Bow', subtitled 'The War Service of Sherlock
Holmes', published in the *Strand*. The recent Holmes short
stories collected as *His Last Bow* and published in book
form.

1918   Death of eldest son Kingsley from pneumonia after being wounded at the Somme. Conan Doyle publishes his first book on spiritualism, *The New Revelation*; begins new career as an ardent global campaigner for spiritualism.

1919   Death of younger brother Innes from pneumonia.

1921–7   New Holmes short stories published in the *Strand*.

1921   Death of Conan Doyle's mother, Mary Foley.

1924   Autobiography, *Memories and Adventures*, published.

1926   Publication of third Professor Challenger story, *The Land of Mist* (narrative with a spiritualist theme).

1927   Recent short stories collected in book form as *The Case-Book of Sherlock Holmes*, the last volume of Holmes stories published.

1929   Appearance of the final Professor Challenger story, 'When the World Screamed', in *The Maracot Deep and Other Stories*.

1930   Arthur Conan Doyle dies on 7 July at home in Crowborough.

NOTE ON THE TEXTS

The Lost World first appeared in serial form in the USA in the *Philadelphia Press* between March and July of 1912, and in Great Britain in the *Strand* magazine (with which Arthur Conan Doyle had had a long and highly successful association) between April and November of the same year. Conan Doyle's British publishers, Hodder & Stoughton, arranged an extensive publicity campaign for the first appearance of the story in a single volume on 15 October 1912, at the price of 6 shillings; on the title-page Conan Doyle is identified not as the author of the phenomenally acclaimed Sherlock Holmes stories but as the creator of historical romances like *Sir Nigel* and *The White Company*, suggesting that he or his publishers regarded *The Lost World* as being in a not totally dissimilar vein. The same day in October 1912 saw the first US book publication (by the George H. Doran Company).

The Poison Belt was serialized in the *Strand* magazine between March and July 1913, and in the New York edition of the *Strand* between April and August of the same year. Hodder & Stoughton issued the first one-volume edition (price 3 shillings and 6 pence) on 13 August 1913, and, in conjunction with the George H. Doran Company, issued the first US edition on 23 August 1913. The novel capitalized on the great success of the earlier volume by advertising itself on the title-page as 'Being an account of another adventure of [. . .] the discoverers of "The Lost World"'. The illustrations for *The Poison Belt* (reproduced in this edition) are attributed on the title-page of the first edition to Harry Rountree.

'The Terror of Blue John Gap' first appeared in August 1910, in the *Strand* magazine and then in the *New York Sun* Sunday magazine in

December 1912, by which time it had appeared in book form as part of a short-story collection. It was featured in *The Last Galley*, published in Britain by Smith, Elder & Co., price 6 shillings (April 1911) and in the USA by Doubleday, Page & Company (September 1911).

'The Horror of the Heights' appeared in the *Strand* magazine and in the New York publication *Everybody's Magazine* in the same month, November 1913. It was included in *Danger! And Other Stories*, published in Britain by John Murray, price 6 shillings (December 1918), and in the USA by the George H. Doran Company (February 1919).

In preparing this edition I have used the first book edition of each narrative, rather than its earlier magazine serialization. Apart from a few cases of standardization or modernized usage (e.g. 'tomorrow' for 'to-morrow', '*The Times*' rather than 'the *Times*') and some minor changes of punctuation, there are only a handful of alterations to evident misprints. These have been checked against later editions. They are: 'opal-tinted' for 'oval-tinted' (*The Lost World*, p. 166); 'the Straits of Sunda' for 'the Straits of Sudan' (*The Poison Belt*, p. 216); 'Macdona' for 'Macdonna' (*The Poison Belt*, p. 268), since the name appears with the first spelling in *The Lost World*; and 'breed' for 'weed' (*The Poison Belt*, p. 297), on the grounds that Challenger has already used 'breed' to characterize the Press in the same speech and that, however much the Professor detests reporters, 'weed' seems to me an un-Challenger-like term!

The Lost World

Being an account of the recent amazing adventures of
Professor George E. Challenger, Lord John Roxton,
Professor Summerlee, and Mr E. D. Malone of
the 'Daily Gazette'.

I have wrought my simple plan
    If I give one hour of joy
To the boy who's half a man,
    Or the man who's half a boy.

Professor Summerlee, F.R.S.

E. D. Malone (*Daily Gazette*) Professor G. E. Challenger, F.R.S., F.R.G.S. Lord John Roxton

The members of the exploring party (From a photograph by William Ransford, Hampstead)

FOREWORD

Mr E. D. Malone[1] desires to state that both the injunction for restraint and the libel action have been withdrawn unreservedly by Professor G. E. Challenger, who, being satisfied that no criticism or comment in this book is meant in an offensive spirit, has guaranteed that he will place no impediment to its publication and circulation. Mr E. D. Malone would wish also to express his gratitude to Mr Patrick L. Forbes, of Rosslyn Hill, Hampstead, for the skill and sympathy with which he has worked up the sketches which were brought from South America, and also to Mr W. Ransford, of Elm Row, Hampstead, for his valuable expert help in dealing with the photographs.

CONTENTS

CHAPTER I

There are Heroisms All Round Us

Mr Hungerton, her father, really was the most tactless person upon earth – a fluffy, feathery, untidy cockatoo of a man, perfectly good-natured, but absolutely centred upon his own silly self. If anything could have driven me from Gladys, it would have been the thought of such a father-in-law. I am convinced that he really believed in his heart that I came round to the Chestnuts three days a week for the pleasure of his company, and very especially to hear his views upon bimetallism[1] – a subject upon which he was by way of being an authority.

For an hour or more that evening I listened to his monotonous chirrup about bad money driving out good, the token value of silver, the depreciation of the rupee, and the true standards of exchange.

'Suppose,' he cried, with feeble violence, 'that all the debts in the world were called up simultaneously and immediate payment insisted upon. What, under our present conditions, would happen then?'

I gave the self-evident answer that I should be a ruined man, upon which he jumped from his chair, reproved me for my habitual levity, which made it impossible for him to discuss any reasonable subject in my presence, and bounced off out of the room to dress for a Masonic meeting.

At last I was alone with Gladys, and the moment of fate had come!

All that evening I had felt like the soldier who awaits the signal which will send him on a forlorn hope, hope of victory and fear of repulse alternating in his mind.

She sat with that proud, delicate profile of hers outlined against the red curtain. How beautiful she was! And yet how aloof! We had been friends, quite good friends; but never could I get beyond the same comradeship which I might have established with one of my fellow-reporters upon the *Gazette* – perfectly frank, perfectly kindly, and perfectly unsexual. My instincts are all against a woman being too frank and at her ease with me. It is no compliment to a man. Where the real sex feeling begins, timidity and distrust are its companions, heritage from old wicked days when love and violence went often hand in hand. The bent head, the averted eye, the faltering voice, the wincing figure – these, and not the unshrinking gaze and frank reply, are the true signals of passion. Even in my short life I had learned as much as that – or had inherited it in that race-memory which we call instinct.

Gladys was full of every womanly quality. Some judged her to be cold and hard, but such a thought was treason. That delicately-bronzed skin, almost Oriental in its colouring, that raven hair, the large liquid eyes, the full but exquisite lips – all the stigmata of passion were there. But I was sadly conscious that up to now I had never found the secret of drawing it forth. However, come what might, I should have done with suspense and bring matters to a head tonight. She could but refuse me, and better be a repulsed lover than an accepted brother.

So far my thoughts had carried me, and I was about to break the long and uneasy silence when two critical dark eyes looked round at me, and the proud head was shaken in smiling reproof.

'I have a presentiment that you are going to propose, Ned. I do wish you wouldn't, for things are so much nicer as they are.'

I drew my chair a little nearer.

'Now, how did you know that I was going to propose?' I asked, in genuine wonder.

'Don't women always know? Do you suppose any woman in the world was ever taken unawares? But, oh, Ned, our friendship has been so good and so pleasant! What a pity to spoil it! Don't you feel how splendid it is that a young man and a young woman should be able to talk face to face as we have talked?'

'I don't know, Gladys. You see, I can talk face to face with – with the station-master.' I can't imagine how that official came into the matter, but in he trotted and set us both laughing. 'That does not satisfy me in the least. I want my arms round you and your head on my breast, and, oh, Gladys, I want –'

She had sprung from her chair as she saw signs that I proposed to demonstrate some of my wants.

'You've spoiled everything, Ned,' she said. 'It's all so beautiful and natural until this kind of thing comes in. It is such a pity. Why can't you control yourself?'

'I didn't invent it,' I pleaded. 'It's nature. It's love.'

'Well, perhaps if both love it may be different. I have never felt it.'

'But you must – you, with your beauty, with your soul! Oh, Gladys, you were made for love! You must love!'

'One must wait till it comes.'

'But why can't you love me, Gladys? Is it my appearance, or what?'

She did unbend a little. She put forward a hand – such a gracious, stooping attitude it was – and she pressed back my head. Then she looked into my upturned face with a very wistful smile.

'No, it isn't that,' she said at last. 'You're not a conceited boy by nature, and so I can safely tell you that it is not that. It's deeper.'

'My character?'

She nodded severely.

'What can I do to mend it? Do sit down and talk it over. No, really I won't, if you'll only sit down!'

She looked at me with a wondering distrust which was much more to my mind than her whole-hearted confidence. How primitive and bestial it looks when you put it down in black and white! And perhaps after all it is only a feeling peculiar to myself. Anyhow, she sat down.

'Now tell me what's amiss with me.'

'I'm in love with somebody else,' said she.

It was my turn to jump out of my chair.

'It's nobody in particular,' she explained, laughing at the expression of my face, 'only an ideal. I've never met the kind of man I mean.'

'Tell me about him. What does he look like?'

'Oh, he might look very much like you.'

'How dear of you to say that! Well, what is it that he does that I don't do? Just say the word – teetotal, vegetarian, aeronaut, Theosophist,[2] Superman[3] – I'll have a try at it, Gladys, if you will only give me an idea what would please you.'

She laughed at the elasticity of my character. 'Well, in the first place, I don't think my ideal would speak like that,' said she. 'He would be a harder, sterner man, not so ready to adopt himself to a silly girl's whim. But above all he must be a man who could do, who could act, who would look Death in the face and have no fear of him – a man of great deeds and strange experiences. It is never a man that I should love, but always the glories he had won, for they would be reflected upon me. Think of Richard Burton![4] When I read his wife's life of him I could so understand her love. And Lady Stanley![5] Did you ever read the wonderful last chapter of that book about her husband? These are the sort of men that a woman could worship with all her soul and yet be the greater, not the less, on account of her love, honoured by all the world as the inspirer of noble deeds.'

She looked so beautiful in her enthusiasm that I nearly brought down the whole level of the interview. I gripped myself hard, and went on with the argument.

'We can't all be Stanleys and Burtons,' said I. 'Besides, we don't get the chance – at least, I never had the chance. If I did I should try to take it.'

'But chances are all around you. It is the mark of the kind of man I mean that he makes his own chances. You can't hold him back. I've never met him, and yet I seem to know him so well. There are heroisms all round us waiting to be done. It's for men to do them, and for women to reserve their love as a reward for such men. Look at that young Frenchman who went up last week in a balloon. It was blowing a gale of wind, but because he was announced to go he insisted on starting. The wind blew him one thousand five hundred miles in twenty-four hours, and he fell in the middle of Russia. That was the kind of man I mean. Think of the woman he loved, and how other women must have envied her! That's what I should like – to be envied for my man.'

'I'd have done it to please you.'

'But you shouldn't do it merely to please me. You should do it because you can't help it, because it's natural to you – because the man in you is crying out for heroic expression. Now, when you described the Wigan coal explosion last month, could you not have gone down and helped those people, in spite of the choke-damp.'[6]

'I did.'

'You never said so.'

'There was nothing worth bucking[7] about.'

'I didn't know.' She looked at me with rather more interest. 'That was brave of you.'

'I had to. If you want to write good copy you must be where the things are.'

'What a prosaic motive! It seems to take all the romance out of it. But still, whatever your motive, I am glad that you went down that mine.' She gave me her hand, but with such sweetness and dignity that I could only stoop and kiss it. 'I dare say I am merely a foolish woman with a young girl's fancies. And yet it is so real with me, so entirely part of my very self, that I cannot help acting upon it. If I marry, I do want to marry a famous man.'

'Why should you not?' I cried. 'It is women like you who brace men up. Give me a chance and see if I will take it! Besides, as you say, men ought to *make* their own chances, and not wait until they are given. Look at Clive[8] – just a clerk, and he conquered India. By George! I'll do something in the world yet!'

She laughed at my sudden Irish effervescence.

'Why not?' she said. 'You have everything a man could have – youth, health, strength, education, energy. I was sorry you spoke. And now I am glad – so glad – if it wakens these thoughts in you.'

'And if I do –?'

Her hand rested like warm velvet upon my lips.

'Not another word, sir. You should have been at the office for evening duty half an hour ago, only I hadn't the heart to remind you. Some day, perhaps, when you have won your place in the world, we shall talk it over again.'

And so it was that I found myself that foggy November evening pursuing the Camberwell tram with my heart glowing within me, and with the eager determination that not another day should elapse before I should find some deed which was worthy of my lady. But who in all this wide world could ever have imagined the incredible shape which that deed was to take, or the strange steps by which I was led to the doing of it?

And, after all, this opening chapter will seem to the reader to have nothing to do with my narrative; and yet there would have been no narrative without it, for it is only when a man goes out into the world with the thought that there are heroisms all round him, and with the desire all alive in his heart to follow any which may come within sight of him, that he breaks away as I did from the life he knows, and ventures forth into the wonderful mystic twilight land where lie the great adventures and the great rewards. Behold me, then, at the office of the *Daily Gazette*, on the staff of which I was a most insignificant unit, with the settled determination that very night, if possible, to find the quest which should be worthy of my Gladys! Was it hardness, was it selfishness, that she should ask me to risk my life for her own glorification? Such thoughts may come to middle age, but never to ardent three-and-twenty in the fever of his first love.

CHAPTER II

Try your Luck with Professor Challenger

I always liked McArdle, the crabbed old, round-backed, red-headed news editor, and I rather hoped that he liked me. Of course, Beaumont was the real boss, but he lived in the rarefied atmosphere of some Olympian height from which he could distinguish nothing smaller than an international crisis or a split in the Cabinet. Sometimes we saw him passing in lonely majesty to his inner sanctum with his eyes staring vaguely and his mind hovering over the Balkans or the Persian Gulf. He was above and beyond us. But McArdle was his first lieutenant, and it was he that we knew. The old man nodded as I entered the room, and he pushed his spectacles far up on his bald forehead.

'Well, Mr Malone, from all I hear, you seem to be doing very well,' said he, in his kindly Scotch accent.

I thanked him.

'The colliery explosion was excellent. So was the Southwark fire. You have the true descreeptive touch. What did you want to see me about?'

'To ask a favour.'

He looked alarmed and his eyes shunned mine.

'Tut! tut! What is it?'

'Do you think, sir, that you could possibly send me on some mission for the paper? I would do my best to put it through and get you some good copy.'

'What sort of a meesion had you in your mind, Mr Malone?'

'Well, sir, anything that had adventure and danger in it. I would really do my very best. The more difficult it was the better it would suit me.'

'You seem very anxious to lose your life.'

'To justify my life, sir.'

'Dear me, Mr Malone, this is very – very exalted. I'm afraid the day for this sort of thing is rather past. The expense of the "special meesion" business hardly justifies the result, and, of course, in any case it would only be an experienced man with a name that would command public confidence who would get such an order. The big blank spaces in the map are all being filled in, and there's no room for romance anywhere. Wait a bit, though!' he added, with a sudden smile upon his face. 'Talking of the blank spaces of the map gives me an idea. What about exposing a fraud – a modern Munchausen[1] – and making him rideeculous? You could show him up as the liar that he is! Eh, man, it would be fine. How does it appeal to you?'

'Anything – anywhere – I care nothing.'

McArdle was plunged in thought for some minutes.

'I wonder whether you could get on friendly – or at least on talking terms with the fellow,' he said, at last. 'You seem to have a sort of genius for establishing relations with people – seempathy, I suppose, or animal magnetism, or youthful vitality, or something. I am conscious of it myself.'

'You are very good, sir.'

'So why should you not try your luck with Professor Challenger, of Enmore Park?'

I dare say I looked a little startled.

'Challenger!' I cried. 'Professor Challenger, the famous zoologist! Wasn't he the man who broke the skull of Blundell, of the *Telegraph*?'

The news editor smiled grimly.

'Do you mind? Didn't you say it was adventures you were after?'

'It is all in the way of business, sir,' I answered.

'Exactly. I don't suppose he can always be so violent as that. I'm thinking that Blundell got him at the wrong moment, maybe, or in the wrong fashion. You may have better luck, or more tact in handling him. There's something in your line there, I am sure, and the *Gazette* should work it.'

'I really know nothing about him,' said I. 'I only remember his name in connection with the police-court proceedings, for striking Blundell.'

'I have a few notes for your guidance, Mr Malone. I've had my eye on the Professor for some little time.' He took a paper from a drawer. 'Here is a summary of his record. I give it you briefly: –

' "Challenger, George Edward. *Born:* Largs, N.B., 1863. *Educ.:* Largs Academy; Edinburgh University. British Museum Assistant, 1892. Assistant-Keeper of Comparative Anthropology Department, 1893. Resigned after acrimonious Correspondence same year. Winner of Crayston Medal for Zoological Research. Foreign Member of" – well, quite a lot of things, about two inches of small type – "Société Belge, American Academy of Sciences, La Plata, etc., etc. Ex-President Palaeontological Society. Section H, British Association" – so on, so on! – "*Publications:* 'Some Observations Upon a Series of Kalmuck Skulls'; 'Outlines of Vertebrate Evolution'; and numerous papers, including 'The Underlying Fallacy of Weissmannism',[2] which caused heated discussion at the Zoological Congress of Vienna. *Recreations:* Walking, Alpine climbing. *Address:* Enmore Park, Kensington, W."

'There, take it with you. I've nothing more for you tonight.'

I pocketed the slip of paper.

'One moment, sir,' I said, as I realized that it was a pink bald head, and not a red face, which was fronting me. 'I am not very clear yet why I am to interview this gentleman. What has he done?'

The face flashed back again.

'Went to South America on a solitary expedeetion two years ago. Came back last year. Had undoubtedly been to South America, but refused to say exactly where. Began to tell his adventures in a vague way, but somebody started to pick holes, and he just shut up like an oyster. Something wonderful happened – or the man's a champion liar, which is the more probable supposeetion. Had some damaged photographs, said to be fakes. Got so touchy that he assaults anyone who asks questions, and heaves reporters doun the stairs. In my opinion he's just a homicidal megalomaniac with a turn for science. That's your man, Mr Malone. Now, off you run, and see what you can make of him. You're big enough to look after yourself. Anyway, you are all safe. Employers' Liability Act, you know.'

A grinning red face turned once more into a pink oval, fringed with gingery fluff; the interview was at an end.

I walked across to the Savage Club,[3] but instead of turning into it I leaned upon the railings of Adelphi Terrace and gazed thoughtfully for a long time at the brown, oily river. I can always think most sanely and clearly in the open air. I took out the list of Professor Challenger's exploits, and I read it over under the electric lamp. Then I had what I can only regard as an inspiration. As a Pressman, I felt sure from what I had been told that I could never hope to get into touch with this cantankerous Professor. But these recriminations, twice mentioned in his skeleton biography, could only mean that he was a fanatic in science. Was there not an exposed margin there upon which he might be accessible? I would try.

I entered the club. It was just after eleven, and the big room was fairly full, though the rush had not yet set in. I noticed a tall, thin, angular man seated in an arm-chair by the fire. He turned as I drew my chair up to him. It was the man of all others whom I should have chosen – Tarp Henry, of the staff of *Nature*,[4] a thin, dry, leathery creature, who was full, to those who knew him, of kindly humanity. I plunged instantly into my subject.

'What do you know of Professor Challenger?'

'Challenger?' He gathered his brows in scientific disapproval. 'Challenger was the man who came with some cock-and-bull story from South America.'

'What story?'

'Oh, it was rank nonsense about some queer animals he had discovered. I believe he has retracted since. Anyhow, he has suppressed it all. He gave an interview to Reuter's, and there was such a howl that he saw it wouldn't do. It was a discreditable business. There were one or two folk who were inclined to take him seriously, but he soon choked them off.'

'How?'

'Well, by his insufferable rudeness and impossible behaviour. There was poor old Wadley, of the Zoological Institute. Wadley sent a message: "The President of the Zoological Institute presents his compliments to Professor Challenger, and would take it as a personal favour if he would do them the honour to come to their next meeting." The answer was unprintable.'

'You don't say?'

'Well, a bowdlerized version of it would run: "Professor Challenger presents his compliments to the President of the Zoological Institute, and would take it as a personal favour if he would go to the devil." '

'Good Lord!'

'Yes, I expect that's what old Wadley said. I remember his wail at the meeting, which began: "In fifty years experience of scientific intercourse – " It quite broke the old man up.'

'Anything more about Challenger?'

'Well, I'm a bacteriologist, you know. I live in a nine-hundred-diameter microscope. I can hardly claim to take serious notice of anything that I can see with my naked eye. I'm a frontiersman from the extreme edge of the Knowable, and I feel quite out of place when I leave my study and come into touch with all you great, rough, hulking creatures. I'm too detached to talk scandal, and yet at scientific conversaziones I *have* heard something of Challenger, for he is one of those men whom nobody can ignore. He's as clever as they make 'em – a full-charged battery of force and vitality, but a quarrelsome, ill-conditioned faddist, and unscrupulous at that. He had gone the length of faking some photographs over the South American business.'

'You say he is a faddist. What is his particular fad?'

'He has a thousand, but the latest is something about Weissmann and Evolution. He had a fearful row about it in Vienna, I believe.'

'Can't you tell me the point?'

'Not at the moment, but a translation of the proceedings exists. We have it filed at the office. Would you care to come?'

'It's just what I want. I have to interview the fellow, and I need some lead up to him. It's really awfully good of you to give me a lift. I'll go with you now, if it is not too late.'

Half an hour later I was seated in the newspaper office with a huge tome in front of me, which had been opened at the article 'Weissmann *versus* Darwin', with the sub-heading, 'Spirited Protest at Vienna. Lively Proceedings.' My scientific education having been somewhat neglected, I was unable to follow the whole argument, but it was evident that the English Professor had handled his subject in a very aggressive fashion, and had thoroughly annoyed his Continental colleagues. 'Protests', 'Uproar', and 'General appeal to the Chairman' were three of the first brackets which caught my eye. Most of the matter might have been written in Chinese for any definite meaning that it conveyed to my brain.

'I wish you could translate it into English for me,' I said, pathetically, to my help-mate.

'Well, it is a translation.'

'Then I'd better try my luck with the original.'

'It is certainly rather deep for a layman.'

'If I could only get a single good, meaty sentence which seemed to convey some sort of definite human idea, it would serve my turn. Ah, yes, this one will do. I seem in a vague way almost to understand it. I'll copy it out. This shall be my link with the terrible Professor.'

'Nothing else I can do?'

'Well, yes; I propose to write to him. If I could frame the letter here, and use your address, it would give atmosphere.'

'We'll have the fellow round here making a row and breaking the furniture.'

'No, no; you'll see the letter – nothing contentious, I assure you.'

'Well, that's my chair and desk. You'll find paper there. I'd like to censor it before it goes.'

It took some doing, but I flatter myself that it wasn't such a bad job when it was finished. I read it aloud to the critical bacteriologist with some pride in my handiwork.

'Dear Professor Challenger,' it said. 'As a humble student of Nature, I have always taken the most profound interest in your speculations as to the differences between Darwin and Weissmann. I have recently had occasion to refresh my memory by re-reading –'

'You infernal liar!' murmured Tarp Henry.

' – by re-reading your masterly address at Vienna. That lucid and admirable statement seems to be the last word in the matter. There is one sentence in it, however – namely: "I protest strongly against the insufferable and entirely dogmatic assertion that each separate *id* is a microcosm possessed of an historical architecture elaborated slowly through the series of generations." Have you no desire, in view of later research, to modify this statement? Do you not think that it is over-accentuated? With your permission, I would ask the favour of an interview, as I feel strongly upon the subject, and have certain suggestions which I could only elaborate in a personal conversation. With your consent, I trust to have the honour of calling at eleven o'clock the day after tomorrow (Wednesday) morning.

'I remain, Sir, with assurances of profound respect, yours very truly, 'EDWARD D. MALONE.'

'How's that?' I asked, triumphantly.

'Well, if your conscience can stand it –'

'It has never failed me yet.'

'But what do you mean to do?'

'To get there. Once I am in his room I may see some opening. I may even go the length of open confession. If he is a sportsman he will be tickled.'

'Tickled, indeed! He's much more likely to do the tickling. Chain mail, or an American football suit – that's what you'll want. Well, goodbye. I'll have the answer for you here on Wednesday morning – if he ever deigns to answer you. He is a violent, dangerous, cantankerous character, hated by everyone who comes across him, and the butt of the students, so far as they dare take a liberty with him. Perhaps it would be best for you if you never heard from the fellow at all.'

CHAPTER III

He is a Perfectly Impossible Person

My friend's fear or hope was not destined to be realized. When I called on Wednesday there was a letter with the West Kensington postmark upon it, and my name scrawled across the envelope in a handwriting which looked like a barbed-wire railing. The contents were as follows:–

'Enmore Park, W.

'Sir, – I have duly received your note, in which you claim to endorse my views, although I am not aware that they are dependent upon endorsement either from you or anyone else. You have ventured to use the word "speculation" with regard to my statement upon the subject of Darwinism, and I would call your attention to the fact that such a word in such a connection is offensive to a degree. The context convinces me, however, that you have sinned rather through ignorance and tactlessness than through malice, so I am content to pass the matter by. You quote an isolated sentence from my lecture, and appear to have some difficulty in understanding it. I should have thought that only a sub-human intelligence could have failed to grasp the point, but if it really needs amplification I shall consent to see you at the hour named, though visits and visitors of every sort are exceedingly distasteful to me. As to your suggestion that I may modify my opinion, I would have you know that it is not my habit to do so after a deliberate expression of my mature views. You will kindly show the envelope of this letter to my man, Austin, when you call, as he has to take every precaution to shield me from the intrusive rascals who call themselves "journalists".

'Yours faithfully.

'GEORGE EDWARD CHALLENGER.'

This was the letter that I read aloud to Tarp Henry, who had come down early to hear the result of my venture. His only remark was, 'There's some new stuff, cuticura or something, which is better than arnica.'[1] Some people have such extraordinary notions of humour.

It was nearly half-past ten before I had received my message, but a taxicab took me round in good time for my appointment. It was an imposing porticoed house at which we stopped, and the heavily-curtained windows gave every indication of wealth upon the part of this formidable Professor. The door was opened by an odd, swarthy, dried-up person of uncertain age, with a dark pilot jacket and brown leather gaiters. I found afterwards that he was the chauffeur, who filled the gaps left by a succession of fugitive butlers. He looked me up and down with a searching light blue eye.

'Expected?' he asked.

'An appointment.'

'Got your letter?'

I produced the envelope.

'Right!' He seemed to be a person of few words. Following him down the passage I was suddenly interrupted by a small woman, who stepped out from what proved to be the dining-room door. She was a bright, vivacious, dark-eyed lady, more French than English in her type.

'One moment,' she said. 'You can wait, Austin. Step in here, sir. May I ask if you have met my husband before?'

'No, madam, I have not had the honour.'

'Then I apologize to you in advance. I must tell you that he is a perfectly impossible person – absolutely impossible. If you are forewarned you will be the more ready to make allowances.'

'It is most considerate of you, madam.'

'Get quickly out of the room if he seems inclined to be violent.

Don't wait to argue with him. Several people have been injured through doing that. Afterwards there is a public scandal, and it reflects upon me and all of us. I suppose it wasn't about South America you wanted to see him?'

I could not lie to a lady.

'Dear me! That is his most dangerous subject. You won't believe a word he says – I'm sure I don't wonder. But don't tell him so, for it makes him very violent. Pretend to believe him, and you may get through all right. Remember he believes it himself. Of that you may be assured. A more honest man never lived. Don't wait any longer or he may suspect. If you find him dangerous – really dangerous – ring the bell and hold him off until I come. Even at his worst I can usually control him.'

With these encouraging words the lady handed me over to the taciturn Austin, who had waited like a bronze statue of discretion during our short interview, and I was conducted to the end of the passage. There was a tap at a door, a bull's bellow from within, and I was face to face with the Professor.

He sat in a rotating chair behind a broad table, which was covered with books, maps, and diagrams. As I entered, his seat spun round to face me. His appearance made me gasp. I was prepared for something strange, but not for so overpowering a personality as this. It was his size which took one's breath away – his size and his imposing presence. His head was enormous, the largest I have ever seen upon a human being. I am sure that his top-hat, had I ever ventured to don it, would have slipped over me entirely and rested on my shoulders. He had the face and beard which I associate with an Assyrian bull;[2] the former florid, the latter so black as almost to have a suspicion of blue, spade-shaped and rippling down over his chest. The hair was peculiar, plastered down in front in a long, curving wisp over his massive forehead. The eyes were blue-grey under great black tufts, very clear, very critical, and very masterful. A huge spread of shoulders and a chest like a barrel were the other parts of him which appeared above the table, save for two enormous hands covered with long black hair. This and a bellowing, roaring, rumbling voice made up my first impression of the notorious Professor Challenger.

'Well?' said he, with a most insolent stare. 'What now?'

I must keep up my deception for at least a little time longer, otherwise here was evidently an end of the interview.

'You were good enough to give me an appointment, sir,' said I, humbly, producing his envelope.

He took my letter from his desk and laid it out before him.

'Oh, you are the young person who cannot understand plain English, are you? My general conclusions you are good enough to approve, as I understand?'

'Entirely, sir – entirely!' I was very emphatic.

'Dear me! That strengthens my position very much, does it not? Your age and appearance make your support doubly valuable. Well, at least you are better than that herd of swine in Vienna, whose gregarious grunt is, however, not more offensive than the isolated effort of the British hog.' He glared at me as the present representative of the beast.

'They seem to have behaved abominably,' said I.

'I assure you that I can fight my own battles, and that I have no possible need of your sympathy. Put me alone, sir, and with my back to the wall. G. E. C. is happiest then. Well, sir, let us do what we can to curtail this visit, which can hardly be agreeable to you, and is inexpressibly irksome to me. You had, as I have been led to believe, some comments to make upon the proposition which I advanced in my thesis.'

There was a brutal directness about his methods which made evasion difficult. I must still make play and wait for a better opening. It had seemed simple enough at a distance. Oh, my Irish wits, could they not help me now, when I needed help so sorely? He transfixed me with two sharp, steely eyes. 'Come, come!' he rumbled.

'I am, of course, a mere student,' said I, with a fatuous smile, 'hardly more, I might say, than an earnest inquirer. At the same time, it seemed to me that you were a little severe upon Weissmann in this matter. Has not the general evidence since that date tended to – well, to strengthen his position?'

'What evidence?' He spoke with a menacing calm.

'Well, of course, I am aware that there is not any what you might call *definite* evidence. I alluded merely to the trend of modern thought and the general scientific point of view, if I might so express it.'

He leaned forward with great earnestness.

'I suppose you are aware,' said he, checking off points upon his fingers, 'that the cranial index is a constant factor?'

'Naturally,' said I.

'And that telegony[3] is still *sub judice*?'

'Undoubtedly.'

'And that the germ plasm is different from the parthenogenetic egg?'[4]

'Why, surely!' I cried, and gloried in my own audacity.

'But what does that prove?' he asked, in a gentle, persuasive voice.

'Ah, what indeed?' I murmured. 'What does it prove?'

'Shall I tell you?' he cooed.

'Pray do.'

'It proves,' he roared, with a sudden blast of fury, 'that you are the rankest impostor in London – a vile, crawling journalist, who has no more science than he has decency in his composition!'

He had sprung to his feet with a mad rage in his eyes. Even at that moment of tension I found time for amazement at the discovery that he was quite a short man, his head not higher than my shoulder – a stunted Hercules whose tremendous vitality had all run to depth, breadth, and brain.

'Gibberish!' he cried, leaning forward, with his fingers on the table and his face projecting. 'That's what I have been talking to you, sir – scientific gibberish! Did you think you could match cunning with me – you with your walnut of a brain? You think you are omnipotent, you infernal scribblers, don't you? That your praise can make a man and your blame can break him? We must all bow to you, and try to get a favourable word, must we? This man shall have a leg up, and this man shall have a dressing down! Creeping vermin, I know you! You've got out of your station. Time was when your ears were clipped. You've lost your sense of proportion. Swollen gas-bags! I'll keep you in your proper place. Yes, sir, you haven't got over G. E. C. There's one man who is still your master. He warned you off, but if you *will* come, by the Lord you do it at your own risk. Forfeit, my good Mr Malone, I claim forfeit! You have played a rather dangerous game, and it strikes me that you have lost it.'

'Look here, sir,' said I, backing to the door and opening it; 'you can be as abusive as you like. But there is a limit. You shall not assault me.'

'Shall I not?' He was slowly advancing in a peculiarly menacing way, but he stopped now and put his big hands into the side-pockets of a rather boyish short jacket which he wore. 'I have thrown several of you out of the house. You will be the fourth or fifth. Three pound fifteen[5] each – that is how it averaged. Expensive, but very necessary. Now, sir, why should you not follow your brethren? I rather think you must.' He resumed his unpleasant and stealthy advance, pointing his toes as he walked, like a dancing master.

I could have bolted for the hall door, but it would have been too ignominious. Besides, a little glow of righteous anger was springing up within me. I had been hopelessly in the wrong before, but this man's menaces were putting me in the right.

'I'll trouble you to keep your hands off, sir. I'll not stand it.'

'Dear me!' His black moustache lifted and a white fang twinkled in a sneer. 'You won't stand it, eh?'

'Don't be such a fool, Professor!' I cried. 'What can you hope for? I'm fifteen stone, as hard as nails, and play centre three-quarter every Saturday for the London Irish.[6] I'm not the man – '

It was at that moment that he rushed me. It was lucky that I had opened the door, or we should have gone through it. We did a Catherine-wheel together down the passage. Somehow we gathered up a chair upon our way, and bounded on with it towards the street. My mouth was full of his beard, our arms were locked, our bodies intertwined, and that infernal chair radiated its legs all round us. The watchful Austin had thrown open the hall door. We went with a back somersault down the front steps. I have seen the two Macs attempt something of the kind at the halls, but it appears to take some practice to do it without hurting oneself. The chair went to matchwood at the bottom, and we rolled apart into the gutter. He sprang to his feet, waving his fists and wheezing like an asthmatic.

'Had enough?' he panted.

'You infernal bully!' I cried, as I gathered myself together.

Then and there we should have tried the thing out, for he was effervescing with fight, but fortunately I was rescued from an odious situation. A policeman was beside us, his notebook in his hand.

'What's all this? You ought to be ashamed,' said the policeman. It was the most rational remark which I had heard in Enmore Park. 'Well,' he insisted, turning to me, 'what is it, then?'

'This man attacked me,' said I.

'Did you attack him?' asked the policeman.

The Professor breathed hard and said nothing.

'It's not the first time, either,' said the policeman, severely, shaking his head. 'You were in trouble last month for the same thing. You've blackened this young man's eye. Do you give him in charge, sir?'

I relented.

'No,' said I, 'I do not.'

'What's that?' said the policeman.

'I was to blame myself. I intruded upon him. He gave me fair warning.'

The policeman snapped up his notebook.

'Don't let us have any more such goings-on,' said he. 'Now, then! Move on, there, move on!' This to a butcher's boy, a maid, and one or two loafers who had collected. He clumped heavily down the street, driving this little flock before him. The Professor looked at me, and there was something humorous at the back of his eyes.

'Come in!' said he. 'I've not done with you yet.'

The speech had a sinister sound, but I followed him none the less into the house. The man-servant, Austin, like a wooden image, closed the door behind us.

CHAPTER IV

It's just the very Biggest Thing in the World

Hardly was it shut than Mrs Challenger darted out from the dining-room. The small woman was in a furious temper. She barred her husband's way like an enraged chicken in front of a bulldog. It was evident that she had seen my exit, but had not observed my return.

'You brute, George!' she screamed. 'You've hurt that nice young man.'

He jerked backwards with his thumb.

'Here he is, safe and sound behind me.'

She was confused, but not unduly so.

'I am so sorry, I didn't see you.'

'I assure you, madam, that it is all right.'

'He has marked your poor face! Oh, George, what a brute you are! Nothing but scandals from one end of the week to the other. Everyone hating and making fun of you. You've finished my patience. This ends it.'

'Dirty linen,' he rumbled.

'It's not a secret,' she cried. 'Do you suppose that the whole street – the whole of London, for that matter – Get away, Austin, we don't want you here. Do you suppose they don't all talk about you? Where is your dignity? You, a man who should have been Regius Professor at a great University with a thousand students all revering you. Where is your dignity, George?'

'How about yours, my dear?'

'You try me too much. A ruffian – a common brawling ruffian – that's what you have become.'

'Be good, Jessie.'

'A roaring, raging bully!'

'That's done it! Stool of penance!' said he.

To my amazement he stooped, picked her up, and placed her sitting upon a high pedestal of black marble in the angle of the hall. It was at least seven feet high, and so thin that she could hardly balance upon it. A more absurd object than she presented cocked up there with her face convulsed with anger, her feet dangling, and her body rigid for fear of an upset, I could not imagine.

'Let me down!' she wailed.

'Say "please".'

'You brute, George! Let me down this instant!'

'Come into the study, Mr Malone.'

'Really, sir –!' said I, looking at the lady.

'Here's Mr Malone pleading for you, Jessie. Say "please", and down you come.'

'Oh, you brute! Please! please!'

He took her down as if she had been a canary.

'You must behave yourself, dear. Mr Malone is a Pressman. He will have it all in his rag tomorrow, and sell an extra dozen among our neighbours. "Strange story of high life" – you felt fairly high on that pedestal, did you not? Then a sub-title, "Glimpse of a singular ménage." He's a foul feeder, is Mr Malone, a carrion eater, like all of his kind – *porcus ex grege diaboli* – a swine from the devil's herd. That's it, Malone – what?'

'You are really intolerable!' said I, hotly.

He bellowed with laughter.

'We shall have a coalition presently,' he boomed, looking from his wife to me and puffing out his enormous chest. Then, suddenly altering his tone, 'Excuse this frivolous family badinage, Mr Malone. I called you back for some more serious purpose than to mix you up with our little domestic pleasantries. Run away, little woman, and don't fret.' He placed a huge hand upon each of her shoulders. 'All that you say is perfectly true. I should be a better man if I did what you advise, but I shouldn't be quite George Edward Challenger. There are plenty of better men, my dear, but only one G. E. C. So make the best of him.' He suddenly gave her a resounding kiss, which embarrassed me even more than his violence had done. 'Now, Mr Malone,' he continued, with a great accession of dignity, 'this way, if *you* please.'

We re-entered the room which we had left so tumultuously ten minutes before. The Professor closed the door carefully behind us, motioned me into an arm-chair, and pushed a cigar-box under my nose.

'Real San Juan Colorado,' he said. 'Excitable people like you are the better for narcotics. Heavens! don't bite it! Cut – and cut with reverence! Now lean back, and listen attentively to whatever I may care to say to you. If any remark should occur to you, you can reserve it for some more opportune time.

'First of all, as to your return to my house after your most justifiable expulsion' – he protruded his beard, and stared at me as one who challenges and invites contradiction – 'after, as I say, your well-merited expulsion. The reason lay in your answer to that most officious police-man, in which I seemed to discern some glimmering of good feeling upon your part – more, at any rate, than I am accustomed to associate with your profession. In admitting that the fault of the incident lay with you, you gave some evidence of a certain mental detachment and breadth of view which attracted my favourable notice. The sub-species of the human race to which you unfortunately belong has always been below my mental horizon. Your words brought you suddenly above it. You swam up into my serious notice. For this reason I asked you to return with me, as I was minded to make your further acquaintance. You will kindly deposit your ash in the small Japanese tray on the bamboo table which stands at your left elbow.'

All this he boomed forth like a professor addressing his class. He had swung round his revolving-chair so as to face me, and he sat all puffed out like an enormous bull-frog, his head laid back, and his eyes half-covered by supercilious lids. Now he suddenly turned himself sideways, and all I could see of him was tangled hair with a red, protruding ear. He was scratching about among the litter of papers upon his desk. He faced me presently with what looked like a very tattered sketch-book in his hand.

'I am going to talk to you about South America,' said he. 'No comments if you please. First of all, I wish you to understand that nothing I tell you now is to be repeated in any public way unless you have my express permission. That permission will, in all human probability, never be given. Is that clear?'

'It is very hard,' said I. 'Surely a judicious account –'

He replaced the notebook upon the table.

'That ends it,' said he. 'I wish you a very good morning.'

'No, no!' I cried. 'I submit to any conditions. So far as I can see, I have no choice.'

'None in the world,' said he.

'Well, then, I promise.'

'Word of honour?'

'Word of honour.'

He looked at me with doubt in his insolent eyes.

'After all, what do I know about your honour?' said he.

'Upon my word, sir,' I cried, angrily, 'you take very great liberties! I have never been so insulted in my life.'

He seemed more interested than annoyed at my outbreak.

'Round-headed,' he muttered. 'Brachycephalic, grey-eyed, black-haired, with suggestion of the negroid. Celtic, I presume?'

'I am an Irishman, sir.'

'Irish Irish?'

'Yes, sir.'

'That, of course, explains it. Let me see; you have given me your promise that my confidence will be respected? That confidence, I may say, will be far from complete. But I am prepared to give you a few indications which will be of interest. In the first place, you are probably aware that two years ago I made a journey to South America – one which will be classical in the scientific history of the world? The object of my journey was to verify some conclusions of Wallace and of Bates,[1] which could only be done by observing their reported facts under the same conditions in which they had themselves noted them. If my expedition had no other results it would still have been noteworthy, but a curious incident occurred to me while there which opened up an entirely fresh line of inquiry.

'You are aware – or probably, in this half-educated age, you are not aware – that the country round some parts of the Amazon is still only partially explored, and that a great number of tributaries, some of them entirely uncharted, run into the main river. It was my business to visit this little-known back-country and to examine its fauna, which furnished me with the materials for several chapters for that great and monumental work upon zoology which will be my life's justification. I was returning, my work accomplished, when I had occasion to spend a night at a small Indian village at a point where a certain tributary – the name and position of which I withhold – opens into the main river. The natives were Cucama Indians, an amiable but degraded race, with mental powers hardly superior to the average Londoner. I had effected some cures among them upon my way up the river, and had impressed them considerably with my personality, so that I was not surprised to find myself eagerly awaited upon my return. I gathered from their signs that someone had urgent need of my medical services, and I followed the chief to one of his huts. When I entered I found that the sufferer to whose aid I had been summoned had that instant expired. He was, to my surprise, no Indian, but a white man; indeed, I may say a very white man, for he was flaxen-haired and had some characteristics of an albino. He was clad in rags, was very emaciated, and bore every trace of prolonged hardship. So far as I could understand the account of the natives, he was a complete stranger to them, and had come upon their village through the woods alone and in the last stage of exhaustion.

'The man's knapsack lay beside the couch, and I examined the contents. His name was written upon a tab within it – Maple White, Lake Avenue, Detroit, Michigan. It is a name to which I am prepared always to lift my hat. It is not too much to say that it will rank level with my own when the final credit of this business comes to be apportioned.

'From the contents of the knapsack it was evident that this man had been an artist and poet in search of effects. There were scraps of verse. I do not profess to be a judge of such things, but they appeared to me to be singularly wanting in merit. There were also some rather commonplace pictures of river scenery, a paint-box, a box of coloured chalks, some brushes, that curved bone which lies upon my inkstand, a volume of Baxter's "Moths and Butterflies", a cheap revolver, and a few cartridges. Of personal equipment he either had none or he had lost it in his journey. Such were the total effects of this strange American Bohemian.

'I was turning away from him when I observed that something projected from the front of his ragged jacket. It was this sketch-book, which was as dilapidated then as you see it now. Indeed, I can assure you that a first folio of Shakespeare could not be treated with greater reverence than this relic has been since it came into my possession. I hand it to you now, and I ask you to take it page by page and to examine the contents.'

He helped himself to a cigar and leaned back with a fiercely critical pair of eyes, taking note of the effect which this document would produce.

I had opened the volume with some expectation of a revelation,

though of what nature I could not imagine. The first page was dis-
appointing, however, as it contained nothing but the picture of a very
fat man in a pea-jacket, with the legend, 'Jimmy Colver on the
Mail-boat,' written beneath it. There followed several pages which
were filled with small sketches of Indians and their ways. Then came
a picture of a cheerful and corpulent ecclesiastic in a shovel hat, sitting
opposite a very thin European, and the inscription: 'Lunch with Fra
Cristofero at Rosario.' Studies of women and babies accounted for
several more pages, and then there was an unbroken series of animal
drawings with such explanations as 'Manatee upon Sandbank',
'Turtles and Their Eggs', 'Black Ajouti under a Miriti Palm' – the
latter disclosing some sort of pig-like animal; and finally came a double
page of studies of long-snouted and very unpleasant saurians. I could
make nothing of it, and said so to the Professor.

'Surely these are only crocodiles?'

'Alligators! Alligators! There is hardly such a thing as a true croco-
dile in South America. The distinction between them –'

'I meant that I could see nothing unusual – nothing to justify what
you have said.'

He smiled serenely.

'Try the next page,' said he.

I was still unable to sympathize. It was a full-page sketch of a
landscape roughly tinted in colour – the kind of painting which an
open-air artist takes as a guide to a future more elaborate effort. There
was a pale-green foreground of feathery vegetation, which sloped
upwards and ended in a line of cliffs dark red in colour, and curiously
ribbed like some basaltic formations which I have seen. They extended
in an unbroken wall right across the background. At one point was an
isolated pyramidal rock, crowned by a great tree, which appeared to
be separated by a cleft from the main crag. Behind it all, a blue tropical
sky. A thin green line of vegetation fringed the summit of the ruddy
cliff. On the next page was another water-colour wash of the same
place, but much nearer, so that one could clearly see the details.

'Well?' he asked.

'It is no doubt a curious formation,' said I, 'but I am not geologist
enough to say that it is wonderful.'

'Wonderful!' he repeated. 'It is unique. It is incredible. No one on earth has ever dreamed of such a possibility. Now the next.'

I turned it over, and gave an exclamation of surprise. There was a full-page picture of the most extraordinary creature that I had ever seen. It was the wild dream of an opium smoker, a vision of delirium. The head was like that of a fowl, the body that of a bloated lizard, the trailing tail was furnished with upward-turned spikes, and the curved back was edged with a high serrated fringe, which looked like a dozen cocks' wattles placed behind each other. In front of this creature was an absurd mannikin, or dwarf in the human form, who stood staring at it.

'Well, what do you think of that?' cried the Professor, rubbing his hands with an air of triumph.

'It is monstrous – grotesque.'

'But what made him draw such an animal?'

'Trade gin, I should think.'

'Oh, that's the best explanation you can give, is it?'

'Well, sir, what is yours?'

'The obvious one that the creature exists. That it is actually sketched from the life.'

I should have laughed only that I had a vision of our doing another Catherine-wheel down the passage.

'No doubt,' said I, 'no doubt,' as one humours an imbecile. 'I confess, however,' I added, 'that this tiny human figure puzzles me. If it were an Indian we could set it down as evidence of some pigmy race in America, but it appears to be a European in a sun-hat.'

The Professor snorted like an angry buffalo. 'You really touch the limit,' said he. 'You enlarge my view of the possible. Cerebral paresis! Mental inertia! Wonderful!'

He was too absurd to make me angry. Indeed, it was a waste of energy, for if you were going to be angry with this man you would be angry all the time. I contented myself with smiling wearily. 'It struck me that the man was small,' said I.

'Look here!' he cried, leaning forward and dabbing a great hairy sausage of a finger on to the picture. 'You see that plant behind the animal; I suppose you thought it was a dandelion or a Brussels sprout – what? Well, it is a vegetable ivory palm, and they run to about fifty or

The monster (From Maple White's sketch-book)

sixty feet. Don't you see that the man is put in for a purpose? He couldn't really have stood in front of that brute and lived to draw it. He sketched himself in to give a scale of heights. He was, we will say, over five feet high. The tree is ten times bigger, which is what one would expect.'

'Good heavens!' I cried. 'Then you think the beast was – Why, Charing Cross station would hardly make a kennel for such a brute!'

'Apart from exaggeration, he is certainly a well-grown specimen,' said the Professor, complacently.

'But,' I cried, 'surely the whole experience of the human race is not to be set aside on account of a single sketch' – I had turned over the leaves and ascertained that there was nothing more in the book – 'a single sketch by a wandering American artist who may have done it under hashish, or in the delirium of fever, or simply in order to gratify a freakish imagination. You can't, as a man of science, defend such a position as that.'

For answer the Professor took a book down from a shelf.

'This is an excellent monograph by my gifted friend, Ray Lankester!'[2] said he. 'There is an illustration here which would interest you. Ah, yes, here it is! The inscription beneath it runs: "Probable appearance in life of the Jurassic Dinosaur Stegosaurus. The hind leg alone is twice as tall as a full-grown man." Well, what do you make of that?'

He handed me the open book. I started as I looked at the picture. In this reconstructed animal of a dead world there was certainly a very great resemblance to the sketch of the unknown artist.

'That is certainly remarkable,' said I.

'But you won't admit that it is final?'

'Surely it might be a coincidence, or this American may have seen a picture of the kind and carried it in his memory. It would be likely to recur to a man in a delirium.'

'Very good,' said the Professor, indulgently; 'we leave it at that. I will now ask you to look at this bone.' He handed over the one which he had already described as part of the dead man's possessions. It was about six inches long, and thicker than my thumb, with some indications of dried cartilege at one end of it.

'To what known creature does that bone belong?' asked the Professor.

I examined it with care, and tried to recall some half-forgotten knowledge.

'It might be a very thick human collar-bone,' I said.

My companion waved his hand in contemptuous deprecation.

'The human collar-bone is curved. This is straight. There is a groove upon its surface showing that a great tendon played across it, which could not be the case with a clavicle.'

'Then I must confess that I don't know what it is.'

'You need not be ashamed to expose your ignorance, for I don't suppose the whole South Kensington staff could give a name to it.' He took a little bone the size of a bean out of a pill-box. 'So far as I am a judge this human bone is the analogue of the one which you hold in your hand. That will give you some idea of the size of the creature. You will observe from the cartilege that this is no fossil specimen, but recent. What do you say to that?'

'Surely in an elephant –'

He winced as if in pain.

'Don't! Don't talk of elephants in South America. Even in these days of Board schools –'

'Well,' I interrupted, 'any large South American animal – a tapir, for example.'

'You may take it, young man, that I am versed in the elements of my business. This is not a conceivable bone either of a tapir or of any other creature known to zoology. It belongs to a very large, a very strong, and, by all analogy, a very fierce animal which exists upon the face of the earth, but has not yet come under the notice of science. You are still unconvinced?'

'I am at least deeply interested.'

'Then your case is not hopeless. I feel that there is reason lurking in you somewhere, so we will patiently grope round for it. We will now leave the dead American and proceed with my narrative. You can imagine that I could hardly come away from the Amazon without probing deeper into the matter. There were indications as to the direction from which the dead traveller had come. Indian legends would alone have been my guide, for I found that rumours of a strange land were common among all the riverine tribes. You have heard, no doubt, of Curupuri?'[3]

'Never.'

'Curupuri is the spirit of the woods, something terrible, something malevolent, something to be avoided. None can describe its shape or nature, but it is a word of terror along the Amazon. Now all tribes agree as to the direction in which Curupuri lives. It was the same direction from which the American had come. Something terrible lay that way. It was my business to find out what it was.'

'What did you do?' My flippancy was all gone. This massive man compelled one's attention and respect.

'I overcame the extreme reluctance of the natives – a reluctance which extends even to talk upon the subject – and by judicious persuasion and gifts, aided, I will admit, by some threats of coercion, I got two of them to act as guides. After many adventures which I need not describe, and after travelling a distance which I will not mention, in a direction which I withhold, we came at last to a tract of country which has never been described, nor, indeed, visited save by my unfortunate predecessor. Would you kindly look at this?'

He handed me a photograph – half-plate size.

'The unsatisfactory appearance of it is due to the fact,' said he, 'that on descending the river the boat was upset and the case which contained the undeveloped films was broken, with disastrous results. Nearly all of them were totally ruined – an irreparable loss. This is one of the few which partially escaped. This explanation of deficiencies or abnormalities you will kindly accept. There was talk of faking. I am not in a mood to argue such a point.'

The photograph was certainly very off-coloured. An unkind critic might easily have misinterpreted that dim surface. It was a dull grey landscape, and as I gradually deciphered the details of it I realized that it represented a long and enormously high line of cliffs exactly like an immense cataract seen in the distance, with a sloping, tree-clad plain in the foreground.

'I believe it is the same place as the painted picture,' said I.

'It *is* the same place,' the Professor answered. 'I found traces of the fellow's camp. Now look at this.'

It was a nearer view of the same scene, though the photograph was

A distant view of the plateau (From a photograph by Professor Challenger)

extremely defective. I could distinctly see the isolated, tree-crowned pinnacle of rock which was detached from the crag.

'I have no doubt of it at all,' said I.

'Well, that is something gained,' said he. 'We progress, do we not? Now, will you please look at the top of that rocky pinnacle? Do you observe something there?'

'An enormous tree.'

'But on the tree?'

'A large bird,' said I.

He handed me a lens.

'Yes,' I said, peering through it, 'a large bird stands on the tree. It appears to have a considerable beak. I should say it was a pelican.'

'I cannot congratulate you upon your eyesight,' said the Professor. 'It is not a pelican, nor, indeed, is it a bird. It may interest you to know that I succeeded in shooting that particular specimen. It was the only absolute proof of my experiences which I was able to bring away with me.'

'You have it, then?' Here at last was tangible corroboration.

'I had it. It was unfortunately lost with so much else in the same boat accident which ruined my photographs. I clutched at it as it disappeared in the swirl of the rapids, and part of its wing was left in my hand. I was insensible when washed ashore, but the miserable remnant of my superb specimen was still intact; I now lay it before you.'

From a drawer he produced what seemed to me to be the upper portion of the wing of a large bat. It was at least two feet in length, a curved bone, with a membranous veil beneath it.

'A monstrous bat!' I suggested.

'Nothing of the sort,' said the Professor, severely. 'Living, as I do, in an educated and scientific atmosphere, I could not have conceived that the first principles of zoology were so little known. Is it possible that you do not know the elementary fact in comparative anatomy, that the wing of a bird is really the forearm, while the wing of a bat consists of three elongated fingers with membranes between? Now, in this case, the bone is certainly not the forearm, and you can see for yourself that this is a single membrane hanging upon a single bone, and therefore that it cannot belong to a bat. But if it is neither bird nor bat, what is it?'

My small stock of knowledge was exhausted.

'I really do not know,' said I.

He opened the standard work to which he had already referred me.

'Here,' said he, pointing to the picture of an extraordinary flying monster, 'is an excellent reproduction of the dimorphodon,[4] or ptero-dactyl, a flying reptile of the Jurassic period.[5] On the next page is a diagram of the mechanism of its wing. Kindly compare it with the specimen in your hand.'

A wave of amazement passed over me as I looked. I was convinced. There could be no getting away from it. The cumulative proof was overwhelming. The sketch, the photographs, the narrative, and now the actual specimen – the evidence was complete. I said so – I said so warmly, for I felt that the Professor was an ill-used man. He leaned back in his chair with drooping eyelids and a tolerant smile, basking in this sudden gleam of sunshine.

'It's just the very biggest thing that I ever heard of!' said I, though it was my journalistic rather than my scientific enthusiasm that was roused. 'It is colossal. You are a Columbus of science who has dis-covered a lost world. I'm really awfully sorry if I seemed to doubt you. It was all so unthinkable. But I understand evidence when I see it, and this should be good enough for anyone.'

The Professor purred with satisfaction.

'And then, sir, what did you do next?'

'It was the wet season, Mr Malone, and my stores were exhausted. I explored some portion of this huge cliff, but I was unable to find any way to scale it. The pyramidal rock upon which I saw and shot the pterodactyl was more accessible. Being something of a cragsman, I did manage to get half way to the top of that. From that height I had a better idea of the plateau upon the top of the crags. It appeared to be very large; neither to east nor to west could I see any end to the vista of green-capped cliffs. Below, it is a swampy, jungly region, full of snakes, insects, and fever. It is a natural protection to this singular country.'

'Did you see any other trace of life?'

'No, sir, I did not; but during the week that we lay encamped at the base of the cliff we heard some very strange noises from above.'

'But the creature that the American drew? How do you account for that?'

'We can only suppose that he must have made his way to the summit and seen it there. We know, therefore, that there *is* a way up. We know equally that it must be a very difficult one, otherwise the creatures would have come down and overrun the surrounding country. Surely that is clear?'

'But how do they come to be there?'

'I do not think that the problem is a very obscure one,' said the Professor; 'there can only be one explanation. South America is, as you may have heard, a granite continent. At this single point in the interior there has been, in some far distant age, a great, sudden volcanic upheaval. These cliffs, I may remark, are basaltic, and therefore plutonic.[6] An area, as large perhaps as Sussex, has been lifted up *en bloc* with all its living contents, and cut off by perpendicular precipices of a hardness which defies erosion from all the rest of the continent. What is the result? Why, the ordinary laws of Nature are suspended. The various checks which influence the struggle for existence in the world at large are all neutralized or altered. Creatures survive which would otherwise disappear. You will observe that both the pterodactyl and the stegosaurus are Jurassic, and therefore of a great age in the order of life. They have been artificially conserved by those strange accidental conditions.'

'But surely your evidence is conclusive. You have only to lay it before the proper authorities.'

'So, in my simplicity, I had imagined,' said the Professor, bitterly. 'I can only tell you that it was not so, that I was met at every turn by incredulity, born partly of stupidity and partly of jealousy. It is not my nature, sir, to cringe to any man, or to seek to prove a fact if my word has been doubted. After the first I have not condescended to show such corroborative proofs as I possess. The subject became hateful to me – I would not speak of it. When men like yourself, who represent the foolish curiosity of the public, came to disturb my privacy I was unable to meet them with dignified reserve. By nature I am, I admit, somewhat fiery, and under provocation I am inclined to be violent. I fear you may have remarked it.'

I nursed my eye and was silent.

'My wife has frequently remonstrated with me upon the subject, and yet I fancy that any man of honour would feel the same. Tonight, however, I propose to give an extreme example of the control of the will over the emotions. I invite you to be present at the exhibition.' He handed me a card from his desk. 'You will perceive that Mr Percival Waldron, a naturalist of some popular repute, is announced to lecture at eight-thirty at the Zoological Institute's Hall upon "The Record of the Ages." I have been specially invited to be present upon the platform, and to move a vote of thanks to the lecturer. While doing so, I shall make it my business, with infinite tact and delicacy, to throw out a few remarks which may arouse the interest of the audience and cause some of them to desire to go more deeply into the matter. Nothing contentious, you understand, but only an indication that there are greater deeps beyond. I shall hold myself strongly in leash, and see whether by this self-restraint I attain a more favourable result.'

'And I may come?' I asked eagerly.

'Why, surely,' he answered, cordially. He had an enormously massive genial manner, which was almost as overpowering as his violence. His smile of benevolence was a wonderful thing, when his cheeks would suddenly bunch into two red apples, between his half-closed eyes and his great black beard. 'By all means, come. It will be a comfort to me to know that I have one ally in the hall, however inefficient and ignorant of the subject he may be. I fancy there will be a large audience, for Waldron, though an absolute charlatan, has a considerable popular following. Now, Mr Malone, I have given you rather more of my time than I had intended. The individual must not monopolize what is meant for the world. I shall be pleased to see you at the lecture tonight. In the meantime, you will understand that no public use is to be made of any of the material that I have given you.'

'But Mr McArdle – my news editor, you know – will want to know what I have done.'

'Tell him what you like. You can say, among other things, that if he sends anyone else to intrude upon me I shall call upon him with a riding-whip. But I leave it to you that nothing of all this appears in print. Very good. Then the Zoological Institute's Hall at eight-thirty tonight.' I had a last impression of red cheeks, blue rippling beard, and intolerant eyes, as he waved me out of the room.

CHAPTER V

Question!

What with the physical shocks incidental to my first interview with Professor Challenger and the mental ones which accompanied the second, I was a somewhat demoralized journalist by the time I found myself in Enmore Park once more. In my aching head the one thought was throbbing that there really *was* truth in this man's story, that it was of tremendous consequence, and that it would work up into inconceivable copy for the *Gazette* when I could obtain permission to use it. A taxicab was waiting at the end of the road, so I sprang into it and drove down to the office. McArdle was at his post as usual.

'Well,' he cried, expectantly, 'what may it run to? I'm thinking, young man, you have been in the wars. Don't tell me that he assaulted you.'

'We had a little difference at first.'

'What a man it is! What did you do?'

'Well, he became more reasonable and we had a chat. But I got nothing out of him – nothing for publication.'

'I'm not so sure about that. You got a black eye out of him, and that's for publication. We can't have this reign of terror, Mr Malone. We must bring the man to his bearings. I'll have a leaderette on him tomorrow that will raise a blister. Just give me the material and I will engage to brand the fellow for ever. Professor Munchausen – how's that for an inset headline? Sir John Mandeville redivivus – Cagliostro[1] – all the impostors and bullies in history. I'll show him up for the fraud he is.'

'I wouldn't do that, sir.'

'Why not?'

'Because he is not a fraud at all.'

'What!' roared McArdle. 'You don't mean to say you really believe this stuff of his about mammoths and mastodons and great sea sairpents?'

'Well, I don't know about that. I don't think he makes any claims of that kind. But I do believe he has got something new.'

'Then for Heaven's sake, man, write it up!'

'I'm longing to, but all I know he gave me in confidence and on condition that I didn't.' I condensed into a few sentences the Professor's narrative. 'That's how it stands.'

McArdle looked deeply incredulous.

'Well, Mr Malone,' he said at last, 'about this scientific meeting tonight; there can be no privacy about that, anyhow. I don't suppose any paper will want to report it, for Waldron has been reported already a dozen times, and no one is aware that Challenger will speak. We may get a scoop, if we are lucky. You'll be there in any case, so you'll just give us a pretty full report. I'll keep space up to midnight.'

My day was a busy one, and I had an early dinner at the Savage Club with Tarp Henry, to whom I gave some account of my adventures. He listened with a sceptical smile on his gaunt face, and roared with laughter on hearing that the Professor had convinced me.

'My dear chap, things don't happen like that in real life. People don't stumble upon enormous discoveries and then lose their evidence. Leave that to the novelists. The fellow is as full of tricks as the monkey-house at the Zoo. It's all absolute bosh.'

'But the American poet?'

'He never existed.'

'I saw his sketch-book.'

'Challenger's sketch-book.'

'You think he drew that animal?'

'Of course he did. Who else?'

'Well, then, the photographs?'

'There was nothing in the photographs. By your own admission you only saw a bird.'

'A pterodactyl.'

'That's what *he* says. He put the pterodactyl into your head.'

'Well, then, the bones?'

'First one out of an Irish stew. Second one vamped up for the occasion. If you are clever and know your business you can fake a bone as easily as you can a photograph.'

I began to feel uneasy. Perhaps, after all, I had been premature in my acquiescence. Then I had a sudden happy thought.

'Will you come to the meeting?' I asked.

Tarp Henry looked thoughtful.

'He is not a popular person, the genial Challenger,' said he. 'A lot of people have accounts to settle with him. I should say he is about the best-hated man in London. If the medical students turn out there will be no end of a rag. I don't want to get into a bear-garden.'

'You might at least do him the justice to hear him state his own case.'

'Well, perhaps, it's only fair. All right. I'm your man for the evening.'

When we arrived at the hall we found a much greater concourse than I had expected. A line of electric broughams discharged their little cargoes of white-bearded professors, while the dark stream of humbler pedestrians, who crowded through the arched doorway, showed that the audience would be popular as well as scientific. Indeed, it became evident to us as soon as we had taken our seats that a youthful and even boyish spirit was abroad in the gallery and the back portions of the hall. Looking behind me, I could see rows of faces of the familiar medical student type. Apparently the great hospitals had each sent down their contingent. The behaviour of the audience at present was good-humoured, but mischievous. Scraps of popular songs were chorused with an enthusiasm which was a strange prelude to a scientific lecture, and there was already a tendency to personal chaff which promised a jovial evening to others, however embarrassing it might be to the recipients of these dubious honours.

Thus, when old Doctor Meldrum, with his well-known curly-brimmed opera-hat, appeared upon the platform, there was such a universal query of 'Where *did* you get that tile?' that he hurriedly removed it, and concealed it furtively under his chair. When gouty Professor Wadley limped down to his seat there were general affectionate inquiries from all parts of the hall as to the exact state of his poor toe, which caused him obvious embarrassment. The greatest demonstration of all, however, was at the entrance of my new acquaintance, Professor Challenger, when he passed down to take his place at the extreme end of the front row of the platform. Such a yell of welcome broke forth when his black beard first protruded round the corner that I began to suspect Tarp Henry was right in his surmise, and that this assemblage was there not merely for the sake of the lecture, but because it had got rumoured abroad that the famous Professor would take part in the proceedings.

There was some sympathetic laughter on his entrance among the front benches of well-dressed spectators, as though the demonstration of the students in this instance was not unwelcome to them. That greeting was, indeed, a frightful outburst of sound, the uproar of the carnivora cage when the step of the bucket-bearing keeper is heard in the distance. There was an offensive tone in it, perhaps, and yet in the main it struck me as mere riotous outcry, the noisy reception of one who amused and interested them, rather than of one they disliked or despised. Challenger smiled with weary and tolerant contempt, as a kindly man would meet the yapping of a litter of puppies. He sat slowly down, blew out his chest, passed his hand caressingly down his beard, and looked with drooping eyelids and supercilious eyes at the crowded hall before him. The uproar of his advent had not yet died away when Professor Ronald Murray, the chairman, and Mr Waldron, the lecturer, threaded their way to the front, and the proceedings began.

Professor Murray will, I am sure, excuse me if I say that he has the common fault of most Englishmen of being inaudible. Why on earth people who have something to say which is worth hearing should not take the slight trouble to learn how to make it heard is one of the strange mysteries of modern life. Their methods are as reasonable as to try to pour some precious stuff from the spring to the reservoir through a non-conducting pipe, which could by the least effort be opened. Professor Murray made several profound remarks to his white tie and to the water-carafe upon the table, with a humorous, twinkling aside to the silver candlestick upon his right. Then he sat down, and Mr Waldron, the famous popular lecturer, rose amid a general murmur of applause. He was a stern, gaunt man, with a harsh voice and an aggressive manner, but he had the merit of knowing how to assimilate the ideas of other men, and to pass them on in a way which was intelligible and even interesting to the lay public, with a happy knack of being funny about the most unlikely objects, so that the precession of the Equinox or the formation of a vertebrate became a highly humorous process as treated by him.

It was a bird's-eye view of creation, as interpreted by science, which, in language always clear and sometimes picturesque, he unfolded before us. He told us of the globe, a huge mass of flaming gas, flaring through the heavens. Then he pictured the solidification, the cooling, the wrinkling which formed the mountains, the steam which turned to water, the slow preparation of the stage upon which was to be played the inexplicable drama of life. On the origin of life itself he was discreetly vague. That the germs of it could hardly have survived the original roasting was, he declared, fairly certain. Therefore it had come later. Had it built itself out of the cooling, inorganic elements of the globe? Very likely. Had the germs of it arrived from outside upon a meteor? It was hardly conceivable. On the whole, the wisest man was the least dogmatic upon the point. We could not – or at least we had not succeeded up to date in making organic life in our laboratories out of inorganic materials. The gulf between the dead and the living was something which our chemistry could not as yet bridge. But there was a higher and subtler chemistry of Nature, which, working with great forces over long epochs, might well produce results which were impossible for us. There the matter must be left.

This brought the lecturer to the great ladder of animal life, beginning low down in molluscs and feeble sea creatures, then up rung by rung through reptiles and fishes, till at last we came to a kangaroo-rat, a creature which brought forth its young alive, the direct ancestor of all mammals, and presumably, therefore, of everyone in the audience. ('No, no,' from a sceptical student in the back row.) If the young gentleman in the red tie who cried 'No, no,' and who presumably claimed to have been hatched out of an egg, would wait upon him after the lecture, he would be glad to see such a curiosity. (Laughter.) It was strange to think that the climax of all the age-long processes of Nature had been the creation of that gentleman in the red tie. But had the process stopped? Was this gentleman to be taken as the final type – the be-all and end-all of development? He hoped that he would not hurt the feelings of the gentleman in the red tie if he maintained that, whatever virtues that gentleman might possess in private life, still the vast processes of the universe were not fully justified if they were to end entirely in his production. Evolution was not a spent force, but one still working, and even greater achievements were in store.

Having thus, amid a general titter, played very prettily with his interrupter, the lecturer went back to his picture of the past, the drying of the seas, the emergence of the sand-bank, the sluggish, viscous life which lay upon their margins, the overcrowded lagoons, the tendency of the sea creatures to take refuge upon the mud-flats, the abundance of food awaiting them, their consequent enormous growth. 'Hence, ladies and gentlemen,' he added, 'that frightful brood of saurians which still affright our eyes when seen in the Wealden or in the Solenhofen slates,[2] but which were fortunately extinct long before the first appearance of mankind upon this planet.'

'Question!' boomed a voice from the platform.

Mr Waldron was a strict disciplinarian with a gift of acid humour, as exemplified upon the gentleman with the red tie, which made it perilous to interrupt him. But this interjection appeared to him so absurd that he was at a loss how to deal with it. So looks the Shakespearean who is confronted by a rancid Baconian,[3] or the astronomer who is assailed by a flat-earth fanatic. He paused for a moment, and then, raising his voice, repeated slowly the words: 'Which were extinct before the coming of man.'

'Question!' boomed the voice once more.

Waldron looked with amazement along the line of professors upon the platform until his eyes fell upon the figure of Challenger, who leaned back in his chair with closed eyes and an amused expression, as if he were smiling in his sleep.

'I see!' said Waldron, with a shrug. 'It is my friend Professor Challenger,' and amid laughter he renewed his lecture as if this was a final explanation and no more need be said.

But the incident was far from being closed. Whatever path the lecturer took amid the wilds of the past seemed invariably to lead him to some assertion as to extinct or prehistoric life which instantly brought the same bull's bellow from the Professor. The audience began to anticipate it and to roar with delight when it came. The packed benches of students joined in, and every time Challenger's beard opened, before any sound could come forth, there was a yell of 'Question!' from a hundred voices, and an answering counter cry of 'Order!' and 'Shame!' from as many more. Waldron, though a hardened lecturer and a strong man, became rattled. He hesitated, stammered, repeated himself, got snarled in a long sentence, and finally turned furiously upon the cause of his troubles.

'This is really intolerable!' he cried, glaring across the platform. 'I must ask you, Professor Challenger, to cease these ignorant and unmannerly interruptions.'

There was a hush over the hall, the students rigid with delight at seeing the high gods on Olympus quarrelling among themselves. Challenger levered his bulky figure slowly out of his chair.

'I must in turn ask you, Mr Waldron,' he said, 'to cease to make assertions which are not in strict accordance with scientific fact.'

The words unloosed a tempest. 'Shame! Shame!' 'Give him a hearing!' 'Put him out!' 'Shove him off the platform!' 'Fair play!' emerged from a general roar of amusement or execration. The chairman was on his feet flapping both his hands and bleating excitedly. 'Professor Challenger – personal – views – later,' were the solid peaks above his clouds of inaudible mutter. The interrupter bowed, smiled, stroked his beard, and relapsed into his chair. Waldron, very flushed and warlike, continued his observations. Now and then, as he made an assertion, he shot a venomous glance at his opponent, who seemed to be slumbering deeply, with the same broad, happy smile upon his face.

At last the lecture came to an end – I am inclined to think that it was a premature one, as the peroration was hurried and disconnected.

The thread of the argument had been rudely broken, and the audience was restless and expectant. Waldron sat down, and, after a chirrup from the chairman, Professor Challenger rose and advanced to the edge of the platform. In the interests of my paper I took down his speech verbatim.

'Ladies and Gentlemen,' he began, amid a sustained interruption from the back. 'I beg pardon – Ladies, Gentlemen, and Children – I must apologize, I had inadvertently omitted a considerable section of this audience' (tumult, during which the Professor stood with one hand raised and his enormous head nodding sympathetically, as if he were bestowing a pontifical blessing upon the crowd), 'I have been selected to move a vote of thanks to Mr Waldron for the very picturesque and imaginative address to which we have just listened. There are points in it with which I disagree, and it has been my duty to indicate them as they arose, but, none the less, Mr Waldron has accomplished his object well, that object being to give a simple and interesting account of what he conceives to have been the history of our planet. Popular lectures are the easiest to listen to, but Mr Waldron' (here he beamed and blinked at the lecturer) 'will excuse me when I say that they are necessarily both superficial and misleading, since they have to be graded to the comprehension of an ignorant audience.' (Ironical cheering.) 'Popular lecturers are in their nature parasitic.' (Angry gesture of protest from Mr Waldron.) 'They exploit for fame or cash the work which has been done by their indigent and unknown brethren. One smallest new fact obtained in the laboratory, one brick built into the temple of science, far outweighs any second-hand exposition which passes an idle hour, but can leave no useful result behind it. I put forward this obvious reflection, not out of any desire to disparage Mr Waldron in particular, but that you may not lose your sense of proportion and mistake the acolyte for the high priest.' (At this point Mr Waldron whispered to the chairman, who half rose and said something severely to his water-carafe.) 'But enough of this!' (Loud and prolonged cheers.) 'Let me pass to some subject of wider interest. What is the particular point upon which I, as an original investigator, have challenged our lecturer's accuracy? It is upon the permanence of certain types of animal life upon the earth. I do not

speak upon this subject as an amateur, nor, I may add, as a popular
lecturer, but I speak as one whose scientific conscience compels him
to adhere closely to facts, when I say that Mr Waldron is very wrong in
supposing that because he has never himself seen a so-called prehistoric
animal, therefore these creatures no longer exist. They are indeed, as
he has said, our ancestors, but they are, if I may use the expression,
our contemporary ancestors, who can still be found with all their
hideous and formidable characteristics if one has but the energy and
hardihood to seek their haunts. Creatures which were supposed to be
Jurassic, monsters who would hunt down and devour our largest and
fiercest mammals, still exist.' (Cries of 'Bosh!' 'Prove it!' 'How do *you*
know?' 'Question!') 'How do I know, you ask me? I know because I
have visited their secret haunts. I know because I have seen some of
them.' (Applause, uproar, and a voice, 'Liar!') 'Am I a liar?' (General
hearty and noisy assent.) 'Did I hear someone say that I was a liar?
Will the person who called me a liar kindly stand up that I may know
him?' (A voice, 'Here he is, sir!' and an inoffensive little person in
spectacles, struggling violently, was held up among a group of students.) 'Did you venture to call me a liar?' ('No, sir, no!' shouted the
accused, and disappeared like a Jack-in-the-box.) 'If any person in this
hall dares to doubt my veracity, I shall be glad to have a few words
with him after the lecture.' ('Liar!') 'Who said that?' (Again the inoffensive one plunging desperately, was elevated high into the air.) 'If I
come down among you –' (General chorus of 'Come, love, come!'
which interrupted the proceedings for some moments, while the chairman, standing up and waving both his arms, seemed to be conducting
the music. The Professor, with his face flushed, his nostrils dilated,
and his beard bristling, was now in a proper Berserk[4] mood.) 'Every
great discoverer has been met with the same incredulity – the sure
brand of a generation of fools. When great facts are laid before you,
you have not the intuition, the imagination which would help you to
understand them. You can only throw mud at the men who have
risked their lives to open new fields to science. You persecute the
prophets! Galileo, Darwin, and I –' (Prolonged cheering and complete
interruption.)

All this is from my hurried notes taken at the time, which give little notion of the absolute chaos to which the assembly had by this time been reduced. So terrific was the uproar that several ladies had already beaten a hurried retreat. Grave and reverend seniors[5] seemed to have caught the prevailing spirit as badly as the students, and I saw white-bearded men rising and shaking their fists at the obdurate Professor. The whole great audience seethed and simmered like a boiling pot. The Professor took a step forward and raised both his hands. There was something so big and arresting and virile in the man that the clatter and shouting died gradually away before his commanding gesture and his masterful eyes. He seemed to have a definite message. They hushed to hear it.

'I will not detain you,' he said. 'It is not worth it. Truth is truth, and the noise of a number of foolish young men – and, I fear I must add, of their equally foolish seniors – cannot affect the matter. I claim that I have opened a new field of science. You dispute it.' (Cheers.) 'Then I put you to the test. Will you accredit one or more of your own number to go out as your representatives and test my statement in your name?'

Mr Summerlee, the veteran Professor of Comparative Anatomy, rose among the audience, a tall, thin, bitter man, with the withered aspect of a theologian. He wished, he said, to ask Professor Challenger whether the results to which he had alluded in his remarks had been obtained during a journey to the head-waters of the Amazon made by him two years before.

Professor Challenger answered that they had.

Mr Summerlee desired to know how it was that Professor Challenger claimed to have made discoveries in those regions which had been overlooked by Wallace, Bates, and other previous explorers of established scientific repute.

Professor Challenger answered that Mr Summerlee appeared to be confusing the Amazon with the Thames; that it was in reality a somewhat larger river; that Mr Summerlee might be interested to know that with the Orinoco, which communicated with it, some fifty thousand miles of country were opened up, and that in so vast a space it was not impossible for one person to find what another had missed.

Mr Summerlee declared, with an acid smile, that he fully appreciated the difference between the Thames and the Amazon, which lay in the fact that any assertion about the former could be tested, while about the latter it could not. He would be obliged if Professor Challenger would give the latitude and the longitude of the country in which prehistoric animals were to be found.

Professor Challenger replied that he reserved such information for good reasons of his own, but would be prepared to give it with proper precautions to a committee chosen from the audience. Would Mr Summerlee serve on such a committee and test his story in person?

Mr Summerlee: 'Yes, I will.' (Great cheering.)

Professor Challenger: 'Then I guarantee that I will place in your hands such material as will enable you to find your way. It is only right, however, since Mr Summerlee goes to check my statement that I should have one or more with him who may check his. I will not disguise from you that there are difficulties and dangers. Mr Summerlee will need a younger colleague. May I ask for volunteers?'

It is thus that the great crisis of a man's life springs out at him. Could I have imagined when I entered that hall that I was about to pledge myself to a wilder adventure than had ever come to me in my dreams? But Gladys – was it not the very opportunity of which she spoke? Gladys would have told me to go. I had sprung to my feet. I was speaking, and yet I had prepared no words. Tarp Henry, my companion, was plucking at my skirts and I heard him whispering, 'Sit down, Malone! Don't make a public ass of yourself.' At the same time I was aware that a tall, thin man, with dark gingery hair, a few seats in front of me, was also upon his feet. He glared back at me with hard angry eyes, but I refused to give way.

'I will go, Mr Chairman,' I kept repeating over and over again.

'Name! Name!' cried the audience.

'My name is Edward Dunn Malone. I am the reporter of the *Daily Gazette*. I claim to be an absolutely unprejudiced witness.'

'What is *your* name, sir?' the chairman asked of my tall rival.

'I am Lord John Roxton. I have already been up the Amazon, I know all the ground, and have special qualifications for this investigation.'

'Lord John Roxton's reputation as a sportsman and a traveller is, of course, world-famous,' said the chairman; 'at the same time it would certainly be as well to have a member of the Press upon such an expedition.'

'Then I move,' said Professor Challenger, 'that both these gentlemen be elected, as representatives of this meeting, to accompany Professor Summerlee upon his journey to investigate and to report upon the truth of my statements.'

And so, amid shouting and cheering, our fate was decided, and I found myself borne away in the human current which swirled towards the door, with my mind half stunned by the vast new project which had risen so suddenly before it. As I emerged from the hall I was conscious for a moment of a rush of laughing students down the pavement, and of an arm wielding a heavy umbrella, which rose and fell in the midst of them. Then, amid a mixture of groans and cheers, Professor Challenger's electric brougham slid from the kerb, and I found myself walking under the silvery lights of Regent Street, full of thoughts of Gladys and of wonder as to my future.

Suddenly there was a touch at my elbow. I turned, and found myself looking into the humorous, masterful eyes of the tall, thin man who had volunteered to be my companion on this strange quest.

'Mr Malone, I understand,' said he. 'We are to be companions – what? My rooms are just over the road, in the Albany. Perhaps you would have the kindness to spare me half an hour, for there are one or two things that I badly want to say to you.'

CHAPTER VI

I was the Flail of the Lord

Lord John Roxton and I turned down Vigo Street together and through the dingy portals of the famous aristocratic rookery.[1] At the end of a long drab passage my new acquaintance pushed open a door and turned on an electric switch. A number of lamps shining through tinted shades bathed the whole great room before us in a ruddy radiance. Standing in the doorway and glancing round me, I had a general impression of extraordinary comfort and elegance combined with an atmosphere of masculine virility. Everywhere there were mingled the luxury of the wealthy man of taste and the careless untidiness of the bachelor. Rich furs and strange iridescent mats from some Oriental bazaar were scattered upon the floor. Pictures and prints which even my unpractised eyes could recognize as being of great price and rarity hung thick upon the walls. Sketches of boxers, of ballet-girls, and of racehorses alternated with a sensuous Fragonard, a martial Girardet, and a dreamy Turner.[2] But amid these varied ornaments there were scattered the trophies which brought back strongly to my recollection the fact that Lord John Roxton was one of the great all-round sportsmen and athletes of his day. A dark-blue oar crossed with a cherry-pink one above his mantelpiece spoke of the old Oxonian and Leander[3] man, while the foils and boxing-gloves above and below them were the tools of a man who had won supremacy with each. Like a dado round the room was the jutting line of splendid heavy game-heads, the best of their sort from every quarter of the world, with the rare white rhinoceros of the Lado Enclave drooping its supercilious lip above them all.

In the centre of the rich red carpet was a black and gold Louis Quinze table, a lovely antique, now sacrilegiously desecrated with marks of glasses and the scars of cigar-stumps. On it stood a silver tray of smokables and a burnished spirit-stand, from which and an adjacent siphon my silent host proceeded to charge two high glasses. Having indicated an arm-chair to me and placed my refreshment near it, he handed me a long, smooth Havana. Then, seating himself opposite to me, he looked at me long and fixedly with his strange, twinkling, reckless eyes – eyes of a cold light blue, the colour of a glacier lake.

Through the thin haze of my cigar-smoke I noted the details of a face which was already familiar to me from many photographs – the strongly-curved nose, the hollow, worn cheeks, the dark, ruddy hair, thin at the top, the crisp, virile moustaches, the small, aggressive tuft upon his projecting chin. Something there was of Napoleon III, something of Don Quixote,[4] and yet again something which was the essence of the English country gentleman, the keen, alert, open-air lover of dogs and of horses. His skin was of a rich flower-pot red from sun and wind. His eyebrows were tufted and overhanging, which gave those naturally cold eyes an almost ferocious aspect, an impression which was increased by his strong and furrowed brow. In figure he was spare, but very strongly built – indeed, he had often proved that there were few men in England capable of such sustained exertions. His height was a little over six feet, but he seemed shorter on account of a peculiar rounding of the shoulders. Such was the famous Lord John Roxton as he sat opposite to me, biting hard upon his cigar and watching me steadily in a long and embarrassing silence.

'Well,' said he, at last, 'we've gone and done it, young fellah my lad.' (This curious phrase he pronounced as if it were all one word – 'young-fellah-me-lad'.) 'Yes, we've take a jump, you an' me. I suppose, now, when you went into that room there was no such notion in your head – what?'

'No thought of it.'

'The same here. No thought of it. And here we are, up to our necks in the tureen. Why I've only been back three weeks from Uganda, and taken a place in Scotland, and signed the lease and all. Pretty goin's on – what? How does it hit you?'

'Well, it is all in the main line of my business. I am a journalist on the *Gazette*.'

'Of course – you said so when you took it on. By the way, I've got a small job for you, if you'll help me.'

'With pleasure.'

'Don't mind takin' a risk, do you?'

'What is the risk?'

'Well, it's Ballinger – he's the risk. You've heard of him?'

'No.'

'Why, young fellah, where *have* you lived? Sir John Ballinger is the best gentleman jock[5] in the north country. I could hold him on the flat at my best, but over jumps he's my master. Well, it's an open secret that when he's out of trainin' he drinks hard – strikin' an average, he calls it. He got delirium on Toosday, and has been ragin' like a devil ever since. His room is above this. The doctors say that it is all up with the old dear unless some food is got into him, but as he lies in bed with a revolver on his coverlet, and swears he will put six of the best through anyone that comes near him, there's been a bit of a strike among the serving-men. He's a hard nail, is Jack, and a dead shot, too, but you can't leave a Grand National[6] winner to die like that – what?'

'What do you mean to do, then?' I asked.

'Well, my idea was that you and I could rush him. He may be dozin', and at the worst he can only wing one of us, and the other should have him. If we can get his bolster-cover round his arms and then 'phone up a stomach-pump, we'll give the old dear the supper of his life.'

It was a rather desperate business to come suddenly into one's day's work. I don't think that I am a particularly brave man. I have an Irish imagination which makes the unknown and the untried more terrible than they are. On the other hand, I was brought up with a horror of cowardice and with a terror of such a stigma. I dare say that I could throw myself over a precipice, like the Hun in the history books, if my courage to do it were questioned, and yet it would surely be pride and fear, rather than courage, which would be my inspiration. Therefore, although every nerve in my body shrank from the whisky-maddened figure which I pictured in the room above, I still answered, in as careless a voice as I could command, that I was ready to go. Some further remark of Lord Roxton's about the danger only made me irritable.

'Talking won't make it any better,' said I. 'Come on.'

I rose from my chair and he from his. Then, with a little confidential chuckle of laughter, he patted me two or three times on the chest, finally pushing me back into my chair.

'All right, sonny my lad – you'll do,' said he.

I looked up in surprise.

'I saw after Jack Ballinger myself this mornin'. He blew a hole in the skirt of my kimono, bless his shaky old hand, but we got a jacket on him, and he's to be all right in a week. I say, young fellah, I hope you don't mind – what? You see, between you an' me close-tiled,[7] I look on this South American business as a mighty serious thing, and if I have a pal with me I want a man I can bank on. So I sized you down, and I'm bound to say that you came well out of it. You see, it's all up to you and me, for this old Summerlee man will want dry-nursin' from the first. By the way, are you by any chance the Malone who is expected to get his Rugby cap for Ireland?'

'A reserve, perhaps.'

'I thought I remembered your face. Why, I was there when you got that try against Richmond – as fine a swervin' run as I saw the whole season. I never miss a Rugby match if I can help it, for it is the manliest game we have left. Well, I didn't ask you in here just to talk sport. We've got to fix our business. Here are the sailin's, on the first page of *The Times*. There's a Booth boat[8] for Para[9] next Wednesday week, and if the Professor and you can work it, I think we should take it – what? Very good, I'll fix it with him. What about your outfit?'

'My paper will see to that.'

'Can you shoot?'

'About average Territorial standard.'

'Good Lord! as bad as that? It's the last thing you young fellahs think of learnin'. You're all bees without stings, so far as lookin' after the hive goes. You'll look silly, some o' these days, when someone comes along an' sneaks the honey. But you'll need to hold your gun straight in South America, for, unless our friend the Professor is a madman or a liar, we may see some queer things before we get back. What gun have you?'

He crossed to an oaken cupboard, and as he threw it open I caught a glimpse of glistening rows of parallel barrels, like the pipes of an organ.

'I'll see what I can spare you out of my own battery,' said he.

One by one he took out a succession of beautiful rifles, opening and shutting them with a snap and a clang, and then patting them as he put them back into the rack as tenderly as a mother would fondle her children.

'This is a Bland's .577 axite express,' said he. 'I got that big fellow with it.' He glanced up at the white rhinoceros. 'Ten more yards, and he'd would have added me to *his* collection.

> "On that conical bullet his once chance hangs,
>   'Tis the weak one's advantage fair."

Hope you know your Gordon,[10] for he's the poet of the horse and the gun and the man that handles both. Now, here's a useful tool – .470, telescopic sight, double ejector, point-blank up to three-fifty. That's the rifle I used against the Peruvian slave-drivers three years ago. I was the flail of the Lord up in those parts, I may tell you, though you won't find it in any Blue-book.[11] There are times, young fellah, when every one of us must make a stand for human right and justice, or you never feel clean again. That's why I made a little war on my own. Declared it myself, waged it myself, ended it myself. Each of those nicks is for a slave murderer – a good row of them – what? That big one is for Pedro Lopez, the king of them all, that I killed in a backwater of the Putomayo River. Now, here's something that would do for you.' He took out a beautiful brown-and-silver rifle. 'Well rubbered at the stock, sharply sighted, five cartridges to the clip. You can trust your life to that.' He handed it to me and closed the door of his oak cabinet. 'By the way,' he continued, coming back to his chair, 'what do you know of this Professor Challenger?'

'I never saw him till today.'

'Well, neither did I. It's funny we should both sail under sealed orders from a man we don't know. He seemed an uppish old bird. His brothers of science don't seem too fond of him, either. How came you to take an interest in the affair?'

I told him shortly my experiences of the morning, and he listened intently. Then he drew out a map of South America and laid it on the table.

'I believe every single word he said to you was the truth,' said he, earnestly, 'and, mind you, I have something to go on when I speak like that. South America is a place I love, and I think, if you take it right through from Darien to Fuego, it's the grandest, richest, most wonderful bit of earth upon this planet. People don't know it yet, and don't realize what it may become. I've been up an' down it from end to end, and had two dry seasons in those very parts, as I told you when I spoke of the war I made on the slave-dealers. Well, when I was up there I heard some yarns of the same kind – traditions of Indians and the like, but with somethin' behind them, no doubt. The more you knew of that country, young fellah, the more you would understand that anythin' was possible – *anythin'*. There are just some narrow water-lanes along which folk travel, and outside that it is all darkness. Now, down here in the Matto Grosso'[12] – he swept his cigar over a part of the map – 'or up in this corner where three countries meet, nothin' would surprise me. As that chap said tonight, there are fifty-thousand miles of water-way runnin' through a forest that is very near the size of Europe. You and I could be as far away from each other as Scotland is from Constantinople, and yet each of us be in the same great Brazilian forest. Man has just made a track here and a scrape there in the maze. Why, the river rises and falls the best part of forty feet, and half the country is a morass that you can't pass over. Why shouldn't somethin' new and wonderful lie in such a country? And why shouldn't we be the men to find it out? Besides,' he added, his queer, gaunt face shining with delight, 'there's a sportin' risk in every mile of it. I'm like an old golf-ball – I've had all the white paint knocked off me long ago. Life can whack me about now and it can't leave a mark. But a sportin' risk, young fellah, that's the salt of existence. Then it's worth livin' again. We're all gettin' a deal too soft and dull and comfy. Give me the great waste lands and the wide spaces, with a gun in my fist and somethin' to look for that's worth findin'. I've tried war and steeplechasin' and aeroplanes, but this huntin' of beasts that look like a lobster-supper dream is a brand-new sensation.' He chuckled with glee at the prospect.

Perhaps I have dwelt too long upon this new acquaintance, but he is to be my comrade for many a day, and so I have tried to set him down as I first saw him, with his quaint personality and his queer little tricks of speech and of thought. It was only the need of getting in the account of my meeting which drew me at last from his company. I left him seated amid his pink radiance, oiling the lock of his favourite rifle, while he still chuckled to himself at the thought of the adventures which awaited us. It was very clear to me that if dangers lay before us I could not in all England have found a cooler head or a braver spirit with which to share them.

That night, wearied as I was after the wonderful happenings of the day, I sat late with McArdle, the news editor, explaining to him the whole situation, which he thought important enough to bring next morning before the notice of Sir George Beaumont, the chief. It was agreed that I should write home full accounts of my adventures in the shape of successive letters to McArdle, and that these should either be edited for the *Gazette* as they arrived, or held back to be published later, according to the wishes of Professor Challenger, since we could not yet know what conditions he might attach to those directions which should guide us to the unknown land. In response to a telephone inquiry, we received nothing more definite than a fulmination against the Press, ending up with the remark that if we would notify our boat he would hand us any directions which he might think it proper to give us at the moment of starting. A second question from us failed to elicit any answer at all, save a plaintive bleat from his wife to the effect that her husband was in a very violent temper already, and that she hoped we would do nothing to make it worse. A third attempt, later in the day, provoked a terrific crash, and a subsequent message from the Central Exchange that Professor Challenger's receiver had been shattered. After that we abandoned all attempt at communication.

And now, my patient readers, I can address you directly no longer. From now onwards (if, indeed, any continuation of this narrative should ever reach you) it can only be through the paper which I represent. In the hands of the editor I leave this account of the events which have led up to one of the most remarkable expeditions of all time, so that if I never return to England there shall be some record as to how the affair came about. I am writing these last lines in the saloon of the Booth liner *Francisca*, and they will go back by the pilot to the keeping of Mr McArdle. Let me draw one last picture before I close the notebook – a picture which is the last memory of the old country which I bear away with me. It is a wet, foggy morning in the late spring; a thin, cold rain is falling. Three shining mackintoshed figures are walking down the quay, making for the gang-plank of the great liner from which the blue-peter is flying. In front of them a porter pushes a trolley piled high with trunks, wraps, and gun-cases. Professor Summerlee, a long, melancholy figure, walks with dragging steps and drooping head, as one who is already profoundly sorry for himself. Lord John Roxton steps briskly, and his thin, eager face beams forth between his hunting-cap and his muffler. As for myself, I am glad to have got the bustling days of preparation and the pangs of leave-taking behind me, and I have no doubt that I show it in my bearing. Suddenly, just as we reach the vessel, there is a shout behind us. It is Professor Challenger, who had promised to see us off. He runs after us, a puffing, red-faced, irascible figure.

'No, thank you,' says he; 'I should much prefer not to go aboard. I have only a few words to say to you, and they can very well be said where we are. I beg you not to imagine that I am in any way indebted to you for making this journey. I would have you to understand that it is a matter of perfect indifference to me, and I refuse to entertain the most remote sense of personal obligation. Truth is truth, and nothing which you can report can affect it in any way, though it may excite the emotions and allay the curiosity of a number of very ineffectual people. My directions for your instruction and guidance are in this sealed envelope. You will open it when you reach a town upon the Amazon which is called Manaos, but not until the date and hour which is marked upon the outside. Have I made myself clear? I leave the strict observance of my conditions entirely to your honour. No, Mr Malone, I will place no restriction upon your correspondence, since the ventilation of the facts is the object of your journey; but I demand that you shall give no particulars as to your exact destination, and that nothing be actually published until your return. Goodbye, sir. You have done something to mitigate my feelings for the loathsome profession to which you unhappily belong. Goodbye, Lord John. Science is, as I understand, a sealed book to you; but you may congratulate yourself upon the hunting-field which awaits you. You will, no doubt, have the opportunity of describing in the *Field* how you brought down the rocketing dimorphodon. And goodbye to you also, Professor Summerlee. If you are still capable of self-improvement, of which I am frankly unconvinced, you will surely return to London a wiser man.'

So he turned upon his heel, and a minute later from the deck I could see his short, squat figure bobbing about in the distance as he made his way back to his train. Well, we are well down Channel now. There's the last bell for letters, and it's goodbye to the pilot. We'll be 'down, hull-down, on the old trail'[13] from now on. God bless all we leave behind us, and send us safely back.

CHAPTER VII

Tomorrow we Disappear into the Unknown

I will not bore those whom this narrative may reach by an account of our luxurious voyage upon the Booth liner, nor will I tell of our week's stay at Para (save that I should wish to acknowledge the great kindness of the Pereira da Pinta Company in helping us to get together our equipment). I will also allude very briefly to our river journey, up a wide, slow-moving, clay-tinted stream, in a steamer which was little smaller than that which had carried us across the Atlantic. Eventually we found ourselves through the narrows of Obidos and reached the town of Manaos.[1] Here we were rescued from the limited attractions of the local inn by Mr Shortman, the representative of the British and Brazilian Trading Company. In his hospitable fazenda[2] we spent our time until the day when we were empowered to open the letter of instructions given to us by Professor Challenger. Before I reach the surprising events of that date I would desire to give a clearer sketch of my comrades in this enterprise, and of the associates whom we had already gathered together in South America. I speak freely, and I leave the use of my material to your own discretion, Mr McArdle, since it is through your hands that this report must pass before it reaches the world.

The scientific attainments of Professor Summerlee are too well known for me to trouble to recapitulate them. He is better equipped for a rough expedition of this sort than one would imagine at first sight. His tall, gaunt, stringy figure is insensible to fatigue, and his dry, half-sarcastic, and often wholly unsympathetic manner is uninfluenced by any change in his surroundings. Though in his sixty-sixth year, I have never heard him express any dissatisfaction at the occasional hardships which we have had to encounter. I had regarded his presence as an encumbrance to the expedition, but, as a matter of fact, I am now well convinced that his power of endurance is as great as my own. In temper he is naturally acid and sceptical. From the beginning

he has never concealed his belief that Professor Challenger is an
absolute fraud, that we are all embarked upon an absurd wild-goose
chase and that we are likely to reap nothing but disappointment and
danger in South America, and corresponding ridicule in England.
Such are the views which, with much passionate distortion of his thin
features and wagging of his thin, goat-like beard, he poured into our
ears all the way from Southampton to Manaos. Since landing from
the boat he has obtained some consolation from the beauty and
variety of the insect and bird life around him, for he is absolutely
whole-hearted in his devotion to science. He spends his days flitting
through the woods with his shot-gun and his butterfly-net, and his
evenings in mounting the many specimens he has acquired. Among
his minor peculiarities are that he is careless as to his attire, unclean
in his person, exceedingly absent-minded in his habits, and addicted
to smoking a short briar pipe, which is seldom out of his mouth. He
has been upon several scientific expeditions in his youth (he was with
Robertson in Papua), and the life of the camp and the canoe is nothing
fresh to him.

Lord John Roxton has some points in common with Professor
Summerlee, and others in which they are the very antithesis to each
other. He is twenty years younger, but has something of the same
spare, scraggy physique. As to his appearance, I have, as I recollect,
described it in that portion of my narrative which I have left behind
me in London. He is exceedingly neat and prim in his ways, dresses
always with great care in white drill suits and high brown mosquito-
boots, and shaves at least once a day. Like most men of action, he is
laconic in speech, and sinks readily into his own thoughts, but he is
always quick to answer a question or join in a conversation, talking in
a queer, jerky, half-humorous fashion. His knowledge of the world,
and very especially of South America, is surprising, and he has a
whole-hearted belief in the possibilities of our journey which is not to
be dashed by the sneers of Professor Summerlee. He has a gentle voice
and a quiet manner, but behind his twinkling blue eyes there lurks
a capacity for furious wrath and implacable resolution, the more
dangerous because they are held in leash. He spoke little of his own
exploits in Brazil and Peru, but it was a revelation to me to find the

excitement which was caused by his presence among the riverine natives, who looked upon him as their champion and protector. The exploits of the Red Chief, as they called him, had become legends among them, but the real facts, as far as I could learn them, were amazing enough.

These were that Lord John had found himself some years before in that no-man's-land which is formed by the half-defined frontiers between Peru, Brazil, and Colombia. In this great district the wild rubber tree flourishes, and has become, as in the Congo, a curse to the natives which can only be compared to their forced labour under the Spaniards upon the old silver mines of Darien. A handful of villainous half-breeds dominated the country, armed such Indians as would support them, and turned the rest into slaves, terrorizing them with the most inhuman tortures in order to force them to gather the india-rubber, which was then floated down the river to Para. Lord John Roxton expostulated on behalf of the wretched victims, and received nothing but threats and insults for his pains. He then formally declared war against Pedro Lopez, the leader of the slave-drivers, enrolled a band of runaway slaves in his service, armed them, and conducted a campaign, which ended by his killing with his own hands the notorious half-breed and breaking down the system which he represented.

No wonder that the ginger-headed man with the silky voice and the free and easy manners was now looked upon with deep interest upon the banks of the great South American river, though the feelings he inspired were naturally mixed, since the gratitude of the natives was equalled by the resentment of those who desired to exploit them. One useful result of his former experiences was that he could talk fluently in the Lingoa Geral, which is the peculiar talk, one-third Portuguese and two-thirds Indian, which is current all over Brazil.

I have said before that Lord John Roxton was a South Americo-maniac. He could not speak of that great country without ardour, and this ardour was infectious, for, ignorant as I was, he fixed my attention and stimulated my curiosity. How I wish I could reproduce the glamour of his discourses, the peculiar mixture of accurate knowledge and of racy imagination which gave them their fascination, until even the Professor's cynical and sceptical smile would gradually vanish from his thin face as he listened. He would tell the history of the mighty river so rapidly explored (for some of the first conquerors of Peru actually crossed the entire continent upon its waters), and yet so unknown in regard to all that lay behind its ever-changing banks.

'What is there?' he would cry, pointing to the north. 'Wood and marsh and unpenetrated jungle. Who knows what it may shelter? And there to the south? A wilderness of swampy forest, where no white man has ever been. The unknown is up against us on every side. Outside the narrow lines of the rivers what does anyone know? Who will say what is possible in such a country? Why should old man Challenger not be right?' At which direct defiance the stubborn sneer would reappear upon Professor Summerlee's face, and he would sit, shaking his sardonic head in unsympathetic silence, behind the cloud of his briar-root pipe.

So much, for the moment, for my two white companions, whose characters and limitations will be further exposed, as surely as my own, as this narrative proceeds. But already we have enrolled certain retainers who may play no small part in what is to come. The first is a gigantic negro named Zambo, who is a black Hercules, as willing as any horse, and about as intelligent. Him we enlisted at Para, on the recommendation of the steamship company, on whose vessels he had learned to speak a halting English.

It was at Para also that we engaged Gomez and Manuel, two half-breeds from up the river, just come down with a cargo of redwood. They were swarthy fellows, bearded and fierce, as active and wiry as panthers. Both of them had spent their lives in those upper waters of the Amazon which we were about to explore, and it was this recommendation which had caused Lord John to engage them. One of them, Gomez, had the further advantage that he could speak excellent English. These men were willing to act as our personal servants, to cook, to row, or to make themselves useful in any way at a payment of fifteen dollars a month. Besides these, we had engaged three Mojo Indians from Bolivia, who are the most skilful at fishing and boat work of all the river tribes. The chief of these we called Mojo, after his tribe, and the others are known as José and Fernando. Three white men, then, two half-breeds, one negro, and three Indians made up the personnel of the little expedition which lay waiting for its instructions at Manaos, before starting upon its singular quest.

At last, after a weary week, the day had come and the hour. I ask you to picture the shaded sitting-room of the Fazenda Santo Ignacio, two miles inland from the town of Manaos. Outside lay the yellow, brassy glare of the sunshine, with the shadows of the palm trees as black and definite as the trees themselves. The air was calm, full of the eternal hum of insects, a tropical chorus of many octaves, from the deep drone of the bee to the high, keen pipe of the mosquito. Beyond the veranda was a small cleared garden, bounded with cactus hedges and adorned with clumps of flowering shrubs, round which the great blue butterflies and the tiny humming-birds fluttered and darted in crescents of sparkling light. Within we were seated round the cane table, on which lay a sealed envelope. Inscribed upon it, in the jagged handwriting of Professor Challenger, were the words: –

'Instructions to Lord John Roxton and party. To be opened at Manaos upon July 15th, at 12 o'clock precisely.'

Lord John had placed his watch upon the table beside him.

'We have seven more minutes,' said he. 'The old dear is very precise.'

Professor Summerlee gave an acid smile as he picked up the envelope in his gaunt hand.

'What can it possibly matter whether we open it now or in seven minutes?' said he. 'It is all part and parcel of the same system of quackery and nonsense, for which I regret to say that the writer is notorious.'

'Oh, come, we must play the game accordin' to rules,' said Lord John. 'It's old man Challenger's show and we are here by his good will, so it would be rotten bad form if we didn't follow his instructions to the letter.'

'A pretty business it is!' cried the Professor, bitterly. 'It struck me as preposterous in London but I'm bound to say that it seems even more so upon closer acquaintance. I don't know what is inside this envelope, but, unless it is something pretty definite, I shall be much tempted to take the next down-river boat and catch the *Bolivia* at Para. After all, I have some more responsible work in the world than to run about disproving the assertions of a lunatic. Now, Roxton, surely it is time.'

'Time it is,' said Lord John. 'You can blow the whistle.' He took up the envelope and cut it with his penknife. From it he drew a folded sheet of paper. This he carefully opened out and flattened on the table. It was a blank sheet. He turned it over. Again it was blank. We looked at each other in a bewildered silence, which was broken by a discordant burst of derisive laughter from Professor Summerlee.

'It is an open admission,' he cried. 'What more do you want? The fellow is a self-confessed humbug. We have only to return home and report him as the brazen impostor that he is.'

'Invisible ink!' I suggested.

'I don't think!' said Lord Roxton, holding the paper to the light. 'No, young fellah my lad, there is no use deceiving yourself. I'll go bail for it that nothing has ever been written upon this paper.'

'May I come in?' boomed a voice from the veranda.

The shadow of a squat figure had stolen across the patch of sunlight. That voice! That monstrous breadth of shoulder! We sprang to our feet with a gasp of astonishment as Challenger, in a round, boyish straw-hat with a coloured ribbon – Challenger, with his hands in his jacket-pockets and his canvas shoes daintily pointing as he walked – appeared in the open space before us. He threw back his head, and there he stood in the golden glow with all his old Assyrian luxuriance of beard, all his native insolence of drooping eyelids and intolerant eyes.

'I fear,' said he, taking out his watch, 'that I am a few minutes too late. When I gave you this envelope I must confess that I had never intended that you should open it, for it had been my fixed intention to be with you before the hour. The unfortunate delay can be apportioned between a blundering pilot and an intrusive sandbank. I fear that it has given my colleague, Professor Summerlee, occasion to blaspheme.'

'I am bound to say, sir,' said Lord John, with some sternness of voice, 'that your turning up is a considerable relief to us, for our mission seemed to have come to a premature end. Even now I can't for the life of me understand why you should have worked it in so extraordinary a manner.'

Instead of answering, Professor Challenger entered, shook hands with myself and Lord John, bowed with ponderous insolence to Professor Summerlee, and sank back into a basket-chair, which creaked and swayed beneath his weight.

'Is all ready for your journey?' he asked.

'We can start tomorrow.'

'Then so you shall. You need no chart of directions now, since you will have the inestimable advantage of my own guidance. From the first I had determined that I would myself preside over your investigation. The most elaborate charts would, as you will readily admit, be a poor substitute for my own intelligence and advice. As to the small ruse which I played upon you in the matter of the envelope, it is clear that, had I told you all my intentions, I should have been forced to resist unwelcome pressure to travel out with you.'

'Not from me, sir!' exclaimed Professor Summerlee, heartily. 'So long as there was another ship upon the Atlantic.'

Challenger waved him away with his great hairy hand.

'Your common sense will, I am sure, sustain my objection and realize that it was better that I should direct my own movements and appear only at the exact moment when my presence was needed.[3] That moment has now arrived. You are in safe hands. You will not now fail to reach your destination. From henceforth I take command of this expedition, and I must ask you to complete your preparations tonight, so that we may be able to make an early start in the morning. My time is of value, and the same thing may be said, no doubt, in a lesser degree of your own. I propose, therefore, that we push on as rapidly as possible, until I have demonstrated what you have come to see.'

Lord John Roxton had chartered a large steam-launch, the *Esmeralda*, which was to carry us up the river. So far as climate goes, it was immaterial what time we chose for our expedition, as the temperature ranges from seventy-five to ninety degrees both summer and winter, with no appreciable difference in heat. In moisture, however, it is otherwise; from December to May is the period of the rains, and during this time the river slowly rises until it attains a height of nearly forty feet above its low-water mark. It floods the banks, extends in great lagoons over a monstrous waste of country, and forms a huge district, called locally the Gapo, which is for the most part too marshy for foot-travel and too shallow for boating. About June the waters begin to fall, and are at their lowest at October or November. Thus our expedition was at the time of the dry season, when the great river and its tributaries were more or less in a normal condition.

The current of the river is a slight one, the drop being not greater than eight inches in a mile. No stream could be more convenient for navigation, since the prevailing wind is south-east, and sailing boats may make a continuous progress to the Peruvian frontier, dropping down again with the current. In our own case the excellent engines of the *Esmeralda* could disregard the sluggish flow of the stream, and we made as rapid progress as if we were navigating a stagnant lake. For three days we steamed north-westwards up a stream which even here, a thousand miles from its mouth, was still so enormous that from its centre the two banks were mere shadows upon the distant skyline. On the fourth day after leaving Manaos we turned into a tributary which at its mouth was little smaller than the main stream. It narrowed rapidly, however, and after two more days' steaming we reached an Indian village, where the Professor insisted that we should land, and that the *Esmeralda* should be sent back to Manaos. We should soon come upon rapids, he explained, which would make its further use impossible. He added privately that we were now approaching the door of the unknown country, and that the fewer whom we took into our confidence the better it would be. To this end also he made each of us give our word of honour that we would publish or say nothing which would give any exact clue as to the whereabouts of our travels, while the servants were all solemnly sworn to the same effect. It is for this reason that I am compelled to be vague in my narrative, and I would warn my readers that in any map or diagram which I may give the relation of places to each other may be correct, but the points of the compass are carefully confused, so that in no way can it be taken as an actual guide to the country. Professor Challenger's reasons for secrecy may be valid or not, but we had no choice but to adopt them, for he was prepared to abandon the whole expedition rather than modify the conditions upon which he would guide us.

It was August 2nd when we snapped our last link with the outer world by bidding farewell to the *Esmeralda*. Since then four days have passed, during which we have engaged two large canoes from the Indians, made of so light a material (skins over a bamboo framework) that we should be able to carry them round any obstacle. These we have loaded with all our effects, and have engaged two additional Indians to help us in the navigation. I understand that they are the very two – Ataca and Ipetu by name – who accompanied Professor Challenger upon his previous journey. They appeared to be terrified at the prospect of repeating it, but the chief has patriarchal powers in these countries, and if the bargain is good in his eyes the clansman has little choice in the matter.

So tomorrow we disappear into the unknown. This account I am transmitting down the river by canoe, and it may be our last word to those who are interested in our fate. I have, according to our arrangement, addressed it to you, my dear Mr McArdle, and I leave it to your discretion to delete, alter, or do what you like with it. From the assurance of Professor Challenger's manner – and in spite of the continued scepticism of Professor Summerlee – I have no doubt that our leader will make good his statement, and that we are really on the eve of some most remarkable experiences.

CHAPTER VIII

The Outlying Pickets of the New World

Our friends at home may well rejoice with us, for we are at our goal, and up to a point, at least, we have shown that the statement of Professor Challenger can be verified. We have not, it is true, ascended the plateau, but it lies before us, and even Professor Summerlee is in a more chastened mood. Not that he will for an instant admit that his rival could be right, but he is less persistent in his incessant objections, and has sunk for the most part into an observant silence. I must hark back, however, and continue my narrative from where I dropped it. We are sending home one of our local Indians who is injured, and I am committing this letter to his charge, with considerable doubts in my mind as to whether it will ever come to hand.

When I wrote last we were about to leave the Indian village where we had been deposited by the *Esmeralda*. I have to begin my report by bad news, for the first serious personal trouble (I pass over the incessant bickerings between the Professors) occurred this evening, and might have had a tragic ending. I have spoken of our English-speaking half-breed, Gomez – a fine worker and a willing fellow, but afflicted, I fancy, with the vice of curiosity, which is common enough among such men. On the last evening he seems to have hid himself near the hut in which we were discussing our plans, and, being observed by our huge negro Zambo, who is as faithful as a dog and has the hatred which all his race bear to the half-breeds, he was dragged out and carried into our presence. Gomez whipped out his knife, however, and but for the huge strength of his captor, which enabled him to disarm him with one hand, he would certainly have stabbed him. The matter has ended in reprimands, the opponents have been compelled to shake hands, and there is every hope that all will be well. As to the feuds of the two learned men, they are continuous and bitter. It must be admitted that Challenger is provocative in the last degree, but Summerlee has an acid tongue, which makes matters worse. Last night Challenger said that he never cared to walk on the Thames Embankment and look up the river, as it was always sad to see one's own eventual goal. He is convinced, of course, that he is destined for Westminster Abbey. Summerlee retorted, however, with a sour smile, by saying that he understood that Millbank Prison had been pulled down. Challenger's conceit is too colossal to allow him to be really annoyed. He only smiled in his beard and repeated 'Really! really!' in the pitying tone one would use to a child. Indeed, they are children both – the one wizened and cantankerous, the other formidable and overbearing, yet each with a brain which has put him in the front rank of his scientific age. Brain, character, soul – only as one sees more of life does one understand how distinct is each.

The very next day we did actually make our start upon this remarkable expedition. We found that all our possessions fitted very easily into the two canoes, and we divided our personnel, six in each, taking the obvious precaution in the interests of peace of putting one Professor into each canoe. Personally, I was with Challenger, who was in a beatific humour, moving about as one in a silent ecstasy and beaming benevolence from every feature. I have had some experience of him in other moods, however, and shall be the less surprised when the thunderstorms suddenly come up amidst the sunshine. If it is impossible to be at your ease, it is equally impossible to be dull in his company, for one is always in a state of half-tremulous doubt as to what sudden turn his formidable temper may take.

For two days we made our way up a good-sized river, some hundreds of yards broad, and dark in colour, but transparent, so that one could usually see the bottom. The affluents of the Amazon are, half of them, of this nature, while the other half are whitish and opaque, the difference depending upon the class of country through which they have flowed. The dark indicate vegetable decay, while the others point to clayey soil. Twice we came across rapids, and in each case made a portage of half a mile or so to avoid them. The woods on either side were primaeval, which are more easily penetrated than woods of the second growth, and we had no great difficulty in carrying our canoes through them. How shall I ever forget the solemn mystery of it? The height of the trees and the thickness of the boles exceeded anything which I in my town-bred life could have imagined, shooting upwards in magnificent columns until, at an enormous distance above our heads, we could dimly discern the spot where they threw out their side-branches into Gothic upward curves which coalesced to form one great matted roof of verdure, through which only an occasional golden ray of sunshine shot downwards to trace a thin dazzling line of light amidst the majestic obscurity. As we walked noiselessly amid the thick, soft carpet of decaying vegetation the hush fell upon our souls which comes upon us in the twilight of the Abbey, and even Professor Challenger's full-chested notes sank into a whisper. Alone, I should have been ignorant of the names of these giant growths, but our men of science pointed out the cedars, the great silk cotton trees, and the redwood trees, with all that profusion of various plants which has made this continent the chief supplier to the human race of those gifts of Nature which depend upon the vegetable world, while it is the most backward in those products which come from animal life. Vivid orchids and wonderful coloured lichens smouldered upon the swarthy tree-trunks, and where a wandering shaft of light fell full upon the golden allamanda, the scarlet star-clusters of the tacsonia, or the rich deep blue of ipomaea the effect was as a dream of fairyland. In these great wastes of forest, life, which abhors darkness, struggles ever upwards to the light. Every plant, even the smaller ones, curls and writhes to the green surface, twining itself round its stronger and taller brethren in the effort. Climbing plants are monstrous and luxuriant, but others which have never been known to climb elsewhere learn the art as an escape from that sombre shadow, so that the common nettle, the jasmine, and even the jacitara palm tree can be seen circling the stems of the cedars and striving to reach their crowns. Of animal life there was no movement amid the majestic vaulted aisles which stretched from us as we walked, but a constant movement far above our heads told of that multitudinous world of snake and monkey, bird and sloth, which lived in the sunshine, and looked down in wonder at our tiny, dark, stumbling figures in the obscure depths immeasurably below them. At dawn and at sunset the howler monkeys screamed together and the parakeets broke into shrill chatter, but during the hot hours of the day only the full drone of insects, like the beat of a distant surf, filled the ear, while nothing moved amid the solemn vistas of stupendous trunks, fading away into the darkness which held us in. Once some bandy-legged, lurching creature, an ant-eater or a bear, scuttled clumsily amid the shadows. It was the only sign of earth life which I saw in this great Amazonian forest.

And yet there were indications that even human life itself was not far from us in those mysterious recesses. On the third day out we were aware of a singular deep throbbing in the air, rhythmic and solemn, coming and going fitfully throughout the morning. The two boats were paddling within a few yards of each other when first we heard it, and our Indians remained motionless, as if they had been turned to bronze, listening intently with expressions of terror upon their faces.

'What is it, then?' I asked.

'Drums,' said Lord John, carelessly; 'war drums. I have heard them before.'

'Yes, sir, war drums,' said Gomez, the half-breed. 'Wild Indians, bravos, not mansos;[1] they watch us every mile of the way; kill us if they can.'

'How can they watch us?' I asked, gazing into the dark, motionless void.

The half-breed shrugged his broad shoulders.

'The Indians know. They have their own way. They watch us. They talk the drum talk to each other. Kill us if they can.'

By the afternoon of that day – my pocket diary shows me that it was Tuesday, August 18th – at least six or seven drums were throbbing from various points. Sometimes they beat quickly, sometimes slowly, sometimes in obvious question and answer, one far to the east breaking out in a high staccato rattle, and being followed after a pause by a deep roll from the north. There was something indescribably nerve-shaking and menacing in that constant mutter, which seemed to shape itself into the very syllables of the half-breed, endlessly repeated, 'We will kill you if we can. We will kill you if we can.' No one ever moved in the silent woods. All the peace and soothing of quiet Nature lay in that dark curtain of vegetation, but away from behind there came ever the one message from our fellow-man. 'We will kill you if we can,' said the men in the east. 'We will kill you if we can,' said the men in the north.

All day the drums rumbled and whispered, while their menace reflected itself in the faces of our coloured companions. Even the hardy, swaggering half-breed seemed cowed. I learned, however, that day once for all that both Summerlee and Challenger possessed that highest type of bravery, the bravery of the scientific mind. Theirs was the spirit which upheld Darwin among the gauchos of the Argentine or Wallace[2] among the head-hunters of Malaya. It is decreed by a merciful Nature that the human brain cannot think of two things simultaneously, so that if it be steeped in curiosity as to science it has no room for merely personal considerations. All day amid that incessant and mysterious menace our two Professors watched every bird upon the wing, and every shrub upon the bank, with many a sharp wordy contention, when the snarl of Summerlee came quick upon the deep growl of Challenger, but with no more sense of danger and no more reference to drum-beating Indians than if they were seated together in the smoking-room of the Royal Society's Club in St James's Street. Once only did they condescend to discuss them.

'Miranha or Amajuaca cannibals,' said Challenger, jerking his thumb towards the reverberating wood.

'No doubt, sir,' Summerlee answered. 'Like all such tribes, I shall expect to find them of polysynthetic speech[3] and of Mongolian type.'

'Polysynthetic certainly,' said Challenger, indulgently. 'I am not aware that any other type of language exists in this continent, and I have notes of more than a hundred. The Mongolian theory[4] I regard with deep suspicion.'

'I should have thought that even a limited knowledge of comparative anatomy would have helped to verify it,' said Summerlee, bitterly.

Challenger thrust out his aggressive chin until he was all beard and hat-rim. 'No doubt, sir, a limited knowledge would have that effect. When one's knowledge is exhaustive, one comes to other conclusions.' They glared at each other in mutual defiance, while all round rose the distant whisper, 'We will kill you – we will kill you if we can.'

That night we moored our canoes with heavy stones for anchors in the centre of the stream, and made every preparation for a possible attack. Nothing came, however, and with the dawn we pushed upon our way, the drum-beating dying out behind us. About three o'clock in the afternoon we came to a very steep rapid, more than a mile long – the very one in which Professor Challenger had suffered disaster upon his first journey. I confess that the sight of it consoled me, for it was really the first direct corroboration, slight as it was, of the truth of his story. The Indians carried first our canoes and then our stores through the brushwood, which is very thick at this point, while we four whites, our rifles on our shoulders, walked between them and any danger coming from the woods. Before evening we had successfully passed the rapids, and made our way some ten miles above them, where we anchored for the night. At this point I reckoned that we had come not less than a hundred miles up the tributary from the main stream.

It was in the early forenoon of the next day, that we made the great departure. Since dawn Professor Challenger had been acutely uneasy, continually scanning each bank of the river. Suddenly he gave an exclamation of satisfaction and pointed to a single tree, which projected at a peculiar angle over the side of the stream.

'What do you make of that?' he asked.

'It is surely an Assai palm,' said Summerlee.

'Exactly. It was an Assai palm which I took for my landmark. The secret opening is half a mile onwards upon the other side of the river. There is no break in the trees. That is the wonder and the mystery of it. There where you see light-green rushes instead of dark-green undergrowth, there between the great cotton woods, that is my private gate into the unknown. Push through, and you will understand.'

It was indeed a wonderful place. Having reached the spot marked by a line of light-green rushes, we poled our two canoes through them for some hundreds of yards, and eventually emerged into a placid and shallow stream, running clear and transparent over a sandy bottom. It may have been twenty yards across, and was banked in on each side by most luxuriant vegetation. No one who had not observed that for a short distance reeds had taken the place of shrubs could possibly have guessed the existence of such a stream or dreamed of the fairyland beyond.

For a fairyland it was – the most wonderful that the imagination of man could conceive. The thick vegetation met overhead, interlacing into a natural pergola, and through this tunnel of verdure in a golden twilight flowed the green, pellucid river, beautiful in itself, but marvellous from the strange tints thrown by the vivid light from above filtered and tempered in its fall. Clear as crystal, motionless as a sheet of glass, green as the edge of an iceberg, it stretched in front of us under its leafy archway, every stroke of our paddles sending a thousand ripples across its shining surface. It was a fitting avenue to a land of wonders. All sign of the Indians had passed away, but animal life was more frequent, and the tameness of the creatures showed that they knew nothing of the hunter. Fuzzy little black-velvet monkeys, with snow-white teeth and gleaming, mocking eyes, chattered at us as we passed. With a dull, heavy splash an occasional cayman plunged in from the bank. Once a dark, clumsy tapir stared at us from a gap in the bushes, and then lumbered away through the forest; once, too, the yellow, sinuous form of a great puma whisked amid the brushwood, and its green, baleful eyes glared hatred at us over its tawny shoulder. Bird life was abundant, especially the wading birds, stork, heron, and ibis gathering in little groups, blue, scarlet, and white, upon every log which jutted from the bank, while beneath us the crystal water was alive with fish of every shape and colour.

For three days we made our way up this tunnel of hazy green sunshine. On the longer stretches one could hardly tell as one looked ahead where the distant green water ended and the distant green archway began. The deep peace of this strange waterway was unbroken by any sign of man.

'No Indian here. Too much afraid. Curupuri,' said Gomez.

'Curupuri is the spirit of the woods,' Lord John explained. 'It's a name for any kind of devil. The poor beggars think that there is something fearsome in this direction, and therefore they avoid it.'

On the third day it became evident that our journey in the canoes could not last much longer, for the stream was rapidly growing more shallow. Twice in as many hours we stuck upon the bottom. Finally we pulled the boats up among the brushwood and spent the night on the bank of the river. In the morning Lord John and I made our way for a couple of miles through the forest, keeping parallel with the stream; but as it grew ever shallower we returned and reported, what Professor Challenger had already suspected, that we had reached the highest point to which the canoes could be brought. We drew them up, therefore, and concealed them among the bushes, blazing a tree with our axes, so that we should find them again. Then we distributed the various burdens among us – guns, ammunition, food, a tent, blankets, and the rest – and, shouldering our packages, we set forth upon the more laborious stage of our journey.

An unfortunate quarrel between our pepperpots marked the outset of our new stage. Challenger had from the moment of joining us issued directions to the whole party, much to the evident discontent of

Summerlee. Now, upon his assigning some duty to his fellow-Professor (it was only the carrying of an aneroid barometer), the matter suddenly came to a head.

'May I ask, sir,' said Summerlee, with vicious calm, 'in what capacity you take it upon yourself to issue these orders?'

Challenger glared and bristled.

'I do it, Professor Summerlee, as leader of this expedition.'

'I am compelled to tell you, sir, that I do not recognize you in that capacity.'

'Indeed!' Challenger bowed with unwieldy sarcasm. 'Perhaps you would define my exact position.'

'Yes, sir. You are a man whose veracity is upon trial, and this committee is here to try it. You walk, sir, with your judges.'

'Dear me!' said Challenger, seating himself on the side of one of the canoes. 'In that case you will, of course, go on your way, and I will follow at my leisure. If I am not the leader you cannot expect me to lead.'

Thank heaven that there were two sane men – Lord John Roxton and myself – to prevent the petulance and folly of our learned Professors from sending us back empty-handed to London. Such arguing and pleading and explaining before we could get them mollified! Then at last Summerlee, with his sneer and his pipe, would move forwards, and Challenger would come rolling and grumbling after. By some good fortune we discovered about this time that both our savants had the very poorest opinion of Dr Illingworth of Edinburgh. Thenceforward that was our one safety, and every strained situation was relieved by our introducing the name of the Scotch zoologist, when both our Professors would form a temporary alliance and friendship in their detestation and abuse of this common rival.

Advancing in single file along the bank of the stream, we soon found that it narrowed down to a mere brook, and finally that it lost itself in a great green morass of sponge-like mosses, into which we sank up to our knees. The place was horribly haunted by clouds of mosquitoes and every form of flying pest, so we were glad to find solid ground again and to make a circuit among the trees, which enabled us to outflank this pestilent morass, which droned like an organ in the distance, so loud was it with insect life.

On the second day after leaving our canoes we found that the whole character of the country changed. Our road was persistently upwards, and as we ascended the woods became thinner and lost their tropical luxuriance. The huge trees of the alluvial Amazonian plain gave place to the Phoenix and coco palms, growing in scattered clumps, with thick brushwood between. In the damper hollows the Mauritia palms threw out their graceful drooping fronds. We travelled entirely by compass, and once or twice there were differences of opinion between Challenger and the two Indians, when, to quote the Professor's indignant words, the whole party agreed to 'trust the fallacious instincts of undeveloped savages rather than the highest product of modern European culture.' That we were justified in doing so was shown upon the third day, when Challenger admitted that he recognized several landmarks of his former journey, and in one spot we actually came upon four fire-blackened stones, which must have marked a camping-place.

The road still ascended, and we crossed a rock-studded slope which took two days to traverse. The vegetation had again changed, and only the vegetable ivory tree remained, with a great profusion of wonderful orchids, among which I learned to recognize the rare *Nuttonia Vexillaria* and the glorious pink and scarlet blossoms of Cattleya and odontoglossum. Occasional brooks with pebbly bottoms and fern-draped banks gurgled down the shallow gorges in the hill, and offered good camping-grounds every evening on the banks of some rock-studded pool, where swarms of little blue-backed fish, about the size and shape of English trout, gave us a delicious supper.

On the ninth day after leaving the canoes, having done, as I reckon, about a hundred and twenty miles, we began to emerge from the trees, which had grown smaller until they were mere shrubs. Their place was taken by an immense wilderness of bamboo, which grew so thickly that we could only penetrate it by cutting a pathway with the machetes and billhooks of the Indians. It took us a long day, travelling from seven in the morning till eight at night, with only two breaks of one hour each, to get through this obstacle. Anything more monotonous and wearying could not be imagined, for, even at the most open places, I could not see more than ten or twelve yards, while usually my vision was limited to the back of Lord John's cotton jacket in front of me, and to the yellow wall within a foot of me on either side. From above came one thin knife-edge of sunshine, and fifteen feet over our heads one saw the tops of the reeds swaying against the deep blue sky. I do not know what kind of creatures inhabit such a thicket, but several times we heard the plunging of large, heavy animals quite close to us. From their sounds Lord John judged them to be some form of wild cattle. Just as night fell we cleared the belt of bamboos, and at once formed our camp, exhausted by the interminable day.

Early next morning we were again afoot, and found that the character of the country had changed once again. Behind us was the wall of bamboo, as definite as if it marked the course of a river. In front was an open plain, sloping slightly upwards and dotted with clumps of tree-ferns, the whole curving before us until it ended in a long, whale-backed ridge. This we reached about midday, only to find a shallow valley beyond, rising once again into a gentle incline which led to a low, rounded sky-line. It was here, while we crossed the first of these hills, that an incident occurred which may or may not have been important.

Professor Challenger, who, with the two local Indians, was in the van of the party, stopped suddenly and pointed excitedly to the right. As he did so we saw, at the distance of a mile or so, something which appeared to be a huge grey bird flap slowly up from the ground and skim smoothly off, flying very low and straight, until it was lost among the tree-ferns.

'Did you see it?' cried Challenger, in exultation. 'Summerlee, did you see it?'

His colleague was staring at the spot where the creature had disappeared.

'What do you claim that it was?' he asked.

'To the best of my belief, a pterodactyl.'

Summerlee burst into derisive laughter. 'A ptero-fiddlestick!' said he. 'It was a stork, if ever I saw one.'

Challenger was too furious to speak. He simply swung his pack upon his back and continued upon his march. Lord John came abreast of me, however, and his face was more grave than was his wont. He had his Zeiss glasses in his hand.

'I focussed it before it got over the trees,' said he. 'I won't undertake to say what it was, but I'll risk my reputation as a sportsman that it wasn't any bird that ever I clapped eyes on in my life.'

So there the matter stands. Are we really just at the edge of the unknown, encountering the outlying pickets of this lost world of which our leader speaks? I give you the incident as it occurred and you will know as much as I do. It stands alone, for we saw nothing more which could be called remarkable.

And now, my readers, if ever I have any, I have brought you up the broad river, and through the screen of rushes, and down the green tunnel, and up the long slope of palm trees, and through the bamboo brake, and across the plain of tree-ferns. At last our destination lay in full sight of us. When we had crossed the second ridge we saw before us an irregular, palm-studded plain, and then the line of high red cliffs which I have seen in the picture. There it lies, even as I write, and there can be no question that it is the same. At the nearest point it is about seven miles from our present camp, and it curves away, stretching as far as I can see. Challenger struts about like a prize peacock, and Summerlee is silent, but still sceptical. Another day should bring some of our doubts to an end. Meanwhile, as José, whose arm was pierced by a broken bamboo, insists upon returning, I send this letter back in his charge, and only hope that it may eventually come to hand. I will write again as the occasion serves. I have enclosed with this a rough chart of our journey, which may have the effect of making the account rather easier to understand.

CHAPTER IX

Who could have Foreseen it?

A dreadful thing has happened to us. Who could have foreseen it? I cannot foresee any end to our troubles. It may be that we are condemned to spend our whole lives in this strange, inaccessible place. I

Malone's rough map of the journey to the cliffs

ROUGH CHART OF JOURNEY. EDN.
(Neither oriented nor to scale)

MAPLE WHITE LAND.

BASALT CLIFF

CAMP

PLAIN OF TREE FERNS

GIANT CANE BRAKE

X strange grey thing seen here.

ROCKY SLOPE

SEMI-TROPICAL VEGETATION

LOW HILLS

SPONGY MORASS

UNEXPLORED

CANOES HIDDEN

Hills 3 m³n (on far horizon)

UNEXPLORED

CONCEALED RIVER

WOOD'S
DRUMBEATING INDIANS

UNEXPLORED

RAPIDS
(where challenge lost Hammocks in first journey)

(where Maple White died) INDIAN VILLAGE UDOD

GAPO or FLOOD

AMAZON

WOODS.

am still so confused that I can hardly think clearly of the facts of the present or of the chances of the future. To my astounded senses the one seems most terrible and the other as black as night.

No men have ever found themselves in a worse position; nor is there any use in disclosing to you our exact geographical situation and asking our friends for a relief party. Even if they could send one, our fate will in all human probability be decided long before it could arrive in South America.

We are, in truth, as far from any human aid as if we were in the moon. If we are to win through, it is only our own qualities which can save us. I have as companions three remarkable men, men of great brain-power and of unshaken courage. There lies our one and only hope. It is only when I look upon the untroubled faces of my comrades that I see some glimmer through the darkness. Outwardly I trust that I appear as unconcerned as they. Inwardly I am filled with apprehension.

Let me give you, with as much detail as I can, the sequence of events which have led us to this catastrophe.

When I finished my last letter I stated that we were within seven miles from an enormous line of ruddy cliffs which encircled, beyond all doubt, the plateau of which Professor Challenger spoke. Their height, as we approached them, seemed to me in some places to be greater than he had stated – running up in parts to at least a thousand feet – and they were curiously striated, in a manner which is, I believe, characteristic of basaltic upheavals. Something of the sort is to be seen in Salisbury Crags at Edinburgh. The summit showed every sign of a luxuriant vegetation, with bushes near the edge, and farther back many high trees. There was no indication of any life that we could see.

That night we pitched our camp immediately under the cliff – a most wild and desolate spot. The crags above us were not merely perpendicular, but curved outwards at the top, so that ascent was out of the question. Close to us was the high, thin pinnacle of rock which I believe I mentioned earlier in this narrative. It is like a broad red church spire, the top of it being level with the plateau, but a great chasm gaping between. On the summit of it there grew one high tree. Both pinnacle and cliff were comparatively low – some five or six hundred feet, I should think.

'It was on that,' said Professor Challenger, pointing to this tree, 'that the pterodactyl was perched. I climbed half-way up the rock before I shot him. I am inclined to think that a good mountaineer like myself could ascend the rock to the top, though he would, of course, be no nearer to the plateau when he had done so.'

As Challenger spoke of his pterodactyl I glanced at Professor Summerlee, and for the first time I seemed to see some signs of a dawning credulity and repentance. There was no sneer upon his thin lips, but, on the contrary, a grey, drawn look of excitement and amazement. Challenger saw it, too, and revelled in the first taste of victory.

'Of course,' said he, with his clumsy and ponderous sarcasm, 'Professor Summerlee will understand that when I speak of a pterodactyl I mean a stork – only it is the kind of stork which has no feathers, a leathery skin, membranous wings, and teeth in its jaws.' He grinned and blinked and bowed until his colleague turned and walked away.

In the morning, after a frugal breakfast of coffee and manioc – we had to be economical of our stores – we held a council of war as to the best method of ascending to the plateau above us.

Challenger presided with a solemnity as if he were the Lord Chief Justice on the Bench. Picture him seated upon a rock, his absurd boyish straw hat tilted on the back of his head, his supercilious eyes dominating us from under his drooping lids, his great black beard wagging as he slowly defined our present situation and our future movements.

Beneath him you might have seen the three of us – myself, sunburnt, young, and vigorous after our open-air tramp; Summerlee, solemn, but still critical, behind his eternal pipe; Lord John, as keen as a razor-edge, with his supple, alert figure leaning upon his rifle, and his eagle eyes fixed eagerly upon the speaker. Behind us were grouped the two swarthy half-breeds and the little knot of Indians, while in front and above us towered those huge, ruddy ribs of rocks which kept us from our goal.

'I need not say,' said our leader, 'that on the occasion of my last visit I exhausted every means of climbing the cliff, and where I failed I do not think that anyone else is likely to succeed, for I am something of a mountaineer. I had none of the appliances of a rock-climber with me, but I have taken the precaution to bring them now. With their aid I am positive I could climb that detached pinnacle to the summit; but so long as the main cliff overhangs, it is vain to attempt ascending that. I was hurried upon my last visit by the approach of the rainy season and by the exhaustion of my supplies. These considerations limited my time, and I can only claim that I have surveyed about six miles of the cliff to the east of us, finding no possible way up. What, then, shall we now do?'

'There seems to be only one reasonable course,' said Professor Summerlee. 'If you have explored the east, we should travel along the base of the cliff to the west, and seek for a practicable point for our ascent.'

'That's it,' said Lord John. 'The odds are that this plateau is of no great size, and we shall travel round it until we either find an easy way up it, or come back to the point from which we started.'

'I have already explained to our young friend here,' said Challenger (he has a way of alluding to me as if I were a school child ten years old), 'that it is quite impossible that there should be an easy way up anywhere, for the simple reason that if there were the summit would not be isolated, and those conditions would not obtain which have effected so singular an interference with the general laws of survival. Yet I admit that there may very well be places where an expert human climber may reach the summit, and yet a cumbrous and heavy animal be unable to descend. It is certain that there *is* a point where an ascent is possible.'

'How do you know that, sir?' asked Summerlee, sharply.

'Because my predecessor, the American Maple White, actually made such an ascent. How otherwise could he have seen the monster which he sketched in his notebook?'

'There you reason somewhat ahead of the proved facts,' said the stubborn Summerlee. 'I admit your plateau, because I have seen it; but I have not as yet satisfied myself that it contains any form of life whatever.'

'What you admit, sir, or what you do not admit, is really of inconceivably small importance. I am glad to perceive that the plateau itself has actually obtruded itself upon your intelligence.' He glanced up at it, and then, to our amazement, he sprang from his rock, and, seizing Summerlee by the neck, he tilted his face into the air. 'Now, sir!' he shouted, hoarse with excitement. 'Do I help you to realize that the plateau contains some animal life?'

I have said that a thick fringe of green overhung the edge of the cliff. Out of this there had emerged a black, glistening object. As it came slowly forth and overhung the chasm, we saw that it was a very large snake with a peculiar flat, spade-like head. It wavered and quivered above us for a minute, the morning sun gleaming upon its sleek, sinuous coils. Then it slowly drew inwards and disappeared.

Summerlee had been so interested that he had stood unresisting while Challenger tilted his head into the air. Now he shook his colleague off and came back to his dignity.

'I should be glad, Professor Challenger,' said he, 'if you could see your way to make any remarks which may occur to you without seizing me by the chin. Even the appearance of a very ordinary rock python does not appear to justify such a liberty.'

'But there is life upon the plateau all the same,' his colleague replied in triumph. 'And now, having demonstrated this important conclusion so that it is clear to anyone, however prejudiced or obtuse, I am of opinion that we cannot do better than break up our camp and travel to westward until we find some means of ascent.'

The ground at the foot of the cliff was rocky and broken, so that the going was slow and difficult. Suddenly we came, however, upon something which cheered our hearts. It was the site of an old encampment, with several empty Chicago meat tins, a bottle labelled 'Brandy', a broken tin-opener, and a quantity of other travellers' débris. A crumpled, disintegrated newspaper revealed itself as the *Chicago Democrat*, though the date had been obliterated.

'Not mine,' said Challenger. 'It must be Maple White's.'

Lord John had been gazing curiously at a great tree-fern which overshadowed the encampment. 'I say, look at this,' said he. 'I believe it is meant for a sign-post.'

A slip of hard wood had been nailed to the tree in such a way as to point to the westward.

'Most certainly a sign-post,' said Challenger. 'What else? Finding himself upon a dangerous errand, our pioneer has left this sign so that any party which follows him may know the way he has taken. Perhaps we shall come upon some other indications as we proceed.'

We did indeed, but they were of a terrible and most unexpected nature. Immediately beneath the cliff there grew a considerable patch of high bamboo, like that which we had traversed in our journey. Many of these stems were twenty feet high, with sharp, strong tops, so that even as they stood they made formidable spears. We were passing along the edge of this cover when my eye was caught by the gleam of something white within it. Thrusting in my head between the stems, I found myself gazing at a fleshless skull. The whole skeleton was there, but the skull had detached itself and lay some feet nearer to the open.

With a few blows from the machetes of our Indians we cleared the spot and were able to study the details of this old tragedy. Only a few shreds of clothes could still be distinguished, but there were the remains of boots upon the bony feet, and it was very clear that the dead man was a European. A gold watch by Hudson, of New York, and a chain which held a stylographic pen, lay among the bones. There was also a silver cigarette-case, with 'J. C., from A. E. S.', upon the lid. The state of the metal seemed to show that the catastrophe had occurred no great time before.

'Who can he be?' asked Lord John. 'Poor devil! every bone in his body seems to be broken.'

'And the bamboo grows through his smashed ribs,' said Summerlee. 'It is a fast-growing plant, but it is surely inconceivable that this body could have been here while the canes grew to be twenty feet in length.'

'As to the man's identity,' said Professor Challenger, 'I have no doubt whatever upon that point. As I made my way up the river before I reached you at the fazenda I instituted very particular inquiries about Maple White. At Para they knew nothing. Fortunately, I had a definite clue, for there was a particular picture in his sketch-book which showed him taking lunch with a certain ecclesiastic at Rosario. This priest I was able to find, and though he proved a very argumentative fellow, who took it absurdly amiss that I should point out to him the corrosive effect which modern science must have upon his beliefs, he none the less gave me some positive information. Maple White passed Rosario four years ago, or two years before I saw his dead body. He was not alone at the time, but there was a friend, an American named James Colver, who remained in the boat and did not meet this ecclesiastic. I think, therefore, that there can be no doubt that we are now looking upon the remains of this James Colver.'

'Nor,' said Lord John, 'is there much doubt as to how he met his death. He has fallen or been chucked from the top, and so been impaled. How else could he come by his broken bones, and how could he have been stuck through by these canes with their points so high above our heads?'

A hush came over us as we stood round these shattered remains and realized the truth of Lord John Roxton's words. The beetling head of the cliff projected over the cane-brake. Undoubtedly he had fallen from above. But *had* he fallen? Had it been an accident? Or – already ominous and terrible possibilities began to form round that unknown land.

We moved off in silence, and continued to coast round the line of cliffs, which were as even and unbroken as some of those monstrous Antarctic icefields which I have seen depicted as stretching from horizon to horizon and towering high above the mast-heads of the exploring vessel. In five miles we saw no rift or break. And then suddenly we perceived something which filled us with new hope. In a hollow of the rock, protected from rain, there was drawn a rough arrow in chalk, pointing still to the westward.

'Maple White again,' said Professor Challenger. 'He had some presentiment that worthy footsteps would follow close behind him.'

'He had chalk, then?'

'A box of coloured chalks was among the effects I found in his knapsack. I remember that the white one was worn to a stump.'

'That is certainly good evidence,' said Summerlee. 'We can only accept his guidance and follow on to the westward.'

We had proceeded some five more miles when again we saw a white arrow upon the rocks. It was at a point where the face of the cliff was for the first time split into a narrow cleft. Inside the cleft was a second guidance mark, which pointed right up it with the tip somewhat elevated, as if the spot indicated were above the level of the ground.

It was a solemn place, for the walls were so gigantic and the slit of blue sky so narrow and so obscured by a double fringe of verdure that only a dim and shadowy light penetrated to the bottom. We had had no food for many hours, and were very weary with the stony and irregular journey, but our nerves were too strung to allow us to halt. We ordered the camp to be pitched, however, and, leaving the Indians to arrange it, we four, with the two half-breeds, proceeded up the narrow gorge.

It was not more than forty feet across at the mouth, but it rapidly closed until it ended in an acute angle, too straight and smooth for an ascent. Certainly it was not this which our pioneer had attempted to indicate. We made our way back – the whole gorge was not more than a quarter of a mile deep – and then suddenly the quick eyes of Lord John fell upon what we were seeking. High up above our heads, amid the dark shadows, there was one circle of deeper gloom. Surely it could only be the opening of a cave.

The base of the cliff was heaped with loose stones at the spot, and it was not difficult to clamber up. When we reached it, all doubt was removed. Not only was it an opening into the rock, but on the side of it there was marked once again the sign of the arrow. Here was the point, and this the means by which Maple White and his ill-fated comrade had made their ascent.

We were too excited to return to the camp, but must make our first exploration at once. Lord John had an electric torch in his knapsack, and this had to serve us as light. He advanced, throwing his little clear circlet of yellow radiance before him, while in single file we followed at his heels.

The cave had evidently been water-worn, the sides being smooth and the floor covered with rounded stones. It was of such a size that a single man could just fit through by stooping. For fifty yards it ran almost straight into the rock, and then it ascended at an angle of forty-five. Presently this incline became even steeper, and we found ourselves climbing upon hands and knees among loose rubble which slid from beneath us. Suddenly an exclamation broke from Lord Roxton.

'It's blocked!' said he.

Clustering behind him we saw in the yellow field of light a wall of broken basalt which extended to the ceiling.

'The roof has fallen in!'

In vain we dragged out some of the pieces. The only effect was that the larger ones became detached and threatened to roll down the gradient and crush us. It was evident that the obstacle was far beyond any efforts which we could make to remove it. The road by which Maple White had ascended was no longer available.

Too much cast down to speak, we stumbled down the dark tunnel and made our way back to the camp.

One incident occurred, however, before we left the gorge, which is of importance in view of what came afterwards.

We had gathered in a little group at the bottom of the chasm, some forty feet beneath the mouth of the cave, when a huge rock rolled suddenly downwards and shot past us with tremendous force. It was the narrowest escape for one or all of us. We could not ourselves see whence the rock had come, but our half-breed servants, who were still at the opening of the cave, said that it had flown past them, and must therefore have fallen from the summit. Looking upwards, we could see no sign of movement above us amidst the green jungle which topped the cliff. There could be little doubt, however, that the stone was aimed at us, so the incident surely pointed to humanity – and malevolent humanity – upon the plateau!

We withdrew hurriedly from the chasm, our minds full of this new development and its bearing upon our plans. The situation was difficult enough before, but if the obstructions of Nature were increased by the deliberate opposition of man, then our case was indeed a hopeless one. And yet, as we looked up at that beautiful fringe of verdure only a few hundreds of feet above our heads, there was not one of us who could conceive the idea of returning to London until we had explored it to its depths.

On discussing the situation, we determined that our best course was to continue to coast round the plateau in the hope of finding some other means of reaching the top. The line of cliffs, which had decreased considerably in height, had already begun to trend from west to north, and if we could take this as representing the arc of a circle, the whole circumference could not be very great. At the worst, then, we should be back in a few days at our starting-point.

We made a march that day which totalled some two-and-twenty miles, without any change in our prospects. I may mention that our aneroid shows us that in the continual incline which we have ascended since we abandoned our canoes we have risen to no less than three thousand feet above sea-level. Hence there is a considerable change both in the temperature and in the vegetation. We have shaken off some of that horrible insect life which is the bane of tropical travel. A few palms still survive, and many tree-ferns, but the Amazonian trees have been all left behind. It was pleasant to see the convolvulus, the passion-flower, and the begonia, all reminding me of home, here among these inhospitable rocks. There was a red begonia just the same colour as one that is kept in a pot in the window of a certain villa in Streatham – but I am drifting into private reminiscence.

That night – I am still speaking of the first day of our circumnavigation of the plateau – a great experience awaited us, and one which for ever set at rest any doubt which we could have had as to the wonders so near us.

You will realize as you read it, my dear Mr McArdle, and possibly for the first time, that the paper has not sent me on a wild-goose chase, and that there is inconceivably fine copy waiting for the world whenever we have the Professor's leave to make use of it. I shall not dare to publish these articles unless I can bring back my proofs to England, or I shall be hailed as the journalistic Munchausen of all time. I have no doubt that you feel the same way yourself, and that you would not care to stake the whole credit of the *Gazette* upon this adventure until we can meet the chorus of criticism and scepticism which such articles must of necessity elicit. So this wonderful incident, which would make such a headline for the old paper, must still wait its turn in the editorial drawer.

And yet it was all over in a flash, and there was no sequel to it, save in our own convictions.

What occurred was this. Lord John had shot an ajouti – which is a small, pig-like animal – and, half of it having been given to the Indians, we were cooking the other half upon our fire. There is a chill in the air after dark, and we had all drawn close to the blaze. The night was moonless, but there were some stars, and one could see for a little distance across the plain. Well, suddenly out of the darkness, out of the night, there swooped something with a swish like an aeroplane. The whole group of us were covered for an instant by a canopy of leathery wings, and I had a momentary vision of a long, snake-like neck, a fierce, red, greedy eye, and a great snapping beak, filled, to my amazement, with little, gleaming teeth. The next instant it was gone – and so was our dinner. A huge black shadow, twenty feet across, skimmed up into the air; for an instant the monster wings blotted out the stars, and then it vanished over the brow of the cliff above us. We all sat in amazed silence round the fire, like the heroes of Virgil when the Harpies[1] came down upon them. It was Summerlee who was the first to speak.

'Professor Challenger,' said he, in a solemn voice, which quavered with emotion, 'I owe you an apology. Sir, I am very much in the wrong, and I beg that you will forget what is past.'

It was handsomely said, and the two men for the first time shook hands. So much we have gained by this clear vision of our first pterodactyl. It was worth a stolen supper to bring two such men together.

But if prehistoric life existed upon the plateau, it was not superabundant, for we had no further glimpse of it during the next three days. During this time we traversed a barren and forbidding country, which alternated between stony desert and desolate marshes full of many wild-fowl, upon the north and east of the cliffs. From that direction the place is really inaccessible, and, were it not for a hardish ledge which runs at the very base of the precipice, we should have had to turn back. Many times we were up to our waists in the slime and blubber of an old, semi-tropical swamp. To make matters worse, the place seemed to be a favourite breeding-place of the Jaracaca snake, the most venomous and aggressive in South America. Again and again these horrible creatures came writhing and springing towards us across the surface of this putrid bog, and it was only by keeping our shot-guns for ever ready that we could feel safe from them. One funnel-shaped depression in the morass, of a livid green in colour from some lichen which festered in it, will always remain as a nightmare memory in my mind. It seems to have been a special nest of these vermin, and the slopes were alive with them, all writhing in our direction, for it is a peculiarity of the Jaracaca that it will always attack man at first sight. There were too many for us to shoot, so we fairly took to our heels and ran until we were exhausted. I shall always remember as we looked back how far behind we could see the heads and necks of our horrible pursuers rising and falling amid the reeds. Jaracaca Swamp we named it in the map which we are constructing.

The cliffs upon the farther side had lost their ruddy tint, being chocolate-brown in colour; the vegetation was more scattered along the top of them, and they had sunk to three or four hundred feet in height, but in no place did we find any point where they could be ascended. If anything, they were more impossible than at the first point where we had met them. Their absolute steepness is indicated in the photograph which I took over the stony desert.

'Surely,' said I, as we discussed the situation, 'the rain must find its way down somehow. There are bound to be water-channels in the rocks.'

'Our young friend has glimpses of lucidity,' said Professor Challenger, patting me upon the shoulder.

'The rain must go somewhere,' I repeated.

'He keeps a firm grip upon actuality. The only drawback is that we have conclusively proved by ocular demonstration that there are *no* water channels down the rocks.'

'Where, then, does it go?' I persisted.

'I think it may be fairly assumed that if it does not come outwards it must run inwards.'

'Then there is a lake in the centre.'

'So I should suppose.'

'It is more than likely that the lake may be an old crater,' said Summerlee. 'The whole formation is, of course, highly volcanic. But however that may be, I should expect to find the surface of the plateau slope inwards with a considerable sheet of water in the centre, which may drain off, by some subterranean channel, into the marshes of the Jaracaca Swamp.'

'Or evaporation might preserve an equilibrium,' remarked Challenger, and the two learned men wandered off into one of their usual

The plateau (Photographed by E. D. Malone, from the stony plain on the N.E.)

scientific arguments, which were as comprehensible as Chinese to the layman.

On the sixth day we completed our circuit of the cliffs, and found ourselves back at the first camp, beside the isolated pinnacle of rock. We were a disconsolate party, for nothing could have been more minute than our investigation, and it was absolutely certain that there was no single point where the most active human being could possibly hope to scale the cliff. The place which Maple White's chalk-marks had indicated as his own means of access was now entirely impassable.

What were we to do now? Our stores of provisions, supplemented by our guns, were holding out well, but the day must come when they would need replenishment. In a couple of months the rains might be expected, and we should be washed out of our camp. The rock was harder than marble, and any attempt at cutting a path for so great a height was more than our time or resources would admit. No wonder that we looked gloomily at each other that night, and sought our blankets with hardly a word exchanged. I remember that as I dropped off to sleep my last recollection was that Challenger was squatting, like a monstrous bull-frog, by the fire, his huge head in his hands, sunk apparently in the deepest thought, and entirely oblivious to the good-night which I wished him.

But it was a very different Challenger who greeted us in the morning – a Challenger with contentment and self-congratulation shining from his whole person. He faced us as we assembled for breakfast with a deprecating false modesty in his eyes, as who should say, 'I know that I deserve all that you can say, but I pray you to spare my blushes by not saying it.' His beard bristled exultantly, his chest was thrown out, and his hand was thrust into the front of his jacket. So, in his fancy, may he see himself sometimes, gracing the vacant pedestal in Trafalgar Square, and adding one more to the horrors of the London streets.

'Eureka!' he cried, his teeth shining through his beard. 'Gentlemen, you may congratulate me and we may congratulate each other. The problem is solved.'

'You have found a way up?'

'I venture to think so.'

'And where?'

For answer he pointed to the spire-like pinnacle upon our right.

Our faces – or mine, at least – fell as we surveyed it. That it could be climbed we had our companion's assurance. But a horrible abyss lay between it and the plateau.

'We can never get across,' I gasped.

'We can at least all reach the summit,' said he. 'When we are up I may be able to show you that the resources of an inventive mind are not yet exhausted.'

After breakfast we unpacked the bundle in which our leader had brought his climbing accessories. From it he took a coil of the strongest and lightest rope, a hundred and fifty feet in length, with climbing irons, clamps, and other devices. Lord John was an experienced mountaineer, and Summerlee had done some rough climbing at various times, so that I was really the novice at rock-work of the party; but my strength and activity may have made up for my want of experience.

It was not in reality a very stiff task, though there were moments which made my hair bristle upon my head. The first half was perfectly easy but from there upwards it became continually steeper, until, for the last fifty feet, we were literally clinging with our fingers and toes to tiny ledges and crevices in the rock. I could not have accomplished it, nor could Summerlee, if Challenger had not gained the summit (it was extraordinary to see such activity in so unwieldy a creature) and there fixed the rope round the trunk of the considerable tree which grew there. With this as our support, we were soon able to scramble up the jagged wall until we found ourselves upon the small grassy platform, some twenty-five feet each way, which formed the summit.

The first impression which I received when I had recovered my breath was of the extraordinary view over the country which we had traversed. The whole Brazilian plain seemed to lie beneath us, extending away and away until it ended in dim blue mists upon the farthest sky-line. In the foreground was the long slope, strewn with rocks and dotted with tree-ferns; farther off in the middle distance, looking over the saddle-back hill, I could just see the yellow and green mass of bamboos through which we had passed; and then, gradually, the vegetation increased until it formed the huge forest which extended as far as the eyes could reach, and for a good two thousand miles beyond.

I was still drinking in this wonderful panorama when the heavy hand of the Professor fell upon my shoulder.

'This way, my young friend,' said he; '*vestigia nulla retrorsum.*[2] Never look rearwards, but always to our glorious goal.'

The level of the plateau, when I turned, was exactly that on which we stood, and the green bank of bushes, with occasional trees, was so near that it was difficult to realize how inaccessible it remained. At a rough guess the gulf was forty feet across, but, so far as I could see, it might as well have been forty miles. I placed one arm round the trunk of the tree and leaned over the abyss. Far down were the small dark figures of our servants, looking up at us. The wall was absolutely precipitous, as was that which faced me.

'This is indeed curious,' said the creaking voice of Professor Summerlee.

I turned, and found that he was examining with great interest the tree to which I clung. That smooth bark and those small, ribbed leaves seemed familiar to my eyes. 'Why,' I cried, 'it's a beech!'

'Exactly,' said Summerlee. 'A fellow-countryman in a far land.'

'Not only a fellow-countryman, my good sir,' said Challenger, 'but also, if I may be allowed to enlarge your simile, an ally of the first value. This beech tree will be our saviour.'

'By George!' cried Lord John, 'a bridge!'

'Exactly, my friends, a bridge! It is not for nothing that I expended an hour last night in focusing my mind upon the situation. I have some recollection of once remarking to our young friend here that G. E. C. is at his best when his back is to the wall. Last night you will admit that all our backs were to the wall. But where will-power and intellect go together, there is always a way out. A drawbridge had to be found which could be dropped across the abyss. Behold it!'

It was certainly a brilliant idea. The tree was a good sixty feet in height, and if it only fell the right way it would easily cross the chasm. Challenger had slung the camp axe over his shoulder when he ascended. Now he handed it to me.

'Our young friend has the thews and sinews,' said he. 'I think he will be the most useful at this task. I must beg, however, that you will kindly refrain from thinking for yourself, and that you will do exactly what you are told.'

Under his direction I cut such gashes in the sides of the tree as would ensure that it should fall as we desired. It had already a strong, natural tilt in the direction of the plateau, so that the matter was not difficult. Finally I set to work in earnest upon the trunk, taking turn and turn with Lord John. In a little over an hour there was a loud crack, the tree swayed forward, and then crashed over, burying its branches among the bushes on the farther side. The severed trunk rolled to the very edge of our platform, and for one terrible second we all thought that it was over. It balanced itself, however, a few inches from the edge, and there was our bridge to the unknown.

All of us, without a word, shook hands with Professor Challenger, who raised his straw hat and bowed deeply to each in turn.

'I claim the honour,' said he, 'to be the first to cross to the unknown land – a fitting subject, no doubt, for some future historical painting.'

He had approached the bridge when Lord John laid his hand upon his coat.

'My dear chap,' said he, 'I really cannot allow it.'

'Cannot allow it, sir!' The head went back and the beard forward.

'When it is a matter of science, don't you know, I follow your lead because you are by way of bein' a man of science. But it's up to you to follow me when you come into my department.'

'Your department, sir?'

'We all have our professions, and soldierin' is mine. We are, accordin' to my ideas, invadin' a new country, which may or may not be chock-full of enemies of sorts. To barge blindly into it for want of a little common sense and patience isn't my notion of management.'

The remonstrance was too reasonable to be disregarded. Challenger tossed his head and shrugged his heavy shoulders.

'Well, sir, what do you propose?'

'For all I know there may be a tribe of cannibals waitin' for lunch-time among those very bushes,' said Lord John, looking across the bridge. 'It's better to learn wisdom before you get into a cookin'-pot; so we will content ourselves with hopin' that there is no trouble waitin' for us, and at the same time we will act as if there were.

Malone and I will go down again, therefore, and we will fetch up the four rifles, together with Gomez and the other. One man can then go across and the rest will cover him with guns, until he sees that it is safe for the whole crowd to come along.'

Challenger sat down upon the cut stump and groaned his impatience; but Summerlee and I were of one mind that Lord John was our leader when such practical details were in question. The climb was a more simple thing now that the rope dangled down the face of the worst part of the ascent. Within an hour we had brought up the rifles and a shot-gun. The half-breeds had ascended also, and under Lord John's orders they had carried up a bale of provisions in case our first exploration should be a long one. We had each bandoliers of cartridges.

'Now, Challenger, if you really insist upon being the first man in,' said Lord John, when every preparation was complete.

'I am much indebted to you for your gracious permission,' said the angry Professor; for never was a man so intolerant of every form of authority. 'Since you are good enough to allow it, I shall most certainly take it upon myself to act as pioneer upon this occasion.'

Seating himself with a leg overhanging the abyss on each side, and his hatchet slung upon his back, Challenger hopped his way across the trunk and was soon at the other side. He clambered up and waved his arms in the air.

'At last!' he cried; 'at last!'

I gazed anxiously at him, with a vague expectation that some terrible fate would dart at him from the curtain of green behind him. But all was quiet, save that a strange, many-coloured bird flew up from under his feet and vanished among the trees.

Summerlee was the second. His wiry energy is wonderful in so frail a frame. He insisted upon having two rifles slung upon his back, so that both Professors were armed when he had made his transit. I came next, and tried hard not to look down into the horrible gulf over which I was passing. Summerlee held out the butt-end of his rifle, and an instant later I was able to grasp his hand. As to Lord John, he walked across – actually walked, without support! He must have nerves of iron.

And there we were, the four of us, upon the dreamland, the lost world, of Maple White. To all of us it seemed the moment of our supreme triumph. Who could have guessed that it was the prelude to our supreme disaster? Let me say in a few words how the crushing blow fell upon us.

We had turned away from the edge, and had penetrated about fifty yards of close brushwood, when there came a frightful rending crash from behind us. With one impulse we rushed back the way that we had come. The bridge was gone!

Far down at the base of the cliff I saw, as I looked over, a tangled mass of branches and splintered trunk. It was our beech tree. Had the edge of the platform crumbled and let it through? For a moment this explanation was in all our minds. The next, from the farther side of the rocky pinnacle before us a swarthy face, the face of Gomez the half-breed, was slowly protruded. Yes, it was Gomez, but no longer the Gomez of the demure smile and the mask-like expression. Here was a face with flashing eyes and distorted features, a face convulsed with hatred and with the mad joy of gratified revenge.

'Lord Roxton!' he shouted. 'Lord John Roxton!'

'Well,' said our companion, 'here I am.'

A shriek of laughter came across the abyss.

'Yes, there you are, you English dog, and there you will remain! I have waited and waited, and now has come my chance. You found it hard to get up; you will find it harder to get down. You cursed fools, you are trapped, every one of you!'

We were too astounded to speak. We could only stand there staring in amazement. A great broken bough upon the grass showed whence he had gained his leverage to tilt over our bridge. The face had vanished, but presently it was up again, more frantic than before.

'We nearly killed you with a stone at the cave,' he cried; 'but this is better. It is slower and more terrible. Your bones will whiten up there, and none will know where you lie or come to cover them. As you lie dying, think of Lopez, whom you shot five years ago on the Putomayo River. I am his brother, and, come what will I will die happy now, for his memory has been avenged.' A furious hand was shaken at us, and then all was quiet.

Had the half-breed simply wrought his vengeance and then escaped, all might have been well with him. It was that foolish, irresistible Latin impulse to be dramatic which brought his own downfall. Roxton, the man who had earned himself the name of the Flail of the Lord through three countries, was not one who could be safely taunted. The half-breed was descending on the farther side of the pinnacle; but before he could reach the ground Lord John had run along the edge of the plateau and gained a point from which he could see his man. There was a single crack of his rifle, and, though we saw nothing, we heard the scream and then the distant thud of the falling body. Roxton came back to us with a face of granite.

'I have been a blind simpleton,' said he, bitterly. 'It's my folly that has brought you all into this trouble. I should have remembered that these people have long memories for blood-feuds, and have been more upon my guard.'

'What about the other one? It took two of them to lever that tree over the edge.'

'I could have shot him, but I let him go. He may have had no part in it. Perhaps it would have been better if I had killed him, for he must, as you say, have lent a hand.'

Now that we had the clue to his action, each of us could cast back and remember some sinister act upon the part of the half-breed – his constant desire to know our plans, his arrest outside our tent when he was overhearing them, the furtive looks of hatred which from time to time one or other of us had surprised. We were still discussing it, endeavouring to adjust our minds to these new conditions, when a singular scene in the plain below arrested our attention.

A man in white clothes, who could only be the surviving half-breed, was running as one does run when Death is the pacemaker. Behind him, only a few yards in his rear, bounded the huge ebony figure of Zambo, our devoted negro. Even as we looked, he sprang upon the back of the fugitive and flung his arms round his neck. They rolled on the ground together. An instant afterwards Zambo rose, looked at the prostrate man, and then, waving his hand joyously to us, came running in our direction. The white figure lay motionless in the middle of the great plain.

Our two traitors had been destroyed, but the mischief that they had done lived after them. By no possible means could we get back to the pinnacle. We had been natives of the world; now we were natives of the plateau. The two things were separate and apart. There was the plain which led to the canoes. Yonder, beyond the violet, hazy horizon, was the stream which led back to civilization. But the link between was missing. No human ingenuity could suggest a means of bridging the chasm which yawned between ourselves and our past lives. One instant had altered the whole conditions of our existence.

It was at such a moment that I learned the stuff of which my three comrades were composed. They were grave, it is true, and thoughtful, but of an invincible serenity. For the moment we could only sit among the bushes in patience and wait the coming of Zambo. Presently his honest black face topped the rocks and his Herculean figure emerged upon the top of the pinnacle.

'What I do now?' he cried. 'You tell me and I do it.'

It was a question which it was easier to ask than to answer. One thing only was clear. He was our one trusty link with the outside world. On no account must he leave us.

'No, no!' he cried. 'I not leave you. Whatever come, you always find me here. But no able to keep Indians. Already they say too much, Curupuri live on this place, and they go home. Now you leave them me no able to keep them.'

It was a fact that our Indians had shown in many ways of late that they were weary of their journey and anxious to return. We realized that Zambo spoke the truth, and that it would be impossible for him to keep them.

'Make them wait till tomorrow, Zambo,' I shouted; 'then I can send letter back by them.'

'Very good, sarr! I promise they wait till tomorrow,' said the negro. 'But what I do for you now?'

There was plenty for him to do, and admirably the faithful fellow did it. First of all, under our directions, he undid the rope from the tree-stump and threw one end of it across to us. It was not thicker than a clothes-line, but it was of great strength, and though we could not make a bridge of it, we might well find it invaluable if we had any climbing to do. He then fastened his end of the rope to the package of supplies which had been carried up, and we were able to drag it across. This gave us the means of life for at least a week, even if we found nothing else. Finally he descended and carried up two other packets of mixed goods – a box of ammunition and a number of other things, all of which we got across by throwing our rope to him and hauling it back. It was evening when he at last climbed down, with a final assurance that he would keep the Indians till next morning.

And so it is that I have spent nearly the whole of this our first night upon the plateau writing up our experiences by the light of a single candle-lantern.

We supped and camped at the very edge of the cliff, quenching our thirst with two bottles of Apollinaris which were in one of the cases. It is vital to us to find water, but I think even Lord John himself had had adventures enough for one day, and none of us felt inclined to make the first push into the unknown. We forbore to light a fire or to make any unnecessary sound.

Tomorrow (or today, rather, for it is already dawn as I write) we shall make our first venture into this strange land. When I shall be able to write again – or if I ever shall write again – I know not. Meanwhile, I can see that the Indians are still in their place, and I am sure that the faithful Zambo will be here presently to get my letter. I only trust that it will come to hand.

P. S. – The more I think the more desperate does our position seem. I see no possible hope of our return. If there were a high tree near the edge of the plateau we might drop a return bridge across, but there is none within fifty yards. Our united strength could not carry a trunk which would serve our purpose. The rope, of course, is far too short that we could descend by it. No, our position is hopeless – hopeless!

CHAPTER X

The Most Wonderful Things have Happened

The most wonderful things have happened and are continually happening to us. All the paper that I possess consists of five old notebooks and a lot of scraps, and I have only the one stylographic pencil; but so long as I can move my hand I will continue to set down our experiences and impressions, for, since we are the only men of the whole human race to see such things, it is of enormous importance that I should record them whilst they are fresh in my memory and before that fate which seems to be constantly impending does actually overtake us. Whether Zambo can at last take these letters to the river, or whether I shall myself in some miraculous way carry them back with me, or, finally, whether some daring explorer, coming upon our tracks, with the advantage, perhaps, of a perfected monoplane, should find this bundle of manuscript, in any case I can see that what I am writing is destined to immortality as a classic of true adventure.

On the morning after our being trapped upon the plateau by the villainous Gomez we began a new stage in our experiences. The first incident in it was not such as to give me a very favourable opinion of the place to which we had wandered. As I roused myself from a short nap after day had dawned, my eyes fell upon a most singular appearance upon my own leg. My trouser had slipped up, exposing a few inches of my skin above my sock. On this there rested a large, purplish grape. Astonished at the sight, I leaned forward to pick it off, when, to my horror, it burst between my finger and thumb, squirting blood in every direction. My cry of disgust had brought the two Professors to my side.

'Most interesting,' said Summerlee, bending over my shin. 'An enormous blood-tick, as yet I believe, unclassified.'

'The first-fruits of our labours,' said Challenger in his booming, pedantic fashion. 'We cannot do less than call it *Ixodes Maloni*. The very small inconvenience of being bitten, my young friend, cannot, I am sure, weigh with you as against the glorious privilege of having your name inscribed in the deathless roll of zoology. Unhappily you have crushed this fine specimen at the moment of satiation.'

'Filthy vermin!' I cried.

Professor Challenger raised his great eyebrows in protest, and placed a soothing paw upon my shoulder.

'You should cultivate the scientific eye and the detached scientific mind,' said he. 'To a man of philosophic temperament like myself the blood-tick, with its lancet-like proboscis and its distending stomach is as beautiful a work of Nature as the peacock or, for that matter, the aurora borealis. It pains me to hear you speak of it in so unappreciative a fashion. No doubt, with due diligence, we can secure some other specimen.'

'There can be no doubt of that,' said Summerlee, grimly, 'for one has just disappeared behind your shirt-collar.'

Challenger sprang into the air bellowing like a bull, and tore frantically at his coat and shirt to get them off. Summerlee and I laughed so that we could hardly help him. At last we exposed that monstrous torso (fifty-four inches, by the tailor's tape). His body was all matted with black hair, out of which jungle we picked the wandering tick before it had bitten him. But the bushes round were full of the horrible pests, and it was clear that we must shift our camp.

But first of all it was necessary to make our arrangements with the faithful negro, who appeared presently on the pinnacle with a number of tins of cocoa and biscuits, which he tossed over to us. Of the stores which remained below he was ordered to retain as much as would keep him for two months. The Indians were to have the remainder as a reward for their services and as payment for taking our letters back to the Amazon. Some hours later we saw them in single file far out upon the plain, each with a bundle on his head, making their way back along the path we had come. Zambo occupied our little tent at the base of the pinnacle, and there he remained, our one link with the world below.

And now we had to decide upon our immediate movements. We shifted our position from among the tick-laden bushes until we came to a small clearing thickly surrounded by trees upon all sides. There were some flat slabs of rock in the centre, with an excellent well close by, and there we sat in cleanly comfort while we made our first plans for the invasion of this new country. Birds were calling among the foliage – especially one with a peculiar whooping cry which was new to us – but beyond these sounds there were no signs of life.

Our first care was to make some sort of list of our own stores, so that we might know what we had to rely upon. What with the things we had ourselves brought up and those which Zambo had sent across on the rope, we were fairly well supplied. Most important of all, in view of the dangers which might surround us, we had our four rifles and one thousand three hundred rounds, also a shot-gun, but not more than a hundred and fifty medium pellet cartridges. In the matter of provisions we had enough to last for several weeks, with a sufficiency of tobacco and a few scientific implements, including a large telescope and a good field-glass. All these things we collected together in the clearing, and as a first precaution, we cut down with our hatchet and knives a number of thorny bushes, which we piled round in a circle some fifteen yards in diameter. This was to be our headquarters for the time – our place of refuge against sudden danger and the guard-house for our stores. Fort Challenger, we called it.

It was midday before we had made ourselves secure, but the heat was not oppressive, and the general character of the plateau, both in its temperature and in its vegetation, was almost temperate. The beech, the oak, and even the birch were to be found among the tangle of trees which girt us in. One huge gingko tree, topping all the others, shot its great limbs and maidenhair foliage over the fort which we had constructed. In its shade we continued our discussion, while Lord John, who had quickly taken command in the hour of action, gave us his views.

'So long as neither man nor beast has seen or heard us, we are safe,' said he. 'From the time they know we are here our troubles begin. There are no signs that they have found us out as yet. So our game surely is to lie low for a time and spy out the land. We want to have a good look at our neighbours before we get on visitin' terms.'

'But we must advance,' I ventured to remark.

'By all means, sonny my boy! We will advance. But with common sense. We must never go so far that we can't get back to our base.

Above all, we must never, unless it is life or death, fire off our guns.'

'But *you* fired yesterday,' said Summerlee.

'Well, it couldn't be helped. However, the wind was strong and blew outwards. It is not likely that the sound could have travelled far into the plateau. By the way, what shall we call this place? I suppose it is up to us to give it a name?'

There were several suggestions, more or less happy, but Challenger's was final.

'It can only have one name,' said he. 'It is called after the pioneer who discovered it. It is Maple White Land.'

Maple White Land it became, and so it is named in that chart which has become my special task. So it will, I trust, appear in the atlas of the future.

The peaceful penetration of Maple White Land was the pressing subject before us. We had the evidence of our own eyes that the place was inhabited by some unknown creatures, and there was that of Maple White's sketch-book to show that more dreadful and more dangerous monsters might still appear. That there might also prove to be human occupants and that they were of a malevolent character was suggested by the skeleton impaled upon the bamboos, which could not have got there had it not been dropped from above. Our situation, stranded without possibility of escape in such a land, was clearly full of danger, and our reasons endorsed every measure of caution which Lord John's experience could suggest. Yet it was surely impossible that we should halt on the edge of this world of mystery when our very souls were tingling with impatience to push forward and to pluck the heart from it.

We therefore blocked the entrance to our zareba[1] by filling it up with several thorny bushes, and left our camp with the stores entirely surrounded by this protecting hedge. We then slowly and cautiously set forth into the unknown, following the course of the little stream which flowed from our spring, as it should always serve us as a guide on our return.

Hardly had we started when we came across signs that there were indeed wonders awaiting us. After a few hundred yards of thick forest, containing many trees which were quite unknown to me, but which

Summerlee, who was the botanist of the party, recognized as forms of conifera and of cycadaceous plants which have long passed away in the world below, we entered a region where the stream widened out and formed a considerable bog. High reeds of a peculiar type grew thickly before us, which were pronounced to be equisetacea, or mare's-tails, with tree-ferns scattered amongst them, all of them swaying in a brisk wind. Suddenly Lord John, who was walking first, halted with uplifted hand.

'Look at this!' said he. 'By George, this must be the trail of the father of all birds!'

An enormous three-toed track was imprinted in the soft mud before us. The creature, whatever it was, had crossed the swamp and had passed on into the forest. We all stopped to examine that monstrous spoor. If it were indeed a bird – and what animal could leave such a mark? – its foot was so much larger than an ostrich's that its height upon the same scale must be enormous. Lord John looked eagerly round him and slipped two cartridges into his elephant-gun.

'I'll stake my good name as a shikarree,'[2] said he, 'that the track is a fresh one. The creature has not passed ten minutes. Look how the water is still oozing into that deeper print! By Jove! See, here is the mark of a little one!'

Sure enough, smaller tracks of the same general form were running parallel to the large ones.

'But what do you make of this?' cried Professor Summerlee, triumphantly, pointing to what looked like the huge print of a five-fingered human hand appearing among the three-toed marks.

'Wealden!' cried Challenger, in an ecstasy. 'I've seen them in the Wealden clay. It is a creature walking erect upon three-toed feet, and occasionally putting one of its five-fingered forepaws upon the ground. Not a bird, my dear Roxton – not a bird.'

'A beast?'

'No; a reptile – a dinosaur. Nothing else could have left such a track. They puzzled a worthy Sussex doctor[3] some ninety years ago; but who in the world could have hoped – hoped – to have seen a sight like that?'

His words died away into a whisper, and we all stood in motionless amazement. Following the tracks, we had left the morass and passed through a screen of brushwood and trees. Beyond was an open glade, and in this were five of the most extraordinary creatures that I have ever seen. Crouching down among the bushes, we observed them at our leisure.

There were, as I say, five of them, two being adults and three young ones. In size they were enormous. Even the babies were as big as elephants, while the two large ones were far beyond all creatures I have ever seen. They had slate-coloured skin, which was scaled like a lizard's and shimmered where the sun shone upon it. All five were sitting up, balancing themselves upon their broad, powerful tails and their huge three-toed hind-feet, while with their small five-fingered front-feet they pulled down the branches upon which they browsed. I do not know that I can bring their appearance home to you better than by saying that they looked like monstrous kangaroos, twenty feet in length, and with skins like black crocodiles.

I do not know how long we stayed motionless gazing at this marvellous spectacle. A strong wind blew towards us and we were well concealed, so there was no chance of discovery. From time to time the little ones played round their parents in unwieldy gambols, the great beasts bounding into the air and falling with dull thuds upon the earth. The strength of the parents seemed to be limitless, for one of them, having some difficulty in reaching a bunch of foliage which grew upon a considerable-sized tree, put his fore-legs round the trunk and tore it down as if it had been a sapling. The action seemed, as I thought, to show not only the great development of its muscles, but also the small one of its brain, for the whole weight came crashing down upon the top of it, and it uttered a series of shrill yelps to show that, big as it was, there was a limit to what it could endure. The incident made it think, apparently, that the neighbourhood was dangerous, for it slowly lurched off through the wood, followed by its mate and its three enormous infants. We saw the shimmering slatey gleam of their skins between the tree-trunks, and their heads undulating high above the brushwood. Then they vanished from our sight.

I looked at my comrades. Lord John was standing at gaze with his finger on the trigger of his elephant-gun, his eager hunter's soul shining

Glade of the iguanodons (Reconstructed by Mr Pat L. Forbes from sketch by E. D. Malone)

from his fierce eyes. What would he not give for one such head to place between the two crossed oars above the mantelpiece in his snuggery at the Albany! And yet his reason held him in, for all our exploration of the wonders of this unknown land depended upon our presence being concealed from its inhabitants. The two Professors were in silent ecstasy. In their excitement they had unconsciously seized each other by the hand, and stood like two little children in the presence of a marvel, Challenger's cheeks bunched up into a seraphic smile, and Summerlee's sardonic face softening for the moment into wonder and reverence.

'*Nunc dimittis!*'[4] he cried at last. 'What will they say in England of this?'

'My dear Summerlee, I will tell you with great confidence exactly what they will say in England,' said Challenger. 'They will say that you are an infernal liar and a scientific charlatan, exactly as you and others said of me.'

'In the face of photographs?'

'Faked, Summerlee! Clumsily faked!'

'In the face of specimens?'

'Ah, there we may have them! Malone and his filthy Fleet Street crew may be all yelping our praises yet. August the twenty-eighth – the day we saw five live iguanodons in a glade of Maple White Land. Put it down in your diary, my young friend, and send it to your rag.'

'And be ready to get the toe-end of the editorial boot in return,' said Lord John. 'Things look a bit different from the latitude of London, young fellah my lad. There's many a man who never tells his adventures, for he can't hope to be believed. Who's to blame them? For this will seem a bit of a dream to ourselves in a month or two. *What* did you say they were?'

'Iguanodons,' said Summerlee. 'You'll find their footmarks all over the Hastings sands, in Kent, and in Sussex. The South of England was alive with them when there was plenty of good lush green-stuff to keep them going. Conditions have changed, and the beasts died. Here it seems that the conditions have not changed, and the beasts have lived.'

'If ever we get out of this alive, I must have a head with me,' said Lord John. 'Lord, how some of that Somaliland–Uganda crowd would turn a beautiful pea-green if they saw it! I don't know what you chaps think, but it strikes me that we are on mighty thin ice all this time.'

I had the same feeling of mystery and danger around us. In the gloom of the trees there seemed a constant menace, and as we looked up into their shadowy foliage vague terrors crept into one's heart. It is true that these monstrous creatures which we had seen were lumbering, inoffensive brutes which were unlikely to hurt anyone, but in this world of wonders what other survivals might there not be – what fierce, active horrors ready to pounce upon us from their lair among the rocks or brushwood? I knew little of prehistoric life, but I had a clear remembrance of one book which I had read in which it spoke of creatures who would live upon our lions and tigers as a cat lives upon mice. What if these also were to be found in the woods of Maple White Land!

It was destined that on this very morning – our first in the new country – we were to find out what strange hazards lay around us. It was a loathsome adventure, and one of which I hate to think. If, as Lord John said, the glade of the iguanodons will remain with us as a dream, then surely the swamp of the pterodactyls will for ever be our nightmare. Let me set down exactly what occurred.

We passed very slowly through the woods, partly because Lord John acted as scout before he would let us advance, and partly because at every second step one or other of our Professors would fall, with a cry of wonder, before some flower or insect which presented him with a new type. We may have travelled two or three miles in all, keeping to the right of the line of the stream, when we came upon a considerable opening in the trees. A belt of brushwood led up to a tangle of rocks – the whole plateau was strewn with boulders. We were walking slowly towards these rocks, among bushes which reached over our waists, when we became aware of a strange low gabbling and whistling sound, which filled the air with a constant clamour and appeared to come from some spot immediately before us. Lord John held up his hand as a signal for us to stop, and he made his way swiftly, stooping and running, to the line of rocks. We saw him peep over them and give a gesture of amazement. Then he stood staring as if forgetting us, so utterly entranced was he by what he saw. Finally he waved us to come on, holding up his hand as a signal for caution. His whole bearing made me feel that something wonderful but dangerous lay before us.

Creeping to his side, we looked over the rocks. The place into which we gazed was a pit, and may, in the early days, have been one of the smaller volcanic blow-holes of the plateau. It was bowl-shaped, and at the bottom, some hundreds of yards from where we lay, were pools of green-scummed, stagnant water, fringed with bullrushes. It was a weird place in itself, but its occupants made it seem like a scene from the Seven Circles of Dante.[5] The place was a rookery of pterodactyls. There were hundreds of them congregated within view. All the bottom area round the water-edge was alive with their young ones, and with hideous mothers brooding upon their leathery, yellow-ish eggs. From this crawling flapping mass of obscene reptilian life came the shocking clamour which filled the air and the mephitic, horrible, musty odour which turned us sick. But above, perched each upon its own stone, tall, grey, and withered, more like dead and dried specimens than actual living creatures, sat the horrible males, absolutely motionless save for the rolling of their red eyes or an occasional snap of their rat-trap beaks as a dragon-fly went past them. Their huge, membranous wings were closed by folding their forearms, so that they sat like gigantic old women, wrapped in hideous web-coloured shawls, and with their ferocious heads protruding above them. Large and small, not less than a thousand of these filthy creatures lay in the hollow before us.

Our Professors would gladly have stayed there all day, so entranced were they by this opportunity of studying the life of a prehistoric age. They pointed out the fish and dead birds lying about among the rocks as proving the nature of the food of these creatures, and I heard them congratulating each other on having cleared up the point why the bones of this flying dragon are found in such great numbers in certain well-defined areas, as in the Cambridge Green-sand, since it was now seen that, like penguins, they lived in gregarious fashion.

Finally, however, Challenger, bent upon proving some point which Summerlee had contested, thrust his head over the rock and nearly brought destruction upon us all. In an instant the nearest male gave a shrill, whistling cry, and flapped its twenty-foot span of leathery wings as it soared up into the air. The females and young ones huddled

The swamp of the pterodactyls (Reconstructed by Pat L. Forbes from sketch by E. D. Malone)

together beside the water, while the whole circle of sentinels rose one after the other and sailed off into the sky. It was a wonderful sight to see at least a hundred creatures of such enormous size and hideous appearance all swooping like swallows with swift, shearing wing-strokes above us; but soon we realized that it was not one on which we could afford to linger. At first the great brutes flew round in a huge ring, as if to make sure what the exact extent of the danger might be. Then, the flight grew lower and the circle narrower, until they were whizzing round and round us, the dry, rustling flap of their huge slate-coloured wings filling the air with a volume of sound that made me think of Hendon aerodrome upon a race day.[6]

'Make for the wood and keep together,' cried Lord John, clubbing his rifle. 'The brutes mean mischief.'

The moment we attempted to retreat the circle closed in upon us, until the tips of the wings of those nearest to us nearly touched our faces. We beat at them with the stocks of our guns, but there was nothing solid or vulnerable to strike. Then suddenly out of the whizzing, slate-coloured circle a long neck shot out, and a fierce beak made a thrust at us. Another and another followed. Summerlee gave a cry and put his hand to his face, from which the blood was streaming. I felt a prod at the back of my neck, and turned dizzy with the shock. Challenger fell, and as I stooped to pick him up I was again struck from behind and dropped on the top of him. At the same instant I heard the crash of Lord John's elephant-gun, and, looking up, saw one of the creatures with a broken wing struggling upon the ground, spitting and gurgling at us with a wide-opened beak and blood-shot, goggled eyes, like some devil in a mediaeval picture. Its comrades had flown higher at the sudden sound, and were circling above our heads.

'Now,' cried Lord John, 'now for our lives!'

We staggered through the brushwood, and even as we reached the trees the harpies were on us again. Summerlee was knocked down, but we tore him up and rushed among the trunks. Once there we were safe, for those huge wings had no space for their sweep beneath the branches. As we limped homewards, sadly mauled and discomfited, we saw them for a long time flying at a great height against the deep blue sky above our heads, soaring round and round, no bigger than wood-pigeons, with their eyes no doubt still following our progress. At last, however, as we reached the thicker woods they gave up the chase, and we saw them no more.

'A most interesting and convincing experience,' said Challenger, as we halted beside the brook and he bathed a swollen knee. 'We are exceptionally well informed, Summerlee, as to the habits of the enraged pterodactyl.'

Summerlee was wiping the blood from a cut in his forehead, while I was tying up a nasty stab in the muscle of the neck. Lord John had the shoulder of his coat torn away, but the creature's teeth had only grazed the flesh.

'It is worth noting,' Challenger continued, 'that our young friend has received an undoubted stab, while Lord John's coat could only have been torn by a bite. In my own case, I was beaten about the head by their wings, so we have had a remarkable exhibition of their various methods of offence.'

'It has been touch and go for our lives,' said Lord John, gravely, 'and I could not think of a more rotten sort of death than to be outed by such filthy vermin. I was sorry to fire my rifle, but, by Jove! there was no great choice.'

'We should not be here if you hadn't,' said I, with conviction.

'It may do no harm,' said he. 'Among these woods there must be many loud cracks from splitting or falling trees which would be just like the sound of a gun. But now, if you are of my opinion, we have had thrills enough for one day, and had best get back to the surgical box at the camp for some carbolic. Who knows what venom these beasts may have in their hideous jaws?'

But surely no men ever had just such a day since the world began. Some fresh surprise was ever in store for us. When, following the course of our brook, we at last reached our glade and saw the thorny barricade of our camp, we thought that our adventures were at an end. But we had something more to think of before we could rest. The gate of Fort Challenger had been untouched, the walls were unbroken, and yet it had been visited by some strange and powerful creature in our absence. No foot-mark showed a trace of its nature, and only the overhanging branch of the enormous gingko tree suggested how it might have come and gone; but of its malevolent strength there was ample evidence in the condition of our stores. They were strewn at random all over the ground, and one tin of meat had been crushed into pieces so as to extract the contents. A case of cartridges had been shattered into matchwood, and one of the brass shells lay shredded into pieces beside it. Again the feeling of vague horror came upon our souls, and we gazed round with frightened eyes at the dark shadows which lay around us, in all of which some fearsome shape might be lurking. How good it was when we were hailed by the voice of Zambo, and, going to the edge of the plateau, saw him sitting grinning at us upon the top of the opposite pinnacle.

'All well, Massa Challenger, all well!' he cried. 'Me stay here. No fear. You always find me when you want.'

His honest black face, and the immense view before us, which carried us half-way back to the affluent of the Amazon, helped us to remember that we really were upon this earth in the twentieth century, and had not by some magic been conveyed to some raw planet in its earliest and wildest state. How difficult it was to realize that the violet line upon the far horizon was well advanced to that great river upon which huge steamers ran, and folk talked of the small affairs of life, while we, marooned among the creatures of a bygone age, could but gaze towards it and yearn for all that it meant!

One other memory remains with me of this wonderful day, and with it I will close this letter. The two Professors, their tempers aggravated no doubt by their injuries, had fallen out as to whether our assailants were of the genus pterodactylus or dimorphodon, and high words had ensued. To avoid their wrangling I moved some little way apart, and was seated smoking upon the trunk of a fallen tree, when Lord John strolled over in my direction.

'I say, Malone,' said he, 'do you remember that place where those beasts were?'

'Very clearly.'

'A sort of volcanic pit, was it not?'

'Exactly,' said I.

'Did you notice the soil?'

'Rocks.'

'But round the water – where the reeds were?'

'It was a bluish soil. It looked like clay.'

'Exactly. A volcanic tube full of blue clay.'

'What of that?' I asked.

'Oh, nothing, nothing,' said he, and strolled back to where the voices of the contending men of science rose in a prolonged duet, the high, strident note of Summerlee rising and falling to the sonorous bass of Challenger. I should have thought no more of Lord John's remark were it not that once again that night I heard him mutter to himself: 'Blue clay – clay in a volcanic tube!' They were the last words I heard before I dropped into an exhausted sleep.

CHAPTER XI

For Once I was the Hero

Lord John Roxton was right when he thought that some specially toxic quality might lie in the bite of the horrible creatures which had attacked us. On the morning after our first adventure upon the plateau, both Summerlee and I were in great pain and fever, while Challenger's knee was so bruised that he could hardly limp. We kept to our camp all day, therefore, Lord John busying himself, with such help as we could give him, in raising the height and thickness of the thorny walls which were our only defence. I remember that during the whole long day I was haunted by the feeling that we were closely observed, though by whom or whence I could give no guess.

So strong was the impression that I told Professor Challenger of it, who put it down to the cerebral excitement caused by my fever. Again and again I glanced round swiftly, with the conviction that I was about to see something, but only to meet the dark tangle of our hedge or the solemn and cavernous gloom of the great trees which arched above our heads. And yet the feeling grew ever stronger in my own mind that something observant and something malevolent was at our very elbow. I thought of the Indian superstition of the Curupuri – the dreadful, lurking spirit of the woods – and I could have imagined that his terrible presence haunted those who had invaded his most remote and sacred retreat.

That night (our third in Maple White Land) we had an experience which left a fearful impression upon our minds, and made us thankful that Lord John had worked so hard in making our retreat impregnable. We were all sleeping round our dying fire when we were aroused – or, rather, I should say, shot out of our slumbers – by a succession of the most frightful cries and screams to which I have ever listened. I know no sound to which I could compare this amazing tumult, which seemed to come from some spot within a few hundred yards of our camp. It was as ear-splitting as any whistle of a railway-engine; but whereas the whistle is a clear, mechanical, sharp-edged sound, this was far deeper in volume and vibrant with the uttermost strain of agony and horror. We clapped our hands to our ears to shut out that nerve-shaking appeal. A cold sweat broke out over my body, and my heart turned sick at the misery of it. All the woes of tortured life, all its stupendous indictment of high heaven, its innumerable sorrows, seemed to be centred and condensed into that one dreadful, agonized cry. And then, under this high-pitched, ringing sound there was another, more intermittent, a low, deep-chested laugh, a growling, throaty gurgle of merriment which formed a grotesque accompaniment to the shriek with which it was blended. For three or four minutes on end the fearsome duet continued, while all the foliage rustled with the rising of startled birds. Then it shut off as suddenly as it began. For a long time we sat in horrified silence. Then Lord John threw a bundle of twigs upon the fire, and their red glare lit up the intent faces of my companions and flickered over the great boughs above our heads.

'What was it?' I whispered.

'We shall know in the morning,' said Lord John. 'It was close to us – not farther than the glade.'

'We have been privileged to overhear a prehistoric tragedy, the sort of drama which occurred among the reeds upon the border of some Jurassic lagoon, when the greater dragon pinned the lesser among the slime,' said Challenger, with more solemnity than I had ever heard in his voice. 'It was surely well for man that he came late in the order of creation. There were powers abroad in earlier days which no courage and no mechanism of his could have met. What could his sling, his throwing-stick, or his arrow avail him against such forces as have been loose tonight? Even with a modern rifle it would be all odds on the monster.'

'I think I should back my little friend,' said Lord John, caressing his Express. 'But the beast would certainly have a good sporting chance.'

Summerlee raised his hand.

'Hush!' he cried. 'Surely I hear something?'

From the utter silence there emerged a deep, regular pat-pat. It was the tread of some animal – the rhythm of soft but heavy pads placed cautiously upon the ground. It stole slowly round the camp, and then halted near our gateway. There was a low, sibilant rise and fall – the breathing of the creature. Only our feeble hedge separated us from this horror of the night. Each of us had seized his rifle, and Lord John had pulled out a small bush to make an embrasure in the hedge.

'By George!' he whispered. 'I think I can see it!'

I stooped and peered over his shoulder through the gap. Yes, I could see it, too. In the deep shadow of the tree there was a deeper shadow yet, black, inchoate, vague – a crouching form full of savage vigour and menace. It was no higher than a horse, but the dim outline suggested vast bulk and strength. That hissing pant, as regular and full-volumed as the exhaust of an engine, spoke of a monstrous organism. Once, as it moved, I thought I saw the glint of two terrible, greenish eyes. There was an uneasy rustling, as if it were crawling slowly forward.

'I believe it is going to spring!' said I, cocking my rifle.

'Don't fire! Don't fire!' whispered Lord John. 'The crash of a gun in this silent night would be heard for miles. Keep it as a last card.'

'If it gets over the hedge we're done,' said Summerlee, and his voice crackled into a nervous laugh as he spoke.

'No, it must not get over,' cried Lord John; 'but hold your fire to the last. Perhaps I can make something of the fellow. I'll chance it, anyhow.'

It was as brave an act as ever I saw a man do. He stooped to the fire, picked up a blazing branch, and slipped in an instant through a sallyport which he had made in our gateway. The thing moved forward with a dreadful snarl. Lord John never hesitated, but, running towards it with a quick, light step, he dashed the flaming wood into the brute's face. For one moment I had a vision of a horrible mask like a giant toad's, of a warty, leprous skin, and of a loose mouth all beslobbered with fresh blood. The next, there was a crash in the underwood and our dreadful visitor was gone.

'I thought he wouldn't face the fire,' said Lord John, laughing, as he came back and threw his branch among the faggots.

'You should not have taken such a risk!' we all cried.

'There was nothin' else to be done. If he had got among us we should have shot each other in tryin' to down him. On the other hand, if we had fired through the hedge and wounded him he would soon have been on the top of us – to say nothin' of giving ourselves away. On the whole, I think that we are jolly well out of it. What was he, then?'

Our learned men looked at each other with some hesitation.

'Personally, I am unable to classify the creature with any certainty,' said Summerlee, lighting his pipe from the fire.

'In refusing to commit yourself you are but showing a proper scientific reserve,' said Challenger, with massive condescension. 'I am not myself prepared to go farther than to say in general terms that we have almost certainly been in contact tonight with some form of carnivorous dinosaur. I have already expressed my anticipation that something of the sort might exist upon this plateau.'

'We have to bear in mind,' remarked Summerlee, 'that there are many prehistoric forms which have never come down to us. It would be rash to suppose that we can give a name to all that we are likely to meet.'

'Exactly. A rough classification may be the best that we can attempt. Tomorrow some further evidence may help us to an identification. Meantime we can only renew our interrupted slumbers.'

'But not without a sentinel,' said Lord John, with decision. 'We can't afford to take chances in a country like this. Two-hour spells in the future, for each of us.'

'Then I'll just finish my pipe in starting the first one,' said Professor Summerlee; and from that time onwards we never trusted ourselves again without a watchman.

In the morning it was not long before we discovered the source of the hideous uproar which had aroused us in the night. The iguanodon glade was the scene of a horrible butchery. From the pools of blood and the enormous lumps of flesh scattered in every direction over the green sward we imagined at first that a number of animals had been killed, but on examining the remains more closely we discovered that all this carnage came from one of these unwieldy monsters, which had been literally torn to pieces by some creature not larger, perhaps, but far more ferocious, than itself.

Our two Professors sat in absorbed argument, examining piece after piece, which showed the marks of savage teeth and of enormous claws.

'Our judgment must still be in abeyance,' said Professor Challenger, with a huge slab of whitish-coloured flesh across his knee. 'The indications would be consistent with the presence of a sabre-toothed tiger, such as are still found among the breccia[1] of our caverns; but the creature actually seen was undoubtedly of a larger and more reptilian character. Personally, I should pronounce for allosaurus.'

'Or megalosaurus,' said Summerlee.

'Exactly. Any one of the larger carnivorous dinosaurs would meet the case. Among them are to be found all the most terrible types of animal life that have ever cursed the earth or blessed a museum.' He laughed sonorously at his own conceit, for, though he had little sense of humour, the crudest pleasantry from his own lips moved him always to roars of appreciation.

'The less noise the better,' said Lord John, curtly. 'We don't know who or what may be near us. If this fellah comes back for his breakfast and catches us here we won't have so much to laugh at. By the way, what is this mark upon the iguanodon's hide?'

On the dull, scaly, slate-coloured skin, somewhere above the shoulder, there was a singular black circle of some substance which looked like asphalt. None of us could suggest what it meant, though Summerlee was of opinion that he had seen something similar upon one of the young ones two days before. Challenger said nothing, but looked pompous and puffy, as if he could if he would, so that finally Lord John asked his opinion direct.

'If your lordship will graciously permit me to open my mouth, I shall be happy to express my sentiments,' said he, with elaborate sarcasm. 'I am not in the habit of being taken to task in the fashion which seems to be customary with your lordship. I was not aware that it was necessary to ask your permission before smiling at a harmless pleasantry.'

It was not until he had received his apology that our touchy friend would suffer himself to be appeased. When at last his ruffled feelings were at ease, he addressed us at some length from his seat upon a fallen tree, speaking, as his habit was, as if he were imparting most precious information to a class of a thousand.

'With regard to the marking,' said he, 'I am inclined to agree with my friend and colleague, Professor Summerlee, that the stains are from asphalt. As this plateau is, in its very nature, highly volcanic, and as asphalt is a substance which one associates with Plutonic forces, I cannot doubt that it exists in the free liquid state, and that the creatures may have come in contact with it. A much more important problem is the question as to the existence of the carnivorous monster which has left its traces in this glade. We know roughly that this plateau is not larger than an average English county. Within this confined space a certain number of creatures, mostly types which have passed away in the world below, have lived together for innumerable years. Now, it is very clear to me that in so long a period one would have expected that the carnivorous creatures, multiplying unchecked, would have exhausted their food supply and have been compelled to either modify their flesh-eating habits or die of hunger. This we see has not been so. We can only imagine, therefore, that the balance of Nature is preserved by some check which limits the numbers of these ferocious creatures. One of the many interesting problems, therefore, which await our solution is to discover what that check may be and how it operates. I venture to trust that we may have some future opportunity for the closer study of the carnivorous dinosaurs.'

'And I venture to trust we may not,' I observed.

The Professor only raised his great eyebrows, as the schoolmaster meets the irrelevant observation of the naughty boy.

'Perhaps Professor Summerlee may have an observation to make,' he said, and the two *savants* ascended together into some rarefied scientific atmosphere, where the possibilities of a modification of the birth-rate were weighed against the decline of the food supply as a check in the struggle for existence.

That morning we mapped out a small portion of the plateau, avoiding the swamp of the pterodactyls, and keeping to the east of our brook instead of to the west. In that direction the country was still thickly wooded, with so much undergrowth that our progress was very slow.

I have dwelt up to now upon the terrors of Maple White Land; but there was another side to the subject, for all that morning we wandered among lovely flowers – mostly, as I observed, white or yellow in colour, these being, as our Professors explained, the primitive flower-shades. In many places the ground was absolutely covered with them, and as we walked ankle-deep on that wonderful yielding carpet, the scent was almost intoxicating in its sweetness and intensity. The homely English bee buzzed everywhere around us. Many of the trees under which we passed had their branches bowed down with fruit, some of which were of familiar sorts, while other varieties were new. By observing which of them were pecked by the birds we avoided all danger of poison and added a delicious variety to our food reserve. In the jungle which we traversed were numerous hard-trodden paths made by the wild beasts, and in the more marshy places we saw a profusion of strange footmarks, including many of the iguanodon. Once in a grove we observed several of these great creatures grazing, and Lord John, with his glass, was able to report that they also were spotted with asphalt, though in a different place to the one which we had examined in the morning. What this phenomenon meant we could not imagine.

We saw many small animals, such as porcupines, a scaly ant-eater, and a wild pig, piebald in colour and with long curved tusks. Once, through a break in the trees, we saw a clear shoulder of green hill some distance away, and across this a large dun-coloured animal was travelling at a considerable pace. It passed so swiftly that we were unable to say what it was; but if it were a deer, as was claimed by Lord John, it must have been as large as those monstrous Irish elk which are still dug up from time to time in the bogs of my native land.

Ever since the mysterious visit which had been paid to our camp we always returned to it with some misgivings. However, on this occasion we found everything in order. That evening we had a grand discussion upon our present situation and future plans, which I must describe at some length, as it led to a new departure by which we were enabled to gain a more complete knowledge of Maple White Land than might have come in many weeks of exploring. It was Summerlee who opened the debate. All day he had been querulous in manner, and now some remark of Lord John's as to what we should do on the morrow brought all his bitterness to a head.

'What we ought to be doing today, tomorrow, and all the time,' said he, 'is finding some way out of the trap into which we have fallen. You are all turning your brains towards getting into this country. I say that we should be scheming how to get out of it.'

'I am surprised, sir,' boomed Challenger, stroking his majestic beard, 'that any man of science should commit himself to so ignoble a sentiment. You are in a land which offers such an inducement to the ambitious naturalist as none ever has since the world began, and you suggest leaving it before we have acquired more than the most superficial knowledge of it or of its contents. I expected better things of you, Professor Summerlee.'

'You must remember,' said Summerlee, sourly, 'that I have a large class in London who are at present at the mercy of an extremely inefficient *locum tenens*.[2] This makes my situation different from yours, Professor Challenger, since, so far as I know, you have never been entrusted with any responsible educational work.'

'Quite so,' said Challenger. 'I have felt it to be a sacrilege to divert a brain which is capable of the highest original research to any lesser object. That is why I have sternly set my face against any proffered scholastic appointment.'

'For example?' asked Summerlee, with a sneer; but Lord John hastened to change the conversation.

'I must say,' said he, 'that I think it would be a mighty poor thing to go back to London before I know a great deal more of this place than I do at present.'

'I could never dare to walk into the back office of my paper and face old McArdle,' said I. (You will excuse the frankness of this report, will you not, sir?) 'He'd never forgive me for leaving such unexhausted copy behind me. Besides, so far as I can see, it is not worth discussing, since we can't get down, even if we wanted.'

'Our young friend makes up for many obvious mental lacunae by some measure of primitive common sense,' remarked Challenger. 'The interests of his deplorable profession are immaterial to us; but, as he observes, we cannot get down in any case, so it is a waste of energy to discuss it.'

'It is a waste of energy to do anything else,' growled Summerlee from behind his pipe. 'Let me remind you that we came here upon a perfectly definite mission, entrusted to us at the meeting of the Zoological Institute in London. That mission was to test the truth of Professor Challenger's statements. Those statements, as I am bound to admit, we are now in a position to endorse. Our ostensible work is therefore done. As to the detail which remains to be worked out upon this plateau, it is so enormous that only a large expedition, with a very special equipment, could hope to cope with it. Should we attempt to do so ourselves, the only possible result must be that we shall never return with the important contribution to science which we have already gained. Professor Challenger has devised means for getting us on to this plateau when it appeared to be inaccessible; I think that we should now call upon him to use the same ingenuity in getting us back to the world from which we came.'

I confess that as Summerlee stated his view it struck me as altogether reasonable. Even Challenger was affected by the consideration that his enemies would never stand confuted if the confirmation of his statements should never reach those who had doubted them.

'The problem of the descent is at first sight a formidable one,' said he, 'and yet I cannot doubt that the intellect can solve it. I am prepared to agree with our colleague that a protracted stay in Maple White Land is at present inadvisable, and that the question of our return will soon have to be faced. I absolutely refuse to leave, however, until we have made at least a superficial examination of this country, and are able to take back with us something in the nature of a chart.'

Professor Summerlee gave a snort of impatience.

'We have spent two long days in exploration,' said he, 'and we are no wiser as to the actual geography of the place than when we started. It is clear that it is all thickly wooded, and it would take months to penetrate it and to learn the relations of one part to another. If there were some central peak it would be different, but it all slopes downwards, so far as we can see. The farther we go the less likely it is that we will get any general view.'

It was at that moment that I had my inspiration. My eyes chanced to light upon the enormous gnarled trunk of the gingko tree which cast its huge branches over us. Surely, if its bole exceeded that of all others, its height must do the same. If the rim of the plateau was indeed the highest point, then why should this mighty tree not prove to be a watch-tower which commanded the whole country? Now, ever since I ran wild as a lad in Ireland I have been a bold and skilled tree-climber. My comrades might be my masters on the rocks, but I knew that I would be supreme among those branches. Could I only get my legs on to the lowest of the giant off-shoots, then it would be strange indeed if I could not make my way to the top. My comrades were delighted at my idea.

'Our young friend,' said Challenger, bunching up the red apples of his cheeks, 'is capable of acrobatic exertions which would be impossible to a man of a more solid, though possibly of a more commanding, appearance. I applaud his resolution.'

'By George, young fellah, you've put your hand on it!' said Lord John, clapping me on the back. 'How we never came to think of it before I can't imagine! There's not more than an hour of daylight left, but if you take your notebook you may be able to get some rough sketch of the place. If we put these three ammunition cases under the branch, I will soon hoist you on to it.'

He stood on the boxes while I faced the trunk, and was gently raising me when Challenger sprang forward and gave me such a thrust with his huge hand that he fairly shot me into the tree. With both arms clasping the branch, I scrambled hard with my feet until I had worked, first my body, and then my knees, on to it. There were three excellent off-shoots, like huge rungs of a ladder, above my head, and a tangle of convenient branches beyond, so that I clambered onwards with such speed that I soon lost sight of the ground and had nothing but foliage beneath me. Now and then I encountered a check, and once I had to shin up a creeper for eight or ten feet, but I made excellent progress, and the booming of Challenger's voice seemed to be a great distance beneath me. The tree was, however, enormous, and, looking upwards, I could see no thinning of the leaves above my head. There was some thick, bush-like clump which seemed to be a parasite upon a branch up which I was swarming. I leaned my head round it in order to see what was beyond, and I nearly fell out of the tree in my surprise and horror at what I saw.

A face was gazing into mine – at the distance of only a foot or two. The creature that owned it had been crouching behind the parasite, and had looked round it at the same instant that I did. It was a human face – or at least it was far more human than any monkey's that I have ever seen.[3] It was long, whitish, and blotched with pimples, the nose flattened, and the lower jaw projecting, with a bristle of coarse whiskers round the chin. The eyes, which were under thick and heavy brows, were bestial and ferocious, and as it opened its mouth to snarl what sounded like a curse at me I observed that it had curved, sharp canine teeth. For an instant I read hatred and menace in the evil eyes. Then, as quick as a flash, came an expression of overpowering fear. There was a crash of broken boughs as it dived wildly down into the tangle of green. I caught a glimpse of a hairy body like that of a reddish pig, and then it was gone amid a swirl of leaves and branches.

'What's the matter?' shouted Roxton from below. 'Anything wrong with you?'

'Did you see it?' I cried, with my arms round the branch and all my nerves tingling.

'We heard a row, as if your foot had slipped. What was it?'

I was so shocked at the sudden and strange appearance of this ape-man that I hesitated whether I should not climb down again and tell my experience to my companions. But I was already so far up the great tree that it seemed a humiliation to return without having carried out my mission.

After a long pause, therefore, to recover my breath and my courage, I continued my ascent. Once I put my weight upon a rotten branch and swung for a few seconds by my hands, but in the main it was all easy climbing. Gradually the leaves thinned around me, and I was aware, from the wind upon my face, that I had topped all the trees of the forest. I was determined, however, not to look about me before I had reached the very highest point, so I scrambled on until I had got so far that the topmost branch was bending beneath my weight. There I settled into a convenient fork, and, balancing myself securely, I found myself looking down at a most wonderful panorama of this strange country in which we found ourselves.

The sun was just above the western sky-line, and the evening was a particularly bright and clear one, so that the whole extent of the plateau was visible beneath me. It was, as seen from this height, of an oval contour, with a breadth of about thirty miles and a width of twenty. Its general shape was that of a shallow funnel, all the sides sloping down to a considerable lake in the centre. This lake may have been ten miles in circumference, and lay very green and beautiful in the evening light, with a thick fringe of reeds at its edges, and with its surface broken by several yellow sandbanks, which gleamed golden in the mellow sunshine. A number of long dark objects, which were too large for alligators and too long for canoes, lay upon the edges of these patches of sand. With my glass I could clearly see that they were alive, but what their nature might be I could not imagine.

From the side of the plateau on which we were, slopes of woodland, with occasional glades, stretched down for five or six miles to the central lake. I could see at my very feet the glade of the iguanodons, and farther off was a round opening in the trees which marked the swamp of the pterodactyls. On the side facing me, however, the plateau presented a very different aspect. There the basalt cliffs of the outside were reproduced upon the inside, forming an escarpment about two hundred feet high, with a woody slope beneath it. Along the base of these red cliffs, some distance above the ground, I could see a number of dark holes through the glass, which I conjectured to be the mouths of caves. At the opening of one of these something white was shimmering, but I was unable to make out what it was. I sat charting the country until the sun had set and it was so dark that I could no longer distinguish details. Then I climbed down to my companions waiting for me so eagerly at the bottom of the great tree. For once I was the hero of the expedition. Alone I had thought of it, and alone I had done it; and here was the chart which would save us a month's blind groping among unknown dangers. Each of them shook me solemnly by the hand. But before they discussed the details of my map I had to tell them of my encounter with the ape-man among the branches.

'He has been there all the time,' said I.

'How do you know that?' asked Lord John.

'Because I have never been without that feeling that something malevolent was watching us. I mentioned it to you, Professor Challenger.'

'Our young friend certainly said something of the kind. He is also the one among us who is endowed with that Celtic temperament which would make him sensitive to such impressions.'

'The whole theory of telepathy –' began Summerlee, filling his pipe.

'Is too vast to be now discussed,' said Challenger, with decision. 'Tell me, now,' he added, with the air of a bishop addressing a Sunday-school, 'did you happen to observe whether the creature could cross its thumb over its palm?'

'No, indeed.'

'Had it a tail?'

'No.'

'Was the foot prehensile?'

'I do not think it could have made off so fast among the branches if it could not get a grip with its feet.'

'In South America there are, if my memory serves me – you will check the observation, Professor Summerlee – some thirty-six species of monkeys, but the anthropoid ape is unknown. It is clear, however, that he exists in this country, and that he is not the hairy, gorilla-like variety, which is never seen out of Africa or the East.' (I was inclined to interpolate, as I looked at him, that I had seen his first cousin

ROUGH CHART OF MAPLE WHITE LAND

EDM.

ROCKY UNKNOWN TRACT MUCH DREADED BY INDIANS

SWAMPY LAND STRANGE WHITE BEAST WAS SEEN

SWAMP

FOREST APE-TOWN

BATTLE

IGUANODON GLADE

ZAMBO'S CAMP

Ö CAMP

PINNACLE OF ASCENT

CENTRAL LAKE [SANDBANKS AND MONSTERS]

CHALLENGER'S GEYSER

CAVES AT BASE OF CLIFF

PIT FOR DINOSAURS

TWO DINOSAURS KILLED HERE.

HIDING PLACE

FOREST

WHERE WE SAW GREAT ELK

FOREST

Rough chart of Maple White Land

in Kensington.) 'This is a whiskered and colourless type, the latter characteristic pointing to the fact that he spends his days in arboreal seclusion. The question which we have to face is whether he approaches more closely to the ape or the man. In the latter case, he may well approximate to what the vulgar have called the "missing link". The solution of this problem is our immediate duty.'

'It is nothing of the sort,' said Summerlee, abruptly. 'Now that, through the intelligence and activity of Mr Malone' (I cannot help quoting the words), 'we have got our chart, our one and only immediate duty is to get ourselves safe and sound out of this awful place.'

'The flesh-pots of civilization,' groaned Challenger.

'The ink-pots of civilization, sir. It is our task to put on record what we have seen, and to leave the further exploration to others. You all agreed as much before Mr Malone got us the chart.'

'Well,' said Challenger, 'I admit that my mind will be more at ease when I am assured that the result of our expedition has been conveyed to our friends. How we are to get down from this place I have not as yet an idea. I have never yet encountered any problem, however, which my inventive brain was unable to solve, and I promise you that tomorrow I will turn my attention to the question of our descent.'

And so the matter was allowed to rest. But that evening, by the light of the fire and of a single candle, the first map of the lost world was elaborated. Every detail which I had roughly noted from my watch-tower was drawn out in its relative place. Challenger's pencil hovered over the great blank which marked the lake.

'What shall we call it?' he asked.

'Why should you not take the chance of perpetuating your own name?' said Summerlee, with his usual touch of acidity.

'I trust, sir, that my name will have other and more personal claims upon posterity,' said Challenger, severely. 'Any ignoramus can hand down his worthless memory by imposing it upon a mountain or a river. I need no such monument.'

Summerlee, with a twisted smile, was about to make some fresh assault when Lord John hastened to intervene.

General view of plateau from top of gingko tree
(Constructed by Mr Pat L. Forbes from Mr Malone's rough sketch)

'It's up to you, young fellah, to name the lake,' said he. 'You saw it first, and, by George, if you choose to put "Lake Malone" on it, no one has a better right.'

'By all means. Let our young friend give it a name,' said Challenger.

'Then,' said I, blushing, I dare say, as I said it, 'let it be named Lake Gladys.'

'Don't you think the Central Lake would be more descriptive?' remarked Summerlee.

'I should prefer Lake Gladys.'

Challenger looked at me sympathetically, and shook his great head in mock disapproval. 'Boys will be boys,' said he. 'Lake Gladys let it be.'

CHAPTER XII

It was Dreadful in the Forest

I have said – or perhaps I have not said, for my memory plays me sad tricks these days – that I glowed with pride when three such men as my comrades thanked me for having saved, or at least greatly helped, the situation. As the youngster of the party, not merely in years, but in experience, character, knowledge, and all that goes to make a man, I had been overshadowed from the first. And now I was coming into my own. I warmed at the thought. Alas! for the pride which goes before a fall! That little glow of self-satisfaction, that added measure of self-confidence, were to lead me on that very night to the most dreadful experience of my life, ending with a shock which turns my heart sick when I think of it.

It came about in this way. I had been unduly excited by the adventure of the tree, and sleep seemed to be impossible. Summerlee was on guard, sitting hunched over our small fire, a quaint, angular figure, his rifle across his knees and his pointed, goat-like beard wagging with each weary nod of his head. Lord John lay silent, wrapped in the South American poncho which he wore, while Challenger snored with a roll and rattle which reverberated through the woods. The full moon was shining brightly, and the air was crisply cold. What a night for a walk! And then suddenly came the thought, 'Why not?' Suppose I stole softly away, suppose I made my way down to the central lake, suppose I was back at breakfast with some record of the place – would I not in that case be thought an even more worthy associate? Then, if Summerlee carried the day and some means of escape were found, we should return to London with first-hand knowledge of the central mystery of the plateau, to which I alone, of all men, would have penetrated. I thought of Gladys, with her 'There are heroisms all round us.' I seemed to hear her voice as she said it. I thought also of McArdle. What a three column article for the paper! What a foundation for a career! A correspondentship in the next great war might be within my reach. I clutched at a gun – my pockets were full of cartridges – and, parting the thorn bushes at the gate of our zareba, I quickly slipped out. My last glance showed me the unconscious Summerlee, most futile of sentinels, still nodding away like a queer mechanical toy in front of the smouldering fire.

I had not gone a hundred yards before I deeply repented my rashness. I may have said somewhere in this chronicle that I am too imaginative to be a really courageous man, but that I have an overpowering fear of seeming afraid. This was the power which now carried me onwards. I simply could not slink back with nothing done. Even if my comrades should not have missed me, and should never know of my weakness, there would still remain some intolerable self-shame in my own soul. And yet I shuddered at the position in which I found myself, and would have given all I possessed at that moment to have been honourably free of the whole business.

It was dreadful in the forest. The trees grew so thickly and their foliage spread so widely that I could see nothing of the moon-light save that here and there the high branches made a tangled filigree against the starry sky. As the eyes became more used to the obscurity one learned that there were different degrees of darkness among the trees – that some were dimly visible, while between and among them there were coal-black shadowed patches, like the mouths of caves, from which I shrank in horror as I passed. I thought of the despairing yell of the tortured iguanodon – that dreadful cry which had echoed through the woods. I thought, too, of the glimpse I had in the light of Lord John's torch of that bloated, warty, blood-slavering muzzle. Even now I was on its hunting-ground. At any instant it might spring upon me from the shadows – this nameless and horrible monster. I stopped, and, picking a cartridge from my pocket, I opened the breech of my gun. As I touched the lever my heart leaped within me. It was the shot-gun, not the rifle, which I had taken!

Again the impulse to return swept over me. Here, surely, was a most excellent reason for my failure – one for which no one would think the less of me. But again the foolish pride fought against that very word. I could not – must not – fail. After all, my rifle would probably have been as useless as a shot-gun against such dangers as I might meet. If I were to go back to camp to change my weapon I could hardly expect to enter and to leave again without being seen. In that case there would be explanations, and my attempt would no longer be all my own. After a little hesitation, then, I screwed up my courage and continued upon my way, my useless gun under my arm.

The darkness of the forest had been alarming, but even worse was the white, still flood of moon-light in the open glade of the iguanodons. Hid among the bushes, I looked out at it. None of the great brutes were in sight. Perhaps the tragedy which had befallen one of them had driven them from their feeding-ground. In the misty, silvery night I could see no sign of any living thing. Taking courage, therefore, I slipped rapidly across it, and among the jungle on the farther side I picked up once again the brook which was my guide. It was a cheery companion, gurgling and chuckling as it ran, like the dear old trout-stream in the West Country where I have fished at night in my boyhood. So long as I followed it down I must come to the lake, and so long as I followed it back I must come to the camp. Often I had to lose sight of it on account of the tangled brushwood, but I was always within earshot of its tinkle and splash.

As one descended the slope the woods became thinner, and bushes, with occasional high trees, took the place of the forest. I could make good progress, therefore, and I could see without being seen. I passed close to the pterodactyl swamp, and as I did so, with a dry, crisp, leathery rattle of wings, one of these great creatures – it was twenty feet at least from tip to tip – rose up from somewhere near me and soared into the air. As it passed across the face of the moon the light shone clearly through the membranous wings, and it looked like a flying skeleton against the white, tropical radiance. I crouched low among the bushes, for I knew from past experience that with a single cry the creature could bring a hundred of its loathsome mates about my ears. It was not until it had settled again that I dared to steal onwards upon my journey.

The night had been exceedingly still, but as I advanced I became conscious of a low, rumbling sound, a continuous murmur, somewhere in front of me. This grew louder as I proceeded, until at last it was clearly quite close to me. When I stood still the sound was constant, so that it seemed to come from some stationary cause. It was like a boiling kettle or the bubbling of some great pot. Soon I came upon the source of it, for in the centre of a small clearing I found a lake – or a pool, rather, for it was not larger than the basin of the Trafalgar Square fountain – of some black, pitch-like stuff, the surface of which rose and fell in great blisters of bursting gas. The air above it was shimmering with heat, and the ground round was so hot that I could hardly bear to lay my hand on it. It was clear that the great volcanic outburst which had raised this strange plateau so many years ago had not yet entirely spent its forces. Blackened rocks and mounds of lava I had already seen everywhere peeping out from amid the luxuriant vegetation which draped them, but this asphalt pool in the jungle was the first sign that we had of actual existing activity on the slopes of the ancient crater. I had no time to examine it further, for I had need to hurry if I were to be back in camp in the morning.

It was a fearsome walk, and one which will be with me so long as memory holds. In the great moonlit clearings I slunk along among the shadows on the margin. In the jungle I crept forward, stopping with a beating heart whenever I heard, as I often did, the crash of breaking branches as some wild beast went past. Now and then great shadows loomed up for an instant and were gone – great, silent shadows which seemed to prowl upon padded feet. How often I stopped with the intention of returning, and yet every time my pride conquered my fear, and sent me on again until my object should be attained.

At last (my watch showed that it was one in the morning) I saw the gleam of water amid the openings of the jungle, and ten minutes later I was among the reeds upon the borders of the central lake. I was exceedingly dry, so I lay down and took a long draught of its waters, which were fresh and cold. There was a broad pathway with many tracks upon it at the spot which I had found, so that it was clearly one of the drinking-places of the animals. Close to the water's edge there was a huge isolated block of lava. Up this I climbed, and, lying on the top, I had an excellent view in every direction.

The first thing which I saw filled me with amazement. When I described the view from the summit of the great tree, I said that on the farther cliff I could see a number of dark spots, which appeared to be the mouths of caves. Now, as I looked up at the same cliffs, I saw discs of light in every direction, ruddy, clearly-defined patches, like the port-holes of a liner in the darkness. For a moment I thought it was the lava-glow from some volcanic action; but this could not be so. Any volcanic action would surely be down in the hollow, and not high among the rocks. What, then, was the alternative? It was wonderful, and yet it must surely be. These ruddy spots must be the reflection of fires within the caves – fires which could only be lit by the hand of man. There were human beings, then, upon the plateau. How gloriously my expedition was justified! Here was news indeed for us to bear back with us to London!

For a long time I lay and watched these red, quivering blotches of light. I suppose they were ten miles off from me, yet even at that distance one could observe how, from time to time, they twinkled or were obscured as someone passed before them. What would I not have given to be able to crawl up to them, to peep in, and to take back some word to my comrades as to the appearance and character of the race who lived in so strange a place! It was out of the question for the moment, and yet surely we could not leave the plateau until we had some definite knowledge upon the point.

Lake Gladys – my own lake – lay like a sheet of quicksilver before me, with a reflected moon shining brightly in the centre of it. It was shallow, for in many places I saw low sandbanks protruding above the water. Everywhere upon the still surface I could see signs of life, sometimes mere rings and ripples in the water, sometimes the gleam of a great silver-sided fish in the air, sometimes the arched, slate-coloured back of some passing monster. Once upon a yellow sandbank I saw a creature like a huge swan, with a clumsy body and a high, flexible neck, shuffling about upon the margin. Presently it plunged in, and for some time I could see the arched neck and darting head undulating over the water. Then it dived, and I saw it no more.

My attention was soon drawn away from these distant sights and brought back to what was going on at my very feet. Two creatures like large armadillos had come down to the drinking-place, and were squatting at the edge of the water, their long, flexible tongues like red ribbons shooting in and out as they lapped. A huge deer, with branching horns, a magnificent creature which carried itself like a king, came down with its doe and two fawns and drank beside the armadillos. No such deer exists anywhere else upon earth, for the moose or elks which I have seen would hardly have reached its shoulders. Presently it gave a warning snort, and was off with its family among the reeds, while the armadillos also scuttled for shelter. A new-comer, a most monstrous animal, was coming down the path.

For a moment I wondered where I could have seen that ungainly shape, that arched back with triangular fringes along it, that strange bird-like head held close to the ground. Then it came back to me. It was the stegosaurus – the very creature which Maple White had preserved in his sketch-book, and which had been the first object which arrested the attention of Challenger! There he was – perhaps the very specimen which the American artist had encountered. The ground shook beneath his tremendous weight, and his gulpings of water resounded through the still night. For five minutes he was so close to my rock that by stretching out my hand I could have touched the hideous waving hackles upon his back. Then he lumbered away and was lost among the boulders.

Looking at my watch, I saw that it was half-past two o'clock, and high time, therefore, that I started upon my homeward journey. There was no difficulty about the direction in which I should return, for all along I had kept the little brook upon my left, and it opened into the central lake within a stone's-throw of the boulder upon which I had been lying. I set off, therefore, in high spirits, for I felt that I had done good work and was bringing back a fine budget of news for my companions. Foremost of all, of course, were the sight of the fiery caves and the certainty that some troglodytic race inhabited them. But besides that I could speak from experience of the central lake. I could testify that it was full of strange creatures, and I had seen several land forms of primaeval life which we had not before encountered. I reflected as I walked that few men in the world could have spent a stranger night or added more to human knowledge in the course of it.

I was plodding up the slope, turning these thoughts over in my mind, and had reached a point which may have been half-way to home, when my mind was brought back to my own position by a strange noise behind me. It was something between a snore and a growl, low, deep, and exceedingly menacing. Some strange creature was evidently near me, but nothing could be seen, so I hastened more rapidly upon my way. I had traversed half a mile or so when suddenly the sound was repeated, still behind me, but louder and more menacing than before. My heart stood still within me as it flashed across me that the beast, whatever it was, must surely be after *me*. My skin grew cold and my hair rose at the thought. That these monsters should tear each other to pieces was a part of the strange struggle for existence, but that they should turn upon modern man, that they should deliberately track and hunt down the predominant human, was a staggering and fearsome thought. I remembered again the blood-beslobbered face which we had seen in the glare of Lord John's torch, like some horrible vision from the deepest circle of Dante's hell. With my knees shaking beneath me, I stood and glared with starting eyes down the moonlit path which lay behind me. All was quiet as in a dream landscape. Silver clearings and the black patches of the bushes – nothing else could I see. Then from out of the silence, imminent and threatening, there came once more that low, throaty croaking, far louder and closer than before. There could no longer be a doubt. Something was on my trail, and was closing in upon me every minute.

I stood like a man paralysed, still staring at the ground which I had traversed. Then suddenly I saw it. There was movement among the bushes at the far end of the clearing which I had just traversed. A great dark shadow disengaged itself and hopped out into the clear moonlight. I say 'hopped' advisedly, for the beast moved like a kangaroo, springing along in an erect position upon its powerful hind-legs, while its front ones were held bent in front of it. It was of enormous size and power, like an erect elephant, but its movements, in spite of its bulk, were exceedingly alert. For a moment, as I saw its shape, I hoped that it was an iguanodon, which I knew to be harmless, but, ignorant as I was, I soon saw that this was a very different creature. Instead of the gentle, deer-shaped head of the great three-toed leaf-eater, this beast had a broad, squat, toad-like face like that which had alarmed us in our camp. His ferocious cry and the horrible energy of his pursuit both assured me that this was surely one of the great flesh-eating dinosaurs, the most terrible beasts which have ever walked this earth. As the huge brute loped along it dropped forward upon its fore-paws and brought its nose to the ground every twenty yards or so. It was smelling out my trail. Sometimes, for an instant, it was at fault. Then it would catch it up again and come bounding swiftly along the path I had taken.

Even now when I think of that nightmare the sweat breaks out upon my brow. What could I do? My useless fowling-piece was in my hand. What help could I get from that? I looked desperately round for some rock or tree, but I was in a bushy jungle with nothing higher than a sapling within sight, while I knew that the creature behind me could tear down an ordinary tree as though it were a reed. My only possible chance lay in flight. I could not move swiftly over the rough, broken ground, but as I looked round me in despair I saw a well-marked, hard-beaten path which ran across in front of me. We had seen several of the sort, the runs of various wild beasts, during our expeditions. Along this I could perhaps hold my own, for I was a fast runner, and in excellent condition. Flinging away my useless gun, I set myself to do such a half-mile as I have never done before or since. My limbs ached, my chest heaved, I felt that my throat would burst for want of air, and yet with that horror behind me I ran and I ran and ran. At last I paused, hardly able to move. For a moment I thought that I had thrown him off. The path lay still behind me. And then suddenly, with a crashing and a rending, a thudding of giant feet and a panting of monster lungs, the beast was upon me once more. He was at my very heels. I was lost.

Madman that I was to linger so long before I fled! Up to then he had hunted by scent, and his movement was slow. But he had actually seen me as I started to run. From then onwards he had hunted by sight, for the path showed him where I had gone. Now, as he came round the curve, he was springing in great bounds. The moonlight shone upon his huge projecting eyes, the row of enormous teeth in his open mouth, and the gleaming fringe of claws upon his short, powerful forearms. With a scream of terror I turned and rushed wildly down the path. Behind me the thick, gasping breathing of the creature sounded louder and louder. His heavy footfall was beside me. Every instant I expected to feel his grip upon my back. And then suddenly there came a crash – I was falling through space, and everything beyond was darkness and rest.

As I emerged from my unconsciousness – which could not, I think, have lasted more than a few minutes – I was aware of a most dreadful and penetrating smell. Putting out my hand in the darkness I came upon something which felt like a huge lump of meat, while my other hand closed upon a large bone. Up above me there was a circle of starlit sky, which showed me that I was lying at the bottom of a deep pit. Slowly I staggered to my feet and felt myself all over. I was stiff and sore from head to foot, but there was no limb which would not move, no joint which would not bend. As the circumstances of my fall came back into my confused brain, I looked up in terror, expecting to see that dreadful head silhouetted against the paling sky. There was no sign of the monster, however, nor could I hear any sound from above. I began to walk slowly round, therefore, feeling in every direction to find out what this strange place could be into which I had been so opportunely precipitated.

It was, as I have said, a pit, with sharply-sloping walls and a level bottom about twenty feet across. This bottom was littered with great gobbets of flesh, most of which was in the last state of putridity. The atmosphere was poisonous and horrible. After tripping and stumbling over these lumps of decay, I came suddenly against something hard, and I found that an upright post was firmly fixed in the centre of the hollow. It was so high that I could not reach the top of it with my hand, and it appeared to be covered with grease.

Suddenly I remembered that I had a tin box of wax-vestas in my pocket. Striking one of them, I was able at last to form some opinion of this place into which I had fallen. There could be no question as to its nature. It was a trap – made by the hand of man. The post in the centre, some nine feet long, was sharpened at the upper end, and was black with the stale blood of the creatures who had been impaled upon it. The remains scattered about were fragments of the victims, which had been cut away in order to clear the stake for the next who might blunder in. I remembered that Challenger had declared that man could not exist upon the plateau, since with his feeble weapons he could not hold his own against the monsters who roamed over it. But now it was clear enough how it could be done. In their narrow-mouthed caves the natives, whoever they might be, had refuges into which the huge saurians could not penetrate, while with their developed brains they were capable of setting such traps, covered with branches, across the paths which marked the run of the animals as would destroy them in spite of all their strength and activity. Man was always the master.

The sloping wall of the pit was not difficult for an active man to climb, but I hesitated long before I trusted myself within reach of the dreadful creature which had so nearly destroyed me. How did I know that he was not lurking in the nearest clump of bushes, waiting for my reappearance? I took heart, however, as I recalled a conversation between Challenger and Summerlee upon the habits of the great saurians. Both were agreed that the monsters were practically brainless, that there was no room for reason in their tiny cranial cavities, and that if they have disappeared from the rest of the world it was assuredly on account of their own stupidity, which made it impossible for them to adapt themselves to changing conditions.

To lie in wait for me now would mean that the creature had appreciated what had happened to me, and this in turn would argue some power connecting cause and effect. Surely it was more likely that a brainless creature, acting solely by vague predatory instinct, would give up the chase when I disappeared, and, after a pause of astonishment, would wander away in search of some other prey? I clambered to the edge of the pit and looked over. The stars were fading, the sky was whitening, and the cold wind of morning blew pleasantly upon my face. I could see or hear nothing of my enemy. Slowly I climbed out and sat for a while upon the ground, ready to spring back into my refuge if any danger should appear. Then, reassured by the absolute stillness and by the growing light, I took my courage in both hands and stole back along the path which I had come. Some distance down it I picked up my gun, and shortly afterwards struck the brook which was my guide. So, with many a frightened backward glance, I made for home.

And suddenly there came something to remind me of my absent companions. In the clear, still morning air there sounded far away the sharp, hard note of a single rifle-shot. I paused and listened, but there was nothing more. For a moment I was shocked at the thought that some sudden danger might have befallen them. But then a simpler and more natural explanation came to my mind. It was now broad daylight. No doubt my absence had been noticed. They had imagined that I was lost in the woods, and had fired this shot to guide me home. It is true that we had made a strict resolution against firing, but if it seemed to them that I might be in danger they would not hesitate. It was for me now to hurry on as fast as possible, and so to reassure them.

I was weary and spent, so my progress was not so fast as I wished; but at last I came into regions which I knew. There was the swamp of the pterodactyls upon my left; there in front of me was the glade of the iguanodons. Now I was in the last belt of trees which separated me from Fort Challenger. I raised my voice in a cheery shout to allay their fears. No answering greeting came back to me. My heart sank at that ominous stillness. I quickened my pace into a run. The zareba rose before me, even as I had left it, but the gate was open. I rushed in. In the cold morning light it was a fearful sight which met my eyes. Our effects were scattered in wild confusion over the ground; my comrades had disappeared, and close to the smouldering ashes of our fire the grass was stained crimson with a hideous pool of blood.

I was so stunned by this sudden shock that for a time I must have nearly lost my reason. I have a vague recollection, as one remembers a bad dream, of rushing about through the woods all round the empty camp, calling wildly for my companions. No answer came back from the silent shadows. The horrible thought that I might never see them again, that I might find myself abandoned all alone in that dreadful place, with no possible way of descending into the world below, that I might live and die in that nightmare country, drove me to desperation. I could have torn my hair and beaten my head in my despair. Only now did I realize how I had learned to lean upon my companions, upon the serene self-confidence of Challenger, and upon the masterful, humorous coolness of Lord Roxton. Without them I was like a child in the dark, helpless and powerless. I did not know which way to turn or what I should do first.

After a period, during which I sat in bewilderment, I set myself to try and discover what sudden misfortune could have befallen my companions. The whole disordered appearance of the camp showed that there had been some sort of attack, and the rifle-shot no doubt marked the time when it had occurred. That there should have been only one shot showed that it had been all over in an instant. The rifles still lay upon the ground, and one of them – Lord John's – had the empty cartridge in the breech. The blankets of Challenger and of Summerlee beside the fire suggested that they had been asleep at the time. The cases of ammunition and of food were scattered about in a wild litter, together with our unfortunate cameras and plate-carriers, but none of them were missing. On the other hand, all the exposed provisions – and I remembered that there were a considerable quantity of them – were gone. They were animals, then, and not natives, who had made the inroad, for surely the latter would have left nothing behind.

But if animals, or some single terrible animal, then what had become of my comrades? A ferocious beast would surely have destroyed them and left their remains. It is true that there was that one hideous pool of blood, which told of violence. Such a monster as had pursued me during the night could have carried away a victim as easily as a cat would a mouse. In that case the others would have followed in pursuit. But then they would assuredly have taken their rifles with them. The more I tried to think it out with my confused and weary brain the less could I find any plausible explanation. I searched round in the forest, but could see no tracks which could help me to a conclusion. Once I lost myself, and it was only by good luck, and after an hour of wandering, that I found the camp once more.

Suddenly a thought came to me and brought some little comfort to my heart. I was not absolutely alone in the world. Down at the bottom of the cliff, and within call of me, was waiting the faithful Zambo. I went to the edge of the plateau and looked over. Sure enough, he was squatting among his blankets beside his fire in his little camp. But, to my amazement, a second man was seated in front of him. For an instant my heart leaped for joy, as I thought that one of my comrades had made his way safely down. But a second glance dispelled the hope. The rising sun shone red upon the man's skin. He was an Indian. I shouted loudly and waved my handkerchief. Presently Zambo looked up, waved his hand, and turned to ascend the pinnacle. In a short time he was standing close to me and listening with deep distress to the story which I told him.

'Devil got them for sure, Massa Malone,' said he. 'You got into the devil's country, sah, and he take you all to himself. You take advice, Massa Malone, and come down quick, else he get you as well.'

'How can I come down, Zambo?'

'You get creepers from trees, Massa Malone. Throw them over here. I make fast to this stump, and so you have bridge.'

'We have thought of that. There are no creepers here which could bear us.'

'Send for ropes, Massa Malone.'

'Who can I send, and where?'

'Send to Indian villages, sah. Plenty hide-rope in Indian village. Indian down below; send him.'

'Who is he?'

'One of our Indians. Other ones beat him and take away his pay. He come back to us. Ready now to take letter, bring rope – anything.'

To take a letter! Why not? Perhaps he might bring help; but in any case he would ensure that our lives were not spent for nothing, and that news of all that we had won for Science should reach our friends at home. I had two completed letters already waiting. I would spend the day in writing a third, which would bring my experiences absolutely up to date. The Indian could bear this back to the world. I ordered Zambo, therefore, to come again in the evening, and I spent my miserable and lonely day in recording my own adventures of the night before. I also drew up a note, to be given to any white merchant or captain of a steam-boat whom the Indian could find, imploring them to see that ropes were sent to us, since our lives must depend upon it. These documents I threw to Zambo in the evening, and also my purse, which contained three English sovereigns. These were to be given to the Indian, and he was promised twice as much if he returned with the ropes.

So now you will understand, my dear Mr McArdle, how this communication reaches you, and you will also know the truth, in case you never hear again from your unfortunate correspondent. Tonight I am too weary and too depressed to make my plans. Tomorrow I must think out some way by which I shall keep in touch with this camp, and yet search round for any traces of my unhappy friends.

CHAPTER XIII

A Sight which I shall Never Forget

Just as the sun was setting upon that melancholy night I saw the lonely figure of the Indian upon the vast plain beneath me, and I watched him, our one faint hope of salvation, until he disappeared in the rising mists of evening which lay, rose-tinted from the setting sun, between the far-off river and me.

It was quite dark when I at last turned back to our stricken camp, and my last vision as I went was the red gleam of Zambo's fire, the one point of light in the wide world below, as was his faithful presence in my own shadowed soul. And yet I felt happier than I had done since this crushing blow had fallen upon me, for it was good to think that the world should know what we had done, so that at the worst our names should not perish with our bodies, but should go down to posterity associated with the result of our labours.

It was an awesome thing to sleep in that ill-fated camp; and yet it was even more unnerving to do so in the jungle. One or the other it must be. Prudence, on the one hand, warned me that I should remain on guard, but exhausted Nature, on the other, declared that I should do nothing of the kind. I climbed up on to a limb of the great gingko tree, but there was no secure perch on its rounded surface, and I should certainly have fallen off and broken my neck the moment I began to doze. I got down, therefore, and pondered over what I should do. Finally, I closed the door of the zareba, lit three separate fires in a triangle, and having eaten a hearty supper dropped off into a profound sleep, from which I had a strange and most welcome awakening. In the early morning, just as day was breaking, a hand was laid upon my arm, and starting up, with all my nerves in a tingle and my hand feeling for a rifle, I gave a cry of joy as in the cold grey light I saw Lord John kneeling beside me.

It was he – and yet it was not he. I had left him calm in his bearing, correct in his person, prim in his dress. Now he was pale and wild-eyed, gasping as he breathed like one who has run far and fast. His gaunt face was scratched and bloody, his clothes were hanging in rags, and his hat was gone. I stared in amazement, but he gave me no chance for questions. He was grabbing at our stores all the time he spoke.

'Quick, young fellah! Quick!' he cried. 'Every moment counts. Get the rifles, both of them. I have the other two. Now, all the cartridges you can gather. Fill up your pockets. Now, some food. Half a dozen tins will do. That's all right! Don't wait to talk or think. Get a move on, or we are done!'

Still half-awake, and unable to imagine what it all might mean, I found myself hurrying madly after him through the wood, a rifle under each arm and a pile of various stores in my hands. He dodged in and out through the thickest of the scrub until he came to a dense clump of brushwood. Into this he rushed, regardless of thorns, and threw himself into the heart of it, pulling me down by his side.

'There!' he panted. 'I think we are safe here. They'll make for the camp as sure as fate. It will be their first idea. But this should puzzle 'em.'

'What is it all?' I asked, when I had got my breath. 'Where are the professors? And who is it that is after us?'

'The ape-men,' he cried. 'My God, what brutes! Don't raise your voice, for they have long ears – sharp eyes, too, but no power of scent, so far as I could judge, so I don't think they can sniff us out. Where have you been, young fellah? You were well out of it.'

In a few sentences I whispered what I had done.

'Pretty bad,' said he, when he had heard of the dinosaur and the pit. 'It isn't quite the place for a rest cure. What? But I had no idea what its possibilities were until those devils got hold of us. The man-eatin' Papuans had me once, but they are Chesterfields[1] compared to this crowd.'

'How did it happen?' I asked.

'It was in the early mornin'. Our learned friends were just stirrin'. Hadn't even begun to argue yet. Suddenly it rained apes. They came down as thick as apples out of a tree. They had been assemblin' in the dark, I suppose, until that great tree over our heads was heavy with them. I shot one of them through the belly, but before we knew where we were they had us spread-eagled on our backs. I call them apes, but they carried sticks and stones in their hands and jabbered talk to each other, and ended up by tyin' our hands with creepers, so they are ahead of any beast that I have seen in my wanderin's. Ape-men – that's what they are – Missin' Links,[2] and I wish they had stayed missin'. They carried off their wounded comrade – he was bleedin' like a pig – and then they sat around us, and if ever I saw frozen murder it was in their faces. They were big fellows, as big as a man and a deal stronger. Curious glassy grey eyes they have, under red tufts, and they just sat and gloated and gloated. Challenger is no chicken, but even he was cowed. He managed to struggle on to his feet, and yelled out at them to have done with it and get it over. I think he had gone a bit off his head at the suddenness of it, for he raged and cursed at them like a lunatic. If they had been a row of his favourite Pressmen he could not have slanged them worse.'

'Well, what did they do?' I was enthralled by the strange story which my companion was whispering into my ear, while all the time his keen eyes were shooting in every direction and his hand grasping his cocked rifle.

'I thought it was the end of us, but instead of that it started them on a new line. They all jabbered and chattered together. Then one of them stood out beside Challenger. You'll smile, young fellah, but 'pon my word they might have been kinsmen. I couldn't have believed it if I hadn't seen it with my own eyes. This old ape-man – he was their chief – was a sort of red Challenger, with every one of our friend's beauty points, only just a trifle more so. He had the short body, the big shoulders, the round chest, no neck, a great ruddy frill of a beard, the tufted eyebrows, the "What do *you* want, damn you!" look about the eyes, and the whole catalogue. When the ape-man stood by Challenger and put his paw on his shoulder, the thing was complete. Summerlee was a bit hysterical, and he laughed till he cried. The ape-men laughed too – or at least they put up the devil of a cacklin' – and then they set to work to drag us off through the forest. They wouldn't touch the guns and things – thought them dangerous, I expect – but they carried away all our loose food. Summerlee and I got some rough handlin' on the way – there's my skin and my clothes to prove it – for they took us a bee-line through the brambles, and their own hides are like leather. But Challenger was all right. Four of them carried him shoulder high, and he went like a Roman emperor. What's that?'

It was a strange clicking noise in the distance, not unlike castanets.

'There they go!' said my companion, slipping cartridges into the second double-barrelled 'Express'. 'Load them all up, young fellah my lad, for we're not going to be taken alive, and don't you think it! That's the row they make when they are excited. By George! they'll have something to excite them if they put us up. The "Last Stand of the Greys"[3] won't be in it. "With their rifles grasped in their stiffened hands, 'mid a ring of the dead and dyin'," as some fathead sings. Can you hear them now?'

'Very far away.'

'That little lot will do no good, but I expect their search parties are all over the wood. Well, I was tellin' you my tale of woe. They got us soon to this town of theirs – about a thousand huts of branches and leaves in a great grove of trees near the edge of the cliff. It's three or four miles from here. The filthy beasts fingered me all over, and I feel as if I should never be clean again. They tied us up – the fellow who handled me could tie like a bo'sun – and there we lay with our toes up, beneath a tree, while a great brute stood guard over us with a club in his hand. When I say "we" I mean Summerlee and myself. Old Challenger was up a tree, eatin' pines and havin' the time of his life. I'm bound to say that he managed to get some fruit to us, and with his own hands he loosened our bonds. If you'd seen him sittin' up in that tree hob-nobbin' with his twin brother – and singin' in that rollin' bass of his, "Ring out wild bells",[4] 'cause music of any kind seemed to put 'em in a good humour, you'd have smiled; but we weren't in much mood for laughin', as you can guess. They were inclined, within limits, to let him do what he liked, but they drew the line pretty sharply at us. It was a mighty consolation to us all to know that you were runnin' loose and had the archives in your keepin'.

'Well, now, young fellah, I'll tell you what will surprise you. You say you saw signs of men, and fires, traps, and the like. Well, we have seen the natives themselves. Poor devils they were, down-faced little chaps, and had enough to make them so. It seems that the humans hold one side of this plateau – over yonder, where you saw the caves – and the ape-men hold this side, and there is bloody war between them all the time. That's the situation, so far as I could follow it. Well, yesterday the ape-men got hold of a dozen of the humans and brought them in as prisoners. You never heard such a jabberin' and shriekin' in your life. The men were little red fellows, and had been bitten and clawed so that they could hardly walk. The ape-men put two of them to death there and then – fairly pulled the arm off one of them – it was perfectly beastly. Plucky little chaps they are, and hardly gave a squeak. But it turned us absolutely sick. Summerlee fainted, and even Challenger had as much as he could stand. I think they have cleared, don't you?'

We listened intently, but nothing save the calling of the birds broke the deep peace of the forest. Lord John went on with his story.

'I think you have had the escape of your life, young fellah my lad. It was catchin' those Indians that put *you* clean out of their heads, else they would have been back to the camp for you as sure as fate and gathered you in. Of course, as you said, they have been watchin' us from the beginnin' out of that tree, and they knew perfectly well that we were one short. However, they could think only of this new haul; so it was I, and not a bunch of apes, that dropped in on you in the morning. Well, we had a horrid business afterwards. My God! what a nightmare the whole thing is! You remember the great bristle of sharp canes down below where we found the skeleton of the American? Well, that is just under Ape-Town, and that's the jumpin'-off place of their prisoners. I expect there's heaps of skeletons there, if we looked for 'em. They have a sort of clear parade-ground on the top, and they make a proper ceremony about it. One by one the poor devils have to jump, and the game is to see whether they are merely dashed to pieces or whether they get skewered on the canes. They took us out to see it, and the whole tribe lined up on the edge. Four of the Indians jumped, and the canes went through 'em like knitting needles through a pat of butter. No wonder we found that poor Yankee's skeleton with the canes growin' between his ribs. It was horrible – but it was doocedly interestin' too. We were all fascinated to see them take the dive, even when we thought it would be our turn next on the spring-board.

'Well, it wasn't. They kept six of the Indians up for today – that's how I understood it – but I fancy we were to be the star performers in the show. Challenger might get off, but Summerlee and I were in the bill. Their language is more than half signs, and it was not hard to follow them. So I thought it was time we made a break for it. I had been plottin' it out a bit, and had one or two things clear in my mind. It was all on me, for Summerlee was useless and Challenger not much better. The only time they got together they got slangin', because they couldn't agree upon the scientific classification of these red-headed devils that had got hold of us. One said it was the dryopithecus of Java, the other said it was pithecanthropus.[5] Madness, I call it – loonies – both. But, as I say, I had thought out one or two points that were helpful. One was that these brutes could not run as fast as a man in the open. They have short, bandy legs, you see, and heavy bodies.

Even Challenger could give a few yards in a hundred to the best of them, and you or I would be a perfect Shrubb.[6] Another point was that they knew nothin' about guns. I don't believe they ever understood how the fellow I shot came by his hurt. If we could get at our guns there was no sayin' what we could do.

'So I broke away early this mornin', gave my guard a kick in the tummy that laid him out, and sprinted for the camp. There I got you and the guns, and here we are.'

'But the Professors!' I cried, in consternation.

'Well, we must just go back and fetch 'em. I couldn't bring 'em with me. Challenger was up the tree, and Summerlee was not fit for the effort. The only chance was to get the guns and try a rescue. Of course they may scupper them at once in revenge. I don't think they would touch Challenger, but I wouldn't answer for Summerlee. But they would have had him in any case. Of that I am certain. So I haven't made matters any worse by boltin'. But we are honour bound to go back and have them out or see it through with them. So you can make up your soul, young fellah my lad, for it will be one way or the other before evenin'.'

I have tried to imitate here Lord Roxton's jerky talk, his short, strong sentences, the half-humorous, half-reckless tone that ran through it all. But he was a born leader. As danger thickened his jaunty manner would increase, his speech become more racy, his cold eyes glitter into ardent life, and his Don Quixote moustache bristle with joyous excitement. His love of danger, his intense appreciation of the drama of an adventure – all the more intense for being held tightly in – his consistent view that every peril in life is a form of sport, a fierce game betwixt you and Fate, with Death as a forfeit, made him a wonderful companion at such hours. If it were not for our fears as to the fate of our companions, it would have been a positive joy to throw myself with such a man into such an affair. We were rising from our brushwood hiding-place when suddenly I felt his grip upon my arm.

'By George!' he whispered, 'here they come!'

From where we lay we could look down a brown aisle, arched with green, formed by the trunks and branches. Along this a party of the ape-men were passing. They went in single file, with bent legs and rounded backs, their hands occasionally touching the ground, their heads turning to left and right as they trotted along. Their crouching gait took away from their height, but I should put them at five feet or so, with long arms and enormous chests. Many of them carried sticks, and at the distance they looked like a line of very hairy and deformed human beings. For a moment I caught this clear glimpse of them. Then they were lost among the bushes.

'Not this time,' said Lord John, who had caught up his rifle. 'Our best chance is to lie quiet until they have given up the search. Then we shall see whether we can't get back to their town and hit 'em where it hurts most. Give 'em an hour and we'll march.'

We filled in the time by opening one of our food tins and making sure of our breakfast. Lord Roxton had had nothing but some fruit since the morning before and ate like a starving man. Then, at last, our pockets bulging with cartridges and a rifle in each hand, we started off upon our mission of rescue. Before leaving it we carefully marked our little hiding-place among the brushwood and its bearing to Fort Challenger, that we might find it again if we needed it. We slunk through the bushes in silence until we came to the very edge of the cliff, close to the old camp. There we halted, and Lord John gave me some idea of his plans.

'So long as we are among the thick trees these swine are our masters,' said he. 'They can see us and we cannot see them. But in the open it is different. There we can move faster than they. So we must stick to the open all we can. The edge of the plateau has fewer large trees than further inland. So that's our line of advance. Go slowly, keep your eyes open and your rifle ready. Above all, never let them get you prisoner while there is a cartridge left – that's my last word to you, young fellah.'

When we reached the edge of the cliff I looked over and saw our good old black Zambo sitting smoking on a rock below us. I would have given a great deal to have hailed him and told him how we were placed, but it was too dangerous, lest we should be heard. The woods seemed to be full of the ape-men; again and again we heard their curious clicking chatter. At such times we plunged into the nearest clump of bushes and lay still until the sound had passed away. Our advance, therefore, was very slow, and two hours at least must have passed before I saw by Lord John's cautious movements that we must be close to our destination. He motioned to me to lie still, and he crawled forward himself. In a minute he was back again, his face quivering with eagerness.

'Come!' said he. 'Come quick! I hope to the Lord we are not too late already!'

I found myself shaking with nervous excitement as I scrambled forward and lay down beside him, looking out through the bushes at a clearing which stretched before us.

It was a sight which I shall never forget until my dying day – so weird, so impossible, that I do not know how I am to make you realize it, or how in a few years I shall bring myself to believe in it if I live to sit once more on a lounge in the Savage Club and look out on the drab solidity of the Embankment. I know that it will seem then to be some wild nightmare, some delirium of fever. Yet I will set it down now, while it is still fresh in my memory, and one at least, the man who lay in the damp grasses by my side, will know if I have lied.

A wide, open space lay before us – some hundreds of yards across – all green turf and low bracken growing to the very edge of the cliff. Round this clearing there was a semi-circle of trees with curious huts built of foliage piled one above the other among the branches. A rookery, with every nest a little house, would best convey the idea. The openings of these huts and the branches of the trees were thronged with a dense mob of ape-people, whom from their size I took to be the females and infants of the tribe. They formed the background of the picture, and were all looking out with eager interest at the same scene which fascinated and bewildered us.

In the open, and near the edge of the cliff, there had assembled a crowd of some hundred of these shaggy, red-haired creatures, many of them of immense size, and all of them horrible to look upon. There was a certain discipline among them, for none of them attempted to break the line which had been formed. In front there stood a small group of Indians – little, clean-limbed, red fellows, whose skins glowed like polished bronze in the strong sunlight. A tall, thin white man was standing beside them, his head bowed, his arms folded, his whole attitude expressive of his horror and dejection. There was no mistaking the angular form of Professor Summerlee.

In front of and around this dejected group of prisoners were several ape-men, who watched them closely and made all escape impossible. Then, right out from all the others and close to the edge of the cliff, were two figures, so strange, and under other circumstances so ludicrous, that they absorbed my attention. The one was our comrade, Professor Challenger. The remains of his coat still hung in strips from his shoulders, but his shirt had been all torn out, and his great beard merged itself in the black tangle which covered his mighty chest. He had lost his hat, and his hair, which had grown long in our wanderings, was flying in wild disorder. A single day seemed to have changed him from the highest product of modern civilization to the most desperate savage in South America. Beside him stood his master the king of the ape-men. In all things he was, as Lord John had said, the very image of our Professor, save that his colouring was red instead of black. The same short, broad figure, the same heavy shoulders, the same forward hang of the arms, the same bristling beard merging itself in the hairy chest. Only above the eyebrows, where the sloping forehead and low, curved skull of the ape-man were in sharp contrast to the broad brow and magnificent cranium of the European, could one see any marked difference. At every other point the king was an absurd parody of the Professor.

All this, which takes me so long to describe, impressed itself upon me in a few seconds. Then we had very different things to think of, for an active drama was in progress. Two of the ape-men had seized one of the Indians out of the group and dragged him forward to the edge of the cliff. The king raised his hand as a signal. They caught the man up by his leg and arm, and swung him three times backwards and forwards with tremendous violence. Then, with a frightful heave they shot the poor wretch over the precipice. With such force did they throw him that he curved high in the air before beginning to drop. As he vanished from sight, the whole assembly, except the guards, rushed forward to the edge of the precipice, and there was a long pause of absolute silence, broken by a mad yell of delight. They sprang about, tossing their long, hairy arms in the air and howling with exultation.

Then they fell back from the edge, formed themselves again into line, and waited for the next victim.

This time it was Summerlee. Two of his guards caught him by the wrists and pulled him brutally to the front. His thin figure and long limbs struggled and fluttered like a chicken being dragged from a coop. Challenger had turned to the king and waved his hands frantically before him. He was begging, pleading, imploring for his comrade's life. The ape-man pushed him roughly aside and shook his head. It was the last conscious movement he was to make upon earth. Lord John's rifle cracked, and the king sank down, a tangled red sprawling thing, upon the ground.

'Shoot into the thick of them! Shoot! sonny, shoot!' cried my companion.

There are strange red depths in the soul of the most commonplace man. I am tender-hearted by nature, and have found my eyes moist many a time over the scream of a wounded hare. Yet the blood lust was on me now. I found myself on my feet emptying one magazine, then the other, clicking open the breech to re-load, snapping it to again, while cheering and yelling with pure ferocity and joy of slaughter as I did so. With our four guns the two of us made a horrible havoc. Both the guards who held Summerlee were down, and he was staggering about like a drunken man in his amazement, unable to realize that he was a free man. The dense mob of ape-men ran about in bewilderment, marvelling whence this storm of death was coming or what it might mean. They waved, gesticulated, screamed, and tripped up over those who had fallen. Then, with a sudden impulse, they all rushed in a howling crowd to the trees for shelter, leaving the ground behind them spotted with their stricken comrades. The prisoners were left for the moment standing alone in the middle of the clearing.

Challenger's quick brain had grasped the situation. He seized the bewildered Summerlee by the arm, and they both ran towards us. Two of their guards bounded after them and fell to two bullets from Lord John. We ran forward into the open to meet our friends, and pressed a loaded rifle into the hands of each. But Summerlee was at the end of his strength. He could hardly totter. Already the ape-men were recovering from their panic. They were coming through the brushwood and threatening to cut us off. Challenger and I ran Summerlee along, one at each of his elbows, while Lord John covered our retreat, firing again and again as savage heads snarled at us out of the bushes. For a mile or more the chattering brutes were at our very heels. Then the pursuit slackened, for they learned our power and would no longer face that unerring rifle. When we had at last reached the camp, we looked back and found ourselves alone.

So it seemed to us; and yet we were mistaken. We had hardly closed the thorn-bush door of our zareba, clasped each other's hands, and thrown ourselves panting upon the ground beside our spring, when we heard a patter of feet and then a gentle, plaintive crying from outside our entrance. Lord Roxton rushed forward, rifle in hand, and threw it open. There, prostrate upon their faces, lay the little red figures of the four surviving Indians, trembling with fear of us and yet imploring our protection. With an expressive sweep of his hands one of them pointed to the woods around them, and indicated that they were full of danger. Then, darting forward, he threw his arms round Lord John's legs and rested his face upon them.

'By George!' cried Lord John, pulling at his moustache in great perplexity, 'I say – what the dooce are we to do with these people? Get up, little chappie, and take your face off my boots.'

Summerlee was sitting up and stuffing some tobacco into his old briar.

'We've got to see them safe,' said he. 'You've pulled us all out of the jaws of death. My word! it was a good bit of work!'

'Admirable!' cried Challenger. 'Admirable! Not only we as individuals, but European science collectively, owe you a deep debt of gratitude for what you have done. I do not hesitate to say that the disappearance of Professor Summerlee and myself would have left an appreciable gap in modern zoological history. Our young friend here and you have done most excellently well.'

He beamed at us with the old paternal smile, but European science would have been somewhat amazed could they have seen their chosen child, the hope of the future, with his tangled, unkempt head, his bare chest, and his tattered clothes. He had one of the meat-tins between his knees, and sat with a large piece of cold Australian mutton between his fingers. The Indian looked up at him, and then, with a little yelp, cringed to the ground and clung to Lord John's leg.

'Don't you be scared, my bonnie boy,' said Lord John, patting the matted head in front of him. 'He can't stick your appearance, Challenger; and, by George! I don't wonder. All right, little chap, he's only a human, just the same as the rest of us.'

'Really, sir!' cried the Professor.

'Well, it's lucky for you, Challenger, that you *are* a little out of the ordinary. If you hadn't been so like the king –'

'Upon my word, Lord John Roxton, you allow yourself great latitude.'

'Well, it's a fact.'

'I beg, sir, that you will change the subject. Your remarks are irrelevant and unintelligible. The question before us is what are we to do with these Indians? The obvious thing is to escort them home, if we knew where their home was.'

'There is no difficulty about that,' said I. 'They live in the caves on the other side of the central lake.'

'Our young friend here knows where they live. I gather that it is some distance.'

'A good twenty miles,' said I.

Summerlee gave a groan.

'I, for one, could never get there. Surely I hear those brutes still howling upon our track.'

As he spoke, from the dark recesses of the woods we heard far away the jibbering cry of the ape-men. The Indians once more set up a feeble wail of fear.

'We must move, and move quick!' said Lord John. 'You help Summerlee, young fellah. These Indians will carry stores. Now, then, come along before they can see us.'

In less than half-an-hour we had reached our brushwood retreat and concealed ourselves. All day we heard the excited calling of the ape-men in the direction of our old camp, but none of them came our way, and the tired fugitives, red and white, had a long, deep sleep. I was dozing myself in the evening when someone plucked my sleeve, and I found Challenger kneeling beside me.

'You keep a diary of these events, and you expect eventually to publish it, Mr Malone,' said he, with solemnity.

'I am only here as a Press reporter,' I answered.

'Exactly. You may have heard some rather fatuous remarks of Lord John Roxton's which seemed to imply that there was some – some resemblance –'

'Yes, I heard them.'

'I need not say that any publicity given to such an idea – any levity in your narrative of what occurred – would be exceedingly offensive to me.'

'I will keep well within the truth.'

'Lord John's observations are frequently exceedingly fanciful, and he is capable of attributing the most absurd reasons to the respect which is always shown by the most undeveloped races to dignity and character. You follow my meaning?'

'Entirely.'

'I leave the matter to your discretion.' Then, after a long pause, he added: 'The king of the ape-men was really a creature of great distinction – a most remarkably handsome and intelligent personality. Did it not strike you?'

'A most remarkable creature,' said I.

And the Professor, much eased in his mind, settled down to his slumber once more.

CHAPTER XIV

Those were the Real Conquests

We had imagined that our pursuers, the ape-men, knew nothing of our brushwood hiding-place, but we were soon to find out our mistake. There was no sound in the woods – not a leaf moved upon the trees, and all was peace around us – but we should have been warned by our first experience how cunningly and how patiently these creatures can watch and wait until their chance comes. Whatever fate may be mine through life, I am very sure that I shall never be nearer death than I was that morning. But I will tell you the thing in its due order.

We all awoke exhausted after the terrific emotions and scanty food of yesterday. Summerlee was still so weak that it was an effort for him to stand; but the old man was full of a sort of surly courage which would never admit defeat. A council was held, and it was agreed that we should wait quietly for an hour or two where we were, have our much-needed breakfast, and then make our way across the plateau and round the central lake to the caves where my observations had shown that the Indians lived. We relied upon the fact that we could count upon the good word of those whom we had rescued to ensure a warm welcome from their fellows. Then, with our mission accomplished and possessing a fuller knowledge of the secrets of Maple White Land, we should turn our whole thoughts to the vital problem of our escape and return. Even Challenger was ready to admit that we should then have done all for which we had come, and that our first duty from that time onwards was to carry back to civilization the amazing discoveries we had made.

We were able now to take a more leisurely view of the Indians whom we had rescued. They were small men, wiry, active, and well-built, with lank black hair tied up in a bunch behind their heads with a leathern thong, and leathern also were their loin-clothes. Their faces were hairless, well formed, and good-humoured. The lobes of their ears, hanging ragged and bloody, showed that they had been pierced for some ornaments which their captors had torn out. Their speech, though unintelligible to us, was fluent among themselves, and as they pointed to each other and uttered the word 'Accala' many times over, we gathered that this was the name of their nation. Occasionally, with faces which were convulsed with fear and hatred, they shook their clenched hands at the woods round and cried: 'Doda! Doda!' which was surely their term for their enemies.

'What do you make of them, Challenger?' asked Lord John. 'One thing is very clear to me, and that is that the little chap with the front of his head shaved is a chief among them.'

It was indeed evident that this man stood apart from the others, and that they never ventured to address him without every sign of deep respect. He seemed to be the youngest of them all, and yet, so proud and high was his spirit, that upon Challenger laying his great hand upon his head he started like a spurred horse and, with a quick flash of his dark eyes, moved further away from the Professor. Then, placing his hand upon his breast and holding himself with great dignity, he uttered the word 'Maretas' several times. The Professor, unabashed, seized the nearest Indian by the shoulder and proceeded to lecture upon him as if he were a potted specimen in a classroom.

'The type of these people,' said he in his sonorous fashion, 'whether judged by cranial capacity, facial angle, or any other test, cannot be regarded as a low one; on the contrary, we must place it as considerably higher in the scale than many South American tribes which I can mention. On no possible supposition can we explain the evolution of such a race in this place. For that matter, so great a gap separates these ape-men from the primitive animals which have survived upon this plateau, that it is inadmissible to think that they could have developed where we find them.'

'Then where the dooce did they drop from?' asked Lord John.

'A question which will, no doubt, be eagerly discussed in every scientific society in Europe, and America,' the Professor answered. 'My own reading of the situation for what it is worth' – he inflated his chest enormously and looked insolently around him at the words – 'is that evolution has advanced under the peculiar conditions of this country up to the vertebrate stage, the old types surviving and living on in company with the newer ones. Thus we find such modern creatures as the tapir – an animal with quite a respectable length of pedigree – the great deer, and the ant-eater in the companionship of reptilian forms of Jurassic type. So much is clear. And now come the ape-man and the Indian. What is the scientific mind to think of their presence? I can only account for it by an invasion from outside. It is probable that there existed an anthropoid ape in South America, who in past ages found his way to this place, and that he developed into the creatures we have seen, some of which' – here he looked hard at me – 'were of an appearance and shape which if it had been accompanied by corresponding intelligence, would, I do not hesitate to say, have reflected credit upon any living race. As to the Indians I cannot doubt that they are more recent immigrants from below. Under the stress of famine or of conquest they have made their way up here. Faced by ferocious creatures which they had never before seen, they took refuge in the caves which our young friend has described, but they have no doubt had a bitter fight to hold their own against wild beasts, and especially against the ape-men who would regard them as intruders, and wage a merciless war upon them with a cunning which the larger beasts would lack. Hence the fact that their numbers appear to be limited. Well, gentlemen, have I read you the riddle aright, or is there any point which you would query?'

Professor Summerlee for once was too depressed to argue, though he shook his head violently as a token of general disagreement. Lord John merely scratched his scanty locks with the remark that he couldn't put up a fight as he wasn't in the same weight or class. For my own part I performed my usual *rôle* of bringing things down to a strictly prosaic and practical level by the remark that one of the Indians was missing.

'He has gone to fetch some water,' said Lord Roxton. 'We fitted him up with an empty beef tin and he is off.'

'To the old camp?' I asked.

'No, to the brook. It's among the trees there. It can't be more than a couple of hundred yards. But the beggar is certainly taking his time.'

'I'll go and look after him,' said I. I picked up my rifle and strolled in the direction of the brook, leaving my friends to lay out the scanty breakfast. It may seem to you rash that even for so short a distance I should quit the shelter of our friendly thicket, but you will remember that we were many miles from Ape-Town, that so far as we knew the creatures had not discovered our retreat, and that in any case with a rifle in my hands I had no fear of them. I had not yet learned their cunning or their strength.

I could hear the murmur of our brook somewhere ahead of me, but there was a tangle of trees and brushwood between me and it. I was making my way through this at a point which was just out of sight of my companions, when, under one of the trees I noticed something red huddled among the bushes. As I approached it, I was shocked to see that it was the dead body of the missing Indian. He lay upon his side, his limbs drawn up, and his head screwed round at a most unnatural angle, so that he seemed to be looking straight over his own shoulder. I gave a cry to warn my friends that something was amiss, and running forwards I stooped over the body. Surely my guardian angel was very near me then, for some instinct of fear, or it may have been some faint rustle of leaves made me glance upwards. Out of the thick green foliage which hung low over my head, two long muscular arms covered with reddish hair were slowly descending. Another instant and the great stealthy hands would have been round my throat. I sprang backwards, but quick as I was, those hands were quicker still. Through my sudden spring they missed a fatal grip, but one of them caught the back of my neck and the other one my face. I threw my hands up to protect my throat, and the next moment the huge paw had slid down my face and closed over them. I was lifted lightly from the ground, and I felt an intolerable pressure forcing my head back and back until the strain upon the cervical spine was more than I could bear. My senses swam, but I still tore at the hand and forced it out from my chin. Looking up I saw a frightful face with cold inexorable light blue eyes looking down into mine. There was something hypnotic in those terrible eyes. I could struggle no longer. As the creature felt me grow limp in his grasp, two white canines gleamed for a moment at each side of the vile mouth, and the grip tightened still more upon my chin, forcing it always upwards and back. A thin, opal-tinted mist formed before my eyes and little silvery bells tinkled in my ears. Dully and far off I heard the crack of a rifle and was feebly aware of the shock as I was dropped to the earth, where I lay without sense or motion.

I awoke to find myself on my back upon the grass in our lair within the thicket. Someone had brought the water from the brook, and Lord John was sprinkling my head with it, while Challenger and Summerlee were propping me up, with concern in their faces. For a moment I had a glimpse of the human spirits behind their scientific masks.[1] It was really shock, rather than any injury, which had prostrated me, and in half-an-hour, in spite of aching head and stiff neck, I was sitting up and ready for anything.

'But you've had the escape of your life, young fellah my lad,' said Lord John. 'When I heard your cry and ran forward, and saw your head twisted half-off and your stohwassers kickin' in the air, I thought we were one short. I missed the beast in my flurry, but he dropped you all right and was off like a streak. By George! I wish I had fifty men with rifles. I'd clear out the whole infernal gang of them and leave this country a bit cleaner than we found it.'

It was clear now that the ape-men had in some way marked us down, and that we were watched on every side. We had not so much to fear from them during the day, but they would be very likely to rush us by night; so the sooner we got away from their neighbourhood the better. On three sides of us was absolute forest, and there we might find ourselves in an ambush. But on the fourth side – that which sloped down in the direction of the lake – there was only low scrub, with scattered trees and occasional open glades. It was, in fact, the route which I had myself taken in my solitary journey, and it led us straight for the Indian caves. This then must for every reason be our road.

One great regret we had, and that was to leave our old camp behind us, not only for the sake of the stores which remained there, but even more because we were losing touch with Zambo, our link with the outside world. However, we had a fair supply of cartridges and all our guns, so, for a time at least, we could look after ourselves, and we hoped soon to have a chance of returning and restoring our communications with our negro. He had faithfully promised to stay where he was, and we had not a doubt that he would be as good as his word.

It was in the early afternoon that we started upon our journey. The young chief walked at our head as our guide, but refused indignantly to carry any burden. Behind him came the two surviving Indians with our scanty possessions upon their backs. We four white men walked in the rear with rifles loaded and ready. As we started there broke from the thick silent woods behind us a sudden great ululation of the ape-men, which may have been a cheer of triumph at our departure or a jeer of contempt at our flight. Looking back we saw only the dense screen of trees, but that long-drawn yell told us how many of our enemies lurked among them. We saw no sign of pursuit, however, and soon we had got into more open country and beyond their power.

As I tramped along, the rearmost of the four, I could not help smiling at the appearance of my three companions in front. Was this the luxurious Lord John Roxton who had sat that evening in the Albany amidst his Persian rugs and his pictures in the pink radiance of the tinted lights? And was this the imposing Professor who had swelled behind the great desk in his massive study at Enmore Park? and, finally, could this be the austere and prim figure which had risen before the meeting at the Zoological Institute? No three tramps that one could have met in a Surrey lane could have looked more hopeless and bedraggled. We had, it is true, been only a week or so upon the top of the plateau, but all our spare clothing was in our camp below, and the one week had been a severe one upon us all, though least to me who had not to endure the handling of the ape-men. My three friends had all lost their hats, and had now bound handkerchiefs round their heads, their clothes hung in ribbons about them, and their unshaven grimy faces were hardly to be recognized. Both Summerlee and Challenger were limping heavily, while I still dragged my feet from weakness after the shock of the morning, and my neck was as stiff as a board from the murderous grip that held it. We were indeed a sorry crew, and I did not wonder to see our Indian companions glance back at us occasionally with horror and amazement on their faces.

In the late afternoon we reached the margin of the lake, and as we emerged from the bush and saw the sheet of water stretching before us our native friends set up a shrill cry of joy and pointed eagerly in front of them. It was indeed a wonderful sight which lay before us. Sweeping over the glassy surface was a great flotilla of canoes coming straight for the shore upon which we stood. They were some miles out when first we saw them, but they shot forward with great swiftness, and were soon so near that the rowers could distinguish our persons. Instantly a thunderous shout of delight burst from them, and we saw them rise from their seats, waving their paddles and spears madly in the air. Then bending to their work once more, they flew across the intervening water, beached their boats upon the sloping sand, and rushed up to us, prostrating themselves with loud cries of greeting before the young chief. Finally one of them, an elderly man, with a necklace and bracelet of great lustrous glass beads and the skin of some beautiful mottled amber-coloured animal slung over his shoulders, ran forward and embraced most tenderly the youth whom we had saved. He then looked at us and asked some questions, after which he stepped up with much dignity and embraced us also each in turn. Then, at his order, the whole tribe lay down upon the ground before us in homage. Personally I felt shy and uncomfortable at this obsequious adoration, and I read the same feeling in the faces of Lord John and Summerlee, but Challenger expanded like a flower in the sun.

'They may be undeveloped types,' said he, stroking his beard and looking round at them, 'but their deportment in the presence of their superiors might be a lesson to some of our more advanced Europeans. Strange how correct are the instincts of the natural man!'

It was clear that the natives had come out upon the war-path, for every man carried his spear – a long bamboo tipped with bone – his bow and arrows, and some sort of club or stone battle-axe slung at his side. Their dark, angry glances at the woods from which we had come, and the frequent repetition of the word 'Doda', made it clear enough that this was a rescue party who had set forth to save or revenge the old chief's son, for such we gathered that the youth must be. A council was now held by the whole tribe squatting in a circle, whilst we sat near on a slab of basalt and watched their proceedings. Two or three warriors spoke, and finally our young friend made a spirited harangue with such eloquent features and gestures that we could understand it all as clearly as if we had known his language.

'What is the use of returning?' he said. 'Sooner or later the thing must be done. Your comrades have been murdered. What if I have returned safe? These others have been done to death. There is no safety for any of us. We are assembled now and ready.' Then he pointed to us. 'These strange men are our friends. They are great fighters, and they hate the ape-men even as we do. They command,' here he pointed up to heaven, 'the thunder and the lightning. When shall we have such a chance again? Let us go forward, and either die now or live for the future in safety. How else shall we go back unashamed to our women?'

The little red warriors hung upon the words of the speaker, and when he had finished they burst into a roar of applause, waving their rude weapons in the air. The old chief stepped forward to us, and asked us some question, pointing at the same time to the woods. Lord John made a sign to him that he should wait for an answer and then he turned to us.

'Well, it's up to you to say what you will do,' said he, 'for my part I have a score to settle with these monkey-folk, and if it ends by wiping them off the face of the earth I don't see that the earth need fret about it. I'm goin' with our little red pals and I mean to see them through the scrap. What do you say, young fellah?'

'Of course I will come.'

'And you, Challenger?'

'I will assuredly co-operate.'

'And you, Summerlee?'

'We seem to be drifting very far from the object of this expedition, Lord John. I assure you that I little thought when I left my professional chair in London that it was for the purpose of heading a raid of savages upon a colony of anthropoid apes.'

'To such base uses do we come,' said Lord John, smiling. 'But we are up against it, so what's the decision?'

'It seems a most questionable step,' said Summerlee, argumentative to the last, 'but if you are all going, I hardly see how I can remain behind.'

'Then it is settled,' said Lord John, and turning to the chief he nodded and slapped his rifle. The old fellow clasped our hands, each in turn, while his men cheered louder than ever. It was too late to advance that night, so the Indians settled down into a rude bivouac. On all sides their fires began to glimmer and smoke. Some of them who had disappeared into the jungle came back presently driving a young iguanodon before them. Like the others, it had a daub of asphalt upon its shoulder, and it was only when we saw one of the natives step forward with the air of an owner and give his consent to the beast's slaughter that we understood at last that these great creatures were as much private property as a herd of cattle, and that these symbols which had so perplexed us were nothing more than the marks of the owner. Helpless, torpid, and vegetarian, with great limbs but a minute brain, they could be rounded up and driven by a child. In a few minutes the huge beast had been cut up and slabs of him were hanging over a dozen camp fires, together with great scaly ganoid fish which had been speared in the lake.

Summerlee had lain down and slept upon the sand, but we others roamed round the edge of the water, seeking to learn something more of this strange country. Twice we found pits of blue clay, such as we had already seen in the swamp of the pterodactyls. These were old volcanic vents, and for some reason excited the greatest interest in Lord John. What attracted Challenger, on the other hand, was a bubbling, gurgling mud geyser, where some strange gas formed great bursting bubbles upon the surface. He thrust a hollow reed into it and cried out with delight like a schoolboy when he was able, on touching it with a lighted match, to cause a sharp explosion and a blue flame at the far end of the tube. Still more pleased was he when, inverting a leathern pouch over the end of the reed, and so filling it with the gas, he was able to send it soaring up into the air.

'An inflammable gas, and one markedly lighter than the atmosphere. I should say beyond doubt that it contained a considerable proportion of free hydrogen. The resources of G. E. C. are not yet exhausted, my young friend. I may yet show you how a great mind moulds all Nature to its use.' He swelled with some secret purpose, but would say no more.

There was nothing which we could see upon the shore which seemed to me so wonderful as the great sheet of water before us. Our numbers and our noise had frightened all living creatures away, and save for a few pterodactyls, which soared round high above our heads while they waited for the carrion, all was still around the camp. But it was different out upon the rose-tinted waters of the central lake. It boiled and heaved with strange life. Great slate-coloured backs and high serrated dorsal fins shot up with a fringe of silver, and then rolled down into the depths again. The sandbanks far out were spotted with uncouth crawling forms, huge turtles, strange saurians, and one great flat creature like a writhing palpitating mat of black greasy leather, which flopped its way slowly to the lake. Here and there high serpent heads projected out of the water, cutting swiftly through it with a little collar of foam in front, and a long swirling wake behind, rising and falling in graceful, swan-like undulations as they went. It was not until one of these creatures wriggled on to a sandbank within a few hundred yards of us, and exposed a barrel-shaped body and huge flippers behind the long serpent neck, that Challenger and Summerlee, who had joined us, broke out into their duet of wonder and admiration.

'Plesiosaurus! A fresh-water Plesiosaurus!' cried Summerlee. 'That I should have lived to see such a sight! We are blessed, my dear Challenger, above all zoologists since the world began!'

It was not until the night had fallen, and the fires of our savage allies glowed red in the shadows, that our two men of science could be dragged away from the fascinations of that primaeval lake. Even in the darkness as we lay upon the strand, we heard from time to time the snort and plunge of the huge creatures who lived therein.

At earliest dawn our camp was astir and an hour later we had started upon our memorable expedition. Often in my dreams have I thought that I might live to be a war correspondent. In what wildest one could I have conceived the nature of the campaign which it should be my lot to report! Here then is my first despatch from a field of battle:

Our numbers had been reinforced during the night by a fresh batch of natives from the caves, and we may have been four or five hundred strong when we made our advance. A fringe of scouts were thrown out in front, and behind them the whole force in a solid column made their way up the long slope of the bush country until we were near the edge of the forest. Here they spread out into a long straggling line of spearmen and bowmen. Roxton and Summerlee took their position upon the right flank, while Challenger and I were on the left. It was a host of the stone age that we were accompanying to battle – we with the last word of the gunsmith's art from St James's Street and the Strand.

We had not long to wait for our enemy. A wild shrill clamour rose from the edge of the wood and suddenly a body of ape-men rushed out with clubs and stones, and made for the centre of the Indian line. It was a valiant move but a foolish one, for the great bandy-legged creatures were slow of foot, while their opponents were as active as cats. It was horrible to see the fierce brutes with foaming mouths and glaring eyes, rushing and grasping, but for ever missing their elusive enemies, while arrow after arrow buried itself in their hides. One great fellow ran past me roaring with pain, with a dozen darts sticking from his chest and ribs. In mercy I put a bullet through his skull, and he fell sprawling among the aloes. But this was the only shot fired, for the attack had been on the centre of the line, and the Indians there had needed no help of ours in repulsing it. Of all the ape-men who had rushed out into the open, I do not think that one got back to cover.

But the matter was more deadly when we came among the trees. For an hour or more after we entered the wood, there was a desperate struggle in which for a time we hardly held our own. Springing out from among the scrub the ape-men with huge clubs broke in upon the Indians and often felled three or four of them before they could be speared. Their frightful blows shattered everything upon which they fell. One of them knocked Summerlee's rifle to matchwood and the next would have crushed his skull had an Indian not stabbed the beast to the heart. Other ape-men in the trees above us hurled down stones and logs of wood, occasionally dropping bodily on to our ranks and fighting furiously until they were felled. Once our allies broke under the pressure, and had it not been for the execution done by our rifles they would certainly have taken to their heels. But they were gallantly rallied by their old chief and came on with such a rush that the ape-men began in turn to give way. Summerlee was weaponless, but I was emptying my magazine as quick as I could fire, and on the further flank we heard the continuous cracking of our companions' rifles. Then in a moment came the panic and the collapse. Screaming and howling, the great creatures rushed away in all directions through the brushwood, while our allies yelled in their savage delight, following swiftly after their flying enemies. All the feuds of countless generations, all the hatreds and cruelties of their narrow history, all the memories of ill-usage and persecution were to be purged that day. At last man was to be supreme and the man-beast to find for ever his allotted place. Fly as they would the fugitives were too slow to escape from the active savages, and from every side in the tangled woods we heard the exultant yells, the twanging of bows, and the crash and thud as ape-men were brought down from their hiding-places in the trees.

I was following the others, when I found that Lord John and Challenger had come across to join us.

'It's over,' said Lord John. 'I think we can leave the tidying up to them. Perhaps the less we see of it the better we shall sleep.'

Challenger's eyes were shining with the lust of slaughter.

'We have been privileged,' he cried, strutting about like a gamecock, 'to be present at one of the typical decisive battles of history – the battles which have determined the fate of the world. What, my friends, is the conquest of one nation by another? It is meaningless. Each produces the same result. But those fierce fights, when in the dawn of the ages the cave-dwellers held their own against the tiger folk, or the elephants first found that they had a master, those were the real conquests – the victories that count. By this strange turn of fate we have seen and helped to decide even such a contest. Now upon this plateau the future must ever be for man.'

It needed a robust faith in the end to justify such tragic means. As we advanced together through the woods we found the ape-men lying thick, transfixed with spears or arrows. Here and there a little group of shattered Indians marked where one of the anthropoids had turned to bay, and sold his life dearly. Always in front of us we heard the yelling and roaring which showed the direction of the pursuit. The ape-men had been driven back to their city, they had made a last stand there, once again they had been broken, and now we were in time to see the final fearful scene of all. Some eighty or a hundred males, the last survivors, had been driven across that same little clearing which led to the edge of the cliff, the scene of our own exploit two days before. As we arrived the Indians, a semi-circle of spearmen, had closed in on them, and in a minute it was over. Thirty or forty died where they stood. The others, screaming and clawing, were thrust over the precipice, and went hurtling down, as their prisoners had of old, on to the sharp bamboos six hundred feet below. It was as Challenger had said, and the reign of man was assured for ever in Maple White Land. The males were exterminated, Ape-Town was destroyed, the females and young were driven away to live in bondage, and the long rivalry of untold centuries had reached its bloody end.

For us the victory brought much advantage. Once again we were able to visit our camp and get at our stores. Once more also we were able to communicate with Zambo, who had been terrified by the spectacle from afar of an avalanche of apes falling from the edge of the cliff.

'Come away, Massas, come away!' he cried, his eyes starting from his head. 'The debbil get you sure if you stay up there.'

'It is the voice of sanity!' said Summerlee with conviction. 'We have had adventures enough and they are neither suitable to our character or our position. I hold you to your word, Challenger. From now onwards you devote your energies to getting us out of this horrible country and back once more to civilization.'

CHAPTER XV

Our Eyes have Seen Great Wonders

I write this from day to day, but I trust that before I come to the end of it, I may be able to say that the light shines, at last, through our clouds. We are held here with no clear means of making our escape, and bitterly we chafe against it. Yet, I can well imagine that the day may come when we may be glad that we were kept, against our will, to see something more of the wonders of this singular place, and of the creatures who inhabit it.

The victory of the Indians and the annihilation of the ape-men marked the turning point of our fortunes. From then onwards, we were in truth masters of the plateau for the natives looked upon us with a mixture of fear and gratitude, since by our strange powers we had aided them to destroy their hereditary foe. For their own sakes they would, perhaps, be glad to see the departure of such formidable and incalculable people, but they have not themselves suggested any way by which we may reach the plains below. There had been, so far as we could follow their signs, a tunnel by which the place could be approached, the lower exit of which we had seen from below. By this, no doubt, both ape-men and Indians had at different epochs reached the top, and Maple White, with his companion, had taken the same way. Only the year before, however, there had been a terrific earthquake, and the upper end of the tunnel had fallen in and completely disappeared. The Indians now could only shake their heads and shrug their shoulders when we expressed by signs, our desire to descend. It may be that they cannot, but it may also be that they will not help us to get away.

At the end of the victorious campaign the surviving ape-folk were driven across the plateau (their wailings were horrible) and established in the neighbourhood of the Indian caves, where they would, from now onwards, be a servile race under the eyes of their masters. It was a rude, raw, primaeval version of the Jews in Babylon or the Israelites in Egypt. At night we could hear from amid the trees the long-drawn cry, as some primitive Ezekiel[1] mourned for fallen greatness and recalled the departed glories of Ape-Town. Hewers of wood and drawers of water, such were they from now onwards.

We had returned across the plateau with our allies two days after the battle, and made our camp at the foot of their cliffs. They would have had us share their caves with them, but Lord John would by no means consent to it, considering that to do so would put us in their power if they were treacherously disposed. We kept our independence therefore, and had our weapons ready for any emergency, while preserving the most friendly relations. We also continually visited their caves, which were most remarkable places, though whether made by man or by Nature we have never been able to determine. They were all on the one stratum, hollowed out of some soft rock which lay between the volcanic basalt forming the ruddy cliffs above them, and the hard granite which formed their base.

The openings were about eighty feet above the ground, and were led up to by long stone stairs, so narrow and steep that no large animal could mount them. Inside they were warm and dry, running in straight passages of varying length into the side of the hill, with smooth grey walls decorated with many excellent pictures done with charred sticks and representing the various animals of the plateau. If every living thing were swept from the country the future explorer would find upon the walls of these caves ample evidence of the strange fauna – the dinosaurs, iguanodons and fish-lizards – which had lived so recently upon earth.

Since we had learned that the huge iguanodons were kept as tame herds by their owners, and were simply walking meat-stores, we had conceived that man, even with his primitive weapons, had established his ascendancy upon the plateau. We were soon to discover that it was not so, and that he was still there upon tolerance. It was on the third day after our forming our camp near the Indian caves that the tragedy occurred. Challenger and Summerlee had gone off together that day to the lake, where some of the natives, under their direction, were engaged in harpooning specimens of the great lizards. Lord John and I had remained in our camp, while a number of the Indians were scattered about upon the grassy slope in front of the caves engaged in different ways. Suddenly there was a shrill cry of alarm, with the word 'Stoa' resounding from a hundred tongues. From every side men, women and children were rushing wildly for shelter, swarming up the staircases and into the caves in a mad stampede.

Looking up, we could see them waving their arms from the rocks above and beckoning to us to join them in their refuge. We had both seized our magazine rifles and ran out to see what the danger could be. Suddenly from the near belt of trees there broke forth a group of twelve or fifteen Indians, running for their lives, and at their very heels two of those frightful monsters which had disturbed our camp and pursued me upon my solitary journey. In shape they were like horrible toads, and moved in a succession of springs, but in size they were of an incredible bulk, larger than the largest elephant. We had never before seen them save at night, and indeed they are nocturnal animals save when disturbed in their lairs, as these had been. We now stood amazed at the sight, for their blotched and warty skins were of a curious fish-like iridescence, and the sunlight struck them with an ever-varying rainbow bloom as they moved.

We had little time to watch them, however, for in an instant they had overtaken the fugitives and were making a dire slaughter among them. Their method was to fall forward with their full weight upon each in turn, and, leaving him crushed and mangled, to bound on after the others. The wretched Indians screamed with terror, but were helpless, run as they would, before the relentless purpose and horrible activity of these monstrous creatures. One after another they went down, and there were not half-a-dozen surviving by the time my companion and I could come to their help. But our aid was of little avail and only involved us in the same peril. At the range of a couple of hundred yards we emptied our magazines, firing bullet after bullet into the beasts, but with no more effect than if we were pelting them with pellets of paper. Their slow reptilian natures cared nothing for wounds, and the springs of their lives, with no special brain centre but scattered throughout their spinal cords, could not be tapped by any modern weapons. The most that we could do was to check their progress by distracting their attention with the flash and roar of our guns, and so to give both the natives and ourselves time to reach the steps which led to safety. But where the conical explosive bullets of the twentieth century were of no avail the poisoned arrows of the natives, dipped in the juice of strophanthus and steeped afterwards in decayed carrion, could succeed. Such arrows were of little avail to the hunter who attacked the beast, because their action in that torpid circulation was slow, and before its powers failed it could certainly overtake and slay its assailant. But now, as the two monsters hounded us to the very foot of the stairs, a drift of darts came whistling from every chink in the cliff above them. In a minute they were feathered with them, and yet with no sign of pain they clawed and slobbered with impotent rage at the steps which would lead them to their victims, mounting clumsily up for a few yards and then sliding down again to the ground. But at last the poison worked. One of them gave a deep rumbling groan and dropped his huge squat head on to the earth. The other bounded round in an eccentric circle with shrill, wailing cries, and then lying down writhed in agony for some minutes before it also stiffened and lay still. With yells of triumph the Indians came flocking down from their caves and danced a frenzied dance of victory round the dead bodies, in mad joy that two more of the most dangerous of all their enemies had been slain. That night they cut up and removed the bodies, not to eat – for the poison was still active – but lest they should breed a pestilence. The great reptilian hearts, however, each as large as a cushion, still lay there, beating slowly and steadily, with a gentle rise and fall, in horrible independent life. It was only upon the third day that the ganglia ran down and the dreadful things were still.

Some day, when I have a better desk than a meat-tin and more helpful tools than a worn stub of pencil and a last, tattered notebook, I will write some fuller account of the Accala Indians – of our life amongst them, and of the glimpses which we had of the strange conditions of wondrous Maple White Land. Memory, at least, will never fail me, for so long as the breath of life is in me every hour and every action of that period will stand out as hard and clear as do the first strange happenings of our childhood. No new impressions could efface those which are so deeply cut. When the time comes I will describe that wondrous moonlit night upon the great lake when a young ichthyosaurus – a strange creature, half-seal, half-fish, to look at, with bone-covered eyes on each side of his snout, and a third eye fixed upon the top of his head – was entangled in an Indian net, and nearly upset our canoe before we towed it ashore; the same night that a green water-snake shot out from the rushes and carried off in its coils the steersman of Challenger's canoe. I will tell, too, of the great nocturnal white thing – to this day we do not know whether it was beast or reptile – which lived in a vile swamp to the east of the lake, and flitted about with a faint phosphorescent glimmer in the darkness. The Indians were so terrified of it that they would not go near the place, and, though we twice made expeditions and saw it each time, we could not make our way through the deep marsh in which it lived. I can only say that it seemed to be larger than a cow and had the strangest musky odour. I will tell also of the huge bird which chased Challenger to the shelter of the rocks one day – a great running bird, far taller than an ostrich, with a vulture-like neck and cruel head which made it a walking death. As Challenger climbed to safety one dart of that savage curving beak shore off the heel of his boot as if it had been cut with a chisel. This time at least modern weapons prevailed and the great creature, twelve feet from head to foot – phororachus its name, according to our panting but exultant Professor – went down before

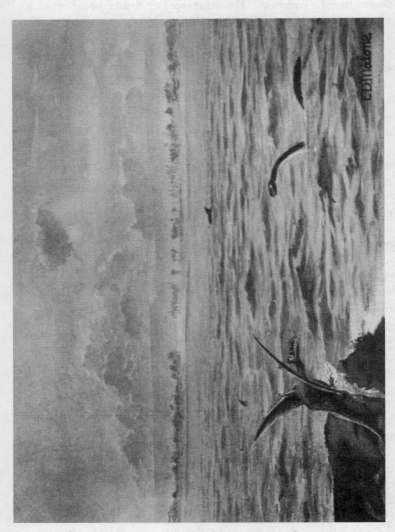

The central lake (Reconstructed by Mr Pat L. Forbes from sketch of E. D. Malone)

Lord Roxton's rifle in a flurry of waving feathers and kicking limbs, with two remorseless yellow eyes glaring up from the midst of it. May I live to see that flattened vicious skull in its own niche amid the trophies of the Albany. Finally, I will surely give some account of the toxodon, the giant ten-foot guinea pig, with projecting chisel teeth, which we killed as it drank in the grey of the morning by the side of the lake.

All this I shall some day write at fuller length, and amidst these more stirring days I would tenderly sketch in those lovely summer evenings, when with the deep blue sky above us we lay in good comradeship among the long grasses by the wood and marvelled at the strange fowl that swept over us and the quaint new creatures which crept from their burrows to watch us, while above us the boughs of the bushes were heavy with luscious fruit, and below us strange and lovely flowers peeped at us from among the herbage; or those long moonlit nights when we lay out upon the shimmering surface of the great lake and watched with wonder and awe the huge circles rippling out from the sudden splash of some fantastic monster; or the greenish gleam, far down in the deep water, of some strange creature upon the confines of darkness. These are the scenes which my mind and my pen will dwell upon in every detail at some future day.

But, you will ask, why these experiences and why this delay, when you and your comrades should have been occupied day and night in the devising of some means by which you could return to the outer world? My answer is, that there was not one of us who was not working for this end, but that our work had been in vain. One fact we had very speedily discovered: The Indians would do nothing to help us. In every other way they were our friends – one might almost say our devoted slaves – but when it was suggested that they should help us to make and carry a plank which would bridge the chasm, or when we wished to get from them thongs of leather or liana to weave ropes which might help us, we were met by a good-humoured, but an invincible, refusal. They would smile, twinkle their eyes, shake their heads, and there was the end of it. Even the old chief met us with the same obstinate denial, and it was only Maretas, the youngster whom we had saved, who looked wistfully at us and told us by his gestures that he was grieved for our thwarted wishes. Ever since their crowning triumph with the ape-men they looked upon us as supermen, who bore victory in the tubes of strange weapons, and they believed that so long as we remained with them good fortune would be theirs. A little red-skinned wife and a cave of our own were freely offered to each of us if we would but forget our own people and dwell for ever upon the plateau. So far all had been kindly, however far apart our desires might be; but we felt well assured that our actual plans of a descent must be kept secret, for we had reason to fear that at the last they might try to hold us by force.

In spite of the danger from dinosaurs (which is not great save at night, for as I may have said before they are mostly nocturnal in their habits) I have twice in the last three weeks been over to our old camp in order to see our negro who still kept watch and ward below the cliff. My eyes strained eagerly across the great plain in the hope of seeing afar off the help for which we had prayed. But the long cactus-strewn levels still stretched away, empty and bare, to the distant line of the cane-brake.

'They will come soon now, Massa Malone. Before another week pass Indian come back and bring rope and fetch you down.' Such was the cheery cry of our excellent Zambo.

I had one strange experience as I came from this second visit which had involved my being away for a night from my companions. I was returning along the well-remembered route, and had reached a spot within a mile or so of the marsh of the pterodactyls, when I saw an extraordinary object approaching me. It was a man who walked inside a framework made of bent canes so that he was enclosed on all sides in a bell-shaped cage. As I drew nearer I was more amazed still to see that it was Lord John Roxton. When he saw me he slipped from under his curious protection and came towards me laughing, and yet, as I thought, with some confusion in his manner.

'Well, young fellah,' said he, 'who would have thought of meetin' you up here?'

'What in the world are you doing?' I asked.

'Visitin' my friends, the pterodactyls,' said he.

'But why?'

'Interestin' beasts, don't you think? But unsociable! Nasty rude ways with strangers, as you may remember. So I rigged this framework which keeps them from bein' too pressin' in their attentions.'

'But what do you want in the swamp?'

He looked at me with a very questioning eye, and I read hesitation in his face.

'Don't you think other people besides Professors can want to know things?' he said at last. 'I'm studyin' the pretty dears. That's enough for you.'

'No offence,' said I.

His good-humour returned and he laughed.

'No offence, young fellah. I'm goin' to get a young devil chick for Challenger. That's one of my jobs. No, I don't want your company. I'm safe in this cage, and you are not. So long, and I'll be back in camp by night-fall.'

He turned away and I left him wandering on through the wood with his extraordinary cage around him.

If Lord John's behaviour at this time was strange, that of Challenger was more so. I may say that he seemed to possess an extraordinary fascination for the Indian women, and that he always carried a large spreading palm branch with which he beat them off as if they were flies, when their attentions became too pressing. To see him walking, like a comic opera Sultan, with this badge of authority in his hand, his black beard bristling in front of him, his toes pointing at each step, and a train of wide-eyed Indian girls behind him, clad in their slender drapery of bark cloth, is one of the most grotesque of all the pictures which I will carry back with me. As to Summerlee, he was absorbed in the insect and bird life of the plateau, and spent his whole time (save that considerable portion which was devoted to abusing Challenger for not getting us out of our difficulties) in cleaning and mounting his specimens.

Challenger had been in the habit of walking off by himself every morning and returning from time to time with looks of portentous solemnity, as one who bears the full weight of a great enterprise upon his shoulders. One day, palm branch in hand, and his crowd of adoring devotees behind him, he led us down to his hidden work-shop and took us into the secret of his plans.

The place was a small clearing in the centre of a palm grove. In this was one of those boiling mud geysers which I have already described. Around its edge were scattered a number of leathern thongs cut from iguanodon hide, and a large collapsed membrane which proved to be the dried and scraped stomach of one of the great fish-lizards from the lake. This huge sack had been sewn up at one end and only a small orifice left at the other. Into this opening several bamboo canes had been inserted and the other ends of these canes were in contact with conical clay funnels which collected the gas bubbling up through the mud of the geyser. Soon the flaccid organ began to slowly expand and show such a tendency to upward move-ments that Challenger fastened the cords which held it to the trunks of the surrounding trees. In half an hour a good-sized gas-bag had been formed, and the jerking and straining upon the thongs showed that it was capable of considerable lift. Challenger, like a glad father in the presence of his first-born, stood smiling and stroking his beard, in silent, self-satisfied content as he gazed at the creation of his brain. It was Summerlee who first broke the silence.

'You don't mean us to go up in that thing, Challenger?' said he, in an acid voice.

'I mean, my dear Summerlee, to give you such a demonstration of its powers that after seeing it you will, I am sure, have no hesitation in trusting yourself to it.'

'You can put it right out of your head now, at once,' said Summerlee with decision, 'nothing on earth would induce me to commit such a folly. Lord John, I trust that you will not countenance such madness?'

'Dooced ingenious, I call it,' said our peer. 'I'd like to see how it works.'

'So you shall,' said Challenger. 'For some days I have exerted my whole brain force upon the problem of how we shall descend from these cliffs. We have satisfied ourselves that we cannot climb down and that there is no tunnel. We are also unable to construct any kind of bridge which may take us back to the pinnacle from which we came. How then shall I find a means to convey us? Some little time ago I had remarked to our young friend here that free hydrogen was evolved from the geyser. The idea of a balloon naturally followed. I was, I will admit, somewhat baffled by the difficulty of discovering an envelope to contain the gas, but the contemplation of the immense entrails of these reptiles supplied me with a solution to the problem. Behold the result!'

He put one hand in the front of his ragged jacket and pointed proudly with the other.

By this time the gas-bag had swollen to a goodly rotundity and was jerking strongly upon its lashings.

'Midsummer madness!' snorted Summerlee.

Lord John was delighted with the whole idea. 'Clever old dear, ain't he?' he whispered to me, and then louder to Challenger, 'What about a car?'

'The car will be my next care. I have already planned how it is to be made and attached. Meanwhile I will simply show you how capable my apparatus is of supporting the weight of each of us.'

'All of us, surely?'

'No, it is part of my plan that each in turn shall descend as in a parachute, and the balloon be drawn back by means which I shall have no difficulty in perfecting. If it will support the weight of one and let him gently down, it will have done all that is required of it. I will now show you its capacity in that direction.'

He brought out a lump of basalt of a considerable size, constructed in the middle so that a cord could be easily attached to it. This cord was the one which we had brought with us on to the plateau after we had used it for climbing the pinnacle. It was over a hundred feet long, and though it was thin it was very strong. He had prepared a sort of collar of leather with many straps depending from it. This collar was placed over the dome of the balloon, and the hanging thongs were gathered together below, so that the pressure of any weight would be diffused over a considerable surface. Then the lump of basalt was fastened to the thongs, and the rope was allowed to hang from the end of it, being passed three times round the Professor's arm.

'I will now,' said Challenger, with a smile of pleased anticipation, 'demonstrate the carrying power of my balloon.' As he said so he cut with a knife the various lashings that held it.

Never was our expedition in more imminent danger of complete annihilation. The inflated membrane shot up with frightful velocity into the air. In an instant Challenger was pulled off his feet and dragged after it. I had just time to throw my arms round his ascending waist when I was myself whipped up into the air. Lord John had me with a rat-trap grip round the legs, but I felt that he also was coming off the ground. For a moment I had a vision of four adventurers floating like a string of sausages over the land that they had explored. But, happily, there were limits to the strain which the rope would stand, though none apparently to the lifting powers of this infernal machine. There was a sharp crack, and we were in a heap upon the ground with coils of rope all over us. When we were able to stagger to our feet we saw far off in the deep blue sky one dark spot where the lump of basalt was speeding upon its way.

'Splendid!' cried the undaunted Challenger, rubbing his injured arm. 'A most thorough and satisfactory demonstration! I could not have anticipated such a success. Within a week, gentlemen, I promise that a second balloon will be prepared, and that you can count upon taking in safety and comfort the first stage of our homeward journey.'

So far I have written each of the foregoing events as it occurred. Now I am rounding off my narrative from the old camp, where Zambo has waited so long, with all our difficulties and dangers left like a dream behind us upon the summit of those vast ruddy crags which tower above our heads. We have descended in safety, though in a most unexpected fashion, and all is well with us. In six weeks or two months we shall be in London, and it is possible that this letter may not reach you much earlier than we do ourselves. Already our hearts yearn and our spirits fly towards the great mother city which holds so much that is dear to us.

It was on the very evening of our perilous adventure with Challenger's home-made balloon that the change came in our fortunes. I have said that the one person from whom we had had some sign of sympathy in our attempts to get away was the young chief whom we had rescued. He alone had no desire to hold us against our will in a strange land. He had told us as much by his expressive language of signs. That evening, after dusk, he came down to our little camp, handed me (for some reason he had always shown his attentions to me, perhaps because I was the one who was nearest his age) a small roll of the bark of a tree, and then pointing solemnly up at the row of caves above him, he had put his finger to his lips as a sign of secrecy and had stolen back again to his people.

I took the slip of bark to the firelight and we examined it together. It was about a foot square, and on the inner side there was a singular arrangement of lines, which I here reproduce:

They were neatly done in charcoal upon the white surface, and looked to me at first sight like some sort of rough musical score.

'Whatever it is, I can swear that it is of importance to us,' said I. 'I could read that on his face as he gave it.'

'Unless we have come upon a primitive practical joker,' Summerlee suggested, 'which I should think would be one of the most elementary developments of man.'

'It is clearly some sort of script,' said Challenger.

'Looks like a guinea puzzle competition,' remarked Lord John, craning his neck to have a look at it. When suddenly he stretched out his hand and seized the puzzle.

'By George!' he cried, 'I believe I've got it. The boy guessed right the very first time. See here! How many marks are on that paper? Eighteen. Well, if you come to think of it there are eighteen cave openings on the hill-side above us.'

'He pointed up to the caves when he gave it to me,' said I.

'Well, that settles it. This is a chart of the caves. What! Eighteen of them all in a row, some short, some deep, some branching, same as we saw them. It's a map, and here's a cross on it. What's the cross for? It is placed to mark one that is much deeper than the others.'

'One that goes through,' I cried.

'I believe our young friend has read the riddle,' said Challenger. 'If the cave does not go through I do not understand why this person, who has every reason to mean us well, should have drawn our attention to it. But if it *does* go through and comes out at the corresponding point on the other side, we should not have more than a hundred feet to descend.'

'A hundred feet!' grumbled Summerlee.

'Well, our rope is still more than a hundred feet long,' I cried. 'Surely we could get down.'

'How about the Indians in the cave?' Summerlee objected.

'There are no Indians in any of the caves above our heads,' said I. 'They are all used as barns and store-houses. Why should we not go up now at once and spy out the land?'

There is a dry bituminous wood upon the plateau – a species of araucaria, according to our botanist – which is always used by the Indians for torches. Each of us picked up a faggot of this, and we made our way up weed-covered steps to the particular cave which was marked in the drawing. It was, as I had said, empty, save for a great number of enormous bats, which flapped round our heads as we advanced into it. As we had no desire to draw the attention of the Indians to our proceedings, we stumbled along in the dark until we had gone round several curves and penetrated a considerable distance into the cavern. Then, at last, we lit our torches. It was a beautiful dry tunnel, with smooth grey walls covered with native symbols, a curved roof which arched over our heads, and white glistening sand beneath our feet. We hurried eagerly along it until, with a deep groan of bitter disappointment, we were brought to a halt. A sheer wall of rock had appeared before us, with no chink through which a mouse could have slipped. There was no escape for us there.

We stood with bitter hearts staring at this unexpected obstacle. It was not the result of any convulsion, as in the case of the ascending tunnel. The end wall was exactly like the side ones. It was, and had always been, a *cul-de-sac*.

'Never mind, my friends,' said the indomitable Challenger. 'You have still my firm promise of a balloon.'

Summerlee groaned.

'Can we be in the wrong cave?' I suggested.

'No use, young fellah,' said Lord John, with his finger on our chart.

'Seventeen from the right and second from the left. This is the cave sure enough.'

I looked at the mark to which his finger pointed, and I gave a sudden cry of joy.

'I believe I have it! Follow me! Follow me!'

I hurried back along the way we had come, my torch in my hand. 'Here,' said I, pointing to some matches upon the ground, 'is where we lit up.'

'Exactly.'

'Well, it is marked as a forked cave, and in the darkness we passed the fork before the torches were lit. On the right side as we go out we should find the longer arm.'

It was as I had said. We had not gone thirty yards before a great black opening loomed in the wall. We turned into it to find that we were in a much larger passage than before. Along it we hurried in breathless impatience for many hundreds of yards. Then, suddenly, in the black darkness of the arch in front of us we saw a gleam of dark red light. We stared in amazement. A sheet of steady flame seemed to cross the passage and to bar our way. We hastened towards it. No sound, no heat, no movement came from it, but still the great luminous curtain glowed before us, silvering all the cave and turning the sand to powdered jewels, until as we drew closer it discovered a circular edge.

'The moon, by George!' cried Lord John. 'We are through, boys! We are through!'

It was indeed the full moon which shone straight down the aperture which opened upon the cliffs. It was a small rift, not larger than a window, but it was enough for all our purposes. As we craned our necks through it we could see that the descent was not a very difficult one, and that the level ground was no very great way below us. It was no wonder that from below we had not observed the place, as the cliffs curved overhead and an ascent at the spot would have seemed so impossible as to discourage close inspection. We satisfied ourselves that with the help of our rope we could find our way down, and then returned, rejoicing, to our camp to make our preparations for the next evening.

What we did we had to do quickly and secretly, since even at this last hour the Indians might hold us back. Our stores we would leave behind us, save only our guns and cartridges. But Challenger had some unwieldy stuff which he ardently desired to take with him, and one particular package, of which I may not speak, which gave us more labour than any. Slowly the day passed, but when the darkness fell we were ready for our departure. With much labour we got our things up the steps, and then, looking back, took one last long survey of that strange land, soon I fear to be vulgarized, the prey of hunter and prospector, but to each of us a dreamland of glamour and romance, a land where we had dared much, suffered much, and learned much – *our* land, as we shall ever fondly call it. Along upon our left the neighbouring caves each threw out its ruddy cheery firelight into the gloom. From the slope below us rose the voices of the Indians as they laughed and sang. Beyond was the long sweep of the woods, and in the centre, shimmering vaguely through the gloom, was the great lake, the mother of strange monsters. Even as we looked a high whickering cry, the call of some weird animal, rang clear out of the darkness. It was the very voice of Maple White Land bidding us goodbye. We turned and plunged into the cave which led to home.

Two hours later, we, our packages, and all we owned, were at the foot of the cliff. Save for Challenger's luggage we had never a difficulty. Leaving it all where we descended, we started at once for Zambo's camp. In the early morning we approached it, but only to find, to our amazement, not one fire but a dozen upon the plain. The rescue party had arrived. There were twenty Indians from the river, with stakes, ropes, and all that could be useful for bridging the chasm. At least we shall have no difficulty now in carrying our packages, when tomorrow we begin to make our way back to the Amazon.

And so, in humble and thankful mood, I close this account. Our eyes have seen great wonders and our souls are chastened by what we have endured. Each is in his own way a better and deeper man. It may be that when we reach Para we shall stop to refit. If we do, this letter will be a mail ahead. If not, it will reach London on the very day that I do. In either case, my dear Mr McArdle, I hope very soon to shake you by the hand.

CHAPTER XVI

A Procession! A Procession!

I should wish to place upon record here our gratitude to all our friends upon the Amazon for the very great kindness and hospitality which was shewn to us upon our return journey. Very particularly would I thank Signor Penalosa and other officials of the Brazilian Government for the special arrangements by which we were helped upon our way, and Signor Pereira of Para, to whose forethought we owe the complete outfit for a decent appearance in the civilized world which we found ready for us at that town. It seemed a poor return for all the courtesy which we encountered that we should deceive our hosts and bene-factors, but under the circumstances we had really no alternative, and I hereby tell them that they will only waste their time and their money if they attempt to follow upon our traces. Even the names have been altered in our accounts, and I am very sure that no one, from the most careful study of them, could come within a thousand miles of our unknown land.

The excitement which had been caused through those parts of South America which we had to traverse was imagined by us to be purely local, and I can assure our friends in England that we had no notion of the uproar which the mere rumour of our experiences had caused through Europe. It was not until the *Ivernia* was within five hundred miles of Southampton that the wireless messages from paper after paper and agency after agency, offering huge prices for a short return message as to our actual results, showed us how strained was the attention not only of the scientific world but of the general public. It was agreed among us, however, that no definite statement should be given to the Press until we had met the members of the Zoological Institute, since as delegates it was our clear duty to give our first report to the body from which we had received our commission of investigation. Thus, although we found Southampton full of Pressmen, we absolutely refused to give any information, which had the natural

effect of focusing public attention upon the meeting which was adver-
tised for the evening of November 7th. For this gathering, the Zoological Hall which had been the scene of the inception of our task was
found to be far too small, and it was only in the Queen's Hall in
Regent Street that accommodation could be found. It is now common
knowledge that the promoters might have ventured upon the Albert
Hall and still found their space too scanty.

It was for the second evening after our arrival that the great meeting
had been fixed. For the first, we had each, no doubt, our own pressing
personal affairs to absorb us. Of mine I cannot yet speak. It may be
that as it stands further from me I may think of it, and even speak of
it, with less emotion. I have shown the reader in the beginning of this
narrative where lay the springs of my action. It is but right, perhaps,
that I should carry on the tale and show also the results. And yet the
day may come when I would not have it otherwise. At least I have
been driven forth to take part in a wondrous adventure, and I cannot
but be thankful to the force that drove me.

And now I turn to the last supreme eventful moment of our
adventure. As I was racking my brain as to how I should best describe
it, my eyes fell upon the issue of my own Journal for the morning of
the 8th of November with the full and excellent account of my friend
and fellow-reporter Macdona. What can I do better than transcribe
his narrative – head-lines and all? I admit that the paper was exuberant
in the matter, out of compliment to its own enterprise in sending a
correspondent, but the other great dailies were hardly less full in their
account. Thus, then, friend Mac in his report:

THE NEW WORLD

GREAT MEETING AT THE QUEEN'S HALL

SCENES OF UPROAR

EXTRAORDINARY INCIDENT

WHAT WAS IT?

NOCTURNAL RIOT IN REGENT STREET

(Special)

'The much-discussed meeting of the Zoological Institute, convened
to hear the report of the Committee of Investigation sent out last year

to South America to test the assertions made by Professor Challenger as to the continued existence of prehistoric life upon that Continent, was held last night in the greater Queen's Hall, and it is safe to say that it is likely to be a red letter date in the history of Science, for the proceedings were of so remarkable and sensational a character that no one present is ever likely to forget them.' (Oh, brother scribe Macdona, what a monstrous opening sentence!) 'The tickets were theoretically confined to members and their friends, but the latter is an elastic term, and long before eight o'clock, the hour fixed for the commencement of the proceedings, all parts of the Great Hall were tightly packed. The general public, however, which most unreasonably entertained a grievance at having been excluded, stormed the doors at a quarter to eight, after a prolonged *mêlée* in which several people were injured, including Inspector Scoble of H Division, whose leg was unfortunately broken. After this unwarrantable invasion, which not only filled every passage, but even intruded upon the space set apart for the Press, it is estimated that nearly five thousand people awaited the arrival of the travellers. When they eventually appeared, they took their places in the front of a platform which already contained all the leading scientific men, not only of this country, but of France and of Germany. Sweden was also represented, in the person of Professor Sergius, the famous Zoologist of the University of Upsala. The entrance of the four heroes of the occasion was the signal for a remarkable demonstration of welcome, the whole audience rising and cheering for some minutes. An acute observer might, however, have detected some signs of dissent amid the applause, and gathered that the proceedings were likely to become more lively than harmonious. It may safely be prophesied, however, that no one could have foreseen the extraordinary turn which they were actually to take.

'Of the appearance of the four wanderers little need be said, since their photographs have for some time been appearing in all the papers. They bear few traces of the hardships which they are said to have undergone. Professor Challenger's beard may be more shaggy, Professor Summerlee's features more ascetic, Lord John Roxton's figure more gaunt, and all three may be burned to a darker tint than when they left our shores, but each appeared to be in most excellent health. As to our own representative, the well-known athlete and international Rugby football player, E. D. Malone, he looks trained to a hair, and as he surveyed the crowd a smile of good-humoured contentment pervaded his honest but homely face.' (All right, Mac, wait till I get you alone!)

'When quiet had been restored and the audience resumed their seats after the ovation which they had given to the travellers, the chairman, the Duke of Durham, addressed the meeting. "He would not," he said, "stand for more than a moment between that vast assembly and the treat which lay before them. It was not for him to anticipate what Professor Summerlee, who was the spokesman of the committee, had to say to them, but it was common rumour that their expedition had been crowned by extraordinary success." (Applause.) "Apparently the age of romance was not dead, and there was common ground upon which the wildest imaginings of the novelist could meet the actual scientific investigations of the searcher for truth. He would only add, before he sat down, that he rejoiced – and all of them would rejoice – that these gentlemen had returned safe and sound from their difficult and dangerous task, for it cannot be denied that any disaster to such an expedition would have inflicted a well-nigh irreparable loss to the cause of zoological science." (Great applause, in which Professor Challenger was observed to join.)

'Professor Summerlee's rising was the signal for another extraordinary outbreak of enthusiasm, which broke out again at intervals throughout his address. That address will not be given *in extenso* in these columns, for the reason that a full account of the whole adventures of the expedition is being published as a supplement from the pen of our own special correspondent. Some general indications will therefore suffice. Having described the genesis of their journey, and paid a handsome tribute to his friend Professor Challenger, coupled with an apology for the incredulity with which his assertions, now fully vindicated, had been received, he gave the actual course of their journey, carefully withholding such information as would aid the public in any attempt to locate this remarkable plateau. Having described, in general terms, their course from the main river up to the time that they actually reached the base of the cliffs, he enthralled his hearers by his account of the difficulties encountered by the expedition in their repeated attempts to mount them, and finally described how they succeeded in their desperate endeavours, which cost the lives of their two devoted half-breed servants. (This amazing reading of the affair was the result of Summerlee's endeavours to avoid raising any questionable matter at the meeting.)

'Having conducted his audience in fancy to the summit, and marooned them there by reason of the fall of their bridge, the Professor proceeded to describe both the horrors and the attractions of that remarkable land. Of personal adventures he said little, but laid stress upon the rich harvest reaped by Science in the observations of the wonderful beast, bird, insect and plant life of the plateau. Peculiarly rich in the coleoptera and in the lepidoptera, forty-six new species of the one and ninety-four of the other had been secured in the course of a few weeks. It was, however, in the larger animals, and especially in the larger animals supposed to have been long extinct, that the interest of the public was naturally centred. Of these he was able to give a goodly list, but had little doubt that it would be largely extended when the place had been more thoroughly investigated. He and his companions had seen at least a dozen creatures, most of them at a distance, which corresponded with nothing at present known to Science. These would in time be duly classified and examined. He instanced a snake, the cast skin of which, deep purple in colour, was fifty-one feet in length, and mentioned a white creature, supposed to be mammalian, which gave forth well-marked phosphorescence in the darkness; also a large black moth, the bite of which was supposed by the Indians to be highly poisonous. Setting aside these entirely new forms of life, the plateau was very rich in known prehistoric forms, dating back in some cases to Early Jurassic times. Among these he mentioned the gigantic and grotesque stegosaurus, seen once by Mr Malone at a drinking-place by the lake, and drawn in the sketch-book of that adventurous American who had first penetrated this unknown world. He described also the iguanodon and the pterodactyl – two of the first of the wonders which they had encountered. He then thrilled the assembly by some account of the terrible carnivorous dinosaurs, which had on more than one occasion pursued members of the party, and which were the most formidable of all the creatures which they had encountered. Thence he passed to the huge and ferocious bird, the phororachus, and to the great elk which still roams upon this upland. It was not, however, until he sketched the mysteries of the central lake that the full interest and enthusiasm of the audience were aroused. One had to pinch oneself to be sure that one was awake as one heard this sane and practical Professor in cold, measured tones describing the monstrous three-eyed fish-lizards and the huge water-snakes which inhabit this enchanted sheet of water. Next he touched upon the Indians, and upon the extraordinary colony of anthropoid apes, which might be looked upon as an advance upon the pithecanthropus of Java, and as coming therefore nearer than any known form to that hypothetical creation, the missing link. Finally he described, amongst some merriment, the ingenious but highly dangerous aeronautic invention of Professor Challenger, and wound up a most memorable address by an account of the methods by which the committee did at last find their way back to civilization.

'It had been hoped that the proceedings would end there, and that a vote of thanks and congratulation, moved by Professor Sergius, of Upsala University, would be duly seconded and carried; but it was soon evident that the course of events was not destined to flow so smoothly. Symptoms of opposition had been evident from time to time during the evening, and now Dr James Illingworth, of Edinburgh, rose in the centre of the hall. Dr Illingworth asked whether an amendment should not be taken before a resolution.

'The Chairman: "Yes, sir, if there must be an amendment."

'Dr Illingworth: "Your Grace, there must be an amendment."

'The Chairman: "Then let us take it at once."

'Professor Summerlee (springing to his feet): "Might I explain, your Grace, that this man is my personal enemy ever since our controversy in the 'Quarterly Journal of Science' as to the true nature of Bathybius?"[1]

'The Chairman: "I fear I cannot go into personal matters. Proceed."

'Dr Illingworth was imperfectly heard in part of his remarks on account of the strenuous opposition of the friends of the explorers. Some attempts were also made to pull him down. Being a man of enormous physique, however, and possessed of a very powerful voice, he dominated the tumult and succeeded in finishing his speech. It was clear, from the moment of his rising, that he had a number of friends and sympathizers in the hall, though they formed a minority in the audience. The attitude of the greater part of the public might be described as one of attentive neutrality.

'Dr Illingworth began his remarks by expressing his high appreciation of the scientific work both of Professor Challenger and of Professor Summerlee. He much regretted that any personal bias should have been read into his remarks, which were entirely dictated by his desire for scientific truth. His position, in fact, was substantially the same as that taken up by Professor Summerlee at the last meeting. At that last meeting Professor Challenger had made certain assertions which had been queried by his colleague. Now this colleague came forward himself with the same assertions and expected them to remain unquestioned. Was this reasonable? ("Yes", "No", and prolonged interruption, during which Professor Challenger was heard from the Press box to ask leave from the chairman to put Dr Illingworth into the street.) A year ago one man said certain things. Now four men said other and more startling ones. Was this to constitute a final proof where the matters in question were of the most revolutionary and incredible character? There had been recent examples of travellers arriving from the unknown with certain tales which had been too readily accepted. Was the London Zoological Institute to place itself in this position? He admitted that the members of the committee were men of character. But human nature was very complex. Even Professors might be misled by the desire for notoriety. Like moths, we all love best to flutter in the light. Heavy-game shots liked to be in a position to cap the tales of their rivals, and journalists were not averse from sensational *coups*, even when imagination had to aid fact in the process. Each member of the committee had his own motive for making the most of his results. ("Shame! shame!") He had no desire to be offensive. ("You are!" and interruption.) The corroboration of these wondrous tales was really of the most slender description. What did it amount to? Some photographs. Was it possible that in this age of ingenious manipulation photographs could be accepted as evidence? What more? We have a story of a flight and a descent by ropes which precluded the production of larger specimens. It was ingenious, but not convincing. It was understood that Lord John Roxton claimed to have the skull of a phororachus. He could only say that he would like to see that skull.

'Lord John Roxton: "Is this fellow calling me a liar?" (Uproar.)

'The Chairman: "Order! order! Dr Illingworth, I must direct you to bring your remarks to a conclusion and to move your amendment."

'Dr Illingworth: "Your Grace, I have more to say, but I bow to your ruling. I move, then, that, while Professor Summerlee be thanked for his interesting address, the whole matter shall be regarded as '*non-proven*', and shall be referred back to a larger, and possibly more reliable Committee of Investigation."

'It is difficult to describe the confusion caused by this amendment. A large section of the audience expressed their indignation at such a slur upon the travellers by noisy shouts of dissent and cries of "Don't put it!" "Withdraw!" "Turn him out!" On the other hand, the malcontents – and it cannot be denied that they were fairly numerous – cheered for the amendment, with cries of "Order!" "Chair!" and "Fair play!" A scuffle broke out in the back benches, and blows were freely exchanged among the medical students who crowded that part of the hall. It was only the moderating influence of the presence of large numbers of ladies which prevented an absolute riot. Suddenly, however, there was a pause, a hush, and then complete silence. Professor Challenger was on his feet. His appearance and manner are peculiarly arresting, and as he raised his hand for order the whole audience settled down expectantly to give him a hearing.

' "It will be within the recollection of many present," said Professor Challenger, "that similar foolish and unmannerly scenes marked the last meeting at which I have been able to address them. On that occasion Professor Summerlee was the chief offender, and though he is now chastened and contrite, the matter could not be entirely forgotten. I have heard tonight similar, but even more offensive, sentiments from the person who has just sat down, and though it is a conscious effort of self-effacement to come down to that person's mental level, I will endeavour to do so, in order to allay any reasonable doubt which could possibly exist in the minds of anyone." (Laughter and interruption.) "I need not remind this audience that, though Professor Summerlee, as the head of the Committee of Investigation, has been put up to speak tonight, still it is I who am the real prime mover in this business, and that it is mainly to me that any successful result must be ascribed. I have safely conducted these three gentlemen to the spot mentioned, and I have, as you have heard, convinced them of the accuracy of my previous account. We had hoped that we should find upon our return that no one was so dense as to dispute our joint conclusions. Warned, however, by my previous experience, I have not come without such proofs as may convince a reasonable man. As explained by Professor Summerlee, our cameras have been tampered with by the ape-men when they ransacked our camp, and most of our negatives ruined." (Jeers, laughter, and "Tell us another!" from the back.) "I have mentioned the ape-men, and I cannot forbear from saying that some of the sounds which now meet my ears bring back most vividly to my recollection my experiences with those interesting creatures." (Laughter.) "In spite of the destruction of so many invaluable negatives, there still remains in our collection a certain number of corroborative photographs showing the conditions of life upon the plateau. Did they accuse them of having forged these photographs?" (A voice, "Yes", and considerable interruption which ended in several men being put out of the hall.) "The negatives were open to the inspection of experts. But what other evidence had they? Under the conditions of their escape it was naturally impossible to bring a large amount of baggage, but they had rescued Professor Summerlee's collections of butterflies and beetles, containing many new species. Was this not evidence?" (Several voices, "No.") "Who said no?"

'Dr Illingworth (rising): "Our point is that such a collection might have been made in other places than a prehistoric plateau." (Applause.)

'Professor Challenger: "No doubt, sir, we have to bow to your scientific authority, although I must admit that the name is unfamiliar. Passing, then, both the photographs and the entomological collection, I come to the varied and accurate information which we bring with us upon points which have never before been elucidated. For example, upon the domestic habits of the pterodactyl – (A voice: "Bosh", and uproar) – I say, that upon the domestic habits of the pterodactyl we can throw a flood of light. I can exhibit to you from my portfolio a picture of that creature taken from life which would convince you – "

'Dr Illingworth: "No picture could convince us of anything."

'Professor Challenger: "You would require to see the thing itself?"

'Dr Illingworth: "Undoubtedly."

'Professor Challenger: "And you would accept that?"

'Dr Illingworth: (Laughing): "Beyond a doubt."

'It was at this point that the sensation of the evening arose – a sensation so dramatic that it can never have been paralleled in the history of scientific gatherings. Professor Challenger raised his hand in the air as a signal, and at once our colleague, Mr E. D. Malone, was observed to rise and to make his way to the back of the platform. An instant later he re-appeared in company of a gigantic negro, the two of them bearing between them a large square packing-case. It was evidently of great weight, and was slowly carried forward and placed in front of the Professor's chair. All sound had hushed in the audience and everyone was absorbed in the spectacle before them. Professor Challenger drew off the top of the case, which formed a sliding lid. Peering down into the box he snapped his fingers several times and was heard from the Press seat to say, "Come, then, pretty, pretty!" in a coaxing voice. An instant later, with a scratching, rattling sound, a most horrible and loathsome creature appeared from below and perched itself upon the side of the case. Even the unexpected fall of the Duke of Durham into the orchestra, which occurred at this moment, could not distract the petrified attention of the vast audience. The face of the creature was like the wildest gargoyle that the imagination of a mad mediaeval builder could have conceived. It was malicious, horrible, with two small red eyes as bright as points of burning coal. Its long, savage mouth, which was held half-open, was full of a double row of sharp-like teeth. Its shoulders were humped, and round them were draped what appeared to be a faded grey shawl. It was the devil of our childhood in person. There was a turmoil in the audience – someone screamed, two ladies in the front row fell senseless from their chairs, and there was a general movement upon the platform to follow their chairman into the orchestra. For a moment there was danger of a general panic. Professor Challenger threw up his hands to still the commotion, but the movement alarmed the creature beside him. Its strange shawl suddenly unfurled, spread, and fluttered as a pair of leathery wings. Its owner grabbed at its legs, but too late to hold it. It had sprung from the perch and was circling slowly round the Queen's Hall with a dry, leathery flapping of its ten-foot wings, while a putrid and insidious odour pervaded the room. The cries of the people in the galleries, who were alarmed at the near approach of those glowing eyes and that murderous beak, excited the creature to a frenzy. Faster and faster it flew, beating against walls and chandeliers in a blind frenzy of alarm. "The window! For heaven's sake shut that window!" roared the Professor from the platform, dancing, and wringing his hands in an agony of apprehension. Alas, his warning was too late! In a moment the creature, beating and bumping along the wall like a huge moth within a gas-shade, came upon the opening, squeezed its hideous bulk through it, and was gone. Professor Challenger fell back into his chair with his face buried in his hands, while the audience gave one long, deep sigh of relief as they realized that the incident was over.

'Then – oh! how shall one describe what took place then – when the full exuberance of the majority and the full reaction of the minority united to make one great wave of enthusiasm, which rolled from the back of the hall, gathering volume as it came, swept over the orchestra, submerged the platform, and carried the four heroes away upon its crest?' (Good for you, Mac!) 'If the audience had done less than justice, surely it made ample amends. Every one was on his feet. Every one was moving, shouting, gesticulating. A dense crowd of cheering men were round the four travellers. "Up with them! up with them!" cried a hundred voices. In a moment four figures shot up above the crowd. In vain they strove to break loose. They were held in their lofty places of honour. It would have been hard to let them down if it had been wished, so dense was the crowd around them. "Regent Street! Regent Street!" sounded the voices. There was a swirl in the packed multitude, and a slow current, bearing the four upon their shoulders, made for the door. Out in the street the scene was extraordinary. An assemblage of not less than a hundred thousand people was waiting. The close-packed throng extended from the other side of the Langham Hotel to

Oxford Circus. A roar of acclamation greeted the four adventurers as they appeared, high above the heads of the people, under the vivid electric lamps outside the hall. "A procession! A procession!" was the cry. In a dense phalanx, blocking the streets from side to side, the crowd set forth, taking the route of Regent Street, Pall Mall, St James's Street, and Piccadilly. The whole central traffic of London was held up, and many collisions were reported between the demonstrators upon the one side and the police and taxi-cabmen upon the other. Finally, it was not until after midnight that the four travellers were released at the entrance to Lord John Roxton's chambers in the Albany, and that the exuberant crowd, having sung "They are Jolly Good Fellows" in chorus, concluded their programme with "God Save the King". So ended one of the most remarkable evenings that London has seen for a considerable time.'

So far my friend Macdona; and it may be taken as a fairly accurate, if florid, account of the proceedings. As to the main incident, it was a bewildering surprise to the audience, but not, I need hardly say, to us. The reader will remember how I met Lord John Roxton upon the very occasion when, in his protective crinoline, he had gone to bring the 'Devil's chick' as he called it, for Professor Challenger. I have hinted also at the trouble which the Professor's baggage gave us when we left the plateau, and had I described our voyage I might have said a good deal of the worry we had to coax with putrid fish the appetite of our filthy companion. If I have not said much about it before, it was, of course, that the Professor's earnest desire was that no possible rumour of the unanswerable argument which we carried should be allowed to leak out until the moment came when his enemies were to be confuted.

One word as to the fate of the London pterodactyl. Nothing can be said to be certain upon this point. There is the evidence of two frightened women that it perched upon the roof of the Queen's Hall and remained there like a diabolical statue for some hours. The next day it came out in the evening papers that Private Miles, of the Coldstream Guards, on duty outside Marlborough House, had deserted his post without leave, and was therefore court-martialled. Private Miles's account, that he dropped his rifle and took to his heels down the Mall because on looking up he had suddenly seen the devil between him and the moon, was not accepted by the Court, and yet it may have a direct bearing upon the point at issue. The only other evidence which I can adduce is from the log of the SS 'Friesland', a Dutch-American liner, which asserts that at nine next morning, Start Point being at the time ten miles upon their starboard quarter, they were passed by something between a flying goat and a monstrous bat, which was heading at a prodigious pace south and west. If its homing instinct led it upon the right line, there can be no doubt that somewhere out in the wastes of the Atlantic the last European pterodactyl found its end.

And Gladys – oh, my Gladys! – Gladys of the mystic lake, now to be re-named the Central, for never shall she have immortality through me. Did I not always see some hard fibre in her nature? Did I not, even at the time when I was proud to obey her behest, feel that it was surely a poor love which could drive a lover to his death or the danger of it? Did I not, in my truest thoughts, always recurring and always dismissed, see past the beauty of the face, and, peering into the soul, discern the twin shadows of selfishness and of fickleness glooming at the back of it? Did she love the heroic and the spectacular for its own noble sake, or was it for the glory which might, without effort or sacrifice, be reflected upon herself? Or are these thoughts the vain wisdom which comes after the event? It was the shock of my life. For a moment it had turned me to a cynic. But already, as I write, a week has passed, and we have had our momentous interview with Lord John Roxton and – well, perhaps things might be worse.

Let me tell it in a few words. No letter or telegram had come to me at Southampton, and I reached the little villa at Streatham about ten o'clock that night in a fever of alarm. Was she dead or alive? Where were all my nightly dreams of the open arms, the smiling face, the words of praise for her man who had risked his life to humour her whim? Already I was down from the high peaks and standing flat-footed upon earth. Yet some good reasons given might still lift me to the clouds once more. I rushed down the garden path, hammered at the door, heard the voice of Gladys within, pushed past the staring maid, and strode into the sitting-room. She was seated in a low settee under the shaded standard lamp by the piano. In three steps I was across the room and had both her hands in mine.

'Gladys!' I cried, 'Gladys!'

She looked up with amazement in her face. She was altered in some subtle way. The expression of her eyes, the hard upward stare, the set of the lips, was new to me. She drew back her hands.

'What do you mean?' she said.

'Gladys!' I cried. 'What is the matter? You are my Gladys, are you not – little Gladys Hungerton?'

'No,' said she, 'I am Gladys Potts. Let me introduce you to my husband.'

How absurd life is! I found myself mechanically bowing and shaking hands with a little ginger-haired man who was coiled up in the deep arm-chair which had once been sacred to my own use. We bobbed and grinned in front of each other.

'Father lets us stay here. We are getting our house ready,' said Gladys.

'Oh, yes,' said I.

'You didn't get my letter at Para, then?'

'No, I got no letter.'

'Oh, what a pity! It would have made all clear.'

'It *is* quite clear,' said I.

'I've told William all about you,' said she. 'We have no secrets. I am so sorry about it. But it couldn't have been so very deep, could it, if you could go off to the other end of the world and leave me here alone. You're not crabby, are you?'

'No, no, not at all. I think I'll go.'

'Have some refreshment,' said the little man, and he added, in a confidential way, 'It's always like this, ain't it? And must be unless you had polygamy, only the other way round; you understand.' He laughed like an idiot, while I made for the door.

I was through it, when a sudden fantastic impulse came upon me, and I went back to my successful rival, who looked nervously at the electric push.

'Will you answer a question?' I asked.

'Well, within reason,' said he.

'How did you do it? Have you searched for hidden treasure, or discovered a pole, or done time on a pirate, or flown the channel, or what? Where is the glamour of romance? How did you get it?'

He stared at me with a hopeless expression upon his vacuous, good-natured, scrubby little face.

'Don't you think all this is a little too personal?' he said.

'Well, just one question,' I cried. 'What are you? What is your profession?'

'I am a solicitor's clerk,' said he. 'Second man at Johnson and Merivale's, 41, Chancery Lane.'

'Goodnight!' said I, and vanished, like all disconsolate and broken-hearted heroes, into the darkness, with grief and rage and laughter all simmering within me like a boiling pot.

One more little scene, and I have done. Last night we all supped at Lord John Roxton's rooms, and sitting together afterwards we smoked in good comradeship and talked our adventures over. It was strange under these altered surroundings to see the old, well-known faces and figures. There was Challenger, with his smile of condescension, his drooping eyelids, his intolerant eyes, his aggressive beard, his huge chest, swelling and puffing as he laid down the law to Summerlee. And Summerlee, too, there he was with his short briar between his thin moustache and his grey goat's-beard, his worn face protruded in eager debate as he queried all Challenger's propositions. Finally, there was our host, with his rugged, eagle face, and his cold, blue, glacier eyes with always a shimmer of devilment and of humour down in the depths of them. Such is the last picture of them that I have carried away.

It was after supper, in his own sanctum – the room of the pink radiance and the innumerable trophies – that Lord John Roxton had something to say to us. From a cupboard he had brought an old cigar-box, and this he laid before him on the table.

'There's one thing,' said he, 'that maybe I should have spoken about before this, but I wanted to know a little more clearly where I was. No use to raise hopes and let them down again. But it's facts, not hopes, with us now. You may remember that day we found the pterodactyl rookery in the swamp – what? Well, somethin' in the lie of the land took my notice. Perhaps it has escaped you, so I will tell you. It was a volcanic vent full of blue clay.'

The Professors nodded.

'Well, now, in the whole world I've only had to do with one place that was a volcanic vent of blue clay. That was the great De Beers Diamond Mine of Kimberley – what? So you see I got diamonds into my head. I rigged up a contraption to hold off those stinking beasts, and I spent a happy day there with a spud.[2] This is what I got.'

He opened his cigar-box, and tilting it over he poured about twenty or thirty rough stones, varying from the size of beans to that of chestnuts, on the table.

'Perhaps you think I should have told you then. Well, so I should, only I know there are a lot of traps for the unwary, and that stones may be of any size and yet of little value where colour and consistency are clean off. Therefore, I brought them back, and on the first day at home I took one round to Spink's, and asked him to have it roughly cut and valued.'

He took a pill-box from his pocket, and spilled out of it a beautiful glittering diamond, one of the finest stones that I have ever seen.

'There's the result,' said he. 'He prices the lot at a minimum of two hundred thousand pounds. Of course it is fair shares between us. I won't hear of anythin' else. Well, Challenger, what will you do with your fifty thousand?'

'If you really persist in your generous view,' said the Professor, 'I should found a private museum, which has long been one of my dreams.'

'And you, Summerlee?'

'I would retire from teaching, and so find time for my final classification of the chalk fossils.'

'I'll use my own,' said Lord John Roxton, 'in fitting a well-formed expedition and having another look at the dear old plateau. As to you, young fellah, you, of course, will spend yours in gettin' married.'

'Not just yet,' said I, with a rueful smile. 'I think, if you will have me, that I would rather go with you.'

Lord Roxton said nothing, but a brown hand was stretched out to me across the table.

THE END

The Poison Belt

Being an account of another adventure of Professor George E.
Challenger, Lord John Roxton, Professor Summerlee, and
Mr E. D. Malone, the discoverers of 'The Lost World'

CONTENTS

'He ran young Alec Simpson, of the Courier, a mile down the high road'

CHAPTER I

The Blurring of the Lines

It is imperative that now at once, while these stupendous events are still clear in my mind, I should set them down with that exactness of detail which time may blur. But even as I do so, I am overwhelmed by the wonder of the fact that it should be our little group of the 'Lost World' – Professor Challenger, Professor Summerlee, Lord John Roxton, and myself – who have passed through this amazing experience.

When, some years ago, I chronicled in the *Daily Gazette* our epoch-making journey in South America, I little thought that it should ever fall to my lot to tell an even stranger personal experience, one which is unique in all human annals, and must stand out in the records of history as a great peak among the humble foothills which surround it. The event itself will always be marvellous, but the circumstances that we four were together at the time of this extraordinary episode came about in a most natural and, indeed, inevitable fashion. I will explain the events which led up to it as shortly and as clearly as I can, though I am well aware that the fuller the detail upon such a subject the more welcome it will be to the reader, for the public curiosity has been and still is insatiable.

It was upon Friday, the twenty-seventh of August – a date for ever memorable in the history of the world – that I went down to the office of my paper and asked for three days' leave of absence from

Mr McArdle, who still presided over our news department. The good old Scotchman shook his head, scratched his dwindling fringe of ruddy fluff, and finally put his reluctance into words.

'I was thinking, Mr Malone, that we could employ you to advantage these days. I was thinking there was a story that you are the only man that could handle as it should be handled.'

'I am sorry for that,' said I, trying to hide my disappointment. 'Of course if I am needed, there is an end of the matter. But the engagement was important and intimate. If I could be spared –'

'Well, I don't see that you can.'

It was bitter, but I had to put the best face I could upon it. After all, it was my own fault, for I should have known by this time that a journalist has no right to make plans of his own.

'Then I'll think no more of it,' said I, with as much cheerfulness as I could assume at so short a notice. 'What was it that you wanted me to do?'

'Well, it was just to interview that deevil of a man down at Rotherfield.'

'You don't mean Professor Challenger?' I cried.

'Aye, it's just him that I do mean. He ran young Alec Simpson, of the *Courier*, a mile down the high road last week by the collar of his coat and the slack of his breeches. You'll have read of it, likely, in the police report. Our boys would as soon interview a loose alligator in the Zoo. But you could do it, I'm thinking – an old friend like you.'

'Why,' said I, greatly relieved, 'this makes it all easy. It so happens that it was to visit Professor Challenger at Rotherfield that I was asking for leave of absence. The fact is, that it is the anniversary of our main adventure on the plateau three years ago, and he has asked our whole party down to his house to see him and celebrate the occasion.'

'Capital!' cried McArdle, rubbing his hands and beaming through his glasses. 'Then you will be able to get his opeenions out of him. In any other man I would say it was all moonshine, but the fellow has made good once, and who knows but he may again!'

'Get what out of him?' I asked. 'What has he been doing?'

'Haven't you seen his letter on "Scientific Possibeelities" in today's *Times*?'

'No.'

McArdle dived down and picked a copy from the floor.

'Read it aloud,' said he, indicating a column with his finger. 'I'd be glad to hear it again, for I am not sure now that I have the man's meaning clear in my head.'

This was the letter which I read to the news editor of the *Gazette*: –

'SCIENTIFIC POSSIBILITIES'

'Sir, – I have read with amusement, not wholly unmixed with some less complimentary emotion, the complacent and wholly fatuous letter of James Wilson MacPhail, which has lately appeared in your columns upon the subject of the blurring of Frauenhofer's lines[1] in the spectra both of the planets and of the fixed stars. He dismisses the matter as of no significance. To a wider intelligence it may well seem of very great possible importance – so great as to involve the ultimate welfare of every man, woman, and child upon this planet. I can hardly hope, by the use of scientific language, to convey any sense of my meaning to those ineffectual people who gather their ideas from the columns of a daily newspaper. I will endeavour, therefore, to condescend to their limitations, and to indicate the situation by the use of a homely analogy which will be within the limits of the intelligence of your readers.'

'Man, he's a wonder – a living wonder!' said McArdle, shaking his head reflectively. 'He'd put up the feathers of a sucking-dove and set up a riot in a Quakers' meeting. No wonder he has made London too hot for him. It's a peety, Mr Malone, for it's a grand brain! Well, let's have the analogy.'

'We will suppose,' I read, 'that a small bundle of connected corks was launched in a sluggish current upon a voyage across the Atlantic. The corks drift slowly on from day to day with the same conditions all round them. If the corks were sentient we could imagine that they would consider these conditions to be permanent and assured. But we, with our superior knowledge, know that many things might happen to surprise the corks. They might possibly float up against a ship, or a sleeping whale, or become tangled in seaweed. In any case, their voyage would probably end by their being thrown up on the rocky coast of Labrador. But what could they know of all this while they drifted so gently day by day in what they thought was a limitless and homogeneous ocean?

'Your readers will possibly comprehend that the Atlantic, in this parable, stands for the mighty ocean of ether[2] through which we drift, and that the bunch of corks represents the little and obscure planetary system to which we belong. A third-rate sun, with its ragtag and bobtail of insignificant satellites, we float under the same daily conditions towards some unknown end, some squalid catastrophe which will overwhelm us at the ultimate confines of space, where we are swept over an etheric Niagara, or dashed upon some unthinkable Labrador. I see no room here for the shallow and ignorant optimism of your correspondent, Mr James Wilson MacPhail, but many reasons why we should watch with a very close and interested attention every indication of change in those cosmic surroundings upon which our own ultimate fate may depend.'

'Man, he'd have made a grand meenister,' said McArdle. 'It just booms like an organ. Let's get doun to what it is that's troubling him.'

'The general blurring and shifting of Frauenhofer's lines of the spectrum point, in my opinion, to a widespread cosmic change of a subtle and singular character. Light from a planet is the reflected light of the sun. Light from a star is a self-produced light. But the spectra both from planets and stars have, in this instance, all undergone the same change. Is it, then, a change in those planets and stars? To me such an idea is inconceivable. What common change could simultaneously come upon them all? Is it a change in our own atmosphere? It is possible, but in the highest degree improbable, since we see no signs of it around us, and chemical analysis has failed to reveal it. What, then, is the third possibility? That it may be a change in the conducting medium, in that infinitely fine ether which extends from star to star and pervades the whole universe. Deep in that ocean we are floating upon a slow current. Might that current not drift us into belts of ether which are novel and have properties of which we have never conceived? There is a change somewhere. This cosmic disturbance of the spectrum proves it. It may be a good change. It may be an evil one. It may be a neutral one. We do not know. Shallow observers may treat the matter as one which can be disregarded, but one who like myself is possessed of the deeper intelligence of the true philosopher will understand that the possibilities of the universe are incalculable and that the wisest man is he who holds himself ready for the unexpected. To take an obvious example, who would undertake to say that the mysterious and universal outbreak of illness, recorded in your columns this very morning as having broken out among the indigenous races of Sumatra, has no connection with some cosmic change to which they may respond more quickly than the more complex peoples of Europe? I throw out the idea for what it is worth. To assert it is, in the present stage, as unprofitable as to deny it, but it is an unimaginative numskull who is too dense to perceive that it is well within the bounds of scientific possibility.

'Yours faithfully,

'GEORGE EDWARD CHALLENGER.

'THE BRIARS, ROTHERFIELD.'

'It's a fine, steemulating letter,' said McArdle, thoughtfully, fitting a cigarette into the long glass tube which he used as a holder. 'What's your opeenion of it, Mr Malone?'

I had to confess my total and humiliating ignorance of the subject at issue. What, for example, were Frauenhofer's lines? McArdle had just been studying the matter with the aid of our tame scientist at the office, and he picked from his desk two of those many-coloured spectral bands which bear a general resemblance to the hat-ribbons of some young and ambitious cricket club. He pointed out to me that there were certain black lines which formed cross-bars upon the series of brilliant colours extending from the red at one end, through gradations of orange, yellow, green, blue, and indigo, to the violet at the other.

'Those dark bands are Frauenhofer's lines,' said he. 'The colours are just light itself. Every light, if you can split it up with a prism, gives the same colours. They tell us nothing. It is the lines that count, because they vary according to what it may be that produces the light. It is these lines that have been blurred instead of clear this last week, and all the astronomers have been quarrelling over the reason. Here's a photograph of the blurred lines for our issue tomorrow. The public have taken no interest in the matter up to now, but this letter of Challenger's in *The Times* will make them wake up, I'm thinking.'

'And this about Sumatra?'

'Well, it's a long cry from a blurred line in a spectrum to a sick nigger in Sumatra. And yet the chiel has shown us once before that he knows what he's talking about. There is some queer illness down yonder, that's beyond all doubt, and today there's a cable just come in from Singapore that the light-houses are out of action in the Straits of Sunda, and two ships on the beach in consequence. Anyhow, it's good enough for you to interview Challenger upon. If you get anything definite, let us have a column by Monday.'

I was coming out from the news editor's room, turning over my new mission in my mind, when I heard my name called from the waiting-room below. It was a telegraph-boy with a wire which had been forwarded from my lodgings at Streatham. The message was from the very man we had been discussing, and ran thus:–

'Malone, 17, Hill Street, Streatham. – Bring oxygen. – CHALLENGER.'

'Bring oxygen!' The Professor, as I remembered him, had an elephantine sense of humour capable of the most clumsy and unwieldy gambollings. Was this one of those jokes which used to reduce him to uproarious laughter, when his eyes would disappear, and he was all gaping mouth and wagging beard, supremely indifferent to the gravity of all around him? I turned the words over, but could make nothing even remotely jocose out of them. Then surely it was a concise order – though a very strange one. He was the last man in the world whose deliberate command I should care to disobey. Possibly some chemical experiment was afoot; possibly – Well, it was no business of mine to speculate upon why he wanted it. I must get it. There was nearly an hour before I should catch the train at Victoria. I took a taxi, and having ascertained the address from the telephone book, I made for the Oxygen Tube Supply Company in Oxford Street.

As I alighted on the pavement at my destination, two youths emerged from the door of the establishment carrying an iron cylinder, which, with some trouble, they hoisted into a waiting motor-car. An elderly man was at their heels scolding and directing in a creaky, sardonic voice. He turned towards me. There was no mistaking those austere features and that goatee beard. It was my old cross-grained companion, Professor Summerlee.

'What!' he cried. 'Don't tell me that *you* have had one of these preposterous telegrams for oxygen?'

I exhibited it.

'Well, well! I have had one, too, and, as you see, very much against the grain, I have acted upon it. Our good friend is as impossible as ever. The need for oxygen could not have been so urgent that he must desert the usual means of supply and encroach upon the time of those who are really busier than himself. Why could he not order it direct?'

I could only suggest that he probably wanted it at once.

'Or thought he did, which is quite another matter. But it is superfluous now for you to purchase any, since I have this considerable supply.'

'Still, for some reason he seems to wish that I should bring oxygen too. It will be safer to do exactly what he tells me.'

Accordingly, in spite of many grumbles and remonstrances from Summerlee, I ordered an additional tube, which was placed with the other in his motor-car, for he had offered me a lift to Victoria.

I turned away to pay off my taxi, the driver of which was very cantankerous and abusive over his fare. As I came back to Professor Summerlee, he was having a furious altercation with the men who had carried down the oxygen, his little white goat's beard jerking with indignation. One of the fellows called him, I remember, 'a silly old bleached cockatoo', which so enraged his chauffeur that he bounded out of his seat to take the part of his insulted master, and it was all we could do to prevent a riot in the street.

These little things may seem trivial to relate, and passed as mere incidents at the time. It is only now, as I look back, that I see their relation to the whole story which I have to unfold.

The chauffeur must, as it seemed to me, have been a novice or else have lost his nerve in this disturbance, for he drove vilely on the way to the station. Twice we nearly had collisions with other equally erratic vehicles, and I remember remarking to Summerlee that the standard of driving in London had very much declined. Once we brushed the

We nearly had collisions with other equally erratic vehicles

very edge of a great crowd which was watching a fight at the corner of the Mall. The people, who were much excited, raised cries of anger at the clumsy driving, and one fellow sprang upon the step and waved a stick above our heads. I pushed him off, but we were glad when we had got clear of them and safe out of the park. These little events, coming one after the other, left me very jangled in my nerves, and I could see from my companion's petulant manner that his own patience had got to a low ebb.

But our good humour was restored when we saw Lord John Roxton waiting for us upon the platform, his tall, thin figure clad in a yellow tweed shooting-suit. His keen face, with those unforgettable eyes, so fierce and yet so humorous, flushed with pleasure at the sight of us. His ruddy hair was shot with grey, and the furrows upon his brow had been cut a little deeper by Time's chisel, but in all else he was the Lord John who had been our good comrade in the past.

'Hullo, Herr Professor! Hullo, young fellah!' he shouted as he came towards us.

He roared with amusement when he saw the oxygen cylinders upon the porter's trolly behind us.

'So you've got them, too!' he cried. 'Mine is in the van. Whatever can the old dear be after?'

'Have you seen his letter in *The Times*?' I asked.

'What was it?'

'Stuff and nonsense!' said Summerlee, harshly.

'Well, it's at the bottom of this oxygen business, or I am mistaken,' said I.

'Stuff and nonsense!' cried Summerlee again, with quite unnecessary violence.

We had all got into a first-class smoker, and he had already lit the short and charred old briar pipe which seemed to singe the end of his long, aggressive nose.

'Friend Challenger is a clever man,' said he, with great vehemence. 'No one can deny it. It's a fool that denies it. Look at his hat. There's a sixty ounce brain inside it – a big engine, running smooth, and turning out clean work. Show me the engine-house and I'll tell you the size of the engine. But he is a born charlatan – you've heard me tell him so to his face – a born charlatan, with a kind of dramatic trick of jumping into the limelight. Things are quiet, so friend Challenger sees a chance to set the public talking about him. You don't imagine that he seriously believes all this nonsense about a change in the ether and a danger to the human race? Was ever such a cock-and-bull story in this life?'

He sat like an old white raven, croaking and shaking with sardonic laughter.

A wave of anger passed through me as I listened to Summerlee. It was disgraceful that he should speak thus of the leader who had been the source of all our fame and given us such an experience as no men have ever enjoyed. I had opened my mouth to utter some hot retort, when Lord John got before me.

'You had a scrap once with old man Challenger,' said he, sternly, 'and you were down and out inside ten seconds. It seems to me, Professor Summerlee, he's beyond your class, and the best you can do with him is to walk wide and leave him alone.'

'Besides,' said I, 'he has been a good friend to every one of us. Whatever his faults may be, he is as straight as a line, and I don't believe he ever speaks evil of his comrades behind their backs.'

'Well said, young fellah my lad,' said Lord John Roxton. Then, with a kindly smile, he slapped Professor Summerlee upon his shoulder. 'Come, Herr Professor, we're not going to quarrel at this time of day. We've seen too much together. But keep off the grass when you get near Challenger, for this young fellah and I have a bit of a weakness for the old dear.'

But Summerlee was in no humour for compromise. His face was screwed up in rigid disapproval, and thick curls of angry smoke rolled up from his pipe.

'As to you, Lord John Roxton,' he creaked, 'your opinion upon a matter of science is of as much value in my eyes as my views upon a new type of shot-gun would be in yours. I have my own judgment, sir, and I use it in my own way. Because it has misled me once, is that any reason why I should accept without criticism anything, however far-fetched, which this man may care to put forward? Are we to have a Pope of science, with infallible decrees laid down *ex cathedrâ*,[3] and accepted without question by the poor humble public? I tell you, sir, that I have a brain of my own, and that I should feel myself to be a snob and a slave if I did not use it. If it pleases you to believe this rigmarole about ether and Frauenhofer's lines upon the spectrum, do so by all means, but do not ask one who is older and wiser than yourself to share in your folly. Is it not evident that if the ether were affected to the degree which he maintains, and if it were obnoxious to human health, the result of it would already be apparent upon ourselves?' Here he laughed with uproarious triumph over his own argument. 'Yes, sir, we should already be very far from our normal selves, and instead of sitting quietly discussing scientific problems in a railway train we should be showing actual symptoms of the poison which was working within us. Where do we see any signs of this poisonous cosmic disturbance? Answer me that, sir! Answer me that! Come, come, no evasion! I pin you to an answer!'

I felt more and more angry. There was something very irritating and aggressive in Summerlee's demeanour.

'I think that if you knew more about the facts you might be less positive in your opinion,' said I.

Summerlee took his pipe from his mouth and fixed me with a stony stare.

'Pray what do you mean, sir, by that somewhat impertinent observation?'

'I mean that when I was leaving the office the news editor told me that a telegram had come in confirming the general illness of the Sumatra natives, and adding that the lights had not been lit in the Straits of Sunda.'

'Really, there should be some limits to human folly!' cried Summerlee, in a positive fury. 'Is it possible that you do not realize that ether, if for a moment we adopt Challenger's preposterous supposition, is a universal substance which is the same here as at the other side of the world? Do you for an instant suppose that there is an English ether and a Sumatran ether? Perhaps you imagine that the ether of Kent is in some way superior to the ether of Surrey, through which this train is now bearing us. There really are no bounds to the credulity and ignorance of the average layman. Is it conceivable that the ether in

Sumatra should be so deadly as to cause total insensibility at the very time when the ether here has had no appreciable effect upon us whatever? Personally, I can truly say that I never felt stronger in body or better balanced in mind in my life.'

'That may be. I don't profess to be a scientific man,' said I, 'though I have heard somewhere that the science of one generation is usually the fallacy of the next. But it does not take much common sense to see that as we seem to know so little about ether it might be affected by some local conditions in various parts of the world, and might show an effect over there which would only develop later with us.'

'With "might" and "may" you can prove anything,' cried Summerlee furiously. 'Pigs may fly. Yes, sir, pigs *may* fly – but they don't. It is not worth arguing with you. Challenger has filled you with his nonsense and you are both incapable of reason. I had as soon lay arguments before those railway cushions.'

'I must say, Professor Summerlee, that your manners do not seem to have improved since I last had the pleasure of meeting you,' said Lord John, severely.

'You lordlings are not accustomed to hear the truth,' Summerlee answered, with a bitter smile. 'It comes as a bit of a shock, does it not, when someone makes you realize that your title leaves you none the less a very ignorant man?'

'Upon my word, sir,' said Lord John, very stern and rigid, 'if you were a younger man you would not dare to speak to me in so offensive a fashion.'

Summerlee thrust out his chin, with its little wagging tuft of goatee beard.

'I would have you know, sir, that, young or old, there has never been a time in my life when I was afraid to speak my mind to an ignorant coxcomb – yes, sir, an ignorant coxcomb, if you had as many titles as slaves could invent and fools could adopt.'

For a moment Lord John's eyes blazed, and then, with a tremendous effort, he mastered his anger and leaned back in his seat with arms folded and a bitter smile upon his face. To me all this was dreadful and deplorable. Like a wave the memory of the past swept over me, the good comradeship, the happy, adventurous days – all that we had suffered and worked for and won. That it should have come to this – to insults and abuse! Suddenly I was sobbing – sobbing in loud, gulping, uncontrollable sobs which refused to be concealed. My companions looked at me in surprise. I covered my face with my hands.

'It's all right,' said I. 'Only – only it *is* such a pity!'

'You're ill, young fellah, that's what's amiss with you,' said Lord John. 'I thought you were queer from the first.'

'Your habits, sir, have not mended in these three years,' said Summerlee, shaking his head. 'I also did not fail to observe your strange manner the moment we met. You need not waste your sympathy, Lord John. These tears are purely alcoholic. The man has been drinking. By the way, Lord John, I called you a coxcomb just now, which was, perhaps, unduly severe. But the word reminds me of a small accomplishment, trivial but amusing, which I used to possess. You know me as the austere man of science. Can you believe that I once had a well-deserved reputation in several nurseries as a farmyard imitator? Perhaps I can help you to pass the time in a pleasant way. Would it amuse you to hear me crow like a cock?'

'No, sir,' said Lord John, who was still greatly offended; 'it would *not* amuse me.'

'My imitation of the clucking hen who had just laid an egg was also considered rather above the average. Might I venture?'

'No, sir, no – certainly not.'

But, in spite of this earnest prohibition, Professor Summerlee laid down his pipe and for the rest of our journey he entertained – or failed to entertain – us by a succession of bird and animal cries which seemed so absurd that my tears were suddenly changed into boisterous laughter, which must have become quite hysterical as I sat opposite this grave Professor and saw him – or rather heard him – in the character of the uproarious rooster or the puppy whose tail had been trodden upon. Once Lord John passed across his newspaper, upon the margin of which he had written in pencil, 'Poor devil! Mad as a hatter.' No doubt it was very eccentric, and yet the performance struck me as extraordinarily clever and amusing.

Whilst this was going on Lord John leaned forward and told me

For the rest of the journey he entertained – or failed to entertain – us by a succession of bird and animal cries

some interminable story about a buffalo and an Indian rajah, which seemed to me to have neither beginning nor end. Professor Summerlee had just begun to chirrup like a canary, and Lord John to get to the climax of his story, when the train drew up at Jarvis Brook, which had been given us as the station for Rotherfield.

And there was Challenger to meet us. His appearance was glorious. Not all the turkey-cocks in creation could match the slow, high-stepping dignity with which he paraded his own railway station, and the benignant smile of condescending encouragement with which he regarded everybody around him. If he had changed in anything since the days of old, it was that his points had become accentuated. The huge head and broad sweep of forehead, with its plastered lock of black hair, seemed even greater than before. His black beard poured forward in a more impressive cascade, and his clear grey eyes, with their insolent and sardonic eyelids, were even more masterful than of yore.

He gave me the amused hand-shake and encouraging smile which the head master bestows upon the small boy, and, having greeted the others and helped to collect their bags and their cylinders of oxygen, he stowed us and them away in a large motor-car which was driven by the same impassive Austin, the man of few words, whom I had seen in the character of butler upon the occasion of my first eventful visit to the Professor. Our journey led us up a winding hill through beautiful country. I sat in front with the chauffeur, but behind me my three comrades seemed to me to be all talking together. Lord John was still struggling with his buffalo story, so far as I could make out, while once again I heard, as of old, the deep rumble of Challenger and the insistent accents of Summerlee, as their brains locked in high and fierce scientific debate. Suddenly Austin slanted his mahogany face towards me without taking his eyes from his steering-wheel.

'I'm under notice,' said he.

'Dear me!' said I.

Everything seemed strange today. Everyone said queer, unexpected things. It was like a dream.

'It's forty-seven times,' said Austin, reflectively.

'When do you go?' I asked, for want of some better observation.

'I don't go,' said Austin.

The conversation seemed to have ended there, but presently he came back to it.

'If I was to go, who would look after 'im?' He jerked his head towards his master. 'Who would 'e get to serve 'im?'

'Someone else,' I suggested, lamely.

'Not 'e. No one would stay a week. If I was to go, that 'ouse would run down like a watch with the mainspring out. I'm telling you because you're 'is friend, and you ought to know. If I was to take 'im at 'is word – but there, I wouldn't have the 'eart. 'E and the missus would be like two babes left out in a bundle. I'm just everything. And then 'e goes and gives me notice.'

'Why would no one stay?' I asked.

'Well, they wouldn't make allowances, same as I do. 'E's a very clever man, the master – so clever that 'e's clean balmy sometimes. I've seen 'im right off 'is onion, and no error. Well, look what 'e did this morning.'

'What did he do?'

Austin bent over to me.

' 'E bit the 'ousekeeper,' said he, in a hoarse whisper.

'Bit her?'

'Yes, sir. Bit 'er on the leg. I saw 'er with my own eyes startin' a Marathon from the 'all-door.'

'Good gracious!'

'So you'd say, sir, if you could see some of the goings-on. 'E don't make friends with the neighbours. There's some of them thinks that when 'e was up among those monsters you wrote about, it was just "'Ome, Sweet 'Ome," for the master, and 'e was never in fitter company. That's what *they* say. But I've served 'im ten years, and I'm fond of 'im, and, mind you, 'e's a great man, when all's said an' done, and it's an honour to serve 'im. But 'e does try one cruel at times. Now look at that, sir. That ain't what you might call old-fashioned 'ospitality, is it now? Just you read it for yourself.'

The car on its lowest speed had ground its way up a steep, curving ascent. At the corner a notice-board peered over a well-clipped hedge.

As Austin said, it was not difficult to read, for the words were few and arresting:–

WARNING

———

**Visitors, Pressmen, and Mendicants
are not encouraged.**

G. E. CHALLENGER

'No, it's not what you might call 'earty,' said Austin, shaking his head and glancing up at the deplorable placard. 'It wouldn't look well in a Christmas-card. I beg your pardon, sir, for I haven't spoke as much as this for many a long year, but today my feelings seem to 'ave got the better of me. 'E can sack me till 'e's blue in the face, but I ain't going, and that's flat. I'm 'is man and 'e's my master, and so it will be, I expect, to the end of the chapter.'

We had passed between the white posts of a gate and up a curving drive, lined with rhododendron bushes. Beyond stood a low brick house, picked out with white woodwork, very comfortable and pretty. Mrs Challenger, a small, dainty, smiling figure, stood in the open doorway to welcome us.

'Well, my dear,' said Challenger, bustling out of the car, 'here are our visitors. It is something new for us to have visitors, is it not? No love lost between us and our neighbours, is there? If they could get rat poison into our baker's cart, I expect it would be there.'

'It's dreadful – dreadful!' cried the lady, between laughter and tears. 'George is always quarrelling with everyone. We haven't a friend on the countryside.'

'It enables me to concentrate my attention upon my incomparable wife,' said Challenger, passing his short, thick arm round her waist. Picture a gorilla and a gazelle, and you have the pair of them. 'Come, come, these gentlemen are tired from the journey, and luncheon should be ready. Has Sarah returned?'

The lady shook her head ruefully, and the Professor laughed loudly and stroked his beard in his masterful fashion.

'Austin,' he cried, 'when you have put up the car you will kindly help your mistress to lay the lunch. Now, gentlemen, will you please step into my study, for there are one or two very urgent things which I am anxious to say to you.'

CHAPTER II

The Tide of Death

As we crossed the hall the telephone-bell rang, and we were the involuntary auditors of Professor Challenger's end of the ensuing dialogue. I say 'we', but no one within a hundred yards could have failed to hear the booming of that monstrous voice, which reverberated through the house. His answers lingered in my mind.

'Yes, yes, of course, it is I. . . . Yes, certainly, *the* Professor Challenger, the famous Professor, who else? . . . Of course, every word of it, otherwise I should not have written it. . . . I shouldn't be surprised. . . . There is every indication of it. . . . Within a day or so at the furthest. . . . Well, I can't help that, can I? . . . Very unpleasant, no doubt, but I rather fancy it will affect more important people than you. There is no use whining about it. . . . No, I couldn't possibly. You must take your chance. . . . That's enough, sir. Nonsense! I have something more important to do than to listen to such twaddle.'

He shut off with a crash and led us upstairs into a large, airy apartment which formed his study. On the great mahogany desk seven or eight unopened telegrams were lying.

'Really,' he said, as he gathered them up, 'I begin to think that it would save my correspondents' money if I were to adopt a telegraphic address. Possibly "Noah, Rotherfield" would be the most appropriate.'

As usual when he made an obscure joke, he leaned against the desk and bellowed in a paroxysm of laughter, his hands shaking so that he could hardly open the envelopes.

'Noah! Noah!' he gasped, with a face of beetroot, while Lord John and I smiled in sympathy, and Summerlee, like a dyspeptic goat, wagged his head in sardonic disagreement. Finally Challenger, still rumbling and exploding, began to open his telegrams. The three of us stood in the bow window and occupied ourselves in admiring the magnificent view.

It was certainly worth looking at. The road in its gentle curves had really brought us to a considerable elevation – seven hundred feet, as we afterwards discovered. Challenger's house was on the very edge of the hill, and from its southern face, in which was the study window, one looked across the vast stretch of the weald to where the gentle curves of the South Downs formed an undulating horizon. In a cleft of the hills a haze of smoke marked the position of Lewes. Immediately at our feet there lay a rolling plain of heather, with the long, vivid green stretches of the Crowborough golf course, all dotted with the players. A little to the south, through an opening in the woods, we could see a section of the main line from London to Brighton. In the immediate foreground, under our very noses, was a small enclosed yard, in which stood the car which had brought us from the station.

An ejaculation from Challenger caused us to turn. He had read his telegrams and had arranged them in a little methodical pile upon his desk. His broad, rugged face, or as much of it as was visible over the matted beard, was still deeply flushed, and he seemed to be under the influence of some strong excitement.

'Well, gentlemen,' he said, in a voice as if he were addressing a public meeting, 'this is indeed an interesting reunion, and it takes place under extraordinary – I may say unprecedented – circumstances. May I ask if you have observed anything upon your journey from town?'

'The only thing which I observed,' said Summerlee, with a sour smile, 'was that our young friend here has not improved in his manners during the years that have passed. I am sorry to state that I have had to seriously complain of his conduct in the train, and I should be wanting in frankness if I did not say that it has left a most unpleasant impression in my mind.'

'Well, well, we all get a bit prosy sometimes,' said Lord John. 'The young fellah meant no real harm. After all, he's an International,[1] so if he takes half an hour to describe a game of football he has more right to do it than most folk.'

'Half an hour to describe a game!' I cried, indignantly. 'Why, it was you that took half an hour with some long-winded story about a buffalo. Professor Summerlee will be my witness.'

'I can hardly judge which of you was the most utterly wearisome,' said Summerlee. 'I declare to you, Challenger, that I never wish to hear of football or of buffaloes so long as I live.'

'I have never said one word today about football,' I protested.

Lord John gave a shrill whistle, and Summerlee shook his head sadly.

'So early in the day, too,' said he. 'It is indeed deplorable. As I sat there in sad but thoughtful silence –'

'In silence!' cried Lord John. 'Why, you were doin' a music-hall turn of imitations all the way – more like a runaway gramophone than a man.'

Summerlee drew himself up in bitter protest.

'You are pleased to be facetious, Lord John,' said he, with a face of vinegar.

'Why, dash it all, this is clear madness,' cried Lord John. 'Each of us seems to know what the others did and none of us knows what he did himself. Let's put it all together from the first. We got into a first-class smoker, that's clear, ain't it? Then we began to quarrel over friend Challenger's letter in *The Times*.'

'Oh, you did, did you?' rumbled our host, his eyelids beginning to droop.

'You said, Summerlee, that there was no possible truth in his contention.'

'Dear me!' said Challenger, puffing out his chest and stroking his beard. 'No possible truth! I seem to have heard the words before. And may I ask with what arguments the great and famous Professor Summerlee proceeded to demolish the humble individual who had ventured to express an opinion upon a matter of scientific possibility? Perhaps before he exterminates that unfortunate nonentity he will condescend to give some reasons for the adverse views which he has formed.'

He bowed and shrugged and spread open his hands as he spoke with his elaborate and elephantine sarcasm.

'The reason was simple enough,' said the dogged Summerlee. 'I contended that, if the ether surrounding the earth was so toxic in one quarter that it produced dangerous symptoms, it was hardly likely that we three in the railway carriage should be entirely unaffected.'

The explanation only brought uproarious merriment from Challenger. He laughed until everything in the room seemed to rattle and quiver.

'Our worthy Summerlee is, not for the first time, somewhat out of touch with the facts of the situation,' said he at last, mopping his heated brow. 'Now, gentlemen, I cannot make my point better than by detailing to you what I have myself done this morning. You will the more easily condone any mental aberration upon your own part when you realize that even I have had moments when my balance has been disturbed. We have had for some years in this household a housekeeper – one Sarah, with whose second name I have never attempted to burden my memory. She is a woman of a severe and forbidding aspect, prim and demure in her bearing, very impassive in her nature, and never known within our experience to show signs of any emotion. As I sat alone at my breakfast – Mrs Challenger is in the habit of keeping to her room of a morning – it suddenly entered my head that it would be entertaining and instructive to see whether I could find any limits to this woman's imperturbability. I devised a simple but effective experiment. Having upset a small vase of flowers which stood in the centre of the cloth, I rang the bell and slipped under the table. She entered, and, seeing the room empty, imagined that I had withdrawn to the study. As I had expected, she approached and leaned over the table to replace the vase. I had a vision of a cotton stocking and an elastic-sided boot. Protruding my head, I sank my teeth into the calf of her leg. The experiment was successful beyond belief. For some moments she stood paralysed, staring down at my head. Then with a shriek she tore herself free and rushed from the room. I pursued her with some thoughts of an explanation, but she flew down the drive, and some minutes afterwards I was able to pick her out with my field-glasses travelling very rapidly in a south-westerly direction. I tell you the anecdote for what it is worth. I drop it into your brains and await its germination. Is it illuminative? Has it conveyed anything to your minds? What do *you* think of it, Lord John?'

Lord John shook his head gravely.

'You'll be gettin' into serious trouble some of these days if you don't put a brake on,' said he.

'Perhaps you have some observation to make, Summerlee?'

'You should drop all work instantly, Challenger, and take three months in a German watering-place,' said he.

'Profound! profound!' cried Challenger. 'Now, my young friend, is it possible that wisdom may come from you where your seniors have so signally failed?'

And it did. I say it with all modesty, but it did. Of course, it all seems obvious enough to you who know what occurred, but it was not so very clear when everything was new. But it came on me suddenly with the full force of absolute conviction.

'Poison!' I cried.

Then, even as I said the word, my mind flashed back over the whole morning's experiences, past Lord John with his buffalo, past my own hysterical tears, past the outrageous conduct of Professor Summerlee, to the queer happenings in London, the row in the park, the driving of the chauffeur, the quarrel at the oxygen warehouse. Everything fitted suddenly into its place.

'Of course,' I cried again. 'It is poison. We are all poisoned.'

'Exactly,' said Challenger, rubbing his hands; 'we are all poisoned. Our planet has swum into the poison belt of ether, and is now flying deeper into it at the rate of some millions of miles a minute. Our young friend has expressed the cause of all our troubles and perplexities in a single word, "Poison".'

We looked at each other in amazed silence. No comment seemed to meet the situation.

'There is a mental inhibition by which such symptoms can be checked and controlled,' said Challenger. 'I cannot expect to find it developed in all of you to the same point which it has reached in me, for I suppose that the strength of our different mental processes bears some proportion to each other. But no doubt it is appreciable even in our young friend here. After the little outburst of high spirits which so alarmed my domestic I sat down and reasoned with myself. I put it to myself that I had never before felt impelled to bite any of my household. The impulse had then been an abnormal one. In an instant I perceived the truth. My pulse upon examination was ten beats above the usual, and my reflexes were increased. I called upon my higher and saner self, the real G. E. C., seated serene and impregnable behind all mere molecular disturbance. I summoned him, I say, to watch the foolish mental tricks which the poison would play. I found that I was indeed the master. I could recognize and control a disordered mind. It was a remarkable exhibition of the victory of mind over matter, for it was a victory over that particular form of matter which is most intimately connected with mind. I might almost say that mind was at fault, and that personality controlled it. Thus, when my wife came downstairs and I was impelled to slip behind the door and alarm her by some wild cry as she entered, I was able to stifle the impulse and to greet her with dignity and restraint. An overpowering desire to quack like a duck was met and mastered in the same fashion. Later, when I descended to order the car and found Austin bending over it absorbed in repairs, I controlled my open hand even after I had lifted it, and refrained from giving him an experience which would possibly have caused him to follow in the steps of the housekeeper. On the contrary, I touched him on the shoulder and ordered the car to be at the door in time to meet your train. At the present instant I am most forcibly tempted to take Professor Summerlee by that silly old beard of his, and to shake his head violently backwards and forwards. And yet, as you see, I am perfectly restrained. Let me commend my example to you.'

'I'll look out for that buffalo,' said Lord John.

'And I for the football match.'

'It may be that you are right, Challenger,' said Summerlee, in a chastened voice. 'I am willing to admit that my turn of mind is critical rather than constructive, and that I am not a ready convert to any new theory, especially when it happens to be so unusual and fantastic as this one. However, as I cast my mind back over the events of the morning, and as I reconsider the fatuous conduct of my companions, I find it easy to believe that some poison of an exciting kind was responsible for their symptoms.'

Challenger slapped his colleague good-humouredly upon the shoulder. 'We progress,' said he. 'Decidedly we progress.'

'And pray, sir,' asked Summerlee, humbly, 'what is your opinion as to the present outlook?'

'With your permission I will say a few words upon that subject.' He seated himself upon his desk, his short, stumpy legs swinging in front of him. 'We are assisting at a tremendous and awful function. It is, in my opinion, the end of the world.'

The end of the world! Our eyes turned to the great bow-window and we looked out at the summer beauty of the countryside, the long slopes of heather, the great country houses, the cosy farms, the pleasure-seekers upon the links. The end of the world! One had often heard the words, but the idea that they could ever have an immediate practical significance, that it should not be at some vague date, but now, today, that was a tremendous, a staggering thought. We were all struck solemn and waited in silence for Challenger to continue. His overpowering presence and appearance lent such force to the solemnity of his words that for a moment all the crudities and absurdities of the man vanished, and he loomed before us as something majestic and beyond the range of ordinary humanity. Then to me, at least, there came back the cheering recollection of how twice since we had entered the room he had roared with laughter. Surely, I thought, there are limits to mental detachment. The crisis cannot be so great or so pressing, after all.

'You will conceive a bunch of grapes,' said he, 'which are covered by some infinitesimal but noxious bacillus. The gardener passes it through a disinfecting medium. It may be that he desires his grapes to be cleaner. It may be that he needs space to breed some fresh bacillus less noxious than the last. He dips it into the poison and they are gone. Our Gardener is, in my opinion, about to dip the solar system, and the human bacillus, the little mortal vibrio[2] which twisted and wriggled upon the outer rind of the earth, will in an instant be sterilized out of existence.'

'It is, in my opinion, the end of the world'

Again there was silence. It was broken by the high trill of the telephone-bell.

'There is one of our bacilli squeaking for help,' said he, with a grim smile. 'They are beginning to realize that their continued existence is not really one of the necessities of the Universe.'

He was gone from the room for a minute or two. I remember that none of us spoke in his absence. The situation seemed beyond all words or comments.

'The medical officer of health for Brighton,' said he, when he returned. 'The symptoms are for some reason developing more rapidly upon the sea-level. Our seven hundred feet of elevation give us an advantage. Folk seem to have learned that I am the first authority upon the question. No doubt it comes from my letter in *The Times*. That was the mayor of a provincial town with whom I talked when we first arrived. You may have heard me upon the telephone. He seemed to put an entirely inflated value upon his own life. I helped him to re-adjust his ideas.'

Summerlee had risen and was standing by the window. His thin, bony hands were trembling with his emotion.

'Challenger,' said he, earnestly, 'this thing is too serious for mere futile argument. Do not suppose that I desire to irritate you by any question I may ask. But I put it to you whether there may not be some fallacy in your information or in your reasoning. There is the sun shining as brightly as ever in a blue sky. There are the heather and the flowers and the birds. There are the folk enjoying themselves upon the golf-links, and the labourers yonder cutting the corn. You tell us that they and we may be upon the very brink of destruction – that this sunlit day may be that day of doom which the human race has so long awaited. So far as we know, you found this tremendous judgment upon what? Upon some abnormal lines in a spectrum – upon rumours from Sumatra – upon some curious personal excitement which we have discerned in each other. This latter symptom is not so marked but that you and we could, by a deliberate effort, control it. You need not stand on ceremony with us, Challenger. We have all faced death together before now. Speak out, and let us know exactly where we stand, and what, in your opinion, are our prospects for our future.'

It was a brave, good speech, a speech from that staunch and strong spirit which lay behind all the acidities and angularities of the old zoologist. Lord John rose and shook him by the hand.

'My sentiment to a tick,' said he. 'Now, Challenger, it's up to you to tell us where we are. We ain't nervous folk, as you know well; but when it comes to makin' a week-end visit and finding you've run full butt into the Day of Judgment, it wants a bit of explainin'. What's the danger, and how much of it is there, and what are we goin' to do to meet it?'

He stood, tall and strong, in the sunshine at the window, with his brown hand upon the shoulder of Summerlee. I was lying back in an arm-chair, an extinguished cigarette between my lips, in that sort of half-dazed state in which impressions become exceedingly distinct. It may have been a new phase of the poisoning, but the delirious promptings had all passed away, and were succeeded by an exceedingly languid and, at the same time, perceptive state of mind. I was a spectator. It did not seem to be any personal concern of mine. But here were three strong men at a great crisis, and it was fascinating to observe them. Challenger bent his heavy brows and stroked his beard before he answered. One could see that he was very carefully weighing his words.

'What was the last news when you left London?' he asked.

'I was at the *Gazette* office about ten,' said I. 'There was a Reuter just come in from Singapore to the effect that the sickness seemed to be universal in Sumatra, and that the lighthouses had not been lit in consequence.'

'Events have been moving somewhat rapidly since then,' said Challenger, picking up his pile of telegrams. 'I am in close touch both with the authorities and with the Press, so that news is converging upon me from all parts. There is, in fact, a general and very insistent demand that I should come to London; but I see no good end to be served. From the accounts the poisonous effect begins with mental excitement; the rioting in Paris this morning is said to have been very violent, and the Welsh colliers are in a state of uproar. So far as the evidence to hand can be trusted, this stimulative stage, which varies much in races and in individuals, is succeeded by a certain exaltation and mental lucidity – I seem to discern some signs of it in our young friend here – which, after an appreciable interval, turns to coma, deepening rapidly into death. I fancy, so far as my toxicology carries me, that there are some vegetable nerve poisons –'

'Datura,'[3] suggested Summerlee.

'Excellent!' cried Challenger. 'It would make for scientific precision if we named our toxic agent. Let it be daturon. To you, my dear Summerlee, belongs the honour – posthumous, alas! but none the less unique – of having given a name to the universal destroyer, the great Gardener's disinfectant. The symptoms of daturon, then, may be taken to be such as I indicate. That it will involve the whole world and that no life can possibly remain behind seems to me to be certain, since ether is a universal medium. Up to now it has been capricious in the places which it has attacked, but the difference is only a matter of a few hours, and it is like an advancing tide which covers one strip of sand and then another, running hither and thither in irregular streams, until at last it has submerged it all. There are laws at work in connection with the action and distribution of daturon which would have been of deep interest had the time at our disposal permitted us to study them. So far as I can trace them' – here he glanced over his telegrams – 'the less developed races have been the first to respond to its influence. There are deplorable accounts from Africa, and the Australian aborigines appear to have been already exterminated. The Northern races have as yet shown greater resisting power than the Southern. This, you see, is dated from Marseilles at nine-forty-five this morning. I give it to you verbatim: –

' "All night delirious excitement throughout Provence. Tumult of vine growers at Nîmes. Socialistic upheaval at Toulon. Sudden illness attended by coma attacked population this morning. *Peste foudroyant*.[4] Great numbers of dead in the streets. Paralysis of business and universal chaos."

'An hour later came the following, from the same source: –

' "We are threatened with utter extermination. Cathedrals and churches full to overflowing. The dead outnumber the living. It is inconceivable and horrible. Decease seems to be painless, but swift and inevitable."

'There is a similar telegram from Paris, where the development is not yet as acute. India and Persia appear to be utterly wiped out. The Slavonic population of Austria is down, while the Teutonic has hardly been affected. Speaking generally, the dwellers upon the plains and upon the seashore seem, so far as my limited information goes, to have felt the effects more rapidly than those inland or on the heights. Even a little elevation makes a considerable difference, and perhaps if there be a survivor of the human race, he will again be found upon the summit of some Ararat.[5] Even our own little hill may presently prove to be a temporary island amid a sea of disaster. But at the present rate of advance a few short hours will submerge us all.'

Lord John Roxton wiped his brow.

'What beats me,' said he, 'is how you could sit there laughin' with that stack of telegrams under your hand. I've seen death as often as most folk; but universal death – it's awful!'

'As to the laughter,' said Challenger, 'you will bear in mind that, like yourselves, I have not been exempt from the stimulating cerebral effects of the etheric poison. But as to the horror with which universal death appears to inspire you, I would put it to you that it is somewhat exaggerated. If you were sent to sea alone in an open boat to some unknown destination, your heart might well sink within you. The isolation, the uncertainty, would oppress you. But if your voyage were made in a goodly ship, which bore within it all your relations and your friends, you would feel that, however uncertain your destination might still remain, you would at least have one common and simultaneous experience which would hold you to the end in the same close communion. A lonely death may be terrible, but a universal one, as painless as this would appear to be, is not, in my judgment, a matter for apprehension. Indeed, I could sympathize with the person who took the view that the horror lay in the idea of surviving when all that is learned, famous, and exalted had passed away.'

'What, then, do you propose to do?' asked Summerlee, who had for once nodded his assent to the reasoning of his brother scientist.

'To take our lunch,' said Challenger, as the boom of a gong sounded through the house. 'We have a cook whose omelettes are only excelled by her cutlets. We can but trust that no cosmic disturbance has dulled

'Cathedrals and churches full to overflowing. The dead outnumber the living'

her excellent abilities. My Scharzberger of '96 must also be rescued, so far as our earnest and united efforts can do it, from what would be a deplorable waste of a great vintage.' He levered his great bulk off the desk, upon which he had sat while he announced the doom of the planet. 'Come,' said he. 'If there is little time left, there is the more need that we should spend it in sober and reasonable enjoyment.'

And, indeed, it proved to be a very merry meal. It is true that we could not forget our awful situation. The full solemnity of the event loomed ever at the back of our minds and tempered our thoughts. But surely it is the soul which has never faced Death which shies strongly from it at the end. To each of us men it had, for one great epoch in our lives, been a familiar presence. As to the lady, she leaned upon the strong guidance of her mighty husband and was well content to go whither his path might lead. The future was with Fate. The present was our own. We passed it in goodly comradeship and gentle merriment. Our minds were, as I have said, singularly lucid. Even I struck sparks at times. As to Challenger, he was wonderful! Never have I so realized the elemental greatness of the man, the sweep and power of his understanding. Summerlee drew him on with his chorus of subacid criticism, while Lord John and I laughed at the contest; and the lady, her hand upon his sleeve, controlled the bellowings of the philosopher. Life, death, fate, the destiny of man – these were the stupendous subjects of that memorable hour, made vital by the fact that as the meal progressed strange, sudden exaltations in my mind and tinglings in my limbs proclaimed that the invisible tide of Death was slowly and gently rising around us. Once I saw Lord John put his hand suddenly to his eyes, and once Summerlee dropped back for an instant in his chair. Each breath we breathed was charged with strange forces. And yet our minds were happy and at ease. Presently Austin laid the cigarettes upon the table and was about to withdraw.

'Austin!' said his master.

'Yes, sir?'

'I thank you for your faithful service.'

A smile stole over the servant's gnarled face.

'I've done my duty, sir.'

'I'm expecting the end of the world today, Austin.'

'Yes, sir. What time, sir?'

'I can't say, Austin. Before evening.'

'Very good, sir.'[6]

The taciturn Austin saluted and withdrew. Challenger lit a cigarette, and, drawing his chair closer to his wife's, he took her hand in his.

'You know how matters stand, dear,' said he. 'I have explained it also to our friends here. You're not afraid, are you?'

'It won't be painful, George?'

'No more than laughing-gas[7] at the dentist's. Every time you have had it you have practically died.'

'But that is a pleasant sensation.'

'So may death be. The worn-out bodily machine can't record its impression, but we know the mental pleasure which lies in a dream or a trance. Nature may build a beautiful door and hang it with many a gauzy and shimmering curtain to make an entrance to the new life for our wondering souls. In all my probings of the actual, I have always found wisdom and kindness at the core; and if ever the frightened mortal needs tenderness, it is surely as he makes the passage perilous from life to life. No, Summerlee, I will have none of your materialism,[8] for I, at least, am too great a thing to end in mere physical constituents, a packet of salts and three bucketfuls of water. Here – here' – and he beat his great head with his huge, hairy fist – 'there is something which uses matter, but is not of it – something which might destroy death, but which Death can never destroy.'

'Talkin' of death,' said Lord John. 'I'm a Christian of sorts, but it seems to me there was somethin' mighty natural in those ancestors of ours, who were buried with their axes and bows and arrows and the like, same as if they were livin' on just the same as they used to. I don't know,' he added, looking round the table in a shamefaced way, 'that I wouldn't feel more homely myself if I was put away with my old .450 Express and the fowlin'-piece, the shorter one with the rubbered stock, and a clip or two of cartridges – just a fool's fancy, of course, but there it is. How does it strike you, Herr Professor?'

'Well,' said Summerlee, 'since you ask my opinion, it strikes me as an indefensible throwback to the Stone Age or before it. I'm of the twentieth century myself, and would wish to die like a reasonable civilized man. I don't know that I am more afraid of death than the rest of you, for I am an oldish man, and, come what may, I can't have very much longer to live; but it is all against my nature to sit waiting without a struggle like a sheep for the butcher. Is it quite certain, Challenger, that there is nothing we can do?'

'To save us – nothing,' said Challenger. 'To prolong our lives a few hours, and thus to see the evolution of this mighty tragedy before we are actually involved in it – that may prove to be within my powers. I have taken certain steps –'

'The oxygen?'

'Exactly. The oxygen.'

'But what can oxygen effect in the face of a poisoning of the ether? There is not a greater difference in quality between a brick-bat and a gas than there is between oxygen and ether. They are different planes of matter. They cannot impinge upon one another. Come, Challenger, you could not defend such a proposition.'

'My good Summerlee, this etheric poison is most certainly influenced by material agents. We see it in the methods and distribution of the outbreak. We should not *a priori* have expected it, but it is undoubtedly a fact. Hence I am strongly of opinion that a gas like oxygen, which increases the vitality and the resisting power of the body, would be extremely likely to delay the action of what you have so happily named the daturon. It may be that I am mistaken, but I have every confidence in the correctness of my reasoning.'

'Well,' said Lord John, 'if we've got to sit suckin' at those tubes like so many babies with their bottles, I'm not takin' any.'

'There will be no need for that,' Challenger answered. 'We have made arrangements – it is to my wife that you chiefly owe it – that her boudoir shall be made as airtight as is practicable. With matting and varnished paper –'

'Good heavens, Challenger, you don't suppose you can keep out ether with varnished paper?'

'Really, my worthy friend, you are a trifle perverse in missing the point. It is not to keep out the ether that we have gone to such trouble. It is to keep in the oxygen. I trust that if we can ensure an atmosphere hyper-oxygenated to a certain point, we may be able to retain our senses. I had two tubes of the gas and you have brought me three more. It is not much, but it is something.'

'How long will they last?'

'I have not an idea. We will not turn them on until our symptoms become unbearable. Then we shall dole the gas out as it is urgently needed. It may give us some hours, possibly even some days, on which we may look out upon a blasted world. Our own fate is delayed to that extent, and we will have the very singular experience, we five, of being, in all probability, the absolute rearguard of the human race upon its march into the unknown. Perhaps you will be kind enough now to give me a hand with the cylinders. It seems to me that the atmosphere already grows somewhat more oppressive.'

CHAPTER III

Submerged

The chamber which was destined to be the scene of our unforgettable experience was a charmingly feminine sitting-room, some fourteen or sixteen feet square. At the end of it, divided by a curtain of red velvet, was a small apartment which formed the Professor's dressing-room. This in turn opened into a large bedroom. The curtain was still hanging, but the boudoir and dressing-room could be taken as one chamber for the purposes of our experiment. One door and the window-frame had been plastered round with varnished paper, so as to be practically sealed. Above the other door, which opened on to the landing, there hung a fanlight which could be drawn by a cord when some ventilation became absolutely necessary. A large shrub in a tub stood in each corner.

'How to get rid of our excessive carbonic dioxide without unduly wasting our oxygen is a delicate and vital question,' said Challenger, looking round him after the five iron tubes had been laid side by side against the wall. 'With longer time for preparation I could have brought the whole concentrated force of my intelligence to bear more fully upon the problem, but as it is we must do what we can. The shrubs will be of some small service. Two of the oxygen tubes are ready to be turned on at an instant's notice, so that we cannot be taken unawares. At the same time, it would be well not to go far from the room, as the crisis may be a sudden and urgent one.'

There was a broad, low window opening out upon a balcony. The view beyond was the same as that which we had already admired from the study. Looking out, I could see no sign of disorder anywhere. There was a road curving down the side of the hill, under my very eyes. A cab from the station, one of those prehistoric survivals which are only to be found in our country villages, was toiling slowly up the hill. Lower down was a nurse-girl, wheeling a perambulator and leading a second child by the hand. The blue reeks of smoke from the cottages gave the whole widespread landscape an air of settled order and homely comfort. Nowhere in the blue heaven or on the sunlit earth was there any foreshadowing of a catastrophe. The harvesters were back in the fields once more and the golfers, in pairs and fours, were still streaming round the links. There was so strange a turmoil within my own head, and such a jangling of my overstrung nerves, that the indifference of these people was amazing.

'Those fellows don't seem to feel any ill effects,' said I, pointing down at the links.

'Have you played golf?' asked Lord John.

'No, I have not.'

'Well, young fellah, when you do you'll learn that once fairly out on a round, it would take the crack of doom to stop a true golfer. Halloa! There's that telephone-bell again.'

From time to time during and after lunch the high, insistent ring had summoned the Professor. He gave us the news as it came through to him in a few curt sentences. Such terrific items had never been registered in the world's history before. The great shadow was creeping up from the South like a rising tide of death. Egypt had gone through its delirium and was now comatose. Spain and Portugal, after a wild frenzy in which the Clericals and the Anarchists[1] had fought most

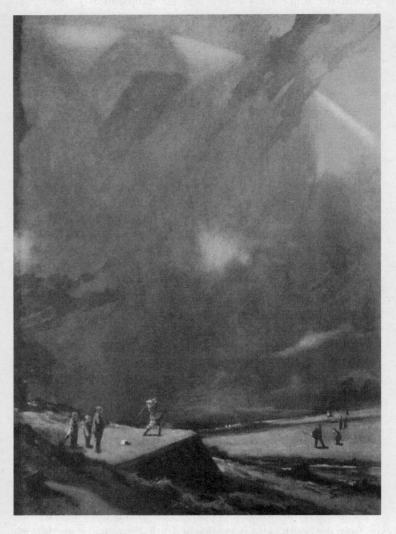

'Once fairly out on a round, it would take the crack of doom to stop a true golfer'

desperately, were now fallen silent. No cable messages were received any longer from South America. In North America the Southern States, after some terrible racial rioting, had succumbed to the poison. North of Maryland the effect was not yet marked, and in Canada it was hardly perceptible. Belgium, Holland, and Denmark had each in turn been affected. Despairing messages were flashing from every quarter to the great centres of learning, to the chemists and the doctors of world-wide repute, imploring their advice. The astronomers, too, were deluged with inquiries. Nothing could be done. The thing was universal and beyond our human knowledge or control. It was death – painless but inevitable – death for young and old, for weak and strong, for rich and poor, without hope or possibility of escape. Such was the news which, in scattered, distracted messages, the telephone had brought us. The great cities already knew their fate, and so far as we could gather were preparing to meet it with dignity and resignation. Yet here were our golfers and labourers like the lambs who gambol under the shadow of the knife. It seemed amazing. And yet how could they know? It had all come upon us in one giant stride. What was there in the morning paper to alarm them? And now it was but three in the afternoon. Even as we looked some rumour seemed to have spread, for we saw the reapers hurrying from the fields. Some of the golfers were returning to the club-house. They were running as if taking refuge from a shower. Their little caddies trailed behind them. Others were continuing their game. The nurse had turned and was pushing her perambulator hurriedly up the hill again. I noticed that she had her hand to her brow. The cab had stopped and the tired horse, with his head sunk to his knees, was resting. Above there was a perfect summer sky – one huge vault of unbroken blue, save for a few fleecy white clouds over the distant downs. If the human race must die today, it was at least upon a glorious deathbed. And yet all that gentle loveliness of Nature made this terrific and wholesale destruction the more pitiable and awful. Surely it was too goodly a residence that we should be so swiftly, so ruthlessly, evicted from it!

But I have said that the telephone-bell had rung once more. Suddenly I heard Challenger's tremendous voice from the hall.

'Malone!' he cried. 'You are wanted.'

I rushed down to the instrument. It was McArdle speaking from London.

'That you, Mr Malone?' cried his familiar voice. 'Mr Malone, there are terrible goings-on in London. For God's sake, see if Professor Challenger can suggest anything that can be done.'

'He can suggest nothing, sir,' I answered. 'He regards the crisis as universal and inevitable. We have some oxygen here, but it can only defer our fate for a few hours.'

'Oxygen!' cried the agonized voice. 'There is no time to get any. The office has been a perfect pandemonium ever since you left in the morning. Now half of the staff are insensible. I am weighed down with heaviness myself. From my window I can see the people lying thick in Fleet Street. The traffic is all held up. Judging by the last telegrams, the whole world –'

His voice had been sinking, and suddenly stopped. An instant later I heard through the telephone a muffled thud, as if his head had fallen forward on the desk.

'Mr McArdle!' I cried. 'Mr McArdle!'

There was no answer. I knew as I replaced the receiver that I should never hear his voice again.

At that instant, just as I took a step backwards from the telephone, the thing was on us. It was as if we were bathers, up to our shoulders in water, who suddenly are submerged by a rolling wave. An invisible hand seemed to have quietly closed round my throat and to be gently pressing the life from me. I was conscious of immense oppression upon my chest, great tightness within my head, a loud singing in my ears, and bright flashes before my eyes. I staggered to the balustrades of the stair. At the same moment, rushing and snorting like a wounded buffalo, Challenger dashed past me, a terrible vision, with red-purple face, engorged eyes, and bristling hair. His little wife, insensible to all appearance, was slung over his great shoulder, and he blundered and thundered up the stair, scrambling and tripping, but carrying himself and her through sheer will-force through that mephitic atmosphere to the haven of temporary safety. At the sight of his effort I too rushed up the steps, clambering, falling, clutching at the rail, until I tumbled half senseless upon my face on the upper landing. Lord John's fingers of steel were in the collar of my coat, and a moment later I was stretched upon my back, unable to speak or move, on the boudoir carpet. The woman lay beside me, and Summerlee was bunched in a chair by the window, his head nearly touching his knees. As in a dream I saw Challenger, like a monstrous beetle, crawling slowly across the floor, and a moment later I heard the gentle hissing of the escaping oxygen. Challenger breathed two or three times with enormous gulps, his lungs roaring as he drew in the vital gas.

'It works!' he cried, exultantly. 'My reasoning has been justified!' He was up on his feet again, alert and strong. With a tube in his hand he rushed over to his wife and held it to her face. In a few seconds she moaned, stirred, and sat up. He turned to me, and I felt the tide of life stealing warmly through my arteries. My reason told me that it was but a little respite, and yet, carelessly as we talk of its value, every hour of existence now seemed an inestimable thing. Never have I known such a thrill of sensuous joy as came with that freshet of life. The weight fell away from my lungs, the band loosened from my brow, a sweet feeling of peace and gentle, languid comfort stole over me. I lay watching Summerlee revive under the same remedy, and finally Lord John took his turn. He sprang to his feet and gave me a hand to rise, while Challenger picked up his wife and laid her on the settee.

'Oh, George, I am so sorry you brought me back,' she said, holding him by the hand. 'The door of death is indeed, as you said, hung with beautiful, shimmering curtains; for, once the choking feeling had passed, it was all unspeakably soothing and beautiful. Why have you dragged me back?'

'Because I wish that we make the passage together. We have been together so many years. It would be sad to fall apart at the supreme moment.'

For a moment in his tender voice I caught a glimpse of a new Challenger, something very far from the bullying, ranting, arrogant man who had alternately amazed and offended his generation. Here in the shadow of death was the innermost Challenger, the man who had won and held a woman's love. Suddenly his mood changed and he was our strong captain once again.

'Alone of all mankind I saw and foretold this catastrophe,' said he, with a ring of exultation and scientific triumph in his voice. 'As to you, my good Summerlee, I trust your last doubts have been resolved as to the meaning of the blurring of the lines in the spectrum, and that you will no longer contend that my letter in *The Times* was based upon a delusion.'

For once our pugnacious colleague was deaf to a challenge. He could but sit gasping and stretching his long, thin limbs, as if to assure himself that he was still really upon this planet. Challenger walked across to the oxygen tube, and the sound of the loud hissing fell away till it was the most gentle sibilation.

'We must husband our supply of the gas,' said he. 'The atmosphere of the room is now strongly hyper-oxygenated, and I take it that none of us feel any distressing symptoms. We can only determine by actual experiments what amount added to the air will serve to neutralize the poison. Let us see how that will do.'

We sat in silent nervous tension for five minutes or more, observing our own sensations. I had just begun to fancy that I felt the constriction round my temples again when Mrs Challenger called out from the sofa that she was fainting. Her husband turned on more gas.

'In pre-scientific days,' said he, 'they used to keep a white mouse in every submarine, as its more delicate organization gave signs of a vicious atmosphere before it was perceived by the sailors. You, my dear, will be our white mouse. I have now increased the supply and you are better.'

'Yes, I am better.'

'Possibly we have hit upon the correct mixture. When we have ascertained exactly how little will serve we shall be able to compute how long we shall be able to exist. Unfortunately, in resuscitating ourselves we have already consumed a considerable proportion of this first tube.'

'Does it matter?' asked Lord John, who was standing with his hands in his pockets close to the window. 'If we have to go, what is the use of holdin' on? You don't suppose there's any chance for us?'

Challenger smiled and shook his head.

'Well, then, don't you think there is more dignity in takin' the jump and not waitin' to be pushed in? If it must be so I'm for sayin' our prayers, turnin' off the gas, and openin' the window.'

'Why not?' said the lady, bravely. 'Surely, George, Lord John is right and it is better so.'

'I most strongly object,' cried Summerlee, in a querulous voice. 'When we must die let us by all means die; but to deliberately anticipate death seems to me to be a foolish and unjustifiable action.'

'What does our young friend say to it?' asked Challenger.

'I think we should see it to the end.'

'And I am strongly of the same opinion,' said he.

'Then, George, if you say so, I think so too,' cried the lady.

'Well, well, I'm only puttin' it as an argument,' said Lord John. 'If you all want to see it through I am with you. It's dooced interestin', and no mistake about that. I've had my share of adventures in my life, and as many thrills as most folk, but I'm endin' on my top note.'

'Granting the continuity of life,' said Challenger.

'A large assumption!' cried Summerlee.

Challenger stared at him in silent reproof.

'Granting the continuity of life,' said he, in his most didactic manner, 'none of us can predicate what opportunities of observation one may have from what we may call the spirit plane to the plane of matter. It surely must be evident to the most obtuse person' (here he glared at Summerlee) 'that it is while we are ourselves material that we are most fitted to watch and form a judgment upon material phenomena. Therefore it is only by keeping alive for these few extra hours that we can hope to carry on with us to some future existence a clear conception of the most stupendous event that the world, or the universe so far as we know it, has ever encountered. To me it would seem a deplorable thing that we should in any way curtail by so much as a minute so wonderful an experience.'

'I am strongly of the same opinion,' cried Summerlee.

'Carried without a division,' said Lord John. 'By George, that poor devil of a chauffeur of yours down in the yard has made his last journey. No use makin' a sally and bringin' him in?'

'It would be absolute madness,' cried Summerlee.

'Well, I suppose it would,' said Lord John. 'It couldn't help him

'That poor devil of a chauffeur of yours down in the yard has made his last journey'

and would scatter our gas all over the house, even if we ever got back alive. My word, look at the little birds under the trees!'

We drew four chairs up to the long, low window, the lady still resting with closed eyes upon the settee. I remember that the monstrous and grotesque idea crossed my mind – the illusion may have been heightened by the heavy stuffiness of the air which we were breathing – that we were in four front seats of the stalls at the last act of the drama of the world.

In the immediate foreground, beneath our very eyes, was the small yard with the half-cleaned motor-car standing in it. Austin, the chauffeur, had received his final notice at last, for he was sprawling beside the wheel, with a great black bruise upon his forehead where it had struck the step or mudguard in falling. He still held in his hand the nozzle of the hose with which he had been washing down his machine. A couple of small plane trees stood in the corner of the yard, and underneath them lay several pathetic little balls of fluffy feathers, with tiny feet uplifted. The sweep of Death's scythe had included everything great and small within its swathe.

Over the wall of the yard we looked down upon the winding road, which led to the station. A group of the reapers whom we had seen running from the fields were lying all pell-mell, their bodies crossing each other, at the bottom of it. Farther up the nurse-girl lay with her head and shoulders propped against the slope of the grassy bank. She had taken the baby from the perambulator, and it was a motionless bundle of wraps in her arms. Close behind her a tiny patch upon the roadside showed where the little boy was stretched. Still nearer to us was the dead cab-horse kneeling between the shafts. The old driver was hanging over the splash-board like some grotesque scarecrow, his arms dangling absurdly in front of him. Through the window we could dimly discern that a young man was seated inside. The door was swinging open, and his hand was grasping the handle, as if he had attempted to leap forth at the last instant. In the middle distance lay the golf links, dotted as they had been in the morning with the dark figures of the golfers, lying motionless upon the grass of the course, or among the heather which skirted it. On one particular green there were eight bodies stretched where a foursome with its caddies had held to their game to the last. No bird flew in the blue vault of heaven, no man or beast moved upon the vast countryside which lay before us. The evening sun shone its peaceful radiance across it, but there brooded over it all the stillness and the silence of universal death – a death in which we were so soon to join. At the present instant that one frail sheet of glass, by holding in the extra oxygen, which counter-acted the poisoned ether, shut us off from the fate of all our kind. For a few short hours the knowledge and foresight of one man could preserve our little oasis of life in the vast desert of death, and save us from participation in the common catastrophe. Then the gas would run low, we too should lie gasping upon that cherry-coloured boudoir carpet, and the fate of the human race and of all earthly life would be complete. For a long time, in a mood which was too solemn for speech, we looked out at the tragic world.

'There is a house on fire,' said Challenger, at last, pointing to a column of smoke which rose above the trees. 'There will, I expect, be many such – possibly whole cities in flames – when we consider how many folk may have dropped with lights in their hands. The fact of combustion is in itself enough to show that the proportion of oxygen in the atmosphere is normal, and that it is the ether which is at fault. Ah, there you see another blaze on the top of Crowborough Hill. It is the golf clubhouse, or I am mistaken. There is the church clock chiming the hour. It would interest our philosophers to know that man-made mechanism has survived the race who made it.'

'By George!' cried Lord John, rising excitedly from his chair. 'What's that puff of smoke? It's a train.'

We heard the roar of it, and presently it came flying into sight, going at what seemed to me to be a prodigious speed. Whence it had come, or how far, we had no means of knowing. Only by some miracle of luck could it have gone any distance. But now we were to see the terrific end of its career. A train of coal-trucks stood motionless upon the line. We held our breath as the express roared along the same track. The crash was horrible. Engine and carriages piled themselves into a hill of splintered wood and twisted iron. Red spurts of flame flickered up from the wreckage until it was all ablaze. For half an hour we sat with hardly a word, stunned by the stupendous sight.

The stillness and the silence of universal death

'Poor, poor people!' cried Mrs Challenger, at last, clinging with a whimper to her husband's arm.

'My dear, the passengers on that train were no more animate than the coals into which they crashed, or the carbon which they have now become,' said Challenger, stroking her hand soothingly. 'It was a train of the living when it left Victoria, but it was driven and freighted by the dead long before it reached its fate.'

'All over the world the same thing must be going on,' said I, as a vision of strange happenings rose before me. 'Think of the ships at sea – how they will steam on and on, until the furnaces die down, or until they run full tilt upon some beach. The sailing ships, too – how they will back and fill with their cargoes of dead sailors, while their timbers rot and their joints leak, till one by one they sink below the surface. Perhaps a century hence the Atlantic may still be dotted with the old drifting derelicts.'

'And the folk in the coal-mines,' said Summerlee, with a dismal chuckle. 'If ever geologists should by any chance live upon earth again they will have some strange theories of the existence of man in carboniferous strata.'

'I don't profess to know about such things,' remarked Lord John, 'but it seems to me the earth will be "To let, empty," after this. When once our human crowd is wiped off it, how will it ever get on again?'

'The world was empty before,' Challenger answered, gravely. 'Under laws which in their inception are beyond and above us, it became peopled. Why may the same process not happen again?'

'My dear Challenger, you can't mean that?'

'I am not in the habit, Professor Summerlee, of saying things which I do not mean. The observation is trivial.' Out went the beard and down came the eyelids.

'Well, you lived an obstinate dogmatist, and you mean to die one,' said Summerlee, sourly.

'And you, sir, have lived an unimaginative obstructionist, and never can hope now to emerge from it.'

'Your worst critics will never accuse you of lacking imagination,' Summerlee retorted.

'Upon my word!' said Lord John. 'It would be like you if you used

A vision of strange happenings

up our last gasp of oxygen in abusing each other. What can it matter whether folk come back or not? It surely won't be in our time.'

'In that remark, sir, you betray your own very pronounced limitations,' said Challenger, severely. 'The true scientific mind is not to be tied down by its own conditions of time and space. It builds itself an observatory erected upon the border line of present, which separates the infinite past from the infinite future. From this sure post it makes its sallies even to the beginning and to the end of all things. As to death, the scientific mind dies at its post working in normal and methodic fashion to the end. It disregards so petty a thing as its own physical dissolution as completely as it does all other limitations upon the plane of matter. Am I right, Professor Summerlee?'

Summerlee grumbled an ungracious assent.

'With certain reservations, I agree,' said he.

'The ideal scientific mind,' continued Challenger – 'I put it in the third person rather than appear to be too self-complacent – the ideal scientific mind should be capable of thinking out a point of abstract knowledge in the interval between its owner falling from a balloon and reaching the earth. Men of this strong fibre are needed to form the conquerors of Nature and the bodyguard of truth.'

'It strikes me Nature's on top this time,' said Lord John, looking out of the window. 'I've read some leadin' articles about you gentlemen controllin' her, but she's gettin' a bit of her own back.'

'It is but a temporary set-back,' said Challenger, with conviction. 'A few million years, what are they in the great cycle of time? The vegetable world has, as you can see, survived. Look at the leaves of that plane tree. The birds are dead, but the plant flourishes. From this vegetable life in pond and in marsh will come, in time, the tiny crawling microscopic slugs which are the pioneers of that great army of life in which for the instant we five have the extraordinary duty of serving as rearguard. Once the lowest form of life has established itself, the final advent of Man is as certain as the growth of the oak from the acorn. The old circle will swing round once more.'

'But the poison?' I asked. 'Will that not nip life in the bud?'

'The poison may be a mere stratum or layer in the ether – a mephitic Gulf Stream across that mighty ocean in which we float. Or tolerance may be established, and life accommodate itself to a new condition. The mere fact that with a comparatively small hyper-oxygenation of our blood we can hold out against it is surely a proof in itself that no very great change would be needed to enable animal life to endure it.'

The smoking house beyond the trees had burst into flames. We could see the high tongues of fire shooting up into the air.

'It's pretty awful,' muttered Lord John, more impressed than I had ever seen him.

'Well, after all, what does it matter?' I remarked. 'The world is dead. Cremation is surely the best burial.'

'It would shorten us up if this house went ablaze.'

'I foresaw the danger,' said Challenger, 'and asked my wife to guard against it.'

'Everything is quite safe, dear. But my head begins to throb again. What a dreadful atmosphere!'

'We must change it,' said Challenger. He bent over his cylinder of oxygen.

'It's nearly empty,' said he. 'It has lasted us some three and a half hours. It is now close on eight o'clock. We shall get through the night comfortably. I should expect the end about nine o'clock tomorrow morning. We shall see one sunrise, which shall be all our own.'

He turned on his second tube and opened for half a minute the fanlight over the door. Then as the air became perceptibly better, but our own symptoms more acute, he closed it once again.

'By the way,' said he, 'man does not live upon oxygen alone. It's dinner-time and over. I assure you, gentlemen, that when I invited you to my home and to what I had hoped would be an interesting reunion, I had intended that my kitchen should justify itself. However, we must do what we can. I am sure that you will agree with me that it would be folly to consume our air too rapidly by lighting an oil-stove. I have some small provision of cold meats, bread, and pickles, which, with a couple of bottles of claret, may serve our turn. Thank you, my dear – now as ever you are the queen of managers.'

It was indeed wonderful how, with the self-respect and sense of propriety of the British housekeeper, the lady had within a few minutes adorned the central table with a snow-white cloth, laid the napkins upon it, and set forth the simple meal with all the elegance of civiliz-ation, including an electric torch lamp in the centre. Wonderful, also, was it to find that our appetites were ravenous.

'It is the measure of our emotion,' said Challenger, with that air of condescension with which he brought his scientific mind to the explanation of humble facts. 'We have gone through a great crisis. That means molecular disturbance. That in turn means the need for repair. Great sorrow or great joy should bring intense hunger – not abstinence from food, as our novelists will have it.'

'That's why the country folk have great feasts at funerals,' I hazarded.

'Exactly. Our young friend has hit upon an excellent illustration. Let me give you another slice of tongue.'

'The same with savages,' said Lord John, cutting away at the beef. 'I've seen them buryin' a chief up the Aruwimi River,[2] and they ate a hippo that must have weighed as much as a tribe. There are some of them down New Guinea way that eat the late-lamented himself, just by way of a last tidy up. Well, of all the funeral feasts on this earth, I suppose the one we are takin' is the queerest.'

'The strange thing is,' said Mrs Challenger, 'that I find it impossible to feel grief for those who are gone. There are my father and mother at Bedford. I know that they are dead, and yet in this tremendous universal tragedy I can feel no sharp sorrow for any individuals, even for them.'

'And my old mother in her cottage in Ireland,' said I. 'I can see her in my mind's eye, with her shawl and her lace cap, lying back with closed eyes in the old high-backed chair near the window, her glasses and her book beside her. Why should I mourn her? She has passed and I am passing, and I may be nearer her in some other life than England is to Ireland. Yet I grieve to think that that dear body is no more.'

'As to the body,' remarked Challenger, 'we do not mourn over the parings of our nails nor the cut locks of our hair, though they were once part of ourselves. Neither does a one-legged man yearn sentimen-tally over his missing member. The physical body has rather been a source of pain and fatigue to us. It is the constant index of our limitations. Why then should we worry about its detachment from our psychical selves?'

'If they can indeed be detached,' Summerlee grumbled. 'But, anyhow, universal death is dreadful.'

'As I have already explained,' said Challenger, 'a universal death must in its nature be far less terrible than an isolated one.'

'Same in a battle,' remarked Lord John. 'If you saw a single man lying on that floor with his chest knocked in and a hole in his face it would turn you sick. But I've seen ten thousand on their backs in the Soudan,[3] and it gave me no such feelin', for when you are makin' history the life of any man is too small a thing to worry over. When a thousand million pass over together, same as happened today, you can't pick your own partic'lar out of the crowd.'

'I wish it were well over with us,' said the lady, wistfully. 'Oh, George, I am so frightened.'

'You'll be the bravest of us all, little lady, when the time comes. I've been a blusterous old husband to you, dear, but you'll just bear in mind that G. E. C. is as he was made and couldn't help himself. After all, you wouldn't have had anyone else?'

'No one in the whole wide world, dear,' said she, and put her arms round his bull neck. We three walked to the window, and stood amazed at the sight which met our eyes.

Darkness had fallen and the dead world was shrouded in gloom. But right across the southern horizon was one long vivid scarlet streak, waxing and waning in vivid pulses of life, leaping suddenly to a crimson zenith and then dying down to a glowing line of fire.

'Lewes is ablaze!' I cried.

'No, it is Brighton which is burning,' said Challenger, stepping across to join us. 'You can see the curved back of the downs against the glow. That fire is miles on the farther side of it. The whole town must be alight.'

There were several red glares at different points, and the pile of *débris* upon the railway line was still smouldering darkly, but they all seemed mere pinpoints of light compared to that monstrous conflagration throbbing beyond the hills. What copy it would all have made for the *Gazette*! Had ever a journalist such an opening and so little chance of using it – the scoop of scoops, and no one to appreciate it? And then, suddenly, the old instinct of recording came over me. If these men of science could be so true to their life's work to the very end, why should not I, in my humble way, be as constant? No human eye might ever rest upon what I had done. But the long night had to be passed somehow, and for me, at least, sleep seemed to be out of the question. My notes would help to pass the weary hours and to occupy my thoughts. Thus it is that now I have before me the notebook with its scribbled pages, written confusedly upon my knee in the dim, waning light of our one electric torch. Had I the literary touch, they might have been worthy of the occasion. As it is, they may still serve to bring to other minds the long-drawn emotions and tremors of that awful night.

CHAPTER IV

A Diary of the Dying

How strange the words look scribbled at the top of the empty page of my book! How stranger still that it is I, Edward Malone, who have written them – I who started only some twelve hours ago from my rooms in Streatham without one thought of the marvels which the day was to bring forth! I look back at the chain of incidents, my interview with McArdle, Challenger's first note of alarm in *The Times*, the absurd journey in the train, the pleasant luncheon, the catastrophe, and now it has come to this – that we linger alone upon an empty planet, and so sure is our fate that I can regard these lines, written from mechanical professional habit and never to be seen by human eyes, as the words of one who is already dead, so closely does he stand to the shadowed borderland over which all outside this one little circle of friends have already gone. I feel how wise and true were the words of Challenger when he said that the real tragedy would be if we were left behind when all that is noble and good and beautiful had passed. But of that there can surely be no danger. Already our second tube of oxygen is drawing to an end. We can count the poor dregs of our lives almost to a minute.

We have just been treated to a lecture, a good quarter of an hour long, from Challenger, who was so excited that he roared and bellowed as if he were addressing his old rows of scientific sceptics in the Queen's Hall. He had certainly a strange audience to harangue: his wife perfectly acquiescent and absolutely ignorant of his meaning, Summerlee seated in the shadow, querulous and critical, but interested, Lord John lounging in a corner somewhat bored by the whole proceeding, and myself beside the window watching the scene with a kind of detached attention as if it were all a dream or something in which I had no personal interest whatever. Challenger sat at the centre table with the electric light illuminating the slide under the microscope which he had brought from his dressing-room. The small vivid circle of white light from the mirror left half of his rugged, bearded face in brilliant radiance, and half in deepest shadow. He had, it seems, been working of late upon the lowest forms of life, and what excited him at the present moment was that in the microscopic slide made up the day before he found the amoeba to be still alive.

'You can see it for yourselves,' he kept repeating, in great excitement. 'Summerlee, will you step across and satisfy yourself upon the point? Malone, will you kindly verify what I say? The little spindle-shaped things in the centre are diatoms,[1] and may be disregarded since they are probably vegetable rather than animal. But at the right-hand side you will see an undoubted amoeba, moving sluggishly across the field. The upper screw is the fine adjustment. Look at it for yourselves.'

Summerlee did so, and acquiesced. So did I, and perceived a little creature which looked as if it were made of ground glass flowing in a sticky way across the lighted circle. Lord John was prepared to take him on trust.

'I'm not troublin' my head whether he's alive or dead,' said he. 'We don't so much as know each other by sight, so why should I take it to heart? I don't suppose he's worryin' himself over the state of *our* health.'

'You can see it for yourselves,' he kept repeating

I laughed at this, and Challenger looked in my direction with his coldest and most supercilious stare. It was a most petrifying experience.

'The flippancy of the half-educated is more obstructive to science than the obtuseness of the ignorant,' said he. 'If Lord John Roxton would condescend –'

'My dear George, don't be so peppery,' said his wife, with her hand on the black mane that drooped over the microscope. 'What can it matter whether the amoeba is alive or not?'

'It matters a great deal,' said Challenger, gruffly.

'Well, let's hear about it,' said Lord John, with a good-humoured smile. 'We may as well talk about that as anything else. If you think I've been too off-hand with the thing, or hurt its feelin's in any way, I'll apologize.'

'For my part,' remarked Summerlee, in his creaky, argumentative voice, 'I can't see why you should attach such importance to the creature being alive. It is in the same atmosphere as ourselves, so naturally the poison does not act upon it. If it were outside of this room it would be dead, like all other animal life.'

'Your remarks, my good Summerlee,' said Challenger, with enormous condescension (oh, if I could paint that overbearing, arrogant face in the vivid circle of reflection from the microscope mirror!) – 'your remarks show that you imperfectly appreciate the situation. This specimen was mounted yesterday and is hermetically sealed. None of our oxygen can reach it. But the ether, of course, has penetrated to it, as to every other point upon the universe. Therefore, it has survived the poison. Hence, we may argue that every amoeba outside this room, instead of being dead, as you have erroneously stated, has really survived the catastrophe.'

'Well, even now I don't feel inclined to hip-hurrah about it,' said Lord John. 'What does it matter?'

'It just matters this, that the world is a living instead of a dead one. If you had the scientific imagination, you would cast your mind forward from this one fact, and you would see some few millions of years hence – a mere passing moment in the enormous flux of the ages – the whole world teeming once more with the animal and human life which will spring from this tiny root. You have seen a prairie fire, where the flames have swept every trace of grass or plant from the surface of the earth and left only a blackened waste. You would think that it must be for ever desert. Yet the roots of growth have been left behind, and when you pass the place a few years hence you can no longer tell where the black scars used to be. Here in this tiny creature are the roots of growth of the animal world, and by its inherent development, and evolution, it will surely in time remove every trace of this incomparable crisis in which we are now involved.'

'Dooced interestin'!' said Lord John, lounging across and looking through the microscope. 'Funny little chap to hang number one among the family portraits. Got a fine big shirt-stud on him!'

'The dark object is his nucleus,' said Challenger, with the air of a nurse teaching letters to a baby.

'Well, we needn't feel lonely,' said Lord John, laughing. 'There's somebody livin' besides us on the earth.'

'You seem to take it for granted, Challenger,' said Summerlee, 'that the object for which this world was created was that it should produce and sustain human life.'

'Well, sir, and what object do you suggest?' asked Challenger, bristling at the least hint of contradiction.

'Sometimes I think that it is only the monstrous conceit of mankind which makes him think that all this stage was erected for him to strut upon.'

'We cannot be dogmatic about it, but at least without what you have ventured to call monstrous conceit we can surely say that we are the highest thing in Nature.'

'The highest of which we have cognizance.'

'That, sir, goes without saying.'

'Think of all the millions and possibly billions of years that the earth swung empty through space – or, if not empty, at least without a sign or thought of the human race. Think of it, washed by the rain and scorched by the sun, and swept by the wind for those unnumbered ages. Man only came into being yesterday so far as geological time goes. Why, then, should it be taken for granted that all this stupendous preparation was for his benefit?'

'For whose then – or for what?'

Summerlee shrugged his shoulders.

'How can we tell? For some reason altogether beyond our conception – and man may have been a mere accident, a by-product evolved
in the process. It is as if the scum upon the surface of the ocean
imagined that the ocean was created in order to produce and sustain
it, or a mouse in a cathedral thought that the building was its own
proper ordained residence.'

I have jotted down the very words of their argument; but now it
degenerates into a mere noisy wrangle with much polysyllabic scientific
jargon upon each side. It is no doubt a privilege to hear two such
brains discuss the highest questions; but as they are in perpetual
disagreement plain folk like Lord John and I get little that is positive
from the exhibition. They neutralize each other and we are left as
they found us. Now the hubbub has ceased, and Summerlee is coiled
up in his chair, while Challenger, still fingering the screws of his
microscope, is keeping up a continual low, deep, inarticulate growl
like the sea after a storm. Lord John comes over to me, and we look
out together into the night.

There is a pale new moon – the last moon that human eyes will
ever rest upon – and the stars are most brilliant. Even in the clear
plateau air of South America I have never seen them brighter. Possibly
this etheric change has some effect upon light. The funeral pyre of
Brighton is still blazing, and there is a very distant patch of scarlet in
the western sky, which may mean trouble at Arundel or Chichester,
possibly even at Portsmouth. I sit and muse and make an occasional
note. There is a sweet melancholy in the air. Youth and beauty and
chivalry and love – is this to be the end of it all? The starlit earth looks
a dreamland of gentle peace. Who would imagine it as the terrible
Golgotha² strewn with the bodies of the human race? Suddenly, I find
myself laughing.

'Halloa, young fellah!' says Lord John, staring at me in surprise.
'We could do with a joke in these hard times. What was it, then?'

'I was thinking of all the great unsolved questions,' I answer; 'the
questions that we spent so much labour and thought over. Think of
Anglo-German competition, for example – or the Persian Gulf³ that
my old chief was so keen about. Whoever would have guessed, when

we fumed and fretted so, how they were to be eventually solved?'

We fall into silence again. I fancy that each of us is thinking of friends that have gone before. Mrs Challenger is sobbing quietly, and her husband is whispering to her. My mind turns to all the most unlikely people, and I see each of them lying white and rigid as poor Austin does in the yard. There is McArdle, for example. I know exactly where he is, with his face upon his writing-desk and his hand on his own telephone, just as I heard him fall. Beaumont, the editor, too – I suppose he is lying upon the blue-and-red Turkey carpet which adorned his sanctum. And the fellows in the reporters' room – Macdona and Murray and Bond. They had certainly died hard at work on their job, with notebooks full of vivid impressions and strange happenings in their hands. I could just imagine how this one would have been packed off to do the doctors, and that other to Westminster, and yet a third to St Paul's. What glorious rows of headlines they must have seen as a last vision beautiful, never destined to materialize in printer's ink! I could see Macdona among the doctors – 'Hope in Harley Street' – Mac had always a weakness for alliteration. 'Interview with Mr Soley Wilson.' 'Famous Specialist says "Never despair!"' 'Our Special Correspondent found the eminent scientist seated upon the roof, whither he had retreated to avoid the crowd of terrified patients who had stormed his dwelling. With a manner which plainly showed his appreciation of the immense gravity of the occasion, the celebrated physician refused to admit that every avenue of hope had been closed.' That's how Mac would start. Then there was Bond; he would probably do St Paul's. He fancied his own literary touch. My word, what a theme for him! 'Standing in the little gallery under the dome, and looking down upon that packed mass of despairing humanity, grovelling at this last instant before a Power which they had so persistently ignored, there rose to my ears from the swaying crowd such a low moan of entreaty and terror, such a shuddering cry for help to the Unknown, that –' and so forth.

Yes, it would be a great end for a reporter, though, like myself, he would die with the treasures still unused. What would Bond not give, poor chap, to see 'J. H. B.' at the foot of a column like that?

But what drivel I am writing! It is just an attempt to pass the weary time. Mrs Challenger has gone to the inner dressing-room, and the Professor says that she is asleep. He is making notes and consulting books at the central table, as calmly as if years of placid work lay before him. He writes with a very noisy quill pen, which seems to be screeching scorn at all who disagree with him.

Summerlee has dropped off in his chair, and gives from time to time a peculiarly exasperating snore. Lord John lies back with his hands in his pockets, and his eyes closed. How people can sleep under such conditions is more than I can imagine.

Three-thirty a.m. I have just wakened with a start. It was five minutes past eleven when I made my last entry. I remember winding up my watch and noting the time. So I have wasted some five hours out of the little span still left to us. Who would have believed it possible? But I feel very much fresher, and ready for my fate – or try to persuade myself that I am. And yet, the fitter a man is, and the higher his tide of life, the more must he shrink from death. How wise and how merciful is that provision of Nature by which his earthly anchor is usually loosened by many little imperceptible tugs, until his consciousness has drifted out of its untenable earthly harbour into the great sea beyond!

Mrs Challenger is still in the dressing-room. Challenger has fallen asleep in his chair. What a picture! His enormous frame leans back, his huge, hairy hands are clasped across his waistcoat, and his head is so tilted that I can see nothing above his collar save a tangled bristle of luxuriant beard. He shakes with the vibration of his own snoring. Summerlee adds his occasional high tenor to Challenger's sonorous bass. Lord John is sleeping also, his long body doubled up sideways in a basket-chair. The first cold light of dawn is just stealing into the room, and everything is grey and mournful.

I look out at the sunrise – that fateful sunrise which will shine upon an unpeopled world. The human race is gone, extinguished in a day, but the planets swing round and the tides rise or fall, and the wind whispers, and all Nature goes her way, down, as it would seem, to the very amoeba, with never a sign that he who styled himself the lord of creation had ever blessed or cursed the universe with his presence. Down in the yard lies Austin with sprawling limbs, his face glimmering white in the dawn, and the hose-nozzle still projecting from his dead hand. The whole of human kind is typified in that one half-ludicrous and half-pathetic figure, lying so helpless beside the machine which it used to control.

Here end the notes which I made at the time. Henceforward events were too swift and too poignant to allow me to write, but they are too clearly outlined in my memory that any detail could escape me.

Some chokiness in my throat made me look at the oxygen cylinders, and I was startled at what I saw. The sands of our lives were running very low. At some period in the night Challenger had switched the tube from the third to the fourth cylinder. Now it was clear that this also was nearly exhausted. That horrible feeling of constriction was closing in upon me. I ran across and, unscrewing the nozzle, I changed it to our last supply. Even as I did so my conscience pricked me, for I felt that perhaps if I had held my hand all of them might have passed in their sleep. The thought was banished, however, by the voice of the lady from the inner room, crying: –

'George, George, I am stifling!'

'It is all right, Mrs Challenger,' I answered, as the others started to their feet. 'I have just turned on a fresh supply.'

Even at such a moment I could not help smiling at Challenger, who with a great hairy fist in each eye was like a huge, bearded baby, new wakened out of sleep. Summerlee was shivering like a man with the ague, human fears, as he realized his position, rising for an instant above the stoicism of the man of science. Lord John, however, was as cool and alert as if he had just been roused on a hunting morning.

'Fifthly and lastly,' said he, glancing at the tube. 'Say, young fellah, don't tell me you've been writin' up your impressions in that paper on your knee.'

'Just a few notes to pass the time.'

'Well, I don't believe anyone but an Irishman would have done that. I expect you'll have to wait till little brother amoeba gets grown up before you'll find a reader. He don't seem to take much stock of things just at present. Well, Herr Professor, what are the prospects?'

Challenger was looking out at the great drifts of morning mist which lay over the landscape. Here and there the wooded hills rose like conical islands out of this woolly sea.

'It might be a winding-sheet,' said Mrs Challenger, who had entered in her dressing-gown. 'There's that song of yours, George, "Ring out the old, ring in the new."[4] It was prophetic. But you are shivering, my poor dear friends. I have been warm under a coverlet all night, and you cold in your chairs. But I'll soon set you right.'

The brave little creature hurried away, and presently we heard the sizzling of a kettle. She was back soon with five steaming cups of cocoa upon a tray.

'Drink these,' said she. 'You will feel so much better.'

And we did. Summerlee asked if he might light his pipe, and we all had cigarettes. It steadied our nerves, I think, but it was a mistake, for it made a dreadful atmosphere in that stuffy room. Challenger had to open the ventilator.

'How long, Challenger?' asked Lord John.

'Possibly three hours,' he answered, with a shrug.

'I used to be frightened,' said his wife. 'But the nearer I get to it, the easier it seems. Don't you think we ought to pray, George?'

'You will pray, dear, if you wish,' the big man answered, very gently. 'We all have our own ways of praying. Mine is a complete acquiescence in whatever Fate may send me – a cheerful acquiescence. The highest religion and the highest science seem to unite on that.'

'I cannot truthfully describe my mental attitude as acquiescence, and far less cheerful acquiescence,' grumbled Summerlee, over his pipe. 'I submit because I have to. I confess that I should have liked another year of life to finish my classification of the chalk fossils.'

'Your unfinished work is a small thing,' said Challenger, pompously, 'when weighed against the fact that my own *magnum opus*, "The Ladder of Life", is still in the first stages. My brain, my reading, my experience – in fact, my whole unique equipment – were to be condensed into that epoch-making volume. And yet, as I say, I acquiesce.'

'I expect we've all left some loose ends stickin' out,' said Lord John. 'What are yours, young fellah?'

'I was working at a book of verses,' I answered.

'Well, the world has escaped that, anyhow,' said Lord John. 'There's always compensation somewhere if you grope around.'

'What about you?' I asked.

'Well, it just so happens, that I was tidied up and ready. I'd promised Merivale to go to Tibet for a snow-leopard in the spring. But it's hard on you, Mrs Challenger, when you have just built up this pretty home.'

'Where George is, there is my home. But, oh, what would I not give for one last walk together in the fresh morning air upon those beautiful downs!'

Our hearts re-echoed her words. The sun had burst through the gauzy mists which veiled it, and the whole broad Weald was washed in golden light. Sitting in our dark and poisonous atmosphere that glorious, clean, windswept countryside seemed a very dream of beauty. Mrs Challenger held her hand stretched out to it in her longing. We drew up chairs and sat in a semicircle in the window. The atmosphere was already very close. It seemed to me that the shadows of death were drawing in upon us – the last of our race. It was like an invisible curtain closing down upon every side.

'That cylinder is not lastin' too well,' said Lord John, with a long gasp for breath.

'The amount contained is variable,' said Challenger, 'depending upon the pressure and care with which it has been bottled. I am inclined to agree with you, Roxton, that this one is defective.'

'So we are to be cheated out of the last hour of our lives,' Summerlee remarked, bitterly. 'An excellent final illustration of the sordid age in which we have lived. Well, Challenger, now is your time if you wish to study the subjective phenomena of physical dissolution.'

'Sit on the stool at my knee and give me your hand,' said Challenger to his wife. 'I think, my friends, that a further delay in this insufferable atmosphere is hardly advisable. You would not desire it, dear, would you?'

His wife gave a little groan and sank her face against his leg.

'I've seen the folk bathin' in the Serpentine in winter,' said Lord John. 'When the rest are in, you see one or two shiverin' on the bank, envyin' the others that have taken the plunge. It's the last that have the worst of it. I'm all for a header and have done with it.'

'You would open the window and face the ether?'

'Better be poisoned than stifled.'

Summerlee nodded his reluctant acquiescence, and held out his thin hand to Challenger.

'We've had our quarrels in our time, but that's all over,' said he. 'We were good friends and had a respect for each other under the surface. Goodbye!'

'Goodbye, young fellah!' said Lord John. 'The window's plastered up. You can't open it.'

Challenger stooped and raised his wife, pressing her to his breast, while she threw her arms round his neck.

'Give me that field-glass, Malone,' said he, gravely.

I handed it to him.

'Into the hands of the Power that made us we render ourselves again!' he shouted in his voice of thunder, and at the words he hurled the field-glass through the window.

Full in our flushed faces, before the last tinkle of falling fragments had died away, there came the wholesome breath of the wind, blowing strong and sweet.

I don't know how long we sat in amazed silence. Then, as in a dream, I heard Challenger's voice once more.

'We are back in normal conditions,' he cried. 'The world has cleared the poison belt, but we alone of all mankind are saved.'

CHAPTER V

The Dead World

I remember that we all sat gasping in our chairs, with that sweet, wet south-western breeze, fresh from the sea, flapping the muslin curtains and cooling our flushed faces. I wonder how long we sat! None of us afterwards could agree at all upon that point. We were bewildered, stunned, semi-conscious. We had all braced our courage for death, but this fearful and sudden new fact – that we must continue to live after we had survived the race to which we belonged – struck us with the shock of a physical blow, and left us prostrate. Then gradually the suspended mechanism began to move once more; the shuttles of memory worked; ideas weaved themselves together in our minds. We saw, with vivid, merciless clearness, the relations between the past, the present, and the future – the lives that we had led and the lives which we would have to live. Our eyes turned in silent horror upon those of our companions and found the same answering look in theirs. Instead of the joy which men might have been expected to feel who had so narrowly escaped an imminent death, a terrible wave of darkest depression submerged us. Everything on earth that we loved had been washed away into the great, infinite, unknown ocean, and here were we marooned upon this desert island of a world, without companions, hopes, or aspirations. A few years' skulking like jackals among the graves of the human race and then our own belated and lonely end would come.

'It's dreadful, George, dreadful!' the lady cried, in an agony of sobs. 'If we had only passed with the others! Oh, why did you save us? I feel as if it is we that are dead and everyone else alive.'

Challenger's great eyebrows were drawn down in concentrated thought, while his huge, hairy paw closed upon the outstretched hand of his wife. I had observed that she always held out her arms to him in trouble as a child would to its mother.

'Without being a fatalist to the point of non-resistance,' said he, 'I have always found that the highest wisdom lies in an acquiescence with the actual.' He spoke slowly, and there was a vibration of feeling in his sonorous voice.

'I do *not* acquiesce,' said Summerlee, firmly.

'I don't see that it matters a row of pins whether you acquiesce or whether you don't,' remarked Lord John. 'You've got to take it, whether you take it fightin' or take it lyin' down, so what's the odds whether you acquiesce or not? I can't remember that anyone asked our permission before the thing began, and nobody's likely to ask it now. So what difference can it make what we may think of it?'

'It is just all the difference between happiness and misery,' said

Challenger, with an abstracted face, still patting his wife's hand. 'You can swim with the tide and have peace in mind and soul, or you can thrust against it and be bruised and weary. This business is beyond us, so let us accept it as it stands and say no more.'

'But what in the world are we to do with our lives?' I asked, appealing in desperation to the blue, empty heaven. 'What am I to do, for example? There are no newspapers, so there's an end of my vocation.'

'And there's nothin' left to shoot, and no more soldierin', so there's an end of mine,' said Lord John.

'And there are no students, so there's an end of mine,' cried Summerlee.

'But I have my husband and my house, so I can thank Heaven that there is no end of mine,' said the lady.

'Nor is there an end of mine,' remarked Challenger, 'for science is not dead, and this catastrophe in itself will offer us many most absorbing problems for investigation.'

He had now flung open the windows and we were gazing out upon the silent and motionless landscape.

'Let me consider,' he continued. 'It was about three, or a little after, yesterday afternoon that the world finally entered the poison belt to the extent of being completely submerged. It is now nine o'clock. The question is, at what hour did we pass out from it?'

'The air was very bad at daybreak,' said I.

'Later than that,' said Mrs Challenger. 'As late as eight o'clock I distinctly felt the same choking at my throat which came at the outset.'

'Then we shall say that it passed just after eight o'clock. For seventeen hours the world has been soaked in the poisonous ether. For that length of time the Great Gardener has sterilized the human mould which had grown over the surface of His fruit. Is it possible that the work is incompletely done – that others may have survived besides ourselves?'

'That's what I was wonderin',' said Lord John. 'Why should we be the only pebbles on the beach?'

'It is absurd to suppose that anyone besides ourselves can possibly have survived,' said Summerlee, with conviction. 'Consider that the poison was so virulent that even a man who is as strong as an ox, and has not a nerve in his body, like Malone here, could hardly get up the stair before he fell unconscious. Is it likely that anyone could stand seventeen minutes of it, far less hours?'

'Unless someone saw it coming and made preparation, same as old friend Challenger did.'

'That, I think, is hardly probable,' said Challenger, projecting his beard and sinking his eyelids. 'The combination of observation, inference, and anticipatory imagination which enabled me to foresee the danger is what one can hardly expect twice in the same generation.'

'Then your conclusion is that everyone is certainly dead?'

'There can be little doubt of that. We have to remember, however, that the poison worked from below upwards, and would possibly be less virulent in the higher strata of the atmosphere. It is strange, indeed, that it should be so; but it presents one of those features which will afford us in the future a fascinating field for study. One could imagine, therefore, that if one had to search for survivors one would turn one's eyes with best hopes of success to some Tibetan village or some Alpine farm, many thousands of feet above the sea-level.'

'Well, considerin' that there are no railroads and no steamers you might as well talk about survivors in the moon,' said Lord John. 'But what I'm askin' myself is whether it's really over or whether it's only half-time.'

Summerlee craned his neck to look round the horizon.

'It seems clear and fine,' said he, in a very dubious voice; 'but so it did yesterday. I am by no means assured that it is all over.'

Challenger shrugged his shoulders.

'We must come back once more to our fatalism,' said he. 'If the world has undergone this experience before, which is not outside the range of possibility, it was certainly a very long time ago. Therefore, we may reasonably hope that it will be very long before it occurs again.'

'That's all very well,' said Lord John; 'but if you get an earthquake shock you are mighty likely to have a second one right on the top of it. I think we'd be wise to stretch our legs and have a breath of air while we have the chance. Since our oxygen is exhausted we may just as well be caught outside as in.'

It was strange the absolute lethargy which had come upon us as a reaction after our tremendous emotions of the last twenty-four hours. It was both mental and physical, a deep-lying feeling that nothing mattered and that everything was a weariness and a profitless exertion. Even Challenger had succumbed to it, and sat in his chair, with his great head leaning upon his hands, and his thoughts far away, until Lord John and I, catching him by each arm, fairly lifted him on to his feet, receiving only the glare and growl of an angry mastiff for our trouble. However, once we had got out of our narrow haven of refuge into the wider atmosphere of everyday life, our normal energy came gradually back to us once more.

But what were we to begin to do in that graveyard of a world? Could ever men have been faced with such a question since the dawn of time? It is true that our own physical needs, and even our luxuries, were assured for the future. All the stores of food, all the vintages of wine, all the treasures of art were ours for the taking. But what were we to *do*? Some few tasks appealed to us at once, since they lay ready to our hands. We descended into the kitchen, and laid the two domestics upon their respective beds. They seemed to have died without suffering, one in the chair by the fire, the other upon the scullery floor. Then we carried in poor Austin from the yard. His muscles were set as hard as a board in the most exaggerated rigor mortis, while the contraction of the fibres had drawn his mouth into a hard sardonic grin. This symptom was prevalent among all who had died from the poison. Wherever we went we were confronted by those grinning faces, which seemed to mock at our dreadful position, smiling silently and grimly at the ill-fated survivors of their race.

'Look here,' said Lord John, who had paced restlessly about the dining-room whilst we partook of some food, 'I don't know how you fellows feel about it, but for my part, I simply *can't* sit here and do nothin'.'

'Perhaps,' Challenger answered, 'you would have the kindness to suggest what you think we ought to do.'

'Get a move on us and see all that has happened.'

'That is what I should myself propose.'

'But not in this little country village. We can see from the window all that this place can teach us.'

'Where should we go, then?'

'To London!'

'That's all very well,' grumbled Summerlee. 'You may be equal to a forty-mile walk, but I'm not so sure about Challenger, with his stumpy legs, and I am perfectly sure about myself.'

Challenger was very much annoyed.

'If you could see your way, sir, to confining your remarks to your own physical peculiarities, you would find that you had an ample field for comment,' he cried.

'I had no intention to offend you, my dear Challenger,' cried our tactless friend. 'You can't be held responsible for your own physique. If Nature has given you a short, heavy body you cannot possibly help having stumpy legs.'

Challenger was too furious to answer. He could only growl and blink and bristle. Lord John hastened to intervene before the dispute became more violent.

'You talk of walking. Why should we walk?' said he.

'Do you suggest taking the train?' asked Challenger, still simmering.

'What's the matter with the motor-car? Why should we not go in that?'

'I am not an expert,' said Challenger, pulling at his beard, reflectively. 'At the same time, you are right in supposing that the human intellect in its higher manifestations should be sufficiently flexible to turn itself to anything. Your idea is an excellent one, Lord John. I myself will drive you all to London.'

'You will do nothing of the kind,' said Summerlee, with decision.

'No, indeed, George!' cried his wife. 'You only tried once, and you remember how you crashed through the gate of the garage.'

'It was a momentary want of concentration,' said Challenger, complacently. 'You can consider the matter settled. I will certainly drive you all to London.'

The situation was relieved by Lord John.

'What's the car?' he asked.

'A twenty-horse Humber.'

'Why, I've driven one for years,' said he. 'By George!' he added. 'I never thought I'd live to take the whole human race in one load.

There's just room for five, as I remember it. Get your things on, and I'll be ready at the door by ten o'clock.'

Sure enough, at the hour named, the car came purring and crackling from the yard with Lord John at the wheel. I took my seat beside him, while the lady, a useful little buffer state, was squeezed in between the two men of wrath at the back. Then Lord John released his brakes, slid his lever rapidly from first to third, and we sped off upon the strangest drive that ever human beings have taken since man first came upon the earth.

You are to picture the loveliness of Nature upon that August day, the freshness of the morning air, the golden glare of the summer sunshine, the cloudless sky, the luxuriant green of the Sussex woods, and the deep purple of the heather-clad downs. As you looked round upon the many-coloured beauty of the scene all thought of a vast catastrophe would have passed from your mind had it not been for one sinister sign – the solemn, all-embracing silence. There is a gentle hum of life which pervades a closely-settled country, so deep and constant that one ceases to observe it as the dweller by the sea loses all sense of the constant murmur of the waves. The twitter of birds, the buzz of insects, the far-off echo of voices, the lowing of cattle, the distant barking of dogs, roar of trains, and rattle of carts – all these form one low, unremitting note, striking unheeded upon the ear. We missed it now. This deadly silence was appalling. So solemn was it, so impressive, that the buzz and rattle of our motor-car seemed an unwarrantable intrusion, an indecent disregard of this reverent stillness which lay like a pall over and round the ruins of humanity. It was this grim hush, and the tall clouds of smoke which rose here and there over the countryside from smouldering buildings, which cast a chill into our hearts as we gazed round at the glorious panorama of the Weald.

And then there were the dead! At first those endless groups of drawn and grinning faces filled us with a shuddering horror. So vivid and mordant was the impression that I can live over again that slow descent of the Station Hill, the passing by the nurse-girl with the two babes, the sight of the old horse on his knees between the shafts, the cabman twisted across his seat, and the young man inside with his

It was this grim hush, and the tall clouds of smoke which rose here and there over the countryside from smouldering buildings, which cast a chill into our hearts

hand upon the open door in the very act of springing out. Lower down were six reapers all in a litter, their limbs crossing, their dead, unwinking eyes gazing upwards at the glare of heaven. These things I see as in a photograph. But soon, by the merciful provision of Nature, the over-excited nerve ceased to respond. The very vastness of the horror took away from its personal appeal. Individuals merged into groups, groups into crowds, crowds into a universal phenomenon which one soon accepted as the inevitable detail of every scene. Only here and there, where some particularly brutal or grotesque incident caught the attention did the mind come back with a sudden shock to the personal and human meaning of it all.

Above all there was the fate of the children. That, I remember, filled us with the strongest sense of intolerable injustice. We could have wept — Mrs Challenger did weep — when we passed a great Council school and saw the long trail of tiny figures scattered down the road which led from it. They had been dismissed by their terrified teachers, and were speeding for their homes when the poison caught them in its net. Great numbers of people were at the open windows of the houses. In Tunbridge Wells there was hardly one which had not its staring, smiling face. At the last instant the need of air, that very craving for oxygen which we alone had been able to satisfy, had sent them flying to the window. The side walks, too, were littered with men and women, hatless and bonnetless, who had rushed out of the houses. Many of them had fallen in the roadway. It was a lucky thing that in Lord John we had found an expert driver, for it was no easy matter to pick one's way. Passing through the villages or towns we could only go at a walking pace, and once, I remember, opposite the school at Tonbridge, we had to halt some time while we carried aside the bodies which blocked our path.

A few small, definite pictures stand out in my memory from amid that long panorama of death upon the Sussex and Kentish high roads. One was that of a great, glittering motor-car standing outside the inn at the village of Southborough. It bore, as I should guess, some pleasure party upon their return from Brighton or from Eastbourne. There were three gaily dressed women, all young and beautiful, one of them with a Peking spaniel upon her lap. With them were a rakish-looking elderly man and a young aristocrat, his eyeglass still in his eye, his cigarette burned down to the stub between the fingers of his begloved hand. Death must have come on them in an instant and fixed them as they sat. Save that the elderly man had at the last moment torn out his collar in an effort to breathe, they might all have been asleep. On one side of the car a waiter with some broken glasses beside a tray was huddled near the step. On the other two very ragged tramps, a man and a woman, lay where they had fallen, the man with his long, thin arm still outstretched, even as he had asked for alms in his lifetime. One instant of time had put aristocrat, waiter, tramp, and dog upon one common footing of inert and dissolving protoplasm.

I remember another singular picture, some miles on the London side of Sevenoaks. There is a large convent upon the left, with a long, green slope in front of it. Upon this slope were assembled a great number of school children, all kneeling at prayer. In front of them was a fringe of nuns, and higher up the slope, facing towards them, a single figure whom we took to be the Mother Superior. Unlike the pleasure-seekers in the motor-car, these people seemed to have had warning of their danger, and to have died beautifully together, the teachers and the taught, assembled for their last common lesson.

My mind is still stunned by that terrific experience, and I grope vainly for means of expression by which I can reproduce the emotions which we felt. Perhaps it is best and wisest not to try, but merely to indicate the facts. Even Summerlee and Challenger were crushed, and we heard nothing of our companions behind us save an occasional whimper from the lady. As to Lord John, he was too intent upon his wheel and the difficult task of threading his way along such roads to have time or inclination for conversation. One phrase he used with such wearisome iteration that it stuck in my memory, and at last almost made me laugh as a comment upon the day of doom.

'Pretty doin's! What!'

That was his ejaculation as each fresh tremendous combination of death and disaster displayed itself before us. 'Pretty doin's! What!' he cried, as we descended the Station Hill at Rotherfield, and it was still 'Pretty doin's! What!' as we picked our way through a wilderness of death in the High Street of Lewisham and the Old Kent Road.

It was here that we received a sudden and amazing shock. Out of the window of a humble corner house there appeared a fluttering handkerchief waving at the end of a long, thin human arm. Never had the sight of unexpected death caused our hearts to stop and then throb so wildly as did this amazing indication of life. Lord John ran the motor to the kerb, and in an instant we had rushed through the open door of the house and up the staircase to the second-floor front room from which the signal proceeded.

A very old lady sat in a chair by the open window, and close to her, laid across a second chair, was a cylinder of oxygen, smaller but of the same shape as those which had saved our own lives. She turned her thin, drawn, bespectacled face towards us as we crowded in at the doorway.

'I feared that I was abandoned here for ever,' said she, 'for I am an invalid and cannot stir.'

'Well, madam,' Challenger answered, 'it is a lucky chance that we happened to pass.'

'I have one all-important question to ask you,' said she. 'Gentlemen, I beg that you will be frank with me. What effect will these events have upon London and North-Western Railway shares?'

We should have laughed had it not been for the tragic eagerness with which she listened for our answer. Mrs Burston, for that was her name, was an aged widow whose whole income depended upon a small holding of this stock. Her life had been regulated by the rise or fall of the dividend, and she could form no conception of existence save as it was affected by the quotation of her shares. In vain we pointed out to her that all the money in the world was hers for the taking, and was useless when taken. Her old mind would not adapt itself to the new idea, and she wept loudly over her vanished stock. 'It was all I had,' she wailed. 'If that is gone I may as well go too.'

Amid her lamentations we found out how this frail old plant had lived where the whole great forest had fallen. She was a confirmed invalid and an asthmatic. Oxygen had been prescribed for her malady, and a tube was in her room at the moment of the crisis. She had naturally inhaled some as had been her habit when there was a difficulty with her breathing. It had given her relief, and by doling out her supply she had managed to survive the night. Finally she had fallen asleep and been awakened by the buzz of our motor-car. As it was impossible to take her on with us, we saw that she had all necessaries of life and promised to communicate with her in a couple of days at the latest. So we left her, still weeping bitterly over her vanished stock.

As we approached the Thames the block in the streets became thicker and the obstacles more bewildering. It was with difficulty that we made our way across London Bridge. The approaches to it upon the Middlesex side were choked from end to end with frozen traffic which made all further advance in that direction impossible. A ship was blazing brightly alongside one of the wharves near the bridge, and the air was full of drifting smuts and of a heavy acrid smell of burning. There was a cloud of dense smoke somewhere near the Houses of Parliament, but it was impossible from where we were to see what was on fire.

'I don't know how it strikes you,' Lord John remarked, as he brought his engine to a standstill, 'but it seems to me the country is more cheerful than the town. Dead London is gettin' on my nerves. I'm for a cast round and then gettin' back to Rotherfield.'

'I confess that I do not see what we can hope for here,' said Professor Summerlee.

'At the same time,' said Challenger, his great voice booming strangely amid the silence, 'it is difficult for us to conceive that out of seven millions of people there is only this one old woman who by some peculiarity of constitution or some accident of occupation has managed to survive this catastrophe.'

'If there should be others, how can we hope to find them, George?' asked the lady. 'And yet I agree with you that we cannot go back until we have tried.'

Getting out of the car, and leaving it by the kerb, we walked with some difficulty along the crowded pavement of King William Street, and entered the open door of a large insurance office. It was a corner house, and we chose it as commanding a view in every direction. Ascending the stair, we passed through what I suppose to have been the board-room, for eight elderly men were seated round a long table

A ship was blazing brightly alongside one of the wharves near the bridge, and the air was full of drifting smuts and of a heavy acrid smell of burning

in the centre of it. The high window was open and we all stepped out upon the balcony. From it we could see the crowded City streets radiating in every direction, while below us the road was black from side to side with the tops of the motionless taxis. All, or nearly all, had their heads pointed outwards, showing how the terrified men of the City had at the last moment made a vain endeavour to rejoin their families in the suburbs or the country. Here and there amid the humbler cabs towered the great brass-spangled motor-car of some wealthy magnate, wedged hopelessly amongst the dammed stream of arrested traffic. Just beneath us there was such a one of great size and luxurious appearance, with its owner, a fat old man, leaning out, half his gross body through the window, and his podgy hand, gleaming with diamonds, outstretched as he urged his chauffeur to make a last effort to break through the press.

A dozen motor-buses towered up like islands in this flood, the passengers who crowded the roofs lying all huddled together and across each others' laps like a child's toys in a nursery. On a broad lamp pedestal, in the centre of the roadway, a burly policeman was standing, leaning his back against the post in so natural an attitude that it was hard to realize that he was not alive, while at his feet there lay a ragged newsboy with his bundle of papers on the ground beside him. A paper-cart had got blocked in the crowd, and we could read in large letters, black upon yellow, 'Scene at Lord's. County match interrupted.' This must have been the earliest edition, for there were other placards bearing the legend, 'Is it the End? Great Scientist's Warning.' And another, 'Is Challenger Justified? Ominous Rumours.'

Challenger pointed the latter placard out to his wife, as it thrust itself like a banner above the throng. I could see him throw out his chest and stroke his beard as he looked at it. It pleased and flattered that complex mind to think that London had died with his name and his words still present in their thoughts. His feelings were so evident that they aroused the sardonic comment of his colleague.

'In the limelight to the last, Challenger,' he remarked.

'So it would appear,' he answered, complacently. 'Well,' he added, as he looked down the long vista of the radiating streets, all silent and all choked up with death, 'I really see no purpose to be served by our

On a broad lamp pedestal, in the centre of the roadway, a burly policeman was standing, leaning his back against the post in so natural an attitude that it was hard to realize that he was not alive

staying any longer in London. I suggest that we return at once to Rotherfield, and then take counsel as to how we shall most profitably employ the years which lie before us.'

Only one other picture shall I give of the scenes which we carried back in our memories from the dead City. It is a glimpse which we had of the interior of the old church of St Mary's, which is at the very point where our car was awaiting us. Picking our way among the prostrate figures upon the steps, we pushed open the swing door and entered. It was a wonderful sight. The church was crammed from end to end with kneeling figures in every posture of supplication and abasement. At the last dreadful moment, brought suddenly face to face with the realities of life, those terrific realities which hang over us even while we follow the shadows, the terrified people had rushed into those old City churches which for generations had hardly ever held a congregation. There they huddled as close as they could kneel, many of them in their agitation still wearing their hats, while above them in the pulpit a young man in lay dress had apparently been addressing them when he and they had been overwhelmed by the same fate. He lay now, like Punch in his booth, with his head and two limp arms hanging over the ledge of the pulpit. It was a nightmare, the grey, dusty church, the rows of agonized figures, the dimness and silence of it all. We moved about with hushed whispers, walking upon our tip-toes.

And then suddenly I had an idea. At one corner of the church, near the door, stood the ancient font, and behind it a deep recess in which there hung the ropes for the bellringers. Why should we not send a message out over London which would attract to us anyone who might still be alive? I ran across, and pulling at the list-covered rope I was surprised to find how difficult it was to swing the bell. Lord John had followed me.

'By George, young fellah!' said he, pulling off his coat. 'You've hit on a dooced good notion. Give me a grip and we'll soon have a move on it.'

But, even then, so heavy was the bell that it was not until Challenger and Summerlee had added their weight to ours that we heard the roaring and clanging above our heads which told us that the great clapper was ringing out its music. Far over dead London resounded our message of comradeship, and hope to any fellow-man surviving. It cheered our own hearts, that strong, metallic call, and we turned the more earnestly to our work, dragged two feet off the earth with each upward jerk of the rope, but all straining together on the downward heave, Challenger the lowest of all, bending all his great strength to the task, and flopping up and down like a monstrous bull-frog, croaking with every pull. It was at that moment that an artist might have taken a picture of the four adventurers, the comrades of many strange perils in the past, whom Fate had now chosen for so supreme an experience. For half an hour we worked, the sweat dropping from our faces, our arms and backs aching with the exertion. Then we went out into the portico of the church, and looked eagerly up and down the silent, crowded streets. Not a sound, not a motion, in answer to our summons.

'It's no use. No one is left,' I cried.

'We can do nothing more,' said Mrs Challenger. 'For God's sake, George, let us get back to Rotherfield. Another hour of this dreadful, silent City would drive me mad.'

We got into the car without another word. Lord John backed her round and turned her to the South. To us the chapter seemed closed. Little did we foresee the strange new chapter which was to open.

CHAPTER VI

The Great Awakening

And now I come to the end of this extraordinary incident so overshadowing in its importance, not only in our own small, individual lives, but in the general history of the human race. As I said when I began my narrative, when that history comes to be written this occurrence will surely stand out among all other events like a mountain towering among its foothills. Our generation has been reserved for a very special fate since it has been chosen to experience so wonderful a thing. How long its effect may last – how long mankind may preserve the humility and reverence which this great shock has taught it, can only be shown by the future. I think it is safe to say that things can never be quite the same again. Never can one realize how powerless and ignorant one is, and how one is upheld by an unseen hand, until for an instant that hand has seemed to close and to crush. Death has been imminent upon us. We know that at any moment it may be again. That grim presence shadows our lives, but who can deny that in that shadow the sense of duty, the feeling of sobriety and responsibility, the appreciation of the gravity and of the objects of life, the earnest desire to develop and improve, have grown and become real with us to a degree that has leavened our whole society from end to end? It is something beyond sects and beyond dogmas. It is rather an alteration of perspective, a shifting of our sense of proportion, a vivid realization that we are insignificant and evanescent creatures, existing on sufferance and at the mercy of the first chill wind from the unknown. But if the world has grown graver with this knowledge it is not, I think, a sadder place in consequence. Surely we are agreed that the more sober and restrained pleasures of the present are deeper as well as wiser than the noisy, foolish hustle which passed so often for enjoyment in the days of old – days so recent and yet already so inconceivable. Those empty lives which were wasted in aimless visiting and being visited, in the worry of great and unnecessary households, in the arranging and eating of elaborate and tedious meals, have now found rest and health in the reading, the music, the gentle family communion which comes from a simpler and saner division of their time. With greater health and greater pleasure they are richer than before, even after they have paid those increased contributions to the common fund which have so raised the standard of life in these islands.

There is some clash of opinion as to the exact hour of the great awakening. It is generally agreed that, apart from the difference of clocks, there may have been local causes which influenced the action of the poison. Certainly, in each separate district the resurrection was practically simultaneous. There are numerous witnesses that Big Ben pointed to ten minutes past six at the moment. The Astronomer Royal has fixed the Greenwich time at twelve past six. On the other hand, Laird Johnson, a very capable East Anglia observer, has recorded six-twenty as the hour. In the Hebrides it was as late as seven. In our own case there can be no doubt whatever, for I was seated in Challenger's study with his carefully-tested chronometer in front of me at the moment. The hour was a quarter-past six.

An enormous depression was weighing upon my spirits. The cumulative effect of all the dreadful sights which we had seen upon our journey was heavy upon my soul. With my abounding animal health and great physical energy any kind of mental clouding was a rare event. I had the Irish faculty of seeing some gleam of humour in every darkness. But now the obscurity was appalling and unrelieved. The others were downstairs making their plans for the future. I sat by the open window, my chin resting upon my hand, and my mind absorbed in the misery of our situation. Could we continue to live? That was the question which I had begun to ask myself. Was it possible to exist upon a dead world? Just as in physics the greater body draws to itself the lesser, would we not feel an overpowering attraction from that vast body of humanity which had passed into the unknown? How would the end come? Would it be from a return of the poison? Or would the earth be uninhabitable from the mephitic products of universal decay? Or, finally, might our awful situation prey upon and unbalance our minds? A group of insane folk upon a dead world! My mind was brooding upon this last dreadful idea when some slight noise caused me to look down upon the road beneath me. The old cab-horse was coming up the hill!

I was conscious at the same instant of the twittering of birds, of someone coughing in the yard below, and of a background of movement in the landscape. And yet I remember that it was that absurd, emaciated, superannuated cab-horse which held my gaze. Slowly and wheezily it was climbing the slope. Then my eye travelled to the driver sitting hunched up upon the box, and finally to the young man who was leaning out of the window in some excitement and shouting a direction. They were all indubitably, aggressively alive!

Everybody was alive once more! Had it all been a delusion? Was it conceivable that this whole poison belt incident had been an elaborate

*The young man . . . leaning out of the window in some excitement and
shouting a direction*

dream? For an instant my startled brain was really ready to believe it. Then I looked down, and there was the rising blister on my hand where it was frayed by the rope of the City bell. It had really been so, then. And yet here was the world resuscitated – here was life come back in an instant full tide to the planet. Now, as my eyes wandered all over the great landscape, I saw it in every direction – and moving, to my amazement, in the very same groove in which it had halted. There were the golfers. Was it possible that they were going on with their game? Yes, there was a fellow driving off from a tee, and that other group upon the green were surely putting for the hole. The reapers were slowly trooping back to their work. The nurse-girl slapped one of her charges and then began to push the perambulator up the hill. Everyone had unconcernedly taken up the thread at the very point where they had dropped it.

I rushed downstairs, but the hall door was open, and I heard the voices of my companions, loud in astonishment and congratulation, in the yard. How we all shook hands and laughed as we came together, and how Mrs Challenger kissed us all in her emotion, before she finally threw herself into the bear-hug of her husband!

'But they could not have been asleep!' cried Lord John. 'Dash it all, Challenger, you don't mean me to believe that those folk were asleep with their staring eyes and stiff limbs, and that awful death-grin on their faces!'

'It can only have been the condition that is called catalepsy,' said Challenger. 'It has been a rare phenomenon in the past and has constantly been mistaken for death. While it endures the temperature falls, the respiration disappears, the heartbeat is indistinguishable – in fact, it *is* death, save that it is evanescent. Even the most comprehensive mind' – here he closed his eyes and simpered – 'could hardly conceive a universal outbreak of it in this fashion.'

'You may label it catalepsy,' remarked Summerlee, 'but, after all, that is only a name, and we know as little of the result as we do of the poison which has caused it. The most we can say is that the vitiated ether has produced a temporary death.'

Austin was seated all in a heap on the step of the car. It was his coughing which I had heard from above. He had been holding his

There were the golfers. Was it possible that they were going on with their game? . . .
The reapers were slowly trooping back to their work

head in silence, but now he was muttering to himself and running his eyes over the car.

'Young fat-head!' he grumbled. 'Can't leave things alone!'

'What's the matter, Austin?'

'Lubricators left running, sir. Someone has been fooling with the car. I expect it's that young garden boy, sir.'

Lord John looked guilty.

'I don't know what's amiss with me,' continued Austin, staggering to his feet. 'I expect I came over queer when I was hosing her down. I seem to remember flopping over by the step. But I'll swear I never left those lubricator taps on.'

In a condensed narrative the astonished Austin was told what had happened to himself and the world. The mystery of the dripping lubricators was also explained to him. He listened with an air of deep distrust when told how an amateur had driven his car, and with absorbed interest to the few sentences in which our experiences of the sleeping City were recorded. I can remember his comment when the story was concluded.

'Was you outside the Bank of England, sir?'

'Yes, Austin.'

'With all them millions inside and everybody asleep?'

'That was so.'

'And I not there!' he groaned, and turned dismally once more to the hosing of his car.

There was a sudden grinding of wheels upon gravel. The old cab had actually pulled up at Challenger's door. I saw the young occupant step out from it. An instant later the maid, who looked as tousled and bewildered as if she had that instant been roused from the deepest sleep, appeared with a card upon a tray. Challenger snorted ferociously as he looked at it, and his thick black hair seemed to bristle up in his wrath.

'A Pressman!' he growled. Then, with a deprecating smile: 'After all, it is natural that the whole world should hasten to know what I think of such an episode.'

'That can hardly be his errand,' said Summerlee, 'for he was on the road in his cab before ever the crisis came.'

Mrs Challenger . . . threw herself into the bear-hug of her husband

I looked at the card: 'James Baxter, London Correspondent, *New York Monitor.*'

'You'll see him?' said I.

'Not I.'

'Oh, George! You should be kinder and more considerate to others. Surely you have learned something from what we have undergone.'

He tut-tutted and shook his big, obstinate head.

'A poisonous breed! Eh, Malone? The worst breed in modern civilization, the ready tool of the quack and the hindrance of the self-respecting man! When did they ever say a good word for me?'

'When did you ever say a good word to them?' I answered. 'Come, sir, this is a stranger who has made a journey to see you. I am sure that you won't be rude to him.'

'Well, well,' he grumbled, 'you come with me and do the talking. I protest in advance against any such outrageous invasion of my private life.' Muttering and mumbling, he came rolling after me like an angry and rather ill-conditioned mastiff.

The dapper young American pulled out his notebook and plunged instantly into his subject.

'I came down, sir,' said he, 'because our people in America would very much like to hear more about this danger which is, in your opinion, pressing upon the world.'

'I know of no danger which is now pressing upon the world,' Challenger answered, gruffly.

The Pressman looked at him in mild surprise.

'I meant, sir, the chances that the world might run into a belt of poisonous ether.'

'I do not now apprehend any such danger,' said Challenger.

The Pressman looked even more perplexed.

'You are Professor Challenger, are you not?' he asked.

'Yes, sir; that is my name.'

'I cannot understand, then, how you can say that there is no such danger. I am alluding to your own letter, published above your name in the London *Times* of this morning.'

It was Challenger's turn to look surprised.

'This morning?' said he. 'No London *Times* was published this morning.'

'Surely, sir,' said the American, in mild remonstrance, 'you must admit that the London *Times* is a daily paper.' He drew out a copy from his inside pocket. 'Here is the letter to which I refer.'

Challenger chuckled and rubbed his hands.

'I begin to understand,' said he. 'So you read this letter this morning?'

'Yes, sir.'

'And came at once to interview me?'

'Yes, sir.'

'Did you observe anything unusual upon the journey down?'

'Well, to tell the truth, your people seemed more lively and generally human than I have ever seen them. The baggage man set out to tell me a funny story, and that's a new experience for me in this country.'

'Nothing else?'

'Why, no, sir, not that I can recall.'

'Well, now, what hour did you leave Victoria?'

The American smiled.

'I came here to interview you, Professor, but it seems to be a case of "Is this nigger fishing, or is this fish niggering?" You're doing most of the work.'

'It happens to interest me. Do you recall the hour?'

'Sure. It was half-past twelve.'

'And you arrived?'

'At a quarter-past two.'

'And you hired a cab?'

'That was so.'

'How far do you suppose it is to the station?'

'Well, I should reckon the best part of two miles.'

'So how long do you think it took you?'

'Well, half an hour, maybe, with that asthmatic in front.'

'So it should be three o'clock?'

'Yes, or a trifle after it.'

'Look at your watch.'

The American did so, and then stared at us in astonishment.

'Say!' he cried. 'It's run down. That horse has broken every record, sure. The sun is pretty low, now that I come to look at it. Well, there's something here I don't understand.'

'Have you no remembrance of anything remarkable as you came up the hill?'

'Well, I seem to recollect that I was mighty sleepy once. It comes back to me that I wanted to say something to the driver, and that I couldn't make him heed me. I guess it was the heat, but I felt swimmy for a moment. That's all.'

'So it is with the whole human race,' said Challenger to me. 'They have all felt swimmy for a moment. None of them have as yet any comprehension of what has occurred. Each will go on with his inter-rupted job as Austin has snatched up his hose-pipe or the golfer continued his game. Your editor, Malone, will continue the issue of his papers, and very much amazed he will be at finding that an issue is missing. Yes, my young friend,' he added, to the American reporter, with a sudden mood of amused geniality, 'it may interest you to know that the world has swum safely through the poisonous current which swirls like the Gulf Stream through the ocean of ether. You will also kindly note for your own future convenience that today is not Friday, August the twenty-seventh, but Saturday, August the twenty-eighth, and that you sat senseless in your cab for twenty-eight hours upon the Rotherfield Hill.'

And 'right here', as my American colleague would say, I may bring this narrative to an end. It is, as you are probably aware, only a fuller and more detailed version of the account which appeared in the Monday edition of the *Daily Gazette* – an account which has been universally admitted to be the greatest journalistic scoop of all time, which sold no fewer than three-and-a-half million copies of the paper. Framed upon the wall of my sanctum I retain those magnificent headlines: –

TWENTY-EIGHT HOURS' WORLD COMA

UNPRECEDENTED EXPERIENCE

CHALLENGER JUSTIFIED

OUR CORRESPONDENT ESCAPES

ENTHRALLING NARRATIVE
THE OXYGEN ROOM
WEIRD MOTOR DRIVE
DEAD LONDON
REPLACING THE MISSING PAGE
GREAT FIRES AND LOSS OF LIFE
WILL IT RECUR?

Underneath this glorious scroll came nine-and-a-half columns of narrative, in which appeared the first, last, and only account of the history of the planet, so far as one observer could draw it, during one long day of its existence. Challenger and Summerlee have treated the matter in a joint scientific paper, but to me alone was left the popular account. Surely I can sing 'Nunc Dimittis'.[1] What is left but anti-climax in the life of a journalist after that!

But let me not end on sensational headlines and a merely personal triumph. Rather let me quote the sonorous passages in which the greatest of daily papers ended its admirable leader upon the subject – a leader which might well be filed for reference by every thoughtful man.

'It has been a well-worn truism,' said *The Times*, 'that our human race are a feeble folk before the infinite latent forces which surround us. From the prophets of old and from the philosophers of our own time the same message and warning have reached us. But, like all oft-repeated truths, it has in time lost something of its actuality and cogency. A lesson, an actual experience, was needed to bring it home. It is from that salutary but terrible ordeal that we have just emerged, with minds which are still stunned by the suddenness of the blow, and with spirits which are chastened by the realization of our own limitations and impotence. The world has paid a fearful price for its schooling. Hardly yet have we learned the full tale of disaster, but the destruction by fire of New York, of Orleans, and of Brighton constitutes in itself one of the greatest tragedies in the history of our race. When the account of the railway and shipping accidents has been completed, it will furnish grim reading, although there is evidence to show that in the vast majority of cases the drivers of trains and engineers of steamers succeeded in shutting off their motive power before succumbing to the poison. But the material damage, enormous as it is both in life and in property, is not the consideration which will be uppermost in our minds today. All this may in time be forgotten. But what will not be forgotten, and what will and should continue to obsess our imaginations, is this revelation of the possibilities of the universe, this destruction of our ignorant self-complacency, and this demonstration of how narrow is the path of our material existence, and what abysses may lie upon either side of it. Solemnity and humility are at the base of all our emotions today. May they be the foundations upon which a more earnest and reverent race may build a more worthy temple.'

THE END

'The Terror of Blue John Gap'

The following narrative was found among the papers of Dr James Hardcastle, who died of phthisis[1] on February 4, 1908, at 36, Upper Coventry Flats, South Kensington. Those who knew him best, while refusing to express an opinion upon this particular statement, are unanimous in asserting that he was a man of a sober and scientific turn of mind, absolutely devoid of imagination, and most unlikely to invent any abnormal series of events. The paper was contained in an envelope, which was docketed, 'A Short Account of the Circumstances which occurred near Miss Allerton's Farm in North-West Derbyshire in the Spring of Last Year.' The envelope was sealed, and on the other side was written in pencil –

'Dear Seaton, – It may interest, and perhaps pain you, to know that the incredulity with which you met my story has prevented me from ever opening my mouth upon the subject again. I leave this record after my death, and perhaps strangers may be found to have more confidence in me than my friend.'

Inquiry has failed to elicit who this Seaton may have been. I may add that the visit of the deceased to Allerton's Farm, and the general nature of the alarm there, apart from his particular explanation, have been absolutely established. With this foreword I append his account exactly as he left it. It is in the form of a diary, some entries in which have been expanded, while a few have been erased.

April 17. – Already I feel the benefit of this wonderful upland air. The farm of the Allertons lies fourteen hundred and twenty feet above sea-level, so it may well be a bracing climate. Beyond the usual morning cough I have very little discomfort, and, what with the fresh milk and the home-grown mutton, I have every chance of putting on weight. I think Saunderson will be pleased.

The two Miss Allertons are charmingly quaint and kind, two dear little hard-working old maids, who are ready to lavish all the heart which might have gone out to husband and to children upon an invalid stranger. Truly, the old maid is a most useful person, one of the reserve forces of the community. They talk of the superfluous woman, but what would the poor superfluous man do without her kindly presence? By the way, in their simplicity they very quickly let out the reason why Saunderson recommended their farm. The Professor rose from the ranks himself, and I believe that in his youth he was not above scaring crows in these very fields.

It is a most lonely spot, and the walks are picturesque in the extreme. The farm consists of grazing land lying at the bottom of an irregular valley. On each side are the fantastic limestone hills, formed of rock so soft that you can break it away with your hands. All this country is hollow. Could you strike it with some gigantic hammer it would boom like a drum, or possibly cave in altogether and expose some huge subterranean sea. A great sea there must surely be, for on all sides the streams run into the mountain itself, never to reappear. There are gaps everywhere amid the rocks, and when you pass through them you find yourself in great caverns, which wind down into the bowels of the earth. I have a small bicycle lamp, and it is a perpetual joy to me to carry it into these weird solitudes, and to see the wonderful silver and black effects when I throw its light upon the stalactites which drape the lofty roofs. Shut off the lamp, and you are in the blackest darkness. Turn it on, and it is a scene from the Arabian Nights.

But there is one of these strange openings in the earth which has a special interest, for it is the handiwork, not of nature, but of man. I had never heard of Blue John[2] when I came to these parts. It is the name given to a peculiar mineral of a beautiful purple shade, which is only found at one or two places in the world. It is so rare that an ordinary vase of Blue John would be valued at a great price. The Romans, with that extraordinary instinct of theirs, discovered that it was to be found in this valley, and sank a horizontal shaft deep into the mountain side. The opening of their mine has been called Blue John Gap, a clean-cut arch in the rock, the mouth all overgrown with bushes. It is a goodly passage which the Roman miners have cut, and it intersects some of the great water-worn caves, so that if you enter Blue John Gap you would do well to mark your steps and to have a good store of candles, or you may never make your way back to the daylight again. I have not yet gone deeply into it, but this very day I stood at the mouth of the arched tunnel, and peering down into the black recesses beyond, I vowed that when my health returned I would devote some holiday to exploring those mysterious depths and finding out for myself how far the Roman had penetrated into the Derbyshire hills.

Strange how superstitious these countrymen are! I should have thought better of young Armitage, for he is a man of some education and character, and a very fine fellow for his station in life. I was standing at the Blue John Gap when he came across the field to me.

'Well, doctor,' said he, 'you're not afraid, anyhow.'

'Afraid!' I answered. 'Afraid of what?'

'Of it,' said he, with a jerk of his thumb towards the black vault, 'of the Terror that lives in the Blue John Cave.'

How absurdly easy it is for a legend to arise in a lonely countryside! I examined him as to the reasons for his weird belief. It seems that from time to time sheep have been missing from the fields, carried bodily away, according to Armitage. That they could have wandered away of their own accord and disappeared among the mountains was an explanation to which he would not listen. On one occasion a pool of blood had been found, and some tufts of wool. That also, I pointed out, could be explained in a perfectly natural way. Further, the nights upon which sheep disappeared were invariably very dark, cloudy nights with no moon. This I met with the obvious retort that those were the nights which a commonplace sheep-stealer would naturally choose for his work. On one occasion a gap had been made in a wall, and some of the stones scattered for a considerable distance. Human agency again, in my opinion. Finally, Armitage clinched all his arguments by telling me that he had actually heard the Creature – indeed, that anyone could hear it who remained long enough at the Gap. It was a distant roaring of an immense volume. I could not but smile at this, knowing, as I do, the strange reverberations which come out of an underground water system running amid the chasms of a limestone formation. My incredulity annoyed Armitage so that he turned and left me with some abruptness.

And now comes the queer point about the whole business. I was still standing near the mouth of the cave, turning over in my mind the various statements of Armitage, and reflecting how readily they could be explained away, when suddenly, from the depth of the tunnel beside me, there issued a most extraordinary sound. How shall I describe it? First of all, it seemed to be a great distance away, far down in the bowels of the earth. Secondly, in spite of this suggestion of distance, it was very loud. Lastly, it was not a boom, nor a crash, such as one would associate with falling water or tumbling rock, but it was a high whine, tremulous and vibrating, almost like the whinnying of a horse. It was certainly a most remarkable experience, and one which for a moment, I must admit, gave a new significance to Armitage's words. I waited by the Blue John Gap for half an hour or more, but there was no return of the sound, so at last I wandered back to the farm-house, rather mystified by what had occurred. Decidedly I shall explore that cavern when my strength is restored. Of course, Armitage's explanation is too absurd for discussion, and yet that sound was certainly very strange. It still rings in my ears as I write.

April 20. – In the last three days I have made several expeditions to the Blue John Gap, and have even penetrated some short distance, but my bicycle lantern is so small and weak that I dare not trust myself very far. I shall do the thing more systematically. I have heard no sound at all, and could almost believe that I had been the victim of some hallucination suggested, perhaps, by Armitage's conversation. Of course, the whole idea is absurd, and yet I must confess that those bushes at the entrance of the cave do present an appearance as if some heavy creature had forced its way through them. I begin to be keenly interested. I have said nothing to the Miss Allertons, for they are quite superstitious enough already, but I have bought some candles, and mean to investigate for myself.

I observed this morning that among the numerous tufts of sheep's wool which lay among the bushes near the cavern there was one which was smeared with blood. Of course, my reason tells me that if sheep wander into such rocky places they are likely to injure themselves, and yet somehow that splash of crimson gave me a sudden shock, and for a moment I found myself shrinking back in horror from the old Roman arch. A fetid breath seemed to ooze from the black depths into which I peered. Could it indeed be possible that some nameless thing, some dreadful presence, was lurking down yonder? I should have been incapable of such feelings in the days of my strength, but one grows more nervous and fanciful when one's health is shaken.

For the moment I weakened in my resolution, and was ready to leave the secret of the old mine, if one exists, for ever unsolved. But tonight my interest has returned and my nerves grown more steady. Tomorrow I trust that I shall have gone more deeply into this matter.

April 22. – Let me try and set down as accurately as I can my extraordinary experience of yesterday. I started in the afternoon, and made my way to the Blue John Gap. I confess that my misgivings returned as I gazed into its depths, and I wished that I had brought a companion to share my exploration. Finally, with a return of resolution, I lit my candle, pushed my way through the briars, and descended into the rocky shaft.

It went down at an acute angle for some fifty feet, the floor being covered with broken stone. Thence there extended a long, straight passage cut in the solid rock. I am no geologist, but the lining of this corridor was certainly of some harder material than limestone, for there were points where I could actually see the tool-marks which the old miners had left in their excavation, as fresh as if they had been done yesterday. Down this strange, old-world corridor I stumbled, my feeble flame throwing a dim circle of light around me, which made the shadows beyond the more threatening and obscure. Finally, I came to a spot where the Roman tunnel opened into a water-worn cavern – a huge hall, hung with long white icicles of lime deposit. From this central chamber I could dimly perceive that a number of passages worn by the subterranean streams wound away into the depths of the earth. I was standing there wondering whether I had better return, or whether I dare venture farther into this dangerous labyrinth, when my eyes fell upon something at my feet which strongly arrested my attention.

The greater part of the floor of the cavern was covered with boulders of rock or with hard incrustations of lime, but at this particular point there had been a drip from the distant roof, which had left a patch of soft mud. In the very centre of this there was a huge mark — an ill-defined blotch, deep, broad and irregular, as if a great boulder had fallen upon it. No loose stone lay near, however, nor was there anything to account for the impression. It was far too large to be caused by any possible animal, and besides, there was only the one, and the patch of mud was of such a size that no reasonable stride could have covered it. As I rose from the examination of that singular mark and then looked round into the black shadows which hemmed me in, I must confess that I felt for a moment a most unpleasant sinking of my heart, and that, do what I could, the candle trembled in my outstretched hand.

I soon recovered my nerve, however, when I reflected how absurd it was to associate so huge and shapeless a mark with the track of any known animal. Even an elephant could not have produced it. I determined, therefore, that I would not be scared by vague and senseless fears from carrying out my exploration. Before proceeding, I took good note of a curious rock formation in the wall by which I could recognize the entrance of the Roman tunnel. The precaution was very necessary, for the great cave, so far as I could see it, was intersected by passages. Having made sure of my position, and reassured myself by examining my spare candles and my matches, I advanced slowly over the rocky and uneven surface of the cavern.

And now I come to the point where I met with such sudden and desperate disaster. A stream, some twenty feet broad, ran across my path, and I walked for some little distance along the bank to find a spot where I could cross dry-shod. Finally, I came to a place where a single flat boulder lay near the centre, which I could reach in a stride. As it chanced, however, the rock had been cut away and made top-heavy by the rush of the stream, so that it tilted over as I landed on it and shot me into the ice-cold water. My candle went out, and I found myself floundering about in utter and absolute darkness.

I staggered to my feet again, more amused than alarmed by my adventure. The candle had fallen from my hand, and was lost in the stream, but I had two others in my pocket, so that it was of no importance. I got one of them ready, and drew out my box of matches to light it. Only then did I realize my position. The box had been soaked in my fall into the river. It was impossible to strike the matches.

A cold hand seemed to close round my heart as I realized my position. The darkness was opaque and horrible. It was so utter that one put one's hand up to one's face as if to press off something solid. I stood still, and by an effort I steadied myself. I tried to reconstruct in my mind a map of the floor of the cavern as I had last seen it. Alas! the bearings which had impressed themselves upon my mind were high on the wall, and not to be found by touch. Still, I remembered in a general way how the sides were situated, and I hoped that by groping my way along them I should at last come to the opening of the Roman tunnel. Moving very slowly, and continually striking against the rocks, I set out on this desperate quest.

But I very soon realized how impossible it was. In that black, velvety darkness one lost all one's bearings in an instant. Before I had made a dozen paces, I was utterly bewildered as to my whereabouts. The rippling of the stream, which was the one sound audible, showed me where it lay, but the moment that I left its bank I was utterly lost. The idea of finding my way back in absolute darkness through that limestone labyrinth was clearly an impossible one.

I sat down upon a boulder and reflected upon my unfortunate plight. I had not told anyone that I proposed to come to the Blue John mine, and it was unlikely that a search party would come after me. Therefore I must trust to my own resources to get clear of the danger. There was only one hope, and that was that the matches might dry. When I fell into the river, only half of me had got thoroughly wet. My left shoulder had remained above the water. I took the box of matches, therefore, and put it into my left armpit. The moist air of the cavern might possibly be counteracted by the heat of my body, but even so, I knew that I could not hope to get a light for many hours. Meanwhile there was nothing for it but to wait.

By good luck I had slipped several biscuits into my pocket before I left the farm-house. These I now devoured, and washed them down with a draught from that wretched stream which had been the cause of all my misfortunes. Then I felt about for a comfortable seat among the rocks, and, having discovered a place where I could get a support for my back, I stretched out my legs and settled myself down to wait. I was wretchedly damp and cold, but I tried to cheer myself with the reflection that modern science prescribed open windows and walks in all weather for my disease. Gradually, lulled by the monotonous gurgle of the stream, and by the absolute darkness, I sank into an uneasy slumber.

How long this lasted I cannot say. It may have been for an hour, it may have been for several. Suddenly I sat up on my rock couch, with every nerve thrilling and every sense acutely on the alert. Beyond all doubt I had heard a sound – some sound very distinct from the gurgling of the waters. It had passed, but the reverberation of it still lingered in my ear. Was it a search party? They would most certainly have shouted, and vague as this sound was which had wakened me, it was very distinct from the human voice. I sat palpitating and hardly daring to breathe. There it was again! And again! Now it had become continuous. It was a tread – yes, surely it was the tread of some living creature. But what a tread it was! It gave one the impression of enormous weight carried upon sponge-like feet, which gave forth a muffled but ear-filling sound. The darkness was as complete as ever, but the tread was regular and decisive. And it was coming beyond all question in my direction.

My skin grew cold, and my hair stood on end as I listened to that steady and ponderous footfall. There was some creature there, and surely, by the speed of its advance, it was one which could see in the dark. I crouched low on my rock and tried to blend myself into it. The steps grew nearer still, then stopped, and presently I was aware of a loud lapping and gurgling. The creature was drinking at the stream. Then again there was silence, broken by a succession of long sniffs and snorts of tremendous volume and energy. Had it caught the scent of me? My own nostrils were filled by a low fetid odour, mephitic and abominable. Then I heard the steps again. They were on my side of the stream now. The stones rattled within a few yards of where I lay.

Hardly daring to breathe, I crouched upon my rock. Then the steps drew away. I heard the splash as it returned across the river, and the sound died away into the distance in the direction from which it had come.

For a long time I lay upon the rock, too much horrified to move. I thought of the sound which I had heard coming from the depths of the cave, of Armitage's fears, of the strange impression in the mud, and now came this final and absolute proof that there was indeed some inconceivable monster, something utterly unearthly and dreadful, which lurked in the hollow of the mountain. Of its nature or form I could frame no conception, save that it was both light-footed and gigantic. The combat between my reason, which told me that such things could not be, and my senses, which told me that they were, raged within me as I lay. Finally, I was almost ready to persuade myself that this experience had been part of some evil dream, and that my abnormal condition might have conjured up an hallucination. But there remained one final experience which removed the last possibility of doubt from my mind.

I had taken my matches from my armpit and felt them. They seemed perfectly hard and dry. Stooping down into a crevice of the rocks, I tried one of them. To my delight it took fire at once. I lit the candle, and, with a terrified backward glance into the obscure depths of the cavern, I hurried in the direction of the Roman passage. As I did so I passed the patch of mud on which I had seen the huge imprint. Now I stood astonished before it, for there were three similar imprints upon its surface, enormous in size, irregular in outline, of a depth which indicated the ponderous weight which had left them. Then a great terror surged over me. Stooping and shading my candle with my hand, I ran in a frenzy of fear to the rocky archway, hastened up it, and never stopped until, with weary feet and panting lungs, I rushed up the final slope of stones, broke through the tangle of briars, and flung myself exhausted upon the soft grass under the peaceful light of the stars. It was three in the morning when I reached the farm-house, and today I am all unstrung and quivering after my terrific adventure. As yet I have told no one. I must move warily in the matter. What would the poor lonely women, or the uneducated yokels here think of it if I were to tell them my experience? Let me go to someone who can understand and advise.

April 25. – I was laid up in bed for two days after my incredible adventure in the cavern. I use the adjective with a very definite meaning, for I have had an experience since which has shocked me almost as much as the other. I have said that I was looking round for someone who could advise me. There is a Dr Mark Johnson who practises some few miles away, to whom I had a note of recommendation from Professor Saunderson. To him I drove, when I was strong enough to get about, and I recounted to him my whole strange experience. He listened intently, and then carefully examined me, paying special attention to my reflexes and to the pupils of my eyes. When he had finished, he refused to discuss my adventure, saying that it was entirely beyond him, but he gave me the card of a Mr Picton at Castleton, with the advice that I should instantly go to him and tell him the story exactly as I had done to himself. He was, according to my adviser, the very man who was pre-eminently suited to help me. I went on to the station, therefore, and made my way to the little town, which is some ten miles away. Mr Picton appeared to be a man of importance, as his brass plate was displayed upon the door of a considerable building on the outskirts of the town. I was about to ring his bell, when some misgiving came into my mind, and, crossing to a neighbouring shop, I asked the man behind the counter if he could tell me anything of Mr Picton. 'Why,' said he, 'he is the best mad doctor in Derbyshire, and yonder is his asylum.' You can imagine that it was not long before I had shaken the dust of Castleton from my feet and returned to the farm, cursing all unimaginative pedants who cannot conceive that there may be things in creation which have never yet chanced to come across their mole's vision. After all, now that I am cooler, I can afford to admit that I have been no more sympathetic to Armitage than Dr Johnson has been to me.

April 27. – When I was a student I had the reputation of being a man of courage and enterprise. I remember that when there was a ghost-hunt at Coltbridge it was I who sat up in the haunted house. Is it advancing years (after all, I am only thirty-five), or is it this physical malady which has caused degeneration? Certainly my heart quails when I think of that horrible cavern in the hill, and the certainty that it has some monstrous occupant. What shall I do? There is not an hour in the day that I do not debate the question. If I say nothing, then the mystery remains unsolved. If I do say anything, then I have the alternative of mad alarm over the whole countryside, or of absolute incredulity which may end in consigning me to an asylum. On the whole, I think that my best course is to wait, and to prepare for some expedition which shall be more deliberate and better thought-out than the last. As a first step I have been to Castleton and obtained a few essentials – a large acetylene lantern for one thing, and a good double-barrelled sporting rifle for another. The latter I have hired, but I have bought a dozen heavy game cartridges, which would bring down a rhinoceros. Now I am ready for my troglodyte friend. Give me better health and a little spate of energy, and I shall try conclusions with him yet. But who and what is he? Ah! there is the question which stands between me and my sleep. How many theories do I form, only to discard each in turn! It is all so utterly unthinkable. And yet the cry, the footmark, the tread in the cavern – no reasoning can get past these. I think of the old-world legends of dragons and of other monsters. Were they, perhaps, not such fairy-tales as we have thought? Can it be that there is some fact which underlies them, and am I, of all mortals, the one who is chosen to expose it?

May 3. – For several days I have been laid up by the vagaries of an English spring, and during those days there have been developments, the true and sinister meaning of which no one can appreciate save myself. I may say that we have had cloudy and moonless nights of late, which according to my information were the seasons upon which sheep disappeared. Well, sheep *have* disappeared. Two of Miss Allerton's, one of old Pearson's of the Cat Walk, and one of Mrs Moulton's. Four in all during three nights. No trace is left of them at all, and the countryside is buzzing with rumours of gipsies and of sheep-stealers.

But there is something more serious than that. Young Armitage has disappeared also. He left his moorland cottage early on Wednesday night and has never been heard of since. He was an unattached man, so there is less sensation than would otherwise be the case. The popular explanation is that he owes money, and has found a situation in some other part of the country, whence he will presently write for his belongings. But I have grave misgivings. Is it not much more likely that the recent tragedy of the sheep has caused him to take some steps which may have ended in his own destruction? He may, for example, have lain in wait for the creature and been carried off by it into the recesses of the mountains. What an inconceivable fate for a civilized Englishman of the twentieth century! And yet I feel that it is possible and even probable. But in that case, how far am I answerable both for his death and for any other mishap which may occur? Surely with the knowledge I already possess it must be my duty to see that something is done, or if necessary to do it myself. It must be the latter, for this morning I went down to the local police-station and told my story. The inspector entered it all in a large book and bowed me out with commendable gravity, but I heard a burst of laughter before I had got down his garden path. No doubt he was recounting my adventure to his family.

June 10. – I am writing this, propped up in bed, six weeks after my last entry in this journal. I have gone through a terrible shock both to mind and body, arising from such an experience as has seldom befallen a human being before. But I have attained my end. The danger from the Terror which dwells in the Blue John Gap has passed never to return. Thus much at least I, a broken invalid, have done for the common good. Let me now recount what occurred as clearly as I may.

The night of Friday, May 3, was dark and cloudy – the very night for the monster to walk. About eleven o'clock I went from the farm-house with my lantern and my rifle, having first left a note upon the table of my bedroom in which I said that, if I were missing, search should be made for me in the direction of the Gap. I made my way to the mouth of the Roman shaft, and, having perched myself among the rocks close to the opening, I shut off my lantern and waited patiently with my loaded rifle ready to my hand.

It was a melancholy vigil. All down the winding valley I could see the scattered lights of the farm-houses, and the church clock of Chapel-le-Dale tolling the hours came faintly to my ears. These tokens of my fellow-men served only to make my own position seem the more lonely, and to call for a greater effort to overcome the terror which tempted me continually to get back to the farm, and abandon for ever this dangerous quest. And yet there lies deep in every man a rooted self-respect which makes it hard for him to turn back from that which he has once undertaken. This feeling of personal pride was my salvation now, and it was that alone which held me fast when every instinct of my nature was dragging me away. I am glad now that I had the strength. In spite of all that it has cost me, my manhood is at least above reproach.

Twelve o'clock struck in the distant church, then one, then two. It was the darkest hour of the night. The clouds were drifting low, and there was not a star in the sky. An owl was hooting somewhere among the rocks, but no other sound, save the gentle sough of the wind, came to my ears. And then suddenly I heard it! From far away down the tunnel came those muffled steps, so soft and yet so ponderous. I heard also the rattle of stones as they gave way under that giant tread. They drew nearer. They were close upon me. I heard the crashing of the bushes round the entrance, and then dimly through the darkness I was conscious of the loom of some enormous shape, some monstrous inchoate creature, passing swiftly and very silently out from the tunnel. I was paralysed with fear and amazement. Long as I had waited, now that it had actually come I was unprepared for the shock. I lay motionless and breathless, whilst the great dark mass whisked by me and was swallowed up in the night.

But now I nerved myself for its return. No sound came from the sleeping countryside to tell of the horror which was loose. In no way could I judge how far off it was, what it was doing, or when it might be back. But not a second time should my nerve fail me, not a second time should it pass unchallenged. I swore it between my clenched teeth as I laid my cocked rifle across the rock.

And yet it nearly happened. There was no warning of approach now as the creature passed over the grass. Suddenly, like a dark, drifting shadow, the huge bulk loomed up once more before me, making for the entrance of the cave. Again came that paralysis of volition which held my crooked forefinger impotent upon the trigger. But with a desperate effort I shook it off. Even as the brushwood rustled, and the monstrous beast blended with the shadow of the Gap,

I fired at the retreating form. In the blaze of the gun I caught a glimpse of a great shaggy mass, something with rough and bristling hair of a withered grey colour, fading away to white in its lower parts, the huge body supported upon short, thick, curving legs. I had just that glance, and then I heard the rattle of the stones as the creature tore down into its burrow. In an instant, with a triumphant revulsion of feeling, I had cast my fears to the wind, and uncovering my powerful lantern, with my rifle in my hand, I sprang down from my rock and rushed after the monster down the old Roman shaft.

My splendid lamp cast a brilliant flood of vivid light in front of me, very different from the yellow glimmer which had aided me down the same passage only twelve days before. As I ran, I saw the great beast lurching along before me, its huge bulk filling up the whole space from wall to wall. Its hair looked like coarse faded oakum, and hung down in long, dense masses which swayed as it moved. It was like an enormous unclipped sheep in its fleece, but in size it was far larger than the largest elephant, and its breadth seemed to be nearly as great as its height. It fills me with amazement now to think that I should have dared to follow such a horror into the bowels of the earth, but when one's blood is up, and when one's quarry seems to be flying, the old primaeval hunting-spirit awakes and prudence is cast to the wind. Rifle in hand, I ran at the top of my speed upon the trail of the monster.

I had seen that the creature was swift. Now I was to find out to my cost that it was also very cunning. I had imagined that it was in panic flight, and that I had only to pursue it. The idea that it might turn upon me never entered my excited brain. I have already explained that the passage down which I was racing opened into a great central cave. Into this I rushed, fearful lest I should lose all trace of the beast. But he had turned upon his own traces, and in a moment we were face to face.

That picture, seen in the brilliant white light of the lantern, is etched for ever upon my brain. He had reared up on his hind legs as a bear would do, and stood above me, enormous, menacing – such a creature as no nightmare had ever brought to my imagination. I have said that he reared like a bear, and there was something bear-like – if one could conceive a bear which was tenfold the bulk of any bear seen upon earth – in his whole pose and attitude, in his great crooked forelegs with their ivory-white claws, in his rugged skin, and in his red, gaping mouth, fringed with monstrous fangs. Only in one point did he differ from the bear, or from any other creature which walks the earth, and even at that supreme moment a shudder of horror passed over me as I observed that the eyes which glistened in the glow of my lantern were huge, projecting bulbs, white and sightless. For a moment his great paws swung over my head. The next he fell forward upon me, I and my broken lantern crashed to the earth, and I remember no more.

When I came to myself I was back in the farm-house of the Allertons. Two days had passed since my terrible adventure in the Blue John Gap. It seems that I had lain all night in the cave insensible from concussion of the brain, with my left arm and two ribs badly fractured. In the morning my note had been found, a search party of a dozen farmers assembled, and I had been tracked down and carried back to my bedroom, where I had lain in high delirium ever since. There was, it seems, no sign of the creature, and no bloodstain which would show that my bullet had found him as he passed. Save for my own plight and the marks upon the mud, there was nothing to prove that what I said was true.

Six weeks have now elapsed, and I am able to sit out once more in the sunshine. Just opposite me is the steep hillside, grey with shaly rock, and yonder on its flank is the dark cleft which marks the opening of the Blue John Gap. But it is no longer a source of terror. Never again through that ill-omened tunnel shall any strange shape flit out into the world of men. The educated and the scientific, the Dr Johnsons and the like, may smile at my narrative, but the poorer folk of the countryside had never a doubt as to its truth. On the day after my recovering consciousness they assembled in their hundreds round the Blue John Gap. As the *Castleton Courier* said:

'It was useless for our correspondent, or for any of the adventurous gentlemen who had come from Matlock, Buxton, and other parts, to offer to descend, to explore the cave to the end, and to finally test the extraordinary narrative of Dr James Hardcastle. The country people had taken the matter into their own hands, and from an early hour of the morning they had worked hard in stopping up the entrance of the tunnel. There is a sharp slope where the shaft begins, and great boulders, rolled along by many willing hands, were thrust down it until the Gap was absolutely sealed. So ends the episode which has caused such excitement throughout the country. Local opinion is fiercely divided upon the subject. On the one hand are those who point to Dr Hardcastle's impaired health, and to the possibility of cerebral lesions of tubercular origin giving rise to strange hallucinations. Some *idée fixe*, according to these gentlemen, caused the doctor to wander down the tunnel, and a fall among the rocks was sufficient to account for his injuries. On the other hand, a legend of a strange creature in the Gap has existed for some months back, and the farmers look upon Dr Hardcastle's narrative and his personal injuries as a final corroboration. So the matter stands, and so the matter will continue to stand, for no definite solution seems to us to be now possible. It transcends human wit to give any scientific explanation which could cover the alleged facts.'

Perhaps before the *Courier* published these words they would have been wise to send their representative to me. I have thought the matter out, as no one else has occasion to do, and it is possible that I might have removed some of the more obvious difficulties of the narrative and brought it one degree nearer to scientific acceptance. Let me then write down the only explanation which seems to me to elucidate what I know to my cost to have been a series of facts. My theory may seem to be wildly improbable, but at least no one can venture to say that it is impossible.

My view is – and it was formed, as is shown by my diary, before my personal adventure – that in this part of England there is a vast subterranean lake or sea, which is fed by the great number of streams which pass down through the limestone. Where there is a large collection of water there must also be some evaporation, mists or rain, and a possibility of vegetation. This in turn suggests that there may be animal life, arising, as the vegetable life would also do, from those seeds and types which had been introduced at an early period of the world's history, when communication with the outer air was more easy. This place had then developed a fauna and flora of its own, including such monsters as the one which I had seen, which may well have been the old cave-bear, enormously enlarged and modified by its new environment. For countless aeons the internal and the external creation had kept apart, growing steadily away from each other. Then there had come some rift in the depths of the mountain which had enabled one creature to wander up and, by means of the Roman tunnel, to reach the open air. Like all subterranean life, it had lost the power of sight, but this had no doubt been compensated for by nature in other directions. Certainly it had some means of finding its way about, and of hunting down the sheep upon the hillside. As to its choice of dark nights, it is part of my theory that light was painful to those great white eyeballs, and that it was only a pitch-black world which it could tolerate. Perhaps, indeed, it was the glare of my lantern which saved my life at that awful moment when we were face to face. So I read the riddle. I leave these facts behind me, and if you can explain them, do so; or if you choose to doubt them, do so. Neither your belief nor your incredulity can alter them, nor affect one whose task is nearly over.

So ended the strange narrative of Dr James Hardcastle.

'The Horror of the Heights'

(WHICH INCLUDES THE MANUSCRIPT KNOWN AS THE
JOYCE-ARMSTRONG FRAGMENT)

The idea that the extraordinary narrative which has been called the Joyce-Armstrong Fragment is an elaborate practical joke evolved by some unknown person, cursed by a perverted and sinister sense of humour, has now been abandoned by all who have examined the matter. The most *macabre* and imaginative of plotters would hesitate before linking his morbid fancies with the unquestioned and tragic facts which reinforce the statement. Though the assertions contained in it are amazing and even monstrous, it is none the less forcing itself upon the general intelligence that they are true, and that we must readjust our ideas to the new situation. This world of ours appears to be separated by a slight and precarious margin of safety from a most singular and unexpected danger. I will endeavour in this narrative, which reproduces the original document in its necessarily somewhat fragmentary form, to lay before the reader the whole of the facts up to date, prefacing my statement by saying that, if there be any who doubt the narrative of Joyce-Armstrong, there can be no question at all as to the facts concerning Lieutenant Myrtle, R.N., and Mr Hay Connor, who undoubtedly met their end in the manner described.

The Joyce-Armstrong Fragment was found in the field which is called Lower Haycock, lying one mile to the westward of the village of Withyham, upon the Kent and Sussex border. It was on the fifteenth of September last that an agricultural labourer, James Flynn, in the employment of Mathew Dodd, farmer, of the Chauntry Farm, Withyham, perceived a briar pipe lying near the footpath which skirts the hedge in Lower Haycock. A few paces farther on he picked up a pair of broken binocular glasses. Finally, among some nettles in the ditch, he caught sight of a flat, canvas-backed book, which proved to be a notebook with detachable leaves, some of which had come loose and were fluttering along the base of the hedge. These he collected, but some, including the first, were never recovered, and leave a deplorable hiatus in this all-important statement. The notebook was taken by the labourer to his master, who in turn showed it to Dr J. H. Atherton, of Hartfield. This gentleman at once recognized the need for an expert examination, and the manuscript was forwarded to the Aero Club[1] in London, where it now lies.

The first two pages of the manuscript are missing. There is also one torn away at the end of the narrative, though none of these affect the general coherence of the story. It is conjectured that the missing opening is concerned with the record of Mr Joyce-Armstrong's qualifications as an aeronaut, which can be gathered from other sources and are admitted to be unsurpassed among the air-pilots of England. For many years he has been looked upon as among the most daring and the most intellectual of flying men, a combination which has enabled him to both invent and test several new devices, including the common gyroscopic attachment which is known by his name. The main body of the manuscript is written neatly in ink, but the last few lines are in pencil and are so ragged as to be hardly legible – exactly, in fact, as they might be expected to appear if they were scribbled off hurriedly from the seat of a moving aeroplane. There are, it may be added, several stains, both on the last page and on the outside cover which have been pronounced by the Home Office experts to be blood – probably human and certainly mammalian. The fact that something closely resembling the organism of malaria was discovered in this blood, and that Joyce-Armstrong is known to have suffered from intermittent fever, is a remarkable example of the new weapons which modern science has placed in the hands of our detectives.

And now a word as to the personality of the author of this epoch-making statement. Joyce-Armstrong, according to the few friends who really knew something of the man, was a poet and a dreamer, as well as a mechanic and an inventor. He was a man of considerable wealth, much of which he had spent in the pursuit of his aeronautical hobby. He had four private aeroplanes in his hangars near Devizes, and is said to have made no fewer than one hundred and seventy ascents in the course of last year. He was a retiring man with dark moods, in which he would avoid the society of his fellows. Captain Dangerfield, who knew him better than anyone, says that there were times when his eccentricity threatened to develop into something more serious. His habit of carrying a shot-gun with him in his aeroplane was one manifestation of it.

Another was the morbid effect which the fall of Lieutenant Myrtle had upon his mind. Myrtle, who was attempting the height record, fell from an altitude of something over thirty thousand feet. Horrible to narrate, his head was entirely obliterated, though his body and limbs preserved their configuration. At every gathering of airmen, Joyce-Armstrong, according to Dangerfield, would ask, with an enigmatic smile: 'And where, pray, is Myrtle's head?'

On another occasion after dinner, at the mess of the Flying School on Salisbury Plain,[2] he started a debate as to what will be the most permanent danger which airmen will have to encounter. Having listened to successive opinions as to air-pockets, faulty construction, and overbanking, he ended by shrugging his shoulders and refusing to put forward his own views, though he gave the impression that they differed from any advanced by his companions.

It is worth remarking that after his own complete disappearance it was found that his private affairs were arranged with a precision which may show that he had a strong premonition of disaster. With these essential explanations I will now give the narrative exactly as it stands, beginning at page three of the blood-soaked notebook:–

'Nevertheless, when I dined at Rheims with Coselli and Gustav Raymond I found that neither of them was aware of any particular danger in the higher layers of the atmosphere. I did not actually say what was in my thoughts, but I got so near to it that if they had any corresponding idea they could not have failed to express it. But then they are two empty, vainglorious fellows with no thought beyond seeing their silly names in the newspaper. It is interesting to note that neither of them had ever been much beyond the twenty-thousand-foot level. Of course, men have been higher than this both in balloons and in the ascent of mountains. It must be well above that point that the aeroplane enters the danger zone – always presuming that my premonitions are correct.

'Aeroplaning has been with us now for more than twenty years,[3] and one might well ask: Why should this peril be only revealing itself in our day? The answer is obvious. In the old days of weak engines, when a hundred horse-power Gnome or Green[4] was considered ample for every need, the flights were very restricted. Now that three hundred horse-power is the rule rather than the exception, visits to the upper layers have become easier and more common. Some of us can remember how, in our youth, Garros[5] made a world-wide reputation by attaining nineteen thousand feet, and it was considered a remarkable achievement to fly over the Alps. Our standard now has been immeasurably raised, and there are twenty high flights for one in former years. Many of them have been undertaken with impunity. The thirty-thousand-foot level has been reached time after time with no discomfort beyond cold and asthma. What does this prove? A visitor might descend upon this planet a thousand times and never see a tiger. Yet tigers exist, and if he chanced to come down into a jungle he might be devoured. There are jungles of the upper air, and there are worse things than tigers which inhabit them. I believe in time they will map these jungles accurately out. Even at the present moment I could name two of them. One of them lies over the Pau-Biarritz district of France. Another is just over my head as I write here in my house in Wiltshire. I rather think there is a third in the Homburg-Wiesbaden district.

'It was the disappearance of the airmen that first set me thinking. Of course, everyone said that they had fallen into the sea, but that did not satisfy me at all. First, there was Verrier in France; his machine was found near Bayonne, but they never got his body. There was the case of Baxter also, who vanished, though his engine and some of the iron fixings were found in a wood in Leicestershire. In that case, Dr Middleton, of Amesbury, who was watching the flight with a telescope, declares that just before the clouds obscured the view he saw the machine, which was at an enormous height, suddenly rise perpendicularly upwards in a succession of jerks in a manner that he would have thought to be impossible. That was the last seen of Baxter. There was a correspondence in the papers, but it never led to anything. There were several other similar cases, and then there was the death of Hay Connor. What a cackle there was about an unsolved mystery of the air, and what columns in the halfpenny papers, and yet how little was ever done to get to the bottom of the business! He came down in a tremendous vol-plané[6] from an unknown height. He never got off his machine and died in his pilot's seat. Died of what? "Heart disease," said the doctors. Rubbish! Hay Connor's heart was as sound as mine is. What did Venables say? Venables was the only man who was at his side when he died. He said that he was shivering and looked like a man who had been badly scared. "Died of fright," said Venables, but could not imagine what he was frightened about. Only said one word to Venables, which sounded like "Monstrous". They could make nothing of that at the inquest. But I could make something of it. Monsters! That was the last word of poor Harry Hay Connor. And he *did* die of fright, just as Venables thought.

'And then there was Myrtle's head. Do you really believe – does anybody really believe – that a man's head could be driven clean into his body by the force of a fall? Well, perhaps it may be possible, but I, for one, have never believed that it was so with Myrtle. And the grease upon his clothes – "all slimy with grease," said somebody at the inquest. Queer that nobody got thinking after that! I did – but, then, I had been thinking for a good long time. I've made three ascents – how Dangerfield used to chaff me about my shot-gun! – but I've never been high enough. Now, with this new, light Paul Veroner machine and its one hundred and seventy-five Robur,[7] I should easily touch the thirty thousand tomorrow. I'll have a shot at the record. Maybe I shall have a shot at something else as well. Of course, it's dangerous. If a fellow wants to avoid danger he had best keep out of flying altogether and subside finally into flannel slippers and a dressing-gown. But I'll visit the air-jungle tomorrow – and if there's anything there I shall know it. If I return, I'll find myself a bit of a celebrity. If I don't, this notebook may explain what I am trying to do, and how I lost my life in doing it. But no drivel about accidents or mysteries, if *you* please.

'I chose my Paul Veroner monoplane for the job. There's nothing like a monoplane when real work is to be done. Beaumont found that out in very early days. For one thing, it doesn't mind damp, and the weather looks as if we should be in the clouds all the time. It's a bonny little model and answers my hand like a tender-mouthed horse. The engine is a ten-cylinder rotary Robur working up to one hundred and seventy-five. It has all the modern improvements – enclosed fuselage, high-curved landing skids, brakes, gyroscopic steadiers, and three speeds, worked by an alteration of the angle of the planes upon the Venetian-blind principle. I took a shot-gun with me and a dozen cartridges filled with buck-shot. You should have seen the face of Perkins, my old mechanic, when I directed him to put them in. I was dressed like an Arctic explorer, with two jerseys under my overalls, thick socks inside my padded boots, a storm-cap with flaps, and my talc goggles. It was stifling outside the hangars, but I was going for the summit of the Himalayas, and had to dress for the part. Perkins knew there was something on and implored me to take him with me. Perhaps I should if I were using the biplane, but a monoplane is a one-man show – if you want to get the last foot of lift out of it. Of course, I took an oxygen bag; the man who goes for the altitude record without one will either be frozen or smothered – or both.

'I had a good look at the planes, the rudder-bar, and the elevating lever before I got in. Everything was in order so far as I could see. Then I switched on my engine and found that she was running sweetly. When they let her go she rose almost at once upon the lowest speed. I circled my home field once or twice just to warm her up, and then, with a wave to Perkins and the others, I flattened out my planes and put her on her highest. She skimmed like a swallow down wind for eight or ten miles until I turned her nose up a little and she began to climb in a great spiral for the cloud-bank above me. It's all-important to rise slowly and adapt yourself to the pressure as you go.

'It was a close, warm day for an English September, and there was the hush and heaviness of impending rain. Now and then there came sudden puffs of wind from the south-west – one of them so gusty and unexpected that it caught me napping and turned me half-round for an instant. I remember the time when gusts and whirls and air-pockets used to be things of danger – before we learned to put an overmastering power into our engines. Just as I reached the cloud-banks, with the altimeter marking three thousand, down came the rain. My word, how it poured! It drummed upon my wings and lashed against my face, blurring my glasses so that I could hardly see. I got down on to a low speed, for it was painful to travel against it. As I got higher it became hail, and I had to turn tail to it. One of my cylinders was out of action – a dirty plug, I should imagine, but still I was rising steadily with plenty of power. After a bit the trouble passed, whatever it was, and I heard the full, deep-throated purr – the ten singing as one. That's where the beauty of our modern silencers comes in. We can at last control our engines by ear. How they squeal and squeak and sob when they are in trouble! All those cries for help were wasted in the old days, when every sound was swallowed up by the monstrous racket of the machine. If only the early aviators could come back to see the beauty and perfection of the mechanism which have been bought at the cost of their lives!

'About nine-thirty I was nearing the clouds. Down below me, all blurred and shadowed with rain, lay the vast expanse of Salisbury Plain. Half a dozen flying machines were doing hackwork at the thousand-foot level, looking like little black swallows against the green background. I dare say they were wondering what I was doing up in cloud-land. Suddenly a grey curtain drew across beneath me and the wet folds of vapours were swirling round my face. It was clammily cold and miserable. But I was above the hail-storm, and that was something gained. The cloud was as dark and thick as a London fog. In my anxiety to get clear, I cocked her nose up until the automatic alarm-bell[8] rang, and I actually began to slide backwards. My sopped and dripping wings had made me heavier than I thought, but presently I was in lighter cloud, and soon had cleared the first layer. There was a second – opal-coloured and fleecy – at a great height above my head, a white, unbroken ceiling above, and a dark, unbroken floor below, with the monoplane labouring upwards upon a vast spiral between them. It is deadly lonely in these cloud-spaces. Once a great flight of some small water-birds went past me, flying very fast to the westwards. The quick whir of their wings and their musical cry were cheery to my ear. I fancy that they were teal, but I am a wretched zoologist. Now that we humans have become birds we must really learn to know our brethren by sight.

'The wind down beneath me whirled and swayed the broad cloud-plain. Once a great eddy formed in it, a whirlpool of vapour, and through it, as down a funnel, I caught sight of the distant world. A large white biplane was passing at a vast depth beneath me. I fancy it was the morning mail service betwixt Bristol and London.[9] Then the drift swirled inwards again and the great solitude was unbroken.

'Just after ten I touched the lower edge of the upper cloud-stratum. It consisted of fine diaphanous vapour drifting swiftly from the west-ward. The wind had been steadily rising all this time and it was now blowing a sharp breeze – twenty-eight an hour by my gauge. Already it was very cold, though my altimeter only marked nine thousand. The engines were working beautifully, and we went droning steadily upwards. The cloud-bank was thicker than I had expected, but at last it thinned out into a golden mist before me, and then in an instant I had shot out from it, and there was an unclouded sky and a brilliant sun above my head – all blue and gold above, all shining silver below, one vast, glimmering plain as far as my eyes could reach. It was a quarter past ten o'clock, and the barograph[10] needle pointed to twelve thousand eight hundred. Up I went and up, my ears concentrated upon the deep purring of my motor, my eyes busy always with the watch, the revolution indicator, the petrol lever, and the oil pump. No wonder aviators are said to be a fearless race. With so many things to think of there is no time to trouble about oneself. About this time I noted how unreliable is the compass when above a certain height from earth. At fifteen thousand feet mine was pointing east and a point south. The sun and the wind gave me my true bearings.

'I had hoped to reach an eternal stillness in these high altitudes, but with every thousand feet of ascent the gale grew stronger. My machine groaned and trembled in every joint and rivet as she faced it, and swept away like a sheet of paper when I banked her on the turn, skimming down wind at a greater pace, perhaps, than ever mortal man has moved. Yet I had always to turn again and tack up in the wind's eye, for it was not merely a height record that I was after. By all my calculations it was above little Wiltshire that my air-jungle lay, and all my labour might be lost if I struck the outer layers at some farther point.

'When I reached the nineteen-thousand-foot level, which was about midday, the wind was so severe that I looked with some anxiety to the stays of my wings, expecting momentarily to see them snap or slacken. I even cast loose the parachute behind me, and fastened its hook into the ring of my leathern belt, so as to be ready for the worst. Now was the time when a bit of scamped work by the mechanic is paid for by the life of the aeronaut. But she held together bravely. Every cord and strut was humming and vibrating like so many harp-strings, but it was glorious to see how, for all the beating and the buffeting, she was still the conqueror of Nature and the mistress of the sky. There is surely something divine in man himself that he should rise so superior to the limitations which Creation seemed to impose – rise, too, by such unselfish, heroic devotion as this air-conquest has shown. Talk of human degeneration! When has such a story as this been written in the annals of our race?

'These were the thoughts in my head as I climbed that monstrous, inclined plane with the wind sometimes beating in my face and sometimes whistling behind my ears, while the cloud-land beneath me fell away to such a distance that the folds and hummocks of silver had all smoothed out into one flat, shining plain. But suddenly I had a horrible and unprecedented experience. I have known before what it is to be in what our neighbours have called a *tourbillon*,[11] but never on such a scale as this. That huge, sweeping river of wind of which I have spoken had, as it appears, whirlpools within it which were as monstrous as itself. Without a moment's warning I was dragged suddenly into the heart of one. I spun round for a minute or two with such velocity that I almost lost my senses, and then fell suddenly, left wing foremost, down the vacuum funnel in the centre. I dropped like a stone, and lost nearly a thousand feet. It was only my belt that kept me in my seat, and the shock and breathlessness left me hanging half-insensible over the side of the fuselage. But I am always capable of a supreme effort – it is my one great merit as an aviator. I was conscious that the descent was slower. The whirlpool was a cone rather than a funnel, and I had come to the apex. With a terrific wrench, throwing my weight all to one side, I levelled my planes and brought her head away from the wind. In an instant I had shot out of the eddies and was skimming down the sky. Then, shaken but victorious, I turned her nose up and began once more my steady grind on the upward spiral. I took a large sweep to avoid the danger-spot of the whirlpool, and soon I was safely above it. Just after one o'clock I was twenty-one thousand feet above the sea-level. To my great joy I had topped the gale, and with every hundred feet of ascent the air grew stiller. On the other hand, it was very cold, and I was conscious of that peculiar nausea which goes with rarefaction of the air. For the first time I unscrewed the mouth of my oxygen bag and took an occasional whiff of the glorious gas. I could feel it running like a cordial through my veins, and I was exhilarated almost to the point of drunkenness. I shouted and sang as I soared upwards into the cold, still outer world.

'It is very clear to me that the insensibility which came upon Glaisher, and in a lesser degree upon Coxwell,[12] when, in 1862, they ascended in a balloon to the height of thirty thousand feet, was due to the extreme speed with which a perpendicular ascent is made. Doing it at an easy gradient and accustoming oneself to the lessened barometric pressure by slow degrees, there are no such dreadful symptoms. At the same great height I found that even without my oxygen inhaler I could breathe without undue distress. It was bitterly cold, however, and my thermometer was at zero, Fahrenheit. At one-thirty I was nearly seven miles above the surface of the earth, and still ascending steadily. I found, however, that the rarefied air was giving markedly less support to my planes, and that my angle of ascent had to be considerably lowered in consequence. It was already clear that even with my light weight and strong engine-power there was a point in front of me where I should be held. To make matters worse, one of my sparking-plugs was in trouble again and there was intermittent misfiring in the engine. My heart was heavy with the fear of failure.

'It was about that time that I had a most extraordinary experience. Something whizzed past me in a trail of smoke and exploded with a loud, hissing sound, sending forth a cloud of steam. For the instant I could not imagine what had happened. Then I remembered that the earth is for ever being bombarded by meteor stones, and would be hardly inhabitable were they not in nearly every case turned to vapour in the outer layers of the atmosphere. Here is a new danger for the high-altitude man, for two others passed me when I was nearing the forty-thousand-foot mark. I cannot doubt that at the edge of the earth's envelope the risk would be a very real one.

'My barograph needle marked forty-one thousand three hundred when I became aware that I could go no farther. Physically, the strain was not as yet greater than I could bear, but my machine had reached its limit. The attenuated air gave no firm support to the wings, and the least tilt developed into side-slip, while she seemed sluggish on her controls. Possibly, had the engine been at its best, another thousand feet might have been within our capacity, but it was still misfiring, and two out of the ten cylinders appeared to be out of action. If I had not already reached the zone for which I was searching then I should never see it upon this journey. But was it not possible that I had attained it? Soaring in circles like a monstrous hawk upon the forty-thousand-foot level I let the monoplane guide herself, and with my Mannheim glass[13] I made a careful observation of my surroundings. The heavens were perfectly clear; there was no indication of those dangers which I had imagined.

'I have said that I was soaring in circles. It struck me suddenly that I would do well to take a wider sweep and open up a new air-tract. If the hunter entered an earth-jungle he would drive through it if he wished to find his game. My reasoning had led me to believe that the air-jungle which I had imagined lay somewhere over Wiltshire. This should be to the south and west of me. I took my bearings from the sun, for the compass was hopeless and no trace of earth was to be seen – nothing but the distant, silver cloud-plain. However, I got my direction as best I might and kept her head straight to the mark. I reckoned that my petrol supply would not last for more than another hour or so, but I could afford to use it to the last drop, since a single magnificent vol-plané could at any time take me to the earth.

'Suddenly I was aware of something new. The air in front of me had lost its crystal clearness. It was full of long, ragged wisps of something which I can only compare to very fine cigarette-smoke. It hung about in wreaths and coils, turning and twisting slowly in the sunlight. As the monoplane shot through it, I was aware of a faint taste of oil upon my lips, and there was a greasy scum upon the woodwork of the machine. Some infinitely fine organic matter appeared to be suspended in the atmosphere. There was no life there. It was inchoate and diffuse, extending for many square acres and then fringing off into the void. No, it was not life. But might it not be the remains of life? Above all, might it not be the food of life, of monstrous life, even as the humble grease of the ocean is the food for the mighty whale? The thought was in my mind when my eyes looked upwards and I saw the most wonderful vision that ever man has seen. Can I hope to convey it to you even as I saw it myself last Thursday?

'Conceive a jelly-fish such as sails in our summer seas, bell-shaped and of enormous size – far larger, I should judge, than the dome of St Paul's. It was of a light pink colour veined with a delicate green, but the whole huge fabric so tenuous that it was but a fairy outline against the dark blue sky. It pulsated with a delicate and regular rhythm. From it there depended two long, drooping, green tentacles, which swayed slowly backwards and forwards. This gorgeous vision passed gently with noiseless dignity over my head, as light and fragile as a soap-bubble, and drifted upon its stately way.

'I had half-turned my monoplane, that I might look after this beautiful creature, when, in a moment, I found myself amidst a perfect fleet of them, of all sizes, but none so large as the first. Some were quite small, but the majority about as big as an average balloon, and with much the same curvature at the top. There was in them a delicacy of texture and colouring which reminded me of the finest Venetian glass. Pale shades of pink and green were the prevailing tints, but all had a lovely iridescence where the sun shimmered through their dainty forms. Some hundreds of them drifted past me, a wonderful fairy squadron of strange, unknown argosies of the sky – creatures whose forms and substance were so attuned to these pure heights that one could not conceive anything so delicate within actual sight or sound of earth.

'But soon my attention was drawn to a new phenomenon – the serpents of the outer air. These were long, thin, fantastic coils of vapour-like material, which turned and twisted with great speed, flying round and round at such a pace that the eyes could hardly follow them. Some of these ghost-like creatures were twenty or thirty feet long, but it was difficult to tell their girth, for their outline was so hazy that it seemed to fade away into the air around them. These air-snakes were of a very light grey or smoke colour, with some darker lines within, which gave the impression of a definite organism. One of them whisked past my very face, and I was conscious of a cold, clammy contact, but their composition was so unsubstantial that I could not connect them with any thought of physical danger, any more than the beautiful bell-like creatures which had preceded them. There was no more solidity in their frames than in the floating spume from a broken wave.

'But a more terrible experience was in store for me. Floating downwards from a great height there came a purplish patch of vapour, small as I saw it first, but rapidly enlarging as it approached me, until it appeared to be hundreds of square feet in size. Though fashioned of some transparent, jelly-like substance, it was none the less of much more definite outline and solid consistence than anything which I had seen before. There were more traces, too, of a physical organization, especially two vast, shadowy, circular plates upon either side, which may have been eyes, and a perfectly solid white projection between them which was as curved and cruel as the beak of a vulture.

'The whole aspect of this monster was formidable and threatening, and it kept changing its colour from a very light mauve to a dark, angry purple so thick that it cast a shadow as it drifted between my monoplane and the sun. On the upper curve of its huge body there were three great projections which I can only describe as enormous bubbles, and I was convinced as I looked at them that they were charged with some extremely light gas which served to buoy up the misshapen and semi-solid mass in the rarefied air. The creature moved swiftly along, keeping pace easily with the monoplane, and for twenty miles or more it formed my horrible escort, hovering over me like a bird of prey which is waiting to pounce. Its method of progression – done so swiftly that it was not easy to follow – was to throw out a long, glutinous streamer in front of it, which in turn seemed to draw forward the rest of the writhing body. So elastic and gelatinous was it that never for two successive minutes was it the same shape, and yet each change made it more threatening and loathsome than the last.

'I knew that it meant mischief. Every purple flush of its hideous body told me so. The vague, goggling eyes which were turned always upon me were cold and merciless in their viscid hatred. I dipped the nose of my monoplane downwards to escape it. As I did so, as quick as a flash there shot out a long tentacle from this mass of floating blubber, and it fell as light and sinuous as a whip-lash across the front of my machine. There was a loud hiss as it lay for a moment across the hot engine, and it whisked itself into the air again, while the huge, flat body drew itself together as if in sudden pain. I dipped to a vol-piqué,[14] but again a tentacle fell over the monoplane and was shorn off by the propeller as easily as it might have cut through a smoke wreath. A long, gliding, sticky, serpent-like coil came from behind and caught me round the waist, dragging me out of the fuselage. I tore at it, my fingers sinking into the smooth, glue-like surface, and for an instant I disengaged myself, but only to be caught round the boot by another coil, which gave me a jerk that tilted me almost on to my back.

'As I fell over I blazed off both barrels of my gun, though, indeed, it was like attacking an elephant with a pea-shooter to imagine that any human weapon could cripple that mighty bulk. And yet I aimed better than I knew, for, with a loud report, one of the great blisters upon the creature's back exploded with the puncture of the buck-shot. It was very clear that my conjecture was right, and that these vast, clear bladders were distended with some lifting gas, for in an instant the huge, cloud-like body turned sideways, writhing desperately to find its balance, while the white beak snapped and gaped in horrible fury. But already I had shot away on the steepest glide that I dared to attempt, my engine still full on, the flying propeller and the force of gravity shooting me downwards like an aerolite.[15] Far behind me I saw a dull, purplish smudge growing swiftly smaller and merging into the blue sky behind it. I was safe out of the deadly jungle of the outer air.

'Once out of danger I throttled my engine, for nothing tears a machine to pieces quicker than running on full power from a height. It was a glorious, spiral vol-plané from nearly eight miles of altitude – first, to the level of the silver cloud-bank, then to that of the storm-cloud beneath it, and finally, in beating rain, to the surface of the earth. I saw the Bristol Channel beneath me as I broke from the clouds, but, having still some petrol in my tank, I got twenty miles inland before I found myself stranded in a field half a mile from the village of Ashcombe. There I got three tins of petrol from a passing motor-car, and at ten minutes past six that evening I alighted gently in my own home meadow at Devizes, after such a journey as no mortal upon earth has ever yet taken and lived to tell the tale. I have seen the beauty and I have seen the horror of the heights – and greater beauty or greater horror than that is not within the ken of man.

'And now it is my plan to go once again before I give my results to the world. My reason for this is that I must surely have something to show by way of proof before I lay such a tale before my fellow-men. It is true that others will soon follow and will confirm what I have said, and yet I should wish to carry conviction from the first. Those lovely iridescent bubbles of the air should not be hard to capture. They drift slowly upon their way, and the swift monoplane could intercept their leisurely course. It is likely enough that they would dissolve in the heavier layers of the atmosphere, and that some small heap of amorphous jelly might be all that I should bring to earth with me. And yet something there would surely be by which I could substantiate my story. Yes, I will go, even if I run a risk by doing so. These purple horrors would not seem to be numerous. It is probable that I shall not see one. If I do I shall dive at once. At the worst there is always the shot-gun and my knowledge of . . .'

Here a page of the manuscript is unfortunately missing. On the next page is written, in large, straggling writing:–

'Forty-three thousand feet. I shall never see earth again. They are beneath me, three of them. God help me; it is a dreadful death to die!'

Such in its entirety is the Joyce-Armstrong Statement. Of the man nothing has since been seen. Pieces of his shattered monoplane have been picked up in the preserves of Mr Budd-Lushington upon the borders of Kent and Sussex, within a few miles of the spot where the notebook was discovered. If the unfortunate aviator's theory is correct that this air-jungle, as he called it, existed only over the south-west of England, then it would seem that he had fled from it at the full speed of his monoplane, but had been overtaken and devoured by these horrible creatures at some spot in the outer atmosphere above the place where the grim relics were found. The picture of that monoplane skimming down the sky, with the nameless terrors flying as swiftly beneath it and cutting it off always from the earth while they gradually closed in upon their victim, is one upon which a man who valued his sanity would prefer not to dwell. There are many, as I am aware, who still jeer at the facts which I have here set down, but even they must admit that Joyce-Armstrong has disappeared, and I would commend to them his own words: 'This note-book may explain what I am trying to do, and how I lost my life in doing it. But no drivel about accidents or mysteries, if *you* please.'

NOTES

The Lost World

FOREWORD

1. *Mr E. D. Malone*: Malone's foreword is part of the half-serious, half-playful business of the authentication of *The Lost World* as an account of a genuine adventure (see Introduction). Challenger's combative, litigious instincts are early hinted at in Malone's reference to 'the injunction for restraint and the libel action'. As in the main text, Conan Doyle mingles real-life and fictional beings. William H. Ransford was a London photographer who had taken several official photographs of Doyle. The illustrations were the work of P. L. Forbes, either Patrick Lewis Forbes (Doyle's brother-in-law) or his son, Patrick Leckie Forbes. Both men appear in the original frontispiece photograph depicting the adventurers: Ransford is Malone, and Forbes is both Summerlee and Roxton. (I am indebted to Richard Lancelyn Green for the biographical information on Doyle's illustrators.)

CHAPTER I

1. *bimetallism*: Monetary doctrine, in vogue at the close of the nineteenth century, which held that currency should be based on silver as well as gold, the two metals being established by international agreement at a fixed ratio of value to each other. This, together with references to other economic topics such as Gresham's Law ('bad money tends to drive out good money from circulation'), indicates the style of Mr Hungerton's suburban theorizing, the antithesis of the novel's world of adventure.

2. *Theosophist*: Follower of the religio-mystic system established by Helena Blavatsky under the aegis of the Theosophical Society in 1875.

3. *Superman*: The term, coined by Friedrich Nietzsche (*Übermensch*), had recently been used by George Bernard Shaw in the title of his 1903 play *Man and Superman*.

4. *Burton*: The life of Richard Burton (1821–90), adventurer, anthropologist, author, could serve – in its more respectable aspects – as a template for the heroes of Haggard, Buchan and Doyle. Burton's wife Isabel produced an idealized biography of her husband in 1893.

5. *Lady Stanley*: Henry Morton Stanley (1841–1904) famously discovered Dr Livingstone but was also an explorer and imperial entrepreneur, helping to establish the Congo Free State and charting much of its interior. After his death, Dorothy Stanley edited her husband's *Autobiography* (1909).

6. *choke-damp*: 'miner's term for the carbonic acid gas (or air largely mixed therewith) which accumulates in old workings in coal' (*OED*).

7. *bucking*: Swaggering, bragging.

8. *Clive*: Robert Clive (1725–74), the victor of the battle of Plassey and twice Governor of Bengal, began his working life as a clerk with the East India Company in Madras in 1744. As Malone's reference indicates, it was the contrast between Clive's humble beginnings and his eventual wealth and status that made him a desirable role model for ambitious aspirants, even 150 years on.

CHAPTER II

1. *Munchausen*: Baron Munchausen (1720–97), a real-life figure, became the type of the tall-story-teller and fraudulent traveller after the publication of the *Narrative of his Marvellous Travels* (1785), compiled by Rudolph Erich Raspe.

2. *Weismannism*: The German biologist August Friedrich Weismann (1834–1914) was one of the founders of genetics. Professor of Zoology at the University of Freiburg, he was a fervent supporter of Charles Darwin (1809–82), but when the originator of evolutionary theory appeared to be modifying his views late in his career Weismann, in effect, out-Darwined Darwin. The author of *The Origin of Species* had become increasingly receptive to Lamarckism (from the French biologist Jean-Baptiste de Lamarck, 1744–1829), a part of which doctrine maintained that characteristics acquired *during* an individual's life could be inherited by its offspring. This contradiction of – or at best deviation from – 'pure' Darwinism was anathema to Weismann, who rejected any dilution of the theory of natural selection. For Weismann, every living organism contained a special hereditary substance which he termed the 'germ plasm'; this (the Victorian equivalent of DNA or chromosomes) could be altered only by chance mutation and recombination, not by characteristics acquired or 'learned' during that organism's existence. The disciple had, in a sense, become the opponent: hence the title of the article – 'Weismann *versus* Darwin' – reporting the Viennese conference in which Challenger was involved.

3. *Savage Club*: Founded in 1857, the Savage Club was 'instituted for the association of gentlemen connected professionally with Literature, Art, Science, the Drama, or Music' (from a 1911 handbook of rules and members).

4. Nature: This magazine, an important forum for scientific discussion, was established in 1869 by the astronomer Sir Joseph Norman Lockyer (1836–1920); he was still editing it at the time of the publication of *The Lost World* in 1912.

CHAPTER III

1. *arnica*: Natural remedy for sprains and bruises.

2. *Assyrian bull*: The specimens brought back to England by Austen Henry Layard (1817–94) from his mid-century excavations at Nineveh and Babylon made up the greater part of the Assyrian collection at the British Museum. Among them was a great winged bull.

3. *telegony*: 'the (imaginary) transmitted influence of a previous mate on the offspring of a female by a later mate' (*Chambers*).

4. *germ plasm . . . parthenogenetic egg*: For Weismann's concept of 'germ plasm' see note 2 to Ch. II above; a parthenogenetic egg is one that reproduces itself without fertilization. Challenger's purpose is to tie Malone in knots rather than to make sense.

5. *Three pound fifteen*: That is, 3 pounds, 15 shillings. This refers to the court-imposed fine or damages which Challenger had to pay for attacking a member of the Press, a not infrequent occurrence as shown by his own remarks and Malone's earlier recalling of 'his name in connection with the police-court proceedings' (p. 26).

6. *the London Irish*: Rugby Union football club founded in 1898 for London's Irish 'exiles'.

CHAPTER IV

1. *Wallace . . . Bates*: The Welsh naturalist Alfred Russel Wallace (1823–1913) began a joint collecting expedition to the Amazon with the English naturalist and explorer Henry Walter Bates (1825–92) in 1848. Wallace, who was to develop evolutionary ideas parallel to and independently of Darwin, later explored the Malay Peninsula.

2. *Lankester*: Sir Edwin Ray Lankester (1847–1929) held professorships in comparative anatomy at Oxford and London before becoming Director of the Natural History Museum in 1898. Challenger shows Malone an 'excellent monograph' that had appeared a few years earlier, a popularizing work by Lankester titled *Extinct Animals* (1905). Conan Doyle may have borrowed more than a book from this real-life figure. The *Dictionary of National Biography* (1937) refers to Lankester's 'impetuous temperament' and describes his imposing physical presence, with its 'tall and massive frame [and] deep booming voice', suggesting a potential source for Challenger.

3. *Curupuri*: In W. H. Hudson's *Green Mansions* (1904) there are several references to this wood-spirit (which Hudson styles Curupitá). 'I recalled some of the Indian beliefs, especially that of the misshapen, man-devouring monster [. . .]. I grew almost afraid to look round lest I should catch sight of him stealing towards me on his huge feet with toes pointing backwards, his mouth snarling horribly to display his great green fangs' (Ch. 3).

4. *dimorphodon*: A type of pterosaur discovered in Dorset; it had a four foot wing-span.

5. *Jurassic period*: The middle period of the Mesozoic era. The Jurassic (between about 190 million and 139 million years) was preceded by the Triassic and followed by the Cretaceous period. The three periods were collectively the 'Age of Reptiles'.

6. *plutonic*: Rocks produced at great depths below the earth's surface.

CHAPTER V

1. *Mandeville redivivus – Cagliostro*: Sir John Mandeville was the supposed author of a medieval book of extravagant traveller's tales set in the Middle East (*redivivus*: resuscitated (Latin)). Similarly, the Count of Cagliostro was a byword for unbelievability. This was the assumed title of Giuseppe Balsamo (1743–95), an Italian adventurer, conman and occult specialist.

2. *Wealden . . . Solenhofen slates*: The Wealden is a series of geological strata of the Cretaceous period (from about 139 million to 65 million years ago) located under and named after the Weald in Sussex. It is a fertile source of remains of the iguanodon, the herbivorous creature later sighted by the Lost World explorers. In the Solenhofen Limestone Formation in Bavaria, dating from the Jurassic period, fossil remains of a wide range of prehistoric animals, from jellyfish to pterosaurs, have been well preserved because of the fine-grained quality of the limestone.

3. *rancid Baconian*: Refers to the theory (which seems to have originated in the middle of the eighteenth century) that Francis Bacon (1561–1626) was the real author of Shakespeare's plays. Conan Doyle obviously did not subscribe to the theory: his application of 'rancid' to the Bacon-supporter is a nice example of the humour which characterizes much of this episode.

4. *Berserk*: A Berserk was a Norse warrior who showed a mad fury on the battlefield.

5. *Grave and reverend seniors*: Allusion to the beginning of Othello's speech to the Venetian Senate: 'Most potent, grave and reverend signiors' (*Othello* I. iii). Like Othello, Challenger has caused an upset to the smooth deliberations of a heavyweight institution.

CHAPTER VI

1. *aristocratic rookery*: The Albany in Piccadilly, originally a single mansion before conversion into bachelor apartments. Its occupation by distinguished literary and political figures, from Lord Byron to Alan Clark, has given the address a certain cachet right up to the present day. Interestingly, Conan Doyle employs the term 'rookery' (here qualified by 'aristocratic' because it usually refers to slums) to describe both the pterodactyl swamp and the Ape-Town later in the novel.

2. *Fragonard . . . Girardet . . . Turner*: Lord John's choice of painters reflects a catholic taste. Jean-Honoré Fragonard (1732–1806) is best known for elegantly erotic paintings such as *The Swing*. Édouard Girardet (1819–80) was a Swiss painter and engraver, now little known; among his paintings is a scene from the Crusades, *The Capture of Jaffa*, the kind of subject-matter that perhaps explains Doyle's description of 'martial'. The controversy surrounding the work of J. M. W. Turner (1775–1851) had long since faded but the application of 'dreamy' to Roxton's picture suggests that his preference was for the more impressionistic, abstract side of that artist. Any sense of unhealthy aestheticism is dispelled by props like the oars, foils and boxing-gloves.

3. *Oxonian and Leander*: Roxton belongs to two famous rowing clubs: the Oxford University Boat Club (signified by the dark-blue oar) and Leander (the cherry-pink), a prestigious club largely made up of Oxford and Cambridge oarsmen and originally based in London, later at Henley-on-Thames.

4. *Napoleon III . . . Don Quixote*: The references are to Napoleon III (1808–73), Emperor of France, and to Cervantes's hero. Doyle is thinking of Lord John's appearance but perhaps also evoking an imperial insouciance as well as an endearing chivalry.

5. *jock*: Jockey.

6. *Grand National*: Famous horse race held every year at Aintree in Liverpool.

7. *close-tiled*: To keep 'close-tiled' is to keep secret. The term comes from freemasonry, a tiler (more usually, tyler) being the 'door-keeper who keeps the uninitiated from intruding upon the secrecy of the lodge or meeting' (*OED*).

8. *a Booth boat*: The brothers Charles and Alfred Booth inaugurated a shipping service between Europe and Brazil in 1866; this was reorganized as the Booth Steamship Company in 1901.

9. *Para*: Port town (now Belém) at the mouth of the Amazon.

10. *Gordon*: The Australian writer, and amateur steeplechase rider, Adam Lindsay Gordon (1833–70), author of three volumes of poetry. The lines Lord John recites are from 'Lex Talionis'.

11. *Blue-book*: Report produced by Parliament. Roger Casement's investigation into the abuses of the Peruvian Amazon Rubber Company appeared as a Blue Book in 1912 (see Introduction).

12. *Matto Grosso*: Roxton makes a sweep over Brazil: the Mato Grosso (modernized spelling) is in the south between the Amazon and River Paraguay basins while the 'corner where three countries meet' is the northern triangle of Brazil, bounded to the north-west by Venezuela and to the east by what was then British Guiana (now Guyana).

13. *'down, hull-down, on the old trail'*: A ship which is 'hull-down' is distant enough from the observer for its hull to be invisible below the horizon. Malone's apparent conflation of journeys by land and sea suggests a mangled memory of some travelling refrain.

CHAPTER VII

1. *Manaos*: Capital of Amazonas state and a substantial inland river-port, Manaus, like Pará (modernized spellings) at the head of the Amazon, was at the time benefiting from a boom in the rubber trade.

2. *fazenda*: Large estate or ranch (Portuguese).

3. *at the exact moment when my presence was needed*: Challenger's dramatic entrance and his not altogether convincing justification of his covert manoeuvres recall Sherlock Holmes's explanation to Watson in *The Hound of the Baskervilles* (1902) of why the great detective has kept his presence on Dartmoor a secret from his associate: ' "As it is, I have been able to get about as I could not possibly have done had I been living at the Hall, and I remain an unknown factor in the business, ready to throw in all my weight at a critical moment" ' (Ch. 12). Challenger's taste for the *coup de théâtre*, his claim to freedom of action and movement, and his general arrogance are all reminiscent of Holmes.

CHAPTER VIII

1. *bravos, not mansos*: Wild, not tame (Portuguese).

2. *Darwin . . . Wallace*: During his voyage on the *Beagle* (1831–6) Darwin made several expeditions on the South American mainland. Attended only by guides, he rode across large tracts of Argentina and Chile, observing and gathering specimens. According to his biographers Adrian Desmond and James Moore, he became 'quite a gaucho himself. The rough-riding suited him perfectly' (*Darwin*, Michael Joseph, 1991). The Welsh naturalist Alfred Russel Wallace, the author of *Malay Archipelago* (dedicated to Darwin), made expeditions to the Malay Peninsula and to Borneo in the 1850s and 1860s (see note 1 to Ch. IV).

3. *polysynthetic speech*: Speech which combines simple words into a single unit, a characteristic of indigenous American languages.

4. *Mongolian theory*: Theory that the native inhabitants of North and South America were the descendants of migrants from eastern Asia. 'Mongolian' was one of the three principal classifications of the human species made by J. F. Blumenbach (in 1795), the others being 'Caucasian' and 'Ethiopian'. The most important consideration in this system of racial classification was the shape of the skull.

CHAPTER IX

1. *heroes of Virgil . . . Harpies*: In book 3 of Virgil's *Aeneid* Aeneas and his followers have their cooked food snatched from them by the Harpies, giant birds with the faces of women. Conan Doyle had the original very much in mind: 'They tear the banquet to pieces, filthying all with their bestial/Touch. Hideous the sounds, nauseous the stench about us' (trans. C. Day-Lewis).

2. vestigia nulla retrorsum: Slightly modified quotation from Horace (*Epistles* I. i. 73–5) meaning '[there are] no footsteps [going] in return': 'olim quod volpes aegroto cauta leoni/respondit, referam: "quia me vestigia terrent,/omnia te adversum spectantia, nulla retrorsum"'. Interestingly, Horace uses an animal analogy to describe his unwillingness to follow the crowd, saying that, if asked why he didn't do so, 'I should reply as once upon a time the prudent fox made answer to the sick lion: "Because these footprints frighten me; they all lead toward your den, and none lead back"' (trans. H. R. Fairclough, 1929). The original context of the quotation is at odds with Challenger's 'glorious goal' rhetoric but, since the group is about to cross into the Lost World, perhaps he is subconsciously influenced by the image of a dangerous wild animal and its potential prey.

CHAPTER X

1. *zareba*: Enclosure made of thorn bushes, etc. The term, used in the Sudan, derives from an Arabic word for a cattle-pen.

2. *shikarree*: Hunter (from Urdu).

3. *a worthy Sussex doctor*: Gideon Martell (1790–1852) was a general practitioner in Lewes, Sussex, but – rather like Conan Doyle – achieved fame in other fields. He wrote and lectured on the palaeontology of the Mesozoic period and uncovered several dinosaur types.

4. Nunc dimittis!: Having seen the ultimate wonder of the living dinosaurs, Summerlee uses the opening phrase of the Song of Simeon (Luke 2: 29–32). A devout inhabitant of Jerusalem, Simeon had been promised that he should not die before seeing Christ. When the infant Christ was presented in the temple, he began his Song: 'Lord, now lettest thou thy servant depart in peace, according to thy word.'

5. *Seven Circles of Dante*: Reference to the description (in canto xiii) of the Harpies in the Seventh Circle of Dante's *Inferno*: 'With broad wings and a human neck and face,/Claws on their feet, and feathers on their breasts,/Perched on the ghastly trees they make lament' (trans. Kenneth Mackenzie). See also note 1 to Ch. IX.

6. *Hendon aerodrome upon a race day*: Hendon (in Middlesex) was the site of one of the earliest aerodromes in Britain. It was used for races and trial flights as well as military reviews.

CHAPTER XI

1. *breccia*: 'a rock composed of angular fragments' (*Chambers*).

2. locum tenens: Deputy, stand-in (Latin).

3. *A face was gazing into mine . . . far more human than any monkey's that I have ever seen*: Compare the similar moment in Hudson's *Green Mansions* when the narrator Abel looks up, alerted by rustling in the foliage: 'High up, where a pale gleam of tempered sunlight fell through the leaves, a grotesque human-like face, black as ebony and adorned with a great red beard, appeared staring down upon me. In another moment it was gone. It was only a large araguato, or howling monkey, but I was so unnerved that I could not get rid of the idea that it was something more than a monkey' (Ch. 3). See also Introduction.

CHAPTER XIII

1. *Chesterfields*: The statesman Philip Dormer Stanhope (1694–1773), 4th Earl of Chesterfield, is best known for his 'Letters' written to his son. Their worldly good sense makes him an exemplar of culture and good manners, as Lord John's comment rather obliquely suggests.

2. *Missin' Links*: The Victorians were much preoccupied by the search for evidence of the hypothetical (and presumably extinct) 'missing' creature which would link man to the anthropoid ape in an unbroken line of descent (see also Introduction). Something of the same mixture of curiosity and fear as to the outcome is shown now in the search for extraterrestrial life.

3. *"Last Stand of the Greys"*: In Rider Haggard's *King Solomon's Mines* (1886), the Greys are 'the pride and glory of the Kukuana army', a Zulu-style people alongside whom the white heroes fight against apparently overwhelming odds. Lord John cites a chapter heading from Haggard's novel.

4. *"Ring out wild bells"*: The words are from Tennyson's *In Memoriam* (cvi, verse 1). Tennyson's poetry was a popular source for late Victorian composers and song-writers. I have not been able to identify the composer but this setting is evidently a favourite with Challenger, since the same song is mentioned in *The Poison Belt* (see note 4 to Ch. IV of *The Poison Belt*).

5. *dryopithecus . . . pithecanthropus*: Fossil remains of these 'ape-men' were discovered, respectively, in 1856 on the French side of the Pyrenees and in 1891 in Java.

6. *Shrubb*: Alfred Shrubb (1878–1964) was a famous long-distance and cross-country runner who broke records and won titles at national and international level in the early years of the twentieth century. His amateur status, which he held until 1905, would have made him a particularly appealing figure to that supreme amateur, Lord John Roxton (as well as to Conan Doyle).

CHAPTER XIV

1. *For a moment I had a glimpse of the human spirits behind their scientific masks*: This moment is echoed and amplified in one of the most famous scenes of the Holmes canon. In the late short story 'The Three Garridebs' (in *The Case-Book of Sherlock Holmes*) Holmes is distraught when Watson is shot: 'It was worth a wound – it was worth many wounds – to know the depth of loyalty and love which lay behind that cold mask. The clear, hard eyes were dimmed for a moment, and the firm lips were shaking. For the one and only time I caught a glimpse of a great heart as well as a great brain.'

CHAPTER XV

1. *Ezekiel*: The Old Testament prophet who was exiled to Babylon (*c.* 597 BC) on the orders of King Nebuchadnezzar and who prophesied the fall of his native Jerusalem because of 'the guilt of the house of Israel'.

CHAPTER XVI

1. *Bathybius*: Thomas Huxley coined this word in 1868 in the *Quarterly Journal of Microscopic Science* to describe a 'gelatinous substance' found at the bottom of the Atlantic Ocean. The reference is a good example of Conan Doyle's adroit use of scientific terminology in *The Lost World*.
2. *spud*: A kind of trowel.

The Poison Belt

CHAPTER I

1. *Frauenhofer's lines*: Joseph von Fraunhofer (*sic*) (1787–1826), a German physicist and optician, was the first to investigate the dark lines of absorption appearing in the sun's spectrum.
2. *ocean of ether*: 'Ether' was the term widely used in the eighteenth and nineteenth centuries to characterize the medium which, it was thought, must fill or permeate interplanetary and interstellar space. Almost magical properties were attributed to this mysterious substance at various times, including the conductivity of light, magnetism, etc. A contemporary scientific equivalent to ether might be the so-called 'dark matter', posited to account for the fact that the mass of the universe is apparently much greater than what can be estimated by direct observation.
3. ex cathedrâ: Literally, 'from the chair of office' (ecclesiastical Latin). When the Pope speaks *ex cathedra* he utters 'infallible decrees'. Summerlee's ironic description of his rival as 'a Pope of science' points to Challenger's taste for dogmatic assertion and his belief in his own rightness.

CHAPTER II

1. *International*: Someone selected to play for his country at international level. Malone has evidently advanced since his days with the London Irish in *The Lost World* (see note 6 to Ch. III of *The Lost World*). The game referred to by Lord John is rugby football.

2. *vibrio*: Bacterium with a spiral curve and tail-like flagellum. Challenger's reductive comparison shows the insignificance of the human species in the face of cosmic disaster.

3. *Datura*: Genus of poisonous plants.

4. Peste foudroyant: Correctly, *peste foudroyante* (French), literally a 'plague striking like lightning' and so, a devastating blow.

5. *Ararat*: Mt. Ararat (in modern Turkey) was where, in the Old Testament (Genesis 8: 4), Noah's Ark came to rest after the Flood, and therefore symbolizes any haven after a universal disaster, as Challenger's next words indicate.

6. *'Very good, sir'*: This exchange between Challenger and his manservant gives strong support to the idea that Austin was the original for P. G. Wodehouse's 'gentleman's gentleman', Jeeves. Certainly, Wodehouse had a profound admiration for Arthur Conan Doyle, both as a writer and as a man: 'I still revere his work as much as ever. I used to think it swell, and I still think it swell' (Wodehouse letter, cited in Owen Dudley Edwards, *The Quest for Sherlock Holmes* (1983)).

7. *laughing-gas*: Gas (nitrous oxide), so called because it may cause laughter when first inhaled. Widely used at the time as an anaesthetic by dentists.

8. *materialism*: Challenger's slighting reference to the philosophical/scientific doctrine that nothing exists apart from matter reflects Conan Doyle's own well-established religious and spiritualist convictions.

CHAPTER III

1. *the Clericals and the Anarchists*: There was much political and social unrest in Spain in the early twentieth century. Conan Doyle may have had in mind the collapse of public order in Barcelona for a period in 1909, during which Anarchists and Radical Republicans burned down churches and convents.

2. *Aruwimi River*: In the Congo (Zaire).

3. *Soudan*: Presumably an allusion to the battle of Omdurman (1898), in which an Anglo-Egyptian army led by Major-General (later Lord) Kitchener inflicted a crushing defeat on the Mahdist forces and re-established British control over the Sudan. There were earlier engagements involving heavy casualties on both sides in 1883 and 1889, but it is likely that Roxton is referring to the most famous as well as the most recent of the battles.

CHAPTER IV

1. *diatoms*: 'a class of microscopic unicellular algae with flinty shells in two halves, fitting like box and lid' (*Chambers*).
2. *Golgotha*: Place of burial, boneyard – literally, 'the place of a skull' (Hebrew). In the New Testament, Golgotha is the site of Christ's crucifixion.
3. *Anglo-German competition . . . the Persian Gulf*: The main manifestation of the intense rivalry between Britain and Germany in the years leading up to the First World War was the struggle for naval supremacy between the two countries. The Persian Gulf was a cockpit of competing superpower interest as the Ottoman Empire entered its final decline.
4. *"Ring out the old, ring in the new"*: The line is from Tennyson's *In Memoriam* (cvi, verse 2). The setting of this particular canto, which deals with change and renewal, is a favourite with the Professor (see note 4 to Ch. XIII of *The Lost World*) and, as Mrs Challenger says, is a 'prophetic' utterance in the context of *The Poison Belt*.

CHAPTER VI

1. *'Nunc Dimittis'*: See *The Lost World*, note 4 to Ch. X.

'The Terror of Blue John Gap'

1. *phthisis*: Tuberculosis.
2. *Blue John*: Variety of the mineral fluorspar, commonly found in Derbyshire and once used in the ornamentation of vases, etc.

'The Horror of the Heights'

1. *Aero Club*: The Aero Club (which became the Royal Aero Club by 1910) was founded in 1901 as a club for balloonists.
2. *Flying School on Salisbury Plain*: The Royal Flying Corps established the Central Flying School in 1912 at Upavon in Wiltshire, on the edge of Salisbury Plain. This remote site, used for basic flying training, was supposedly chosen

so that the new art of aviation could be practised away from prying eyes.

3. *Aeroplaning has been with us now for more than twenty years*: The Wright brothers' flight (the first powered, manned flight in history) took place in 1902, only eleven years before the publication of 'The Horror of the Heights'. This is one of several details which indicate that Conan Doyle intended the narrative to be set a few years ahead of its publication date.

4. *a hundred horse-power Gnome or Green*: The 'Gnome' engine, a French design, was commonly found in aircraft of the time (i.e. the 'old days' of the same sentence). An engineer, Gustavus Green, won a British government-sponsored competition for engine design in 1912, but the heaviness of the engine caused most fliers to prefer the French model. 100 hp would have been the norm for power output, rather than the 300 hp mentioned by the narrator of 'The Horror of the Heights'.

5. *Garros*: Roland Garros (1888–1918) was a French pilot who made his name with a flight across the Mediterranean from France to Tunisia and who went on to establish several aviation records. He was shot down weeks before the end of the First World War.

6. *vol-plané*: Downwards glide (French).

7. *Paul Veroner . . . Robur*: There seems to be no record of either name and they are probably Conan Doyle's invention.

8. *automatic alarm-bell*: This is presumably a stall-warning device. In the early days of aviation all efforts were concentrated in avoiding stalls by maintaining speed, but research into an instrument to detect and warn of them does not appear to have begun until after the First World War.

9. *morning mail service betwixt Bristol and London*: There were no regular official airmail flights until 1915 (when soldiers' mail was first carried by air between Folkestone and the Western Front). This is another detail which suggests that Conan Doyle set his story some years after the date of its composition. (See also notes 3, 8 above.)

10. *barograph*: Barometer linked to a device which makes a record of atmospheric pressure.

11. tourbillon: Whirlwind, vortex (French).

12. *Glaisher . . . Coxwell*: James Glaisher, a meteorologist, and Henry Coxwell, a professional balloonist, made a higher-than-intended ascent over Wolverhampton in 1862. Glaisher passed out as a result; later he estimated their height as being 36,000 feet (although it was probably around 20,000 feet).

13. *Mannheim glass*: This reference to some kind of telescoping or sighting device is almost certainly an invention by Conan Doyle.

14. *vol-piqué*: Dive (French).

15. *aerolite*: Meteorite.